FIONA MCINTOSH was born and raised in Sussex in the UK, but spent her early childhood commuting with her family between England and West Africa where her father worked. She left a PR career in London to travel, and found herself in Australia where she fell in love with the country, its people and one person in particular. She has since roamed the world working for her own travel publishing company, which she runs with her husband. Fiona lives with her family in Adelaide.

You can find out more information about
Fiona or chat to her on her bulletin board via her website:
www.fionamcintosh.com
Email: fiona@fionamcintosh.com

For information about Fiona McIntosh and her books, plus all the latest science fiction news, visit 'Voyager Online': www.voyageronline.com.au — the website for lovers of science fiction and fantasy.

Praise for The Quickening
MYRREN'S GIFT; BLOOD AND MEMORY; BRIDGE OF SOULS

'Enchanting ... McIntosh manages to sustain suspense while deftly handling a large cast of characters and an intricate plot' *Publishers Weekly*

'Fiona McIntosh is a seductress. I have not moved from the sofa for three days ...' *Sydney Morning Herald*

'It's a "just one more chapter" sort of book. Don't start reading *Myrren's Gift* in the evening if you have to get up early the next morning!' *Robin Hobb*

'Relentless, twisty plotting ... offers full sensory immersion ... compulsively readable' *Kirkus Reviews*

'Stunning ... Nothing short of astonishing. McIntosh weaves a captivating web of action, escapes, and intrigue from which you cannot break free ... *Myrren's Gift* is a refreshing breath of fresh air' *Bookreporter.com*

'Reminiscent of Raymond E. Feist's classic *Prince of the Blood* and John Marco's *Tyrants and Kings* trilogy ... McIntosh's utterly readable *Myrren's Gift* is a book fantasy fans will have a hard time putting down ... this fantasy has it all. Highly recommended' *Barnes & Noble Explorations*

'there's an extremely visual, if somewhat brutal, quality to her work ... a very promising start to an engaging tale' *SFX Magazine*

'Strongly conceived, believable characters and a swift plot make this fantasy epic a good addition to most libraries' *Library Journal*

Praise for Trinity
BETRAYAL; REVENGE; DESTINY

'a rattling good adventure that fulfils all the requirements of fantasy' Adelaide *Advertiser*

'as good as Sara Douglass' *Good Reading*

'Slick, hard and dark fantasy at its blistering best ... *Destiny* ends the Trinity series ... with a punch in the guts and a slap in the face. [The] story line is crisp and crackling with explosive power.' *Altair*

ALSO BY FIONA McINTOSH

TRINITY
Betrayal
Revenge
Destiny

THE QUICKENING
Myrren's Gift (Book One)
Blood and Memory (Book Two)
Bridge of Souls (Book Three)

ODALISQUE

∽ PERCHERON ∽
BOOK ONE

Fiona McIntosh

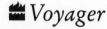
Voyager

An imprint of HarperCollins*Publishers*

Voyager
An imprint of HarperCollins*Publishers*, Australia

First published in Australia in 2005
by HarperCollins*Publishers* Australia Pty Limited
ABN 36 009 913 517
www.harpercollins.com.au

HarperCollins*Publishers*
25 Ryde Road, Pymble, Sydney, NSW 2073, Australia
31 View Road, Glenfield, Auckland 10, New Zealand
77–85 Fulham Palace Road, London, W6 8JB, United Kingdom
2 Bloor Street East, 20th floor, Toronto, Ontario M4W 1A8, Canada
10 East 53rd Street, New York NY 10022, USA

National Library of Australia Cataloguing-in-Publication data:

McIntosh, Fiona, 1960- .
   Odalisque.
   ISBN 0 7322 8180 6.
   I. Title. (Series: McIntosh, Fiona, 1960- Percheron; bk. 1).
A823.4

Cover illustration by Greg Bridges
Cover design by Darren Holt, HarperCollins Design Studio
Map by Fiona McIntosh and Darren Holt
Internal design by HarperCollins Design Studio
Typeset in 11/15 Sabon by HarperCollins Design Studio
Printed and bound in Australia by Griffin Press on 70gsm Bulky Book Ivory

5 4 3 2 1   05 06 07 08

For Ian . . .
who gave me an old dusty book one evening to browse through,
knowing the Topkapi Palace and its harem would prove
irresistible to this writer.

ACKNOWLEDGMENTS

This new adventure is the result of browsing through a centuries-old travel writer's account of his visit to Constantinople. He was particularly taken by the Topkapi Palace and the once-forbidden hallways of its harem. I followed in his footsteps in 2004 with a lively, wonderful few days in Istanbul and experienced my own awe at this same palace ... a setting just begging to be absorbed into a fantasy tale.

I admit that I am in love with Lazar and that bits of him are shamelessly borrowed from Colin Firth's characterisation of Mr Darcy. I refuse to give those bits back by the way. Trophies of a serial fantasist! But thank you, Colin, and especially Jane Austen.

The usual suspects need a mention here — Gary Havelberg, Sonya Caddy, Pip Klimentou and Judy Downs for their early reading of the draft and giving the thumbs up when I was feeling nervous about leaving my comfort zone and heading off to more exotic climes.

Thanks also to Apolonia Niemirowski for her encouragement and international sleuthing skills in finding every kind of reference material this author could possibly need.

A nod to the booksellers around Australia and New Zealand for their boundless enthusiasm for the genre — and to the national sales force from HarperCollins who are so generous to me. In fact to all at Harpers — there are too many of you to list these days who are involved with my books — but you know how much I appreciate your guidance and constant encouragement.

Special thanks to Chris Lotts in New York for helping to take my work to new readers around the globe.

Finally to Ian, Will and Jack ... who keep me firmly in the real world despite my wanderings through make-believe ones and who all brew great tea.   Fx

PERCHERON

GREAT WASTE DESERT

FOOTHILLS

TO WESTERN FOOTHILLS

BARRACKS

STONE PALACE COMPLEX

LAZAR'S HOUSE

SLAVE MARKETS

PERCHERON BAY

THE FARANEL SEA

EZRAM

THE BAZAAR

PERCHERON
BAY

SPICE MARKETS

BELOCH

SEA TEMPLE
of LYANA

STAR ISLAND

✃ PROLOGUE ✄

The prisoners, chained together, shuffled awkwardly into the main square of the slave market of Percheron; six men, all strangers and all captives of a trader called Varanz, who had a reputation for securing the more intriguing product for sale. And this group on offer was no exception, although most onlookers' attention was helplessly drawn to the tall man whose searing, pale-eyed stare, at odds with his long dark hair, seemed to challenge everyone brave enough to lock gazes with him.

Varanz knew it too; knew this one was special and he sensed a good price coming for the handsome foreigner he had ensnared, although it had taken the help of six of his henchmen to firstly bring the man down and then rope him securely. It puzzled him why the man had been travelling across the desert of all places — that in itself a perilous journey but moving alone meant almost certain trouble, particularly from slavers renowned in the region.

But Varanz had a policy of not enquiring into the background of his captives; perhaps to ease his conscience he didn't want to know anything about them, save what was obvious to his own eye. And this one, who refused to name himself, or indeed mutter much more than curses, was clearly in good health. That was enough for this merchant.

Trading for this cluster of slaves opened at the sound of the gong. The Master of the Market called the milling crowd of buyers to order. 'Brothers, this is Varanz Set Number Eight.' His voice droned on extolling the virtues of each on offer but already the majority of potential buyers were in the thrall of the angry-eyed man, the pick of the bunch and the only one of the six who held his head defiantly high. When it came to his turn, the Master of the Market, also sensing a lively auction, decided to state more than the obvious of healthy appearance, strong structure, good teeth and so on. 'He was found emerging from the golden sands of our desert alone, not even a camel for company. Brothers, I'd hazard this one will make a fine bodyguard. If he's canny enough to travel our wasteland and remain as well as he looks, then I imagine he has excellent survival skills.'

'Can he fight?' one buyer called out.

Varanz arched an eyebrow and looked towards the slave, wondering whether he'd finally get something out of the man. His instincts were right.

'I can fight,' the man replied. 'In fact I demand to fight for my freedom,' he challenged.

This set up a fresh murmuring amongst the crowd. An oddity in Percheron's slave market was its ancient and somewhat quaint rule that a slave who was captured as a free person could agree to a death fight that would, if they survived it, buy their freedom. The Crown covered the cost of his loss, either way, to the trader. It was one of the Market's oldest customs, set up by a Zar many centuries previous who understood that such a contest from time to time would provide entertainment for the otherwise tedious business of trading in human cargo.

Such fights were rare, of course, as most prisoners took their chances with a new life as a slave. But now and then one would risk death in the bid to win back their independence.

Varanz strolled over to the man now that he knew his tongue was loosened. 'You understand what you ask for?'

'I do. It was explained to us on the journey here by one of your aides. I wish to fight for my freedom. I also wish to speak with your Zar.'

At this Varanz smirked. 'I can't imagine he will want to speak with you.'

'He might after he watches me fight. He will probably enjoy the spectacle of witnessing me best twelve of his best warriors.'

Varanz was speechless at the man's arrogance. He shook his head and walked to the Master, briefly explaining in a quiet mutter what the slave was proposing. Now both of them returned to stand before the man.

'Don't try and talk me out of it. I want my freedom back. I will pay the price if I fail to win it,' he warned them.

The Master had no intention of attempting to thwart the proposition of some sport after an already long and wearying day in the market. He could see that Varanz was unfazed, knowing that he would get a good price either way.

'What is your reserve, Varanz?' he asked.

'No less than 200 karels for this one.'

He nodded. 'I will send a message to the palace for authorisation,' he said, now turning to the man. 'You must give us your name,' the Master insisted.

He knifed them with a cold gaze. 'My name is Lazar.'

The palace did more than give authorisation. A runner returned swiftly with the news that Zar Joreb, his interest piqued, would be in attendance for this contest. Varanz was not as surprised as the Master of the Market at this news but he understood how unusual it was for the Zar of Percheron to visit the slave traders. He mentioned as much to Lazar.

The foreigner was unmoved. 'I wish to speak with him if I succeed.'

Varanz nodded. 'That is up to our Zar. We have told him twelve of his men will fight you to the death. This is no doubt why he is coming to witness the contest.'

'It is why I suggested so many.'

Varanz showed exasperation in his expression. 'How can you best a dozen fighters, man? There's still time to change your mind and not waste your life. I will ensure a cosy position for you. A fellow like you will find himself in high demand by a rich man to escort his wives, families ... take care of their security.'

Lazar snorted. 'I'm no nursery maid.'

'All right.' Varanz tried again. 'I know I can sell you as a high calibre bodyguard to a man who needs protection whilst he travels. I'll find you a good owner.'

'I don't want to be owned,' Lazar snarled. 'I want my freedom.'

The trader shrugged. 'Well you'll have it, my friend, but you'll be carried off in a sack.'

'So be it. I slave for no-one.'

Their conversation was ended by the Master of the Market hissing for silence — the Zar's karak was apparently just moments away and he knew this by the arrival of a troop of Percheron's guard. Varanz nodded to one of his aides to escort the rest of the prisoners away. Trading would resume once this piece of theatre was done with.

'I wish you luck, brother,' he said to Lazar and moved away to stand with the Master, who was marshalling all of the other traders into a formal line of welcome. The Zar finally arrived flanked by more of the Percherese Guard, but his karak was carried by six of the red-shrouded Elim the elite guardians of the Zar's harem. The Elim also provided bodyguard duties to royalty. The Zar's entry between the slave market's carved pillars of two gryphons was heralded by the sound of several of the curled Percherese horns being blown furiously, and everyone who was not attached to this royal retinue instantly humbled themselves.

No-one dared raise their eyes to the Zar until given formal permission.

No-one but Lazar that is.

He was on his knees because he had been pushed into this position but he brazenly watched the Zar being helped out of the karak; their gazes met and held momentarily across the dust of the slave market. Then Lazar dipped his head, just a fraction, but it was enough that the Zar knew the brash young man had acknowledged the person who was the closest thing to the god Zarab that walked this earth. The Zar did not acknowledge him.

A special seat that was brought by the Guard was set up and the Elim unfurled a canopy over it, beneath which Zar Joreb settled himself. He had a wry smile on his face as the Master of the Market followed protocol and made the official announcement that the prisoner, Lazar, captured by Trader Varanz, had opted to fight for his freedom against a dozen of the warriors from the Percherese Guard. No-one watched the Master or even the Zar. All eyes were riveted on the dark foreigner, whose wrists and ankles were now unshackled and who was disrobing down to the once white, but now dirty loose pants he wore beneath. They watched his measured movements, but mostly they watched him study the twelve men who followed suit before taking some practice swipes with their glinting swords. They all bore smirks, none prepared to take the ridiculously outnumbered opposition seriously.

The gong was once again sounded for silence and the Master outlined what was about to happen. It was a superfluous pronouncement but strict protocol was a way of life for Percheron's various markets and especially in the hallowed presence of the Zar.

'. . . or to the prisoner's death,' he finished sombrely. He looked now to Zar Joreb who, with an almost imperceptible nod, gave the signal for combat to begin.

Those who were present at the slave market that day would talk about this fight for years to come. No-one had ever seen anything like it or were likely to again as Lazar accepted the weapon thrown towards him and without so much as a hurried prayer to his god of choice, strode out to meet the first of the warriors. The Guard had decided on one man at a time — it seemed there would be no sport otherwise and the plan presumably was to keep wounding the arrogant prisoner until he begged for mercy and the death blow. However, by the time the first three men were groaning and bleeding on the ground, their most senior man hurriedly sent in four at a time.

It didn't make much difference to Lazar, who appeared to the audience to be unintimidated by numbers. His face wore the grim countenance of someone who was utterly focused; he made no sound, never once backed away, always threatening his enemy rather than the other way around. It was soon obvious that his sword skills could not be matched by any of the Percherese, not even fighting in tandem. His fighting arm became a blur of silver that weaved a path of wreckage through flesh, turning the dozen men, one after another, into writhing, crying heaps as they gripped torn shoulders, slashed legs, or profusely bleeding fighting arms. To their credit the final two fought superbly but neither could mark Lazar with his own blood, let alone best him. He fought without fear, his focused expression never changing, and his speed only increasing. He finished one off by cutting him down by the ankle and then stomping on his sword wrist, breaking it, to ensure he did not return to the fray, and finally fought the other into exhaustion until the man was on his knees. Lazar flicked the guard's sword away and gave a calculated slash across his chest. The man fell, almost grateful.

The slave market was uncharacteristically quiet, save for the cries of bleeding, paining men. Varanz looked around at the carnage, his nostrils flaring with the raw metallic smell of blood thick in the air, and he raised his eyebrows with surprise. No-one was dead. Lazar had mercilessly and precisely disabled each of his rivals but claimed the life of none. He threw his sword down and stood in the circle of hurt warriors, a light sheen of perspiration on his body the only indication that he had exerted himself. His chest rose and sank steadily, calmly. He turned to the Zar and bowed long and deeply.

'Zar Joreb, will you now grant my freedom?' he spoke finally into the hush that had fallen on everyone, including the wounded.

'My men would surely seek death than live with losing this fight,' was Joreb's response.

Varanz watched Lazar's curiously light eyes cloud with defiance. 'They are innocent. I will not take their lives in what was purely a piece of entertainment for those gathered.'

'They are soldiers! This was a fight to the death.'

'Zar Joreb, this was a fight to *my* death, as I understood it, not theirs. It was made clear that I either win my freedom through death or through survival. I survived. No-one impressed upon me that anyone had to die as part of the rules of this custom.'

'Arrogant pup,' Joreb murmured into the silence. Then he laughed. To Varanz, who was holding his breath, it seemed impossible but their Zar was laughing at the prisoner's audacity. 'Stand before me, young man.'

Lazar took two long strides and then went down on one knee, finally his head bowed.

'What is it you want, stranger?' the Zar demanded.

'I want to live in Percheron as a free man,' Lazar replied, not lifting his head.

'Look at me.' Lazar did so. 'You've humiliated my Guard. You will need to rectify that before I grant you anything.'

'How can I do this, Zar Joreb?'

'By teaching them.'

Lazar stared at the Zar, a quizzical look taking over his normally deadpan expression, but he said nothing.

'Become my Spur,' Zar Joreb offered. 'Our present Spur must retire soon. We need to inject a fresh approach. A young approach. You fight like you're chasing away demons, man. I want you to teach my army how to do that.'

Lazar's gaze narrowed. His tone sounded guarded. 'You're offering to pay me to live as a free man in Percheron?'

'Be my Spur,' Zar Joreb urged, this time there was no humour in his voice, only passion.

'I accept, but first you owe Varanz over there 200 karels apparently.'

Joreb laughed loudly in genuine amusement. 'I like you, Lazar. Follow me back to the palace. We have much to speak of. I must say, I'm impressed how you put your life in danger to get what you want.'

'It was never in danger,' Lazar replied and the semblance of a smile twitched briefly at his mouth.

The Spur of Percheron was oblivious to the clandestine attention he was being paid from the city's favourite ratha emporium. Inside its kitchens a pair of women feasted their eyes on Percheron's most eligible bachelor whilst their patrons took similar pleasure in the sisters' celebrated spicy pancakes.

The two women had been preparing since before sunrise for the busy morning trade. For years they had created what was considered by many to be Percheron's finest hot rathas, and as a result it was commonplace to see a long queue patiently shuffling closer to the counter where the women's husbands took the orders.

The wealthier patrons often sat at some of the small tables on offer and paid a premium for the privilege of being served their steaming rathas on warmed plates with mouth-watering sambas and chutneys to accompany.

But the sisters never had any dealings with the customers and yet they seemed to know them as well as their husbands did. This was because the open windows that allowed fresh air to blow through the busy kitchen also afforded them a splendid close-up view of Percheron's city folk at work and play. And with their hands lively about their work, so skilled in it now their fingers required no thought or supervision, the sisters had instead become keen observers.

And no-one gave them greater pleasure to watch than the revered Spur of Percheron, the long-legged, raven-haired former prisoner turned brother-friend of royalty, who was in their sights at this moment.

'Why do you think he looks at that stone carving each time he passes this way?' asked the woman expertly kneading the dough into mounds between both hands.

'That carving is Iridor, isn't it, and the Spur's been doing that for years,' came the reply over the flattened rolls of dough sizzling in the melted butter. 'Keep fanning those flames now,' the woman urged a young lad who sat between her legs, ensuring the smouldering lumps of knotwood never lost their heat.

'I know that.' The first sister raised her eyebrows in mock exasperation. 'I'm asking you what you think he sees in it.'

'Your guess is as good as mine, Mara. Perhaps he casts a silent prayer to it. Now I come to think on it, I'm sure that owl has something to do with the old stories of the Goddess.'

'Hoosh,' said a man bustling in from behind. 'You know not to speak her name.'

'No-one can hear us back here, Bal. And it's only an old myth. No-one believes in all that Goddess stuff and the owl messenger any more. You go about your business, man, and let us get on with ours. There's a lot of customers queuing.'

'And you stop flapping your gums, woman, and keep frying those rathas up.'

'Oh, be gone,' Mara said, shooing her husband back to the front of the shop. 'You could be right, Hasha.' She returned to her chore, the dough piling up in a neat, glistening pyramid. 'The Spur's such a secretive sort, perhaps he's atoning for something.'

'I'll show him atonement.' Her sister rubbed her breasts and grinned wickedly. The look of shock on Mara's face made Hasha laugh out loud. 'Don't tell me you haven't thought it at least once? Every woman in Percheron daydreams of a roll with the Spur.' The child below sensibly remained silent but his soft smile suggested this was not the first time his mother and aunt had discussed this man and would surely not be the last. The Spur of Percheron prompted more conjecture than any other; the man with the curiously light-coloured eyes was not just every woman's dream but was spoken of admiringly by the men too.

'I haven't,' Mara lied, and stifled her laughter. 'Oh, but if I were younger, I would.'

Hasha flipped the four oiled pancakes currently in the pan and a delicious new aroma of cooked ratha spiced the air. 'He always looks so serious, though. I don't think I've ever seen him laugh.'

Mara stopped kneading the dough. 'Oh, he's got secrets, that one, but he never seems to put a foot wrong. I'm told the Zar holds him in higher esteem than any of his council and his men in the protectorate would die for him. That sort of loyalty isn't won easily.'

Her sister looked up and exclaimed. 'Zarab save us, Mara, he's coming this way!'

Both sisters watched in genuine pleasure as the familiar long stride of the Spur brought him to the door of their husbands' shop and the chance to serve the highest-ranking soldier in the land became reality.

As he entered the shop Lazar was already planning to order a dish known tantalisingly as The Emporium Breakfast Feast. Of course, if he had known that what was to come this day would set off a chain of events so monumental and painful his life would change forever, he might have found good reason to ignore the hunger pangs that made him so accessible to the Elim runner sent from the palace with such dire news.

Ignorant of what was coming, Lazar sat down at a small table and even found a smile for the two middle-aged ladies who giggled coquettishly behind their veils from the kitchen, as if being visited by Zarab himself.

∽ 2 ∽

It was going to be unpleasant, she thought, tapping perfectly rouged lips with the tips of manicured nails buffed by a slave until they shone. But it must be done ... and swiftly.

The First Wife and Absolute Favourite glanced down into the exquisite private garden where boys played amongst the cypresses with a ball made from an inflated pig's bladder. Their laughter prompted a smile, but anyone looking at this woman would have sensed no warmth. Herezah was already imagining how different those childish squeals would be when the order was given.

An agonised groan dragged her from her thoughts. Taking a moment to settle an appropriate look of sorrow on her face, Herezah turned from the beautifully sculpted window of the Stone Palace to where Zar Joreb, Percheron's high ruler, King of the Seas, Ruler of the Deserts, Mightiest of the Mighty, lay dying. The man had been treated as a god these past thirty years. *But even gods have to die*, Herezah thought with fierce joy as she flicked a glance of summons to a slightly stooped man standing nearby.

Tariq spoke softly from behind the oiled beard carefully split into two narrow plaits and ostentatiously hung with a ruby at each end. These audacious accessories spoke much to Herezah about Tariq's designs for personal grandeur. She knew he wanted the title of Grand Vizier and she was sure he had never felt himself closer to his goal than now. That was good. He was well connected; she would feed his ambition, make him her puppet.

He kept his voice low enough for her ears only. 'My lady Herezah?'

'Fetch Boaz,' she whispered. The Vizier understood, bowing and withdrawing silently.

Herezah looked around the fabulously ornate chamber, gilded recklessly with gold at every turn. This was not the Zar's usual bedroom but Herezah had had him moved here because the room, already crowded, would only get more thick with people as the day drew on, for her husband would most likely die, if not this hour then within the next few.

Joreb had very particular tastes in art, which thankfully his Absolute Favourite shared, although in truth he had given her that appreciation, guiding her since childhood as to what constituted beauty. And it was certainly not this gold-laden room with its rich, gaudy colours. No, Joreb liked subtlety and understatement. His preference was for paler hues and simpler design. Herezah felt a fleeting pang that the man who had given her the opportunity to rise out of the slush of the harem would give up his soul in a room as vulgar as this. Her regret passed quickly, however, replaced by the thrill that her ultimate goal, the one she had been striving towards these past two decades, would be achieved in barely hours.

She calmed her racing pulse and tried to focus on the Zar. Despite her thrill at what her husband's death meant for her, Herezah had been shocked to learn that his injuries were, in fact, fatal.

The large chamber might be ungainly but it was cooled by a gentle breeze blowing from the massive, semi-circular aquamarine harbour the famed city of Percheron overlooked. It was here that for thousands of years cultures had collided and mingled to yield the Percheron of today. Its strategic position and seemingly endless reserves of precious stones and metals gave the city riches beyond most realms' dreams.

But while those elements had once given Percheron such power, they were now its greatest threat. Herezah — keenly in tune with national security — was well aware that Joreb had begun fretting about Galinsea in particular. He had disclosed his concerns to her that their warlike neighbour to the west had designs on Percheron.

Herezah's wandering attention was arrested by the worried expressions of the court's most senior physicians. The Zar would not see sunset, that much was obvious, and in turn their lives were forfeit for failing His Majesty. Understandably they continued to consult each other and desperately consider new strategies.

At the foot of the Zar's bed cavorted a dwarf, sumptuously outfitted but looking ridiculous all the same. Herezah quelled a scowl. The fool was a constant annoyance in her life. He was 'closed' too, which only served to irritate Herezah further. Not even a blood-telling by her crone, Yozem, had revealed anything about him. A blank. Even though the crone claimed there could be no such thing and yet it was true, the dwarf offered no clues about himself to the practitioner of the Blood Arts. Herezah felt sickened to see his awkward antics on thick, short legs and cursed his popularity.

If Percheron was credited as the most idyllic cove in the Faranel Sea, then its Stone Palace was the most breathtaking aspect of that cove. And within that Stone Palace its harem was the magnificent prize where beauty ruled supreme. It disturbed Herezah constantly that amongst the beauty roamed such vulgar deformity as this dwarf. He was the flaw in Percheron's jewel. Pez — she wasn't even sure whether that was his real name — had been a favourite clown of the Zar's for too many years for Herezah to get rid of him. She despaired that her son adored Pez in equal measure to her hatred.

She sighed; at least the palace buffoon, with his strange yellow eyes, would keep Boaz amused during the difficult times ahead.

He may even prove a blessing, for there were occasions when time spent with Pez seemed to help her only child understand things. She couldn't imagine how. The dwarf could hardly string a single sensible sentence together without breaking into song, or acrobatics, or his mind wandering elsewhere. How Boaz and Pez ever held even a simple conversation was a mystery to her.

A small movement at the corner of the room distracted her. She glanced over at the silent mountain of black flesh that went by the name of Salmeo. He put the fear of a thousand angry gods into most people around the palace, including herself. She had lost count of the times the giant man had reduced her to a shaking wreck. But never again, she promised, not now that absolute power was within her grasp.

Salmeo was the cleverest, most sly man she had ever known — no doubt ever would. He was as cunning as he was dangerous. He was also cruelty personified ... but then you didn't become Grand Master of the Eunuchs without some of those qualities.

Salmeo embodied so many unpalatable characteristics, it was hard to imagine how they all came together in one person. For the umpteenth time her amazement was triggered by the sheer size of him beneath the richly patterned garments he draped over the folds of loose, flabby skin. Heavy folds, she knew all too well from her own experience, that had to be lifted away in order for him to be cleaned. He matched his revolting looks with a vicious demeanour more befitting a scorned woman. Which wasn't far from the truth perhaps. Salmeo had been cut at the age of seven when his height and size fooled the chief eunuch of the day into believing he was older. He was an 'almost complete'. Nothing much was left of his manhood save the painful yearning of desire. No toys, no tricks, no magicks helped Salmeo with his frustrations, so he took his pleasures in other ways.

Herezah's gaze was helplessly drawn towards the sinister, sharply pointed nail on the index finger of his right hand. He stained it red, so no woman could ever forget its purpose and no naive boy went beyond wondering at its use. She masked the shudder of the memory of that nail's cruel touch when she was twelve.

Salmeo must have sensed her attention and she just had time, before hurriedly looking away, to see the pale rope of a scar that ran the length of one of his fleshy cheeks pull as he raised an eyebrow at her interest.

In turning away, Herezah's focus finally fell upon the Zar himself. He groaned and moved restlessly beneath silken sheets, fighting unseen spirits who had come to claim him.

Death is ugly indeed, Herezah thought, watching the great one's lips draw back in a silent howl as a fresh wave of punishment rode his body. The door opened and to her relief she saw her son ushered in by Vizier Tariq.

'My lion,' she said softly to the boy, reaching out her arms theatrically.

'Mother.' He dutifully kissed her cheek but twisted away from the embrace.

Herezah did not react to his cloaked rejection and made a promise to herself that she would try harder with Boaz. After all, within hours she would be his regent, quietly ruling from behind the figurehead Zar of so few summers. She watched his intelligent dark eyes observing her and felt a momentary loss of guard, as if he understood precisely what she had been thinking before his gaze slid away to his father moaning on the bed.

'You must be brave, Boaz,' she warned. 'He will not last long.'

'Can we not stop his pain?' he asked tersely, ignoring her concern.

'The physicians minimise it,' Tariq offered, eager to include himself in the royal conversation.

Boaz ignored the sycophantic Vizier as well. It was shock enough for him to see his father in this state — especially as he had seemed to rally in the early days of the fall — but having his mother displaying her new-found devotion and feeling his

16

emotions used as some sort of circus ground for everyone else's benefit was making him angry.

'Come, my son,' Herezah said, taking his soft hand. 'You are fifteen now and old enough to witness your father's final breaths.'

Final breaths? Boaz scowled. He could hear the predatory tone in his mother's voice. He knew only too well what his father's death meant — especially for his mother who had comforted him to sleep when he was a young child with stories about how one day the two of them would rule Percheron. That was all well and good if love existed between them, but his mother had, for the past six or seven years, essentially ignored him and he had learned to live without the maternal love he craved. Instead he had been raised by royal servants. Still, it amused him that both parents adored him: his mother because of the power he could bring her, and his father because he recognised in Boaz a future leader. Boaz knew the Zar loved his sharp mind and especially his scholarly pursuits and love of the arts. It didn't hurt that he was described as handsome these days either — he could see how all of these attributes made him the most eligible heir. Nevertheless, it was sickening to watch his mother revelling in this same knowledge and using it to get precisely what she wanted, not for his benefit, but for hers.

Yet she was his only ally — not friend, not loved one, but someone he could count on to look after his interests because they served hers so well. It was a terrible thing to admit but he needed Herezah and her bright, agile mind that could plot and plan faster and more skilfully than anyone he knew.

Accepting this only made him angrier still, but these dark thoughts were put on hold as Pez scampered up. Boaz smiled inwardly at the dwarf's oversized pantaloons which, because they had insufficient length to billow properly, instead pooled comically around his thick ankles. Nevertheless, the swathe of fabric hid the savage bow of his legs that made Pez's gait sway so oddly. He arrived pulling silk squares from his nose. It was a trick that had always amused Boaz, but not today.

'Hello, Pez,' Boaz muttered.

'Master,' Pez replied.

The boy looked sadly at the dwarf. 'Is he truly dying?' he said, as if, by asking his friend rather than those he disliked, the reality might be different.

'We all die,' Pez replied in a singsong voice. 'You, birds, fish, me ... your parents too.' Herezah glared at the dwarf as Pez's gaze slid past her in a deliberate provocation. 'You must carry yourself proudly now, young prince. Do you know why?'

Boaz looked at his friend — the only one he trusted in this room — and nodded. 'Because I'm to be Zar.'

'That's right, my darling.' Herezah gushed, clearly surprised that the dwarf was making sense for once. 'Your father awaits,' she urged, pulling Boaz away from the jester.

The young man glanced at Pez, who blinked slowly in that curious manner of his. Then the dwarf bowed theatrically, the bells on his velvet cap tinkling into strained silence, for the groaning had now subsided.

Aware that all eyes in the room were trained upon him, Boaz took his father's hand. It felt dry, too cold, as if death had indeed arrived, although a rasping groan put an end to that fright. Through puffy eyes, the King of Kings tried to focus.

'My lord,' Herezah spoke lovingly near the Zar's ear, 'our son, Boaz.'

The man rallied ever so slightly, a brief smile immediately replaced by another grimace. 'Boaz.'

'Father, I —'

'Hush. Listen now,' he growled and it took all his effort to load his weak voice with the tone needed to make the youngster pay attention. 'You are the Chosen One. No-one else! You alone. Never forget it!' he forced out. The stricken physicians watched the last struggling breath arrive and expel in a desperate gasp. The head of the Zar lolled to one side; spittle escaped to run down his chin. Herezah looked away in pretend despair, the action hiding her triumph. The men of medicine hung their heads, imagining what their own last words would be that evening when their throats would be cut. No point in fighting it now. Their wills were written and they knew their families would be looked after well. They had enjoyed position and wealth for many years and had always understood that when Joreb died, they would too, if they were in attendance at the time of death.

They went about their duty now, one checking that no pulse was present whilst the other held a small mirror against the Zar's mouth and nose. As a final precaution a large pin was drawn from a pouch and his body was pricked repeatedly. Herezah was busy removing the large ring from her husband's finger. Boaz, his ears ringing from his father's clear message about his mother, his eyes stinging from tears, could not believe his father had lost the fight.

He objected to the pin angrily and Pez, sensing his distress, suddenly dropped to his knees before him. As if the dwarf's sudden movement was a signal, everyone in the chamber came out of the mental paralysis the Zar's death had prompted and also dropped. They bent to touch their heads on the floor before Boaz, for all in the room knew of Joreb's decree, that the son of his Absolute Favourite would succeed him.

Salmeo took longer than anyone to kneel, but after much grunting he too paid the new Zar appropriate homage.

Boaz was stunned; he wasn't ready to accept this new role, even though he had been groomed for many years to take his father's crown. If not for the sly wink that Pez gave him from under a short arm, he might have fled the chamber.

'Your Majesty,' they cried as one. 'Hail the Zar!' They repeated it several times until the new King of Kings commanded them to stop.

Into the instant silence that followed Pez broke wind, his rear pointing suspiciously towards the new Valide Zara and her bejewelled Vizier. Boaz knew this sort of lewd behaviour should have made his father sit up from death and roar with laughter.

Joreb had so loved Pez's wickedness. Boaz felt a nervous flutter of amusement threaten to explode from his own throat but he controlled it with effort and focused on his scowling, clearly offended parent. He ignored the mortified Vizier who deserved all the bad smells that came his way.

'Mother,' he said. 'Rise.'

And she did, first crawling forward — as one should to the Zar — before straightening on her knees to place the diamond-encrusted emerald ring onto her son's finger. She nodded reassurance before bowing her head over her son's hand and kissing the ring fervently.

'My lord Zar,' she said, pride catching in her throat. 'How may I serve?'

'Hail, Valide Zara,' Boaz said and Herezah basked in the words she had longed to hear for so many years. Now, as the Zar's mother, her very name would strike fear into the hearts of those around her.

She took their obeisance, noticed the wry smile on Salmeo's normally unreadable face, and gave the first of many orders as the most powerful woman in the land.

'Rise all,' she said, turning to Tariq. 'Where is Lazar?'

'Waiting, Valide Zara,' the Vizier replied, fully recovered from the dwarf's insult and barely able to contain his glee at the thought of the potential riches and power spreading out before him. Hail the Valide! He had aligned himself well.

'Admit him alone,' she ordered and resisted smiling at the notion that Lazar would share this moment of high joy with her. 'The passing of the old Zar is a secret until I say differently.'

The physicians were instructed to tidy the body of their ruler and were laying out the formerly rumpled sheets neatly over his corpse as the tall, sun-browned Spur entered the chamber.

'Lazar,' Boaz said, his expression lightening. This was the only other person who walked the palace corridors whom he could truly consider a friend.

The Spur spared only a fleeting glance towards the prone figure on the bed, for his shock at the news of imminent death had already been suffered at the Ratha Emporium and then, with effort, concealed as he strode in disbelieving stony silence ahead of the runner who had brought the terrible news of the Zar's relapse. It was something he could only think of in private. Right now his focus was firmly on the new Zar and not allowing his emotions to creep through as Herezah stared at him with the hungry gaze of a hunter.

In an instant Lazar was on his knees and reaching to the huge ring that was barely able to sit straight on the slender fingers of the young man's hand. 'Zar Boaz, Your High One, I offer my services and my life to you.'

In a show of affection, Boaz covered Lazar's hand with his own, pale and unblemished against the tanned, strong fingers of the bowed man. 'I hope we never claim it, Spur.'

The Spur of Percheron stood and nodded at Boaz, proud of the boy's composure. The light grey eyes that marked Lazar as something for curiosity — and certainly a foreigner — looked now to Herezah before he bowed low. 'Valide Zara.'

She stifled her pleasure, hiding it behind the grave expression she had contrived; plenty of time ahead to enjoy Lazar's new fealty to her. Right now there were urgent arrangements to make and she revelled in the thrill of finally being able to give him a direct order.

'Take the physicians away and do what you must,' she said coldly, glad she was not veiled on this occasion as it was not insisted upon within the palace confines, so long as the Zar was present. It pleased her hugely that the Spur could see her beauty and what he was missing.

If he could sense her pleasure he did not show it, but then Lazar gave little away to anyone.

'May I pay my respects?' he asked, looking towards the body draped in silken sheets.

The new Valide inclined her head and watched the Spur cross the room in four strides and then kneel to kiss the hand of the dead Zar. He took a moment in silence before he stood and soberly turned towards the men who had tried to prevent death. 'Physicians,' was all he said.

'You must be gentle with the gentlemen's throats,' Pez began to sing. He cartwheeled once before an exasperated look from Herezah told Lazar that it was in the dwarf's interest to be removed as well.

'Come, Pez. You can keep us company,' the soldier suggested.

The dwarf agreed but not before a loud and long farewell belch to those gathered.

Upstaged, Herezah had to delay her chilling warning to Lazar until he was ready to depart. 'Do it immediately, Spur, but no word of the old Zar's death is to get out until I sanction it.'

Lazar noted how Joreb, still warm on his deathbed, had already been dismissed as the old Zar and the new Zar was already being overlooked. 'As you wish, Valide,' and he bowed. The Faranel Sea below blew a sweet wind into the room but could not cover the stench of ambition. It revolted him and he was grateful to escape even with the unpalatable task ahead of having the physicians executed.

After the door had closed on the four men, Herezah turned and said, 'Tariq, Salmeo.'

'Valide?'

'You understand what needs to be done.' It was not a question.

'I do,' the avaricious Vizier replied.

'Salmeo?'

The huge black man sighed. 'Enemies will be made, Valide Zara.'

She could smell on his breath the violet-fragranced tablets that he habitually sucked. 'The enemies of Boaz will be dead. The other kind will be helpless.'

'Mother? What's going on?' Boaz had been too lost in his grieving thoughts to follow the conversation.

'Come with me, Boaz, I want to explain something to you.'
She took his hand, looking pointedly at the two men who were
charged with the ugly task.

She did not need to say any more. The darkly ambitious eyes
of the woman, who now essentially ruled Percheron, said it all.

~ 3 ~

Boaz was deeply disturbed. This morning had begun like any other in the palace and then, during a language lesson, Vizier Tariq had arrived looking grave. Initially the son of the Zar's First Wife and Absolute Favourite had leapt at the interruption. Any distraction that released him from Galinsean verbs and tenses was a blessing. It was a language that tested even the most accomplished linguists in Percheron. His mother had told him that very few could master the strange tongue. She had explained that she had also tried to learn the tiresome language for many years but failed. Boaz couldn't imagine his mother failing at anything and he'd initially thought she was just saying as much to flatter him, but others had confirmed it. The language of the people from the west was seemingly impossible for a Percherese to speak fluently. His mother jested that should a Galinsean suddenly arrive in the city then not a soul in Percheron could conduct a worthwhile conversation with the visitor. Boaz felt sure she was exaggerating and they had laughed about it. In any case, he reasoned, any Galinsean landing in Percheron meant trouble, not conversation.

The golden-haired race with their pale eyes allegedly wanted Percheron so badly that Lazar had set up a special spy network throughout the city just to keep the Zar constantly updated on every item of news that could be gleaned from the trading ships. It had got to the point where no ship with Galinsean registration, or even a Galinsean aboard, was permitted to pass between the giants let alone dock in the harbour.

Lazar seemed to know something about Galinsea, having roamed it for a number of years apparently, and he agreed that its King would certainly have designs on beautiful Percheron. He remembered how the Spur had scowled when he spoke.

'... not that the Galinsean royals would know art from their arses,' he had warned. 'They want one thing only and that's the harbour. They'd sack the city and then raze it without so much as a look backwards.'

Boaz didn't believe this but grasped the sentiment behind it. It was obvious Lazar held nothing but loathing for their neighbours.

'Our good fortune is that they may be good sailors but we can protect our waters and the desert to our back is the best protection of all. No Galinsean would know how to survive in that unforgiving landscape.'

At the Vizier's interruption Boaz had briefly entertained the thought that it might mean he would be allowed to play pigball with his brothers. But his anticipation of a fun afternoon was immediately dampened by the Vizier's solemn request for Boaz to accompany him.

The day had got much worse, however, than discovering that pigball was not on the agenda. Having witnessed his father take his last breath, he had not only had to deal with everyone suddenly on their knees to him but he had learned something so terrible he had fled his father's chamber. The new Valide's whispered words had set off such a panic within him that he had to run to the only person he knew might soothe his mind, assure him it was some terrible game his power-obsessed mother had dreamed up to frighten him. This was why he now found himself in the private chamber of the court jester, someone he could genuinely call friend.

Pez sat cross-legged and cross-eyed, but he was not winning any smiles from the new Zar.

'I thought my fart well timed,' the dwarf offered into the silence.

'My mother didn't.'

The dwarf sighed and for a rare moment became serious. 'You cannot escape this, Boaz.'

'It's barbaric!'

Pez nodded his oversized head.

Boaz begged. 'There must be another way?'

'Well, certainly not one your mother would entertain. You know this is her way of protecting you.'

'My father would never have condoned this.'

'Boaz,' Pez said mildly. 'This is precisely how your father's throne was won and held.'

The Zar had not expected this. 'I never knew that.'

Pez shrugged. 'It's hardly something he was proud of and it was something he deliberately asked that his own sons be shielded from until his death came about. You are Zar now and your mother can't keep the harsh realities of life from touching you.'

'You sound as if you support her,' Boaz replied sourly. Pez said nothing and the Zar looked chagrined. 'They're my brothers,' he appealed.

'And also your murderers if the shoe was on the other foot. Boaz, don't be naive. Every wife in the harem thinks the same way as your mother. She is doing what she must to protect you and Percheron's throne.'

'She is doing this for her own chance at power!'

The dwarf shook his head sadly. 'Your father chose you for succession. She only dreamed it. He made it so.'

'Why can't I re-write the history books and magnanimously send them away?'

'And watch your back for evermore? No, child, they each have a rightful claim to the throne — the older ones every bit as eligible as you — and you might not think so now, but each of those boys is your enemy. Their mothers would see to it.'

26

The new Zar made a sound of anguished disgust. 'I cannot be there. I will not witness it!'

'You must!' Pez countered equally firmly, 'or you will be viewed as weak.'

'So be it!' Boaz shouted, slamming his hand onto the table. He regretted the raised voice and his tone softened to a plea. 'Save me, Pez — don't allow me to bear witness. I cannot.'

The dwarf was torn. He understood the young man's fear but conspiring against the Valide Zara would be tantamount to treason. He began to shake his head when an idea struck him. It was unpleasant but effective, and hopefully without repercussions.

'Hold out your arm.'

'What?'

'Do it.'

Boaz obeyed, nervously. 'Only Lazar and I know the real you, Pez. Everyone else thinks you're demented.'

Pez decided not to enlighten his friend that there were others who knew the truth. 'Why don't you tell?'

'Because you're my secret. The only thing truly mine that my mother can't spoil or interfere with. I don't share it because you're true; there is no-one else I trust in the way that I trust you.'

Pez smiled and his collection of odd features seemed to blend and become, not handsome — not by any stretch — but suddenly right. The warmth and beauty in his smile revealed his heart.

'There will be, son.'

Boaz frowned, confused. 'Who?'

Pez burped theatrically for his answer and Boaz had experienced the dwarf's evasive tactics enough times to know he would get nothing more from his friend on the subject.

'This is going to hurt, Zar Boaz, but not nearly as much as watching your brothers die.'

The new Zar instinctively closed his eyes.

'How did this happen?' Herezah yelled at Tariq. 'Today of all days!'

She'd donned an exquisite black tunic over matching silk trousers, presumably her mourning garb, but neither man present missed how the cut of the outfit showed off her sensuous figure. Even in grief Herezah intended to take everyone's breath away.

To his credit, the sombre expression of the Vizier did not falter at the outburst. 'Pez found him, Valide Zara. Apparently Boaz had been running to find the jester when he fell and sustained the injury.'

She made a sound of disgust at the Vizier's pointless explanation. That much she had worked out for herself. Herezah's eyes blazed anger towards the Spur instead. It was his turn to answer for her plan going awry. 'Spur Lazar?'

'Pez fetched me when it happened. I could see Boaz's arm was broken and I sent for one of the city's physicians immediately. I didn't have much choice, Valide,' he said. He did not wish to anger her further by reminding her that it was she who had called for the palace physicians' deaths to be carried out immediately.

The men had died bravely as it turned out. They had said their prayers and written notes to their families before kneeling calmly in the execution courtyard and together chanting the mantra to send their souls safely to the Garden of Zarab.

Lazar would not permit the palace soldiers to handle this sort of killing. He had assembled a small team of executioners to carry out any deaths ordered by the royals or their agents. In this instance two experienced men had arrived quietly to stand behind the physicians. A third, the most senior man, gave the signal when the mantra had been cast. The executioners had reached a blade around each victim's throat and expertly slashed the jugular. It was not pretty but it was swift and it was honourable. Their heads were later fully severed but would not be pushed onto spikes until the Valide gave permission for the city to learn of the Zar's passing.

Lazar privately scoffed at the Percherese claim to be peace-loving. He had personally witnessed countless barbaric acts within the palace walls alone. By the same token, Galinsea, hailed as a warlike nation, had never executed its doctors for not being able to cure someone.

'Well, I've sent the city physician away,' Herezah said, exasperated. 'Yozem will take care of Boaz. We shall need to hire a new team of physicians for the Zar.'

'As you wish,' Lazar murmured, still wondering at the senseless waste of life. Those dead doctors would have made fine physicians for Boaz.

'Nothing is as I wish,' she replied acidly. It was galling that Boaz would not be present, but having seen the grey-faced Zar sweating from the pain of his damaged arm, she knew it was impossible. Yozem had already mixed the pain-relieving opium paste including the crushed dust of diamonds, emeralds and rubies accorded royalty, although, from now on, Boaz would take his opiate in the gilded tablets prepared for the Zar alone.

'If not for Pez —' Lazar began but the Valide cut across his words angrily.

'Yes, yes, if not for Pez! If I didn't know he was so feeble-minded, I could almost believe he works against me.' Both men made noises of gentle admonishment. She ignored them. 'What have people been told?'

Lazar answered. 'They know only that the Zar is injured and that he is with his physicians. No-one knows of his death yet.'

She nodded, seemingly no longer interested. 'So, is everything ready, Tariq?'

'As ordered, Valide. Salmeo is with them.'

Herezah knew Lazar would find her latest scheme heinous but he would hide his disgust behind that irritating mask. Hoping this man would ever show any emotion seemed a lost cause. The gods knew she had been trying for long enough. Why he intrigued her so much she couldn't say; perhaps it was his remoteness that made her yearn to be able to reach him. All her life men had looked at her with lust. But this man hardly looked at her at all. If he did, she felt as if he was looking through her. She hated him for that; it was a worse kind of humiliation, insulting her far more cruelly than being wanted purely for fleshly desires. Even a kind word beyond those courtesies he was bound to show would be something to cling to. Still, she thought, everything had changed as of this morning. It was obvious Lazar knew it too, which would explain his reluctant manner. Good. It was high time the dark eagle, as she thought of him, had his feathers ruffled.

'Your men will secure the area, Spur Lazar. I trust I can count on them to be discreet?'

He bowed his head in acknowledgement but not before she saw the unhappiness flit across his face, so briefly anyone else might believe they had imagined it. But not Herezah. She knew the planes and nuances of that face as well as she knew her own; had imagined herself touching it often enough, kissing those angry lips, staring into those furious silver-grey eyes.

'Valide —' Lazar started.

'Don't,' she warned. 'I will not be swayed. It is the only way to protect Boaz. You know that as well as anyone. Now, where are the women?'

'At the pools, Valide,' the Vizier answered.

She turned away from Lazar to make sure he understood who was controlling the power now. Boaz might be Zar but his mother was the ruler. She deliberately made sure she could still see the Spur from the corner of her eye though. Why waste any opportunity to feast on the looks of a man who genuinely fuelled her own desire. Zarab knew there was no other man around her who could. Too long had she had been forced to serve the whims of Joreb; old, fleshy Joreb and his strange sexual habits. And then of course there were the half-men, the eunuchs, with their soft tongues, who illegally satisfied many in the harem, but not her. She found them repulsive. As for finding solace in another woman she felt her stomach twist at the thought, although she knew a number of the odalisques and wives took their pleasures in each other. She scowled to push the notion away. Lazar alone made her heart pound.

'Good. And the wives?' she asked her Vizier.

'Salmeo arranged for them also to go swimming this afternoon, Valide. It is such a warm day. Everyone but Ameera took advantage of him opening up a long-unused gate to the Sapphire Pools.'

She raised an eyebrow in response. 'He *is* spoiling them,' she said, pretending not to notice Lazar's grimace at her condescension. 'And Ameera?'

'Unwell. Confined to her quarters.'

'Set a guard upon her.' The Vizier nodded. Herezah continued. 'So to the boys.'

'At the Lion Fountain,' Tariq confirmed. 'Salmeo is meeting them.'

'We're ready then.' She turned to the Spur and levelled him with a flinty gaze. 'Wipe that scowl from your face, Lazar. You take your commands from me now and, as distasteful as you find this, your men will see it done properly.'

'Yes, Valide Zara.' The words were dutiful but she heard the contempt; saw it flash angrily in his eyes. Still her cold heart leapt, enjoying that ferocity in him, and yes, the defiance. He was the only man in Percheron surely who wore his face clean-shaven, save the youngsters waiting desperately for stubble to show as their voices deepened. But this was no adolescent and he deliberately wore no beard with pride. The nakedness showed his firm jaw; he wore his dark hair loose and longer than any Percherese dared, and that, she knew, was another refusal to relinquish his independence. No jewels or adornments for Lazar either. No, she thought, he is dazzling enough.

Too many of the harem's women committed hours of conversation to how it might feel to bed Lazar. Not once had he shown the usual foibles of men though, and fallen for their charms. To do so was an offence of the highest order, of course, and would have meant instant execution.

Love it was not, she would be the first to admit this, but Herezah desired him with an irresistible passion, and she was the only woman of the harem who could now compel him to do her bidding. It made for interesting times ahead.

'Good,' she said, hoping her cheeks were not as flushed as they suddenly felt. 'Let's finish it.'

The princes of the harem wives, ranging in age from fifteen to just seven moons, were rounded up after midday; the baby seized from his wet nurse. It was she who set off the alarm with her terrible wails. She couldn't guess what might be occurring but she instinctively went running for the Sapphire Pools and the child's mother. The news of the snatching set the wives screaming as the reality of their fragile existence became clear. The Zar must have succumbed to his injuries, and that meant only one thing. Why else would the baby be taken so carelessly? They began clambering out of the pools and running wildly in the direction of where they last saw their sons, their eunuch servants throwing cloaks over bared flesh in a desperate attempt to protect the modesty of these women who were not permitted to show their face, let alone naked bodies.

But it was already too late for the mothers. Their lions were gone, vanished away to a secret place from where they would not return . . . not alive anyway.

The Grand Master Eunuch had quickly overcome any reservations he harboured at the Valide Zara's orders. He should not have been surprised at her choice of action and regretted his subtle warning of earlier. Salmeo made a promise never to underestimate Herezah again, certainly not now that she held his future in the palm of her hand. Oh, how the tables had turned!

Life had been near perfect for him with the old Zar. No-one, not even calculating Salmeo, could have foreseen the accident that had ended the Zar's life. A fall from a horse of all things! And Joreb such an accomplished horseman. He had been showing off for his sons; two men on horses charging towards the same flag stuck in the ground. Joreb had made the same race countless times, had gleefully wagered five of his prettiest odalisques against that crimson flag. And he had won this time, but paid handsomely with his life. Who could have known he would slip off his saddle as he reached down to grab the prize? Or that the other horse would arrive not even a full second later without any opportunity to avoid trampling the Zar's body so viciously that he would never recover from the massive internal bleeding?

Salmeo sighed. All was not lost. He was still the most powerful man next to Boaz within the palace, despite what that ambitious Vizier might believe. His wealth was so vast and his influence so far reaching that Salmeo feared no-one. No-one that is, except Herezah.

He must ingratiate himself swiftly. They'd had their differences but Herezah was not a foolish woman. Better the devil you know, as the old adage said. He could count on her knowing how to play the game. It was why she was today Valide Zara. He admired her in spite of their mutual distrust. They were similar creatures, both prisoners, both wildly ambitious, both with sufficient survival instinct to beat off their rivals.

Perhaps they could start again and she might let the past remain just that? He had hurt her physically and emotionally but that was life in the harem, she knew that, all the women did. If she would permit him to work with her, then together they would be a formidable pair supporting the Zar. Boaz was still so young, it would be up to Herezah to run the realm for him. Oh yes, she would initially rely on Tariq but soon she would need Salmeo's influence and he would give it gladly.

He would start by pleasing her with today's event. It was regrettable but necessary. No-one appreciated the need for absolute supremacy more than Salmeo. He thought about the harem and the great pity that it would be dismantled. It was one of the finest gatherings for several centuries, and he had had everyone in it in their place.

He was pulled from his thoughts by the sound of approaching children. It was time. He hoped Herezah would appreciate the symmetry between the old Zar's injuries and the spectacle he had hastily planned for the execution. He was sure she would.

Salmeo met the youngsters in a long-unused pavilion. The slaves, who had been given their sorrowful orders, herded the boys towards the huge Grand Master Eunuch who took the baby into his own arms and placed the infant into a crimson velvet sack.

'Is this a game?' one boy asked eagerly.

Salmeo's scar twisted as his mouth widened into a grin revealing his massive pearly teeth. There was a gap — as wide as a child's finger — between his front teeth that never failed to fascinate in a macabre way, for his tongue would flick in and out of the hole and cause a lisp to his speech. 'That's right, my prince. It's a new game we've devised just for this afternoon.'

'What's it called?' another boy yelled, cheerfully climbing into his own velvet bag.

'It's called Trample,' Salmeo replied in his effeminate, lisping way. 'Now hurry, boys.'

Giggling and pushing at each other, the boys — even the eldest — managed to wriggle into their sacks.

'Now we're going to tie you in,' Salmeo warned, keeping his voice light. 'Just loosely,' he lied.

He nodded and the slaves obliged, securing the children tightly into the velvet pouches.

'Everyone be still now,' the fat eunuch warned. 'The Zar will be present,' he added untruthfully as a threat.

Each velvet bag with its precious cargo was picked up by a eunuch slave and carried to a large empty pond. It was the ideal pit in which to place the children. Within moments, however, the baby began to cry and this set off some of the smaller boys who had tired of the heat and the dark of the bags. The game wasn't fun any more.

Ꭿ 4 Ꮀ

Herezah did not need to be veiled amongst the privacy of the harem courtyards or, indeed, anywhere that was considered the realm of the harem proper. Nonetheless, she wore a silken gauze draped over her head. She knew those present would think it was her showing respect but her intention was to hide her expression. It was precaution only. Herezah had little doubt that she would handle the spectacle with grace, unpleasant though it was bound to be.

Salmeo had sent a unit of his eunuchs to carry a silken canopy to shade her from the sun and to add to the mystery of the new royal she had become this day. It was a special honour he was paying her.

Striding unhappily behind her was the Spur. She felt sure Lazar was angry by nature. He was abrupt and distant with everyone except Boaz and the hated dwarf. Those two alone won amusement, even the spark of friendship in those fathomless grey eyes. She knew Lazar had liked Joreb and there had been a closeness between the two of them, but they had not had much to do with one another in recent years as the Zar had slumped into a lazier lifestyle. His slide into more carnal activity had disappointed the Spur, or so she guessed. It was just another reason, she was sure, for Lazar's fury at the world.

He was young for head of Percheron's security. Joreb had admitted as much one night after she had satisfied his latest in a line of curious fetishes.

The Zar had been relaxing in the pleasant stupor that usually followed a long session of sexual release. Her work was not done, though. Herezah, just an odalisque then, had offered to massage the Zar's spent body into sleep. She always preferred him in this mood, when his mouth seemed as relaxed as the rest of him.

Herezah took her chance. 'Tell me about the Spur.'

'Lazar?' he asked in a lazy voice. 'What a find he is for us. He was a prisoner, actually.'

Herezah knew from Lazar's looks that he was a foreigner. No Percherese had such light eyes or the aquiline nose, the sharp angles to their face. If not for the dark hair he could have been Galinsean.

'Where is he from?' she asked, intrigued.

'Guess?' the Zar suggested playfully.

'I cannot, High One. I am not experienced in lands beyond our shores ... I know only life in the palace.'

Joreb reached under his silk pillow and slowly withdrew the lightest of sapphires which sparkled in the soft glow of the lamps. A smile stretched across his mouth. 'If you guess right, this is yours.'

She stopped her massage and looked at her Zar sombrely. 'I don't want jewels, High One.'

'What is it you want, then, Herezah, my ambitious slave?'

She hated that word. Odalisque was bad enough but at least it sounded prettier. Nevertheless her expression did not betray her feelings. 'I want the status of Zaradine.'

And he had laughed with genuine pleasure. 'I knew it. Wife you shall be then, if you guess correctly.'

'And the sapphire?'

'Is yours anyway for amusing me.'

'Tell me about him first and let me guess after.' Her hands were working slowly, rhythmically once again.

'You know that a captured prisoner can fight his way to freedom?' She nodded. 'Although most don't take that option for the fights are to the death.'

'Between how many, my Zar?'

'Six is usual. As you can gather, not much chance for the prisoner.' He rested his chin on his fists as he recalled the incident. 'Ha!' he laughed, 'Lazar demanded twelve and the chance to speak with me. It was his audacity that won my interest. It amused me to watch the confidence being beaten from the pup so I asked the then Spur to choose a dozen of his best swordsmen and pit them against the prisoner.'

Herezah's dark eyes glowed as she had pictured the scene. 'He obviously won, Great One,' she said, reaching to pour the Zar a sweet wine.

Joreb turned, sat up and sipped. 'He barely broke a sweat, leaving each with broken limbs or groaning from some gash or injury, all disabling but none life threatening, which was the amazing part. He told me later, when I fulfilled his wish for an audience, that he thought it a waste of good men to kill for exhibition purposes only. And when I asked him whether he thought it a waste to risk his own life, do you know what he answered?'

Herezah shook her head; she hardly knew Lazar even though they were of similar age, but she did know her body craved him.

Joreb grinned. 'He said his life was never at risk! The cheek of it.'

'And what did he want with you, my Zar?'

'He wanted the freedom to live in Percheron. I offered him more — he accepted the position of Spur.'

'Why did he choose Percheron?'

'He told me that the city was a thing of such beauty it lifted his spirits. Our language, culture, people, art, architecture — he wanted to be a part of it.'

'He must have come from a place sorely lacking in all the loveliness we take for granted.'

Joreb had swallowed the goblet's contents and laid back again on his pillows. 'You are crafty, Herezah,' he said and moved her hands to his sex. 'Massage me there, but guess quickly, or I'll forget our bargain.'

Herezah remembered how her mind had raced that evening to seek the right answer. The prize meant more to her than anything and was the first major step towards her goal. As Zaradine, wife to the Zar, she could bear him a son, a prince, and that meant a chance to become Valide Zara. She knew she would cast her fate with her answer and that the Zar would never enter into such a curious bargain again.

'Well?' he asked. 'My mind is drifting, pretty one. It is heading south to where your fingers are calling me.'

She took a deep breath, remembering something she had overheard horrid Salmeo once airing about getting his greatest pleasure from making a Galinsean a eunuch. *'I've only experienced such a joy once and the wretch died anyway but it was wonderful to watch a Galinsean's manhood removed,'* he had explained. *'They are the most arrogant of races and the hardest to tame.'*

She risked it. 'You know, my lord, if I didn't know better I would think your Spur was Galinsean.'

'You know that cannot be, Herezah.' He yawned. 'True Galinseans are golden of hair and curiously light of eye but he is dark, although I grant you his facial structure and bearing are certainly typical of our warlike neighbour. Besides, Lazar has no animosity towards Percheron — he begged to be allowed to remain here.'

'May I have one more try, my Zar?' She tried not to beg but she had to win this contest.

'Why not? But I warn you, Herezah, although you arouse me I tire of conversation and should I fall asleep before I can take my pleasure, your guess will not count, so be swift.' He yawned to make his point.

'Zar Joreb, I would hazard that Lazar hails from somewhere near to Galinsea, then. I would guess at Merlinea.' She knew her geography of the region well and held her breath after giving her answer.

Joreb had moved fast and twisted her over onto her back, amusement twinkling in his no-longer-tired dark eyes. 'I shall give you a son tonight, wife,' and Herezah had arched her back with unrestrained joy as the Zar kept his promise.

Later still, as the Zar curled himself around her to sleep, she suggested he call another exhibition so the women could appreciate Lazar's fighting prowess. Joreb refused.

'Not even for your Favourite?' she begged, relishing the thought of seeing a half-naked Lazar oiled and made to do combat.

Joreb shook his head sleepily. 'A bond between two men.'

'He hardly counts, my Zar, he's only a Merlinean, barely one step better, in my opinion, than a Galinsean barbarian.'

Her new husband was wide awake then. 'We should never underestimate them, oh my beautiful, ambitious one. We must teach our son the same. Yes, we are a cultivated nation with art and language to impress. Galinseans may seem vulgar in comparison. But, Herezah, you should fear them, not poke fun at them.'

She listened and nodded, knowing she had pleased the Zar this night. The jewels that would be left for her tomorrow would be enough to send the other wives into a frenzy of jealousy. But Herezah wanted only one jewel now. She wanted a son and for him alone to take the title of Zar. The rest meant little to her. Power was everything — riches could follow.

She had pleased him enough that night almost thirteen years ago not only to be showered with jewels but to be called back for the next four nights. This was unheard of for Joreb and this was the moment Herezah signalled her intention to take the title of Absolute Favourite. It was during these torrid nights of sexual play and favour that she became pregnant with Boaz. She had not reached fourteen and the Zar was an old man by her standards but that had not mattered. She had given him a prince nine months later and he had given her the ultimate reward, calling her Absolute Favourite.

Someone cleared their throat and interrupted her private musings. It was Tariq.

'We're here, Valide,' the Vizier said.

She wanted to say she already knew this much from the unhappy moans of children. 'Remove the canopy,' she ordered and it was done.

Salmeo bowed his enormous bulk before her. She noticed he was wearing all black silks in honour of the soon-to-be-dead. His painted nail was the only patch of colour amongst the dark of his skin and robes. She glanced briefly to her left and saw the grinding jaw of Lazar. He had already given his orders to his men and so need not remain except out of a reluctant sense of honour, but she knew that honour was not for her; it was for the young princes.

'Shall we call for the creatures, Valide?' It was Tariq again, determined to take charge of proceedings.

She saw Salmeo scowl. 'Grand Master of the Eunuchs,' she called, deciding in that moment that as much as she detested Salmeo, he would be vital to her success. Despite her new status Herezah did not relish him as an enemy and was far-sighted enough to realise he would be a powerful ally. 'Please take charge.' She refused to look at the Vizier, who she was sure was visibly fuming at being overlooked.

Again the huge man bowed and as he straightened the look that passed between him and the Valide Zara spoke much of what never needed to be said out loud. An understanding had been reached. They were now a partnership. The past set aside.

'Bring the elephants,' he bellowed in a voice the harem rarely heard. Salmeo preferred to intimidate with his gentle, lisping lilt. Herezah felt sure the booming tone came from the very tips of his black satin slippers.

At the order fresh screams erupted from the imprisoned children. Suddenly none of them felt comforted by the notion of a game. Somehow things had turned sinister. Elephants were neither cuddly nor playful. Why were they being called? All of the children had marvelled at them in their father's magnificent private zoo but the lumbering giants were dangerous, especially the four males.

The tamed females had been left behind in the zoo. Only a mother enraged by threat to her baby could be persuaded to step amongst the restless velvet sacks. But the males had no qualms. They were led by their keepers to the pit where the noise of the children's terror intensified at the trumpeting of elephants.

At Salmeo's signal the huge animals were run into the pit and encouraged to raise themselves on hind legs and stomp down. This was a trick they had been taught to entertain the children; it was now being used to kill them.

The first bag to stop moving had only a small bundle contained within. Herezah winced. Her thoughts went to Ayeesha. It was her baby. After that death she promised she would wince no more. These were all potential murderers of her son. Even the other wives, demented by grief as they were, would ultimately understand, as she too would have had to had she not been the mother of Joreb's Chosen One.

Soon enough all the bags stopped their writhing and pitiful screams. Odd moans were quickly dealt with by an elephant's strategically placed foot. The Vizier, Herezah noticed, did look away when one sack broke and bright blood splashed the dazzling white cotton robes of one of the handlers. She recognised the face of that child, but only just — he was Boaz's closest stepbrother. They had been born just weeks apart. The back of the boy's head was smashed, its wet contents leaking out. She did not look away but cast quiet thanks to the gods for saving Boaz this trial.

Lazar had not spoken or moved beside her but she felt sure if it were quieter she would be able to hear his teeth grinding, for his jaw was working furiously. However, her stolen glance from beneath the gauze told her he did not cower but stared straight ahead at the grisly scene until Salmeo called a halt to proceedings. The Grand Master Eunuch had decided that the bags contained little more than pulp now. No bodies would be handed back to grieving mothers. They would be burned immediately, following the Valide Zara's instructions.

Herezah sighed, relieved it was done. The throne was safe.

As if reading her thoughts, Lazar turned slowly, deliberately, and looked straight into her eyes as though he could see through the veil and deep into her soul. 'Satisfied, Valide?'

She would not be baited but took pleasure in knowing she had managed to break through his well-constructed defences. 'Careful, Lazar. A new Spur can be appointed as easily as I blink.'

'As you see fit, Valide Zara,' he said, not intimidated at all. 'Excuse me, duty calls,' he added before she could return his brittle reply.

Herezah reined in her natural reaction. She might suddenly be the most powerful woman in Percheron but she was far too mindful of the Zar's warning when he had called for her earlier that day.

'Keep Lazar close to our son. He alone understands the Galinsean mind.'

No, she would not be replacing this Spur when he might be all that stood between Percheron and a Galinsean uprising, especially now that a boy sat the throne. She would let him have his anger for now. Herezah was clever enough to work out more subtle ways to have her revenge and she would exercise those as soon as the old Zar was cremated.

In fact, a wonderful notion was already taking shape in her mind for how next to impress upon the Spur of Percheron her power over him.

ᵔ 5 ᵔ

Lazar shaded his eyes and squinted into the shimmering scene below. They had been directed here by scouts. Out to the west the sun was already past its high point, and the fiercest heat of the day was scorching. He wrapped the tail of the white turban around his face. It was purely habit, for in the foothills sand was not a problem unless the feared Samazen whipped up, but that was a month away at least. It would get hotter still today before it cooled but time was against them. Night fell fast across the desert plains and although these were only the western foothills, barely fifteen miles from Percheron, the darkness would race to claim them faster than they could ride home. Not that being away bothered Lazar. They had been out on the ridges for days and he was happiest when he was away from people.

Home! He scorned himself for thinking of it that way. Percheron had, however, become a sanctuary. It still had its distasteful elements, and immediately Herezah came to mind, but surely there could be no realm more beautiful? Percheron had seduced him and he had become her willing lover. He wondered, as he gazed down at a tiny dwelling that clung to the steppes, whether he could ever leave the stone city. Until recently he would have answered no. Now he wasn't so sure. Herezah's influence was already being felt and he sensed her bite was only going to get worse.

44

She had disbanded the harem the same day as Joreb's funeral procession. Once more he had been forced to grind his teeth and sit out the second of Herezah's unpleasant spectacles. The Valide Zara had masterminded the event down to the tiniest detail, to the point of ordering that the horses which pulled the open-topped carriage and the old Zar's corpse should have the underneath of their eyelids smeared with pepper paste, so even dumb beasts had shed tears for the Great One's passing.

Lazar had never heard of anything quite so ridiculous but there was plenty more to come, such as the four virgins, holy women chosen for their beauty, drugged and thrown into the flames of the pyre. This was supposedly to symbolise each season of the old Zar's life, from birth through childhood, to adolescence and manhood. It was also a sly reminder that Joreb was the god Zarab's appointed representative on the land. By burning the holy women it reinforced the destruction of the goddess Lyana and the pointlessness of those who still privately worshipped her.

Herezah's third and final spectacle was to have the women of his harem unveiled, which was the most painful humiliation she could impose. It was more grievous than death for most of these women who were put into ordinary clothes before being paraded on foot and forced out of the palace and into the streets. Each one was given a pouch of gold and effectively cut loose from the protection of the harem and the lavish, lazy world they had known. They could sew, make fine quishtar and gossip. That was the sum total of their accomplishments ... unless, of course, one counted their ability to pleasure men to heights of ecstasy. If they looked after their money, hopefully that talent would not need to be promoted in the outside world that these confused wretches now inhabited.

Where they went, how they lived, or even if they survived, Herezah could not care less. They were no longer required. Their role as servants of the Zar died with him. As for those who claimed the title of wife, they no longer had status. That had died with the Zar and his eleven precious offspring.

Her next step was to assemble a new harem. Displaying her dark sense of humour, she had ordered the Spur of Percheron to join the hunt for suitable young girls. Fuming at his orders, personally delivered by the Valide, he had considered riding out of the city gates and never returning.

To calm himself he had strode in the direction of the harbour, knowing he would pass some of the city's inexplicably beautiful sculpted beasts on his way. They seemed to him to be so real and warm despite their implacable silence and stone flesh. They were creatures of myth and the only humanlike sculptures were the twin giants, Beloch and Ezram, who presided over the city's busy harbour, a massive horseshoe-shaped sparkling bay.

No, despite Herezah's presence, Percheron's enchantment for him had not waned over the years. In fact, he felt more connected to this city than his own.

His own. The thought made him sigh inwardly; it was his homeland across the ocean he was thinking about as he had reached to touch his favourite creature — Iridor, the owl ... the messenger of the Goddess Lyana.

Iridor had always attracted him and he could rarely pass any of the bird's images dotted around the city, without pausing momentarily to admire the owl or share a thought. He could never admit it to anyone but Iridor felt like an old friend. It was the first of the stone sculptures he had seen when brought through the vast Golden Gates of Percheron and the memory of that knowing expression on the owl's face had left a lasting impression. He had often thought somewhat whimsically that it was the secretive bird who had urged him to put forward the reckless challenge to the Zar that had won him favour.

No-one else, or so it appeared, bothered with the owl or any of the other magnificent engravings or sculptures. Some argued that Percheron was spoilt for art treasures and that if you grew up surrounded by such beauty you tended to take it for granted.

But there was more to it than that.

Lazar knew that the people had been taught from childhood that the ornate statues of the beasts and giants were linked to the Goddess and Lyana had no place in Percheron. Her followers had long ago been dismissed as cranks, and although some women still continued to worship at her shrine, they were few and far between.

Percheron's spiritual wellbeing had been cared for by the priesthood for many centuries now and Lyana had faded to myth. It was thought that the statues themselves dated back to the last occasion when the cyclical battle of the gods had erupted, but no-one knew for sure.

Nevertheless, whether it was truth or folklore, Lazar loved this story. He thought about it again as he stared at Iridor, sworn enemy of Lyana's nemesis, Maliz, the demon warlock granted eternal life by the jealous god, Zarab. Hating Lyana's popularity Zarab had offered Maliz the ultimate prize if he would rid the world of the Goddess and give men ultimate ruling over the matriarchal society in which Percheron had thrived.

Lazar gave a rare smile as he thought about the rising of Iridor which signified the return of Lyana and triggered the reincarnation of Maliz. They would do battle every four or five centuries, or so the story went. But it had been too many battles since Lyana had prevailed, her memory all but wiped out due to constant defeat; only the statues attested to her once powerful hold over Percheron. The story told that these were part of her army, supposedly turned to stone by Maliz in the last great battle.

The few true believers swore she would rise again to fight another battle. Lazar liked the notion of this spirit in Lyana.

He left behind the city proper to stroll into the more seedy area of Percheron down to the harbour, always a hive of activity and somewhere to lose oneself. He could be anonymous here in the mass of twisting lanes that had sprung up haphazardly around the eastern rim of the harbour. This was not a place where the wealthy or famous went. It was the haunt of the peasant

Percherese and thieves, sailors, low-class merchants and prostitutes. Lazar, wearing the common robes of the streets, moved swiftly through the market area and beyond to an open road that led to a lonely temple. A tiny one. It sat on a narrow strip of a peninsula that jutted a mile into the bay. Not as far out as Beloch, of course, but only people on boats could get close enough to the brothers. He looked out to where the enormous stone giant stood proudly on a plinth soaring upwards from the clear waters, guarding his city. Opposite him, flanking the other tip of the harbour's horseshoe shape, was Beloch's twin, Ezram.

Arriving at the tiny place of worship he climbed the short flight of stairs into the small vaulted space of simple design. This was a temple that harked back to the old ways, of a time when goddesses were worshipped and priestesses led prayers. Although he had never been inside it before Lazar liked its remoteness, and as Lyana had been in his mind, it seemed a good enough place to go for some quiet. He lit a small candle and kneeled at the altar below a sculpture of a serene woman who looked down upon him. He should have bowed his head in prayer but he could not take his eyes from the statue. Her soft smile was so tranquil, her eyes so sad, reflecting his mood. He fancied that her expression had been carved just for him, for this very day when he entered her temple with a heavy heart and a question. On her right shoulder sat an owl — it was Iridor — and amongst the folds of her dress flitted an assortment of birds and strange symbols.

Just looking at her soothed his anger.

'She's beautiful, isn't she?' a voice said, and when he turned a tiny hunched woman emerged from the shadows. She was dressed in aquamarine robes — the colour of the sea over which her tiny temple looked.

'I am Lazar, Spur of Percheron, priestess,' he said, standing and bowing.

When he straightened she was smiling. 'We have been expecting you.'

He was taken aback. 'We?'

Her answer was to look to the sculpture. 'This is Lyana. She especially welcomes you.'

'She is the loveliest of all the stone sculptures in Percheron, I'm sure,' he replied, knowing this to be a high compliment.

'Has she helped?'

'Pardon?'

'Did she answer your question?'

He frowned. 'I haven't asked anything of her.'

Again the soft knowing smile. 'Not yet perhaps. Forgive my disturbance, son. Please continue,' and the old woman made to leave.

'Wait.' When she turned to look at him, he hesitated. 'What did you mean, you were expecting me?'

'We have been waiting many years to meet you, Lazar. You have a reason for being in Percheron. You are welcome here always.'

He had no idea what she was talking about but her soft voice was mesmerising, as soothing as her sculpture's smile. 'I don't know your name.'

'I am Zafira. We shall meet another time soon.' Once more she turned to leave and again he stopped her.

'What can she tell me?' he asked.

She didn't turn this time. 'Please stay — you are needed here,' she said as the shadows swallowed her.

Lazar had puzzled over that brief conversation for many days now. How could the old priestess have known he was thinking of leaving the city? In fact it was her words that had convinced him not to ride out of the city in anger but to remain in Percheron — for now anyway. There was something about the certainty of the way she spoke to him that made him obey, although even her suggestion that 'they' had been waiting for him was confusing. He put it down to coincidence. Perhaps everyone in Percheron ultimately visited the Sea Temple, although in his heart he knew he was clutching at the thinnest of explanations. The Sea Temple was as unfashionable as it was redundant in the lives of the Percherese. They had no use for priestesses these days. Zafira was a remnant of a past long gone.

Jumo arrived now to disturb his thoughts of that day. 'Is all well, master?' he asked, guiding his horse to stand alongside.

Lazar smiled. He and Jumo had long ago ceased being slave and master, ever since Lazar granted the reed-thin man his freedom. But Jumo had neither refrained from the title nor from serving Lazar. They were now the closest of friends, their deep bond an unspoken commitment between them. Lazar had once described to Pez that losing Jumo would be like losing his limbs or his sight. 'I would be useless without him,' he recalled saying. And Pez had understood ... but then Pez understood everything.

'All is well,' he answered, looking into his friend's swarthy face, the colour of molasses and creased in bemusement. Jumo came from an exotic land far to the north that Lazar had never seen and was unlikely to. 'Am I making you nervous?' he asked, knowing full well that very little, least of all silence, unsettled Jumo.

They had been a party of twelve but as each girl had been found, she had been sent off with two escorts to the city. Herezah had demanded six girls from Lazar's foray into the foothills. He had sent five safely on their way.

Jumo's face broke into the smile he reserved for very few. 'No, your quiet manner is not making me nervous. What is troubling you, master?'

Lazar sighed. 'Nothing, my friend. I'm fine. Just still questioning this unpleasant task of ours.'

'They will fill a harem with or without your help,' Jumo offered. 'We need only one more girl to fill our quota. Her family will be happy, the Valide will be happy, surely the Zar will be happy and you, master, you will be happy to be returning to your proper duties. Everyone will be happy.'

'Typical Jumo reasoning,' Lazar replied dryly. 'You're right, although I don't know why I feel so reluctant to disturb that gentle scene down there.'

They both looked at the hut, its chimney cheerfully smoking. Outside two young girls, presumably sisters, sat, their backs to the men. The older of the two was brushing the other one's hair; they were as different as two sisters could be. The eldest was dark, whilst the younger one was lighter; the sunlight picked up fiery glints in her hair as her sister brushed it. The girls were singing. A much smaller child, a boy, buzzed around them like a fly. Nearby someone squatted, sorting rice in a large basin, her repetitive action one they had often seen in the neighbourhoods of Percheron. They watched her drag her hand flat across the surface of the grains, spreading them, then begin sorting grit and stones from the rice.

'Is that the mother, master?'

'Looks rather young,' Lazar replied, slightly mesmerised by the simple toil that she somehow managed to make elegant with her slim arms, long fingers. 'No, this would be the mother,' he added as a broader, clearly older woman emerged from the hut. He watched her squint as her eyes adjusted to the brightness.

'The father is a goatherd, I gather,' Jumo said, nodding towards the small pens beside the dwelling.

Lazar nodded. 'The scouts warned he would probably be away.'

'Does that bother you?'

'To take one of his children in his absence? It is up to the mother, I suppose.'

'You will offer a high sum for the lighter-coloured child, of course,' Jumo said, referring to the youngest girl.

'We need to see her face first,' Lazar answered and his tone rang with gathering anger. 'Herezah might blame me for not selecting suitably but I know how her mind works — she'd punish the child to get to me. No, we've done well so far, even the Valide could not complain, but I'll be damned if I'll give her anything to gripe about. I've seen what she's capable of and age is of no relevance to her.'

'Let us see for ourselves, then. Come,' Jumo replied. 'It is getting late.'

Lazar sighed. He looked out from the foothills and through the hazy heat he could just see the whitish sprawl that was Percheron but the sea and the sky blended into a mass of bright blue. It made him wonder whether he should take a voyage. It had been a long time since he'd seen his parents and siblings. His mother might even have forgiven him by now, although he doubted it. She was carved from the same block as Herezah. His mother would never forgive.

'You love the desert too much to leave it, master,' Jumo said softly beside him, and their eyes met.

'You frighten me the way you can read my mind.'

Jumo grinned. 'I've just known you long enough to guess.'

Lazar thought otherwise. It was uncanny how often Jumo seemed to know his private thoughts. But he left it alone, as he always did. 'Lead the way,' he said, and as he did so the younger of the two girls turned and looked directly at them. She did not seem troubled by their presence but the others were when she pointed, the mother gathering up her family around her and watching them wide-eyed, ready to flee like a startled animal.

Lazar pressed on doggedly down the incline, for even from this distance he could see the child was pleasant enough to look upon. Herezah would certainly have nothing to complain about.

'Don't be frightened, woman,' Lazar assured the mother as the land flattened out and he was able to dismount. He made no move closer to them. 'I am the Spur of Percheron; my name is Lazar. This,' he said, nodding behind him, 'is Jumo.'

The mother nodded at both of them. 'What do you want?'

Lazar had already done this five times in the last few days but it never got easier. It was unlikely that anyone had brought these people news of the Zar's death so it was not as though they could even guess at his purpose. How he hated this task.

'May I know your name?' he asked the mother.

'Felluj,' she said abruptly.

'Well, I bring a proposal from the palace, Felluj.'

Felluj looked momentarily startled. 'No-one in the palace knows us.'

Lazar cleared his throat. 'That's probably true. But I have offered this same proposal successfully to several families in the foothills in the last few days.'

'You come for my girls, don't you? My brother-in-law warned you might.'

There was no point in denying it or hedging around it. He nodded. 'Not all of them.'

Her solemn expression did not change but he saw something flash in the dark eyes. 'You can have only Ana.'

'No, mother!' the middle daughter cried and Lazar turned to her, despising himself for the pain he had caused to rack her features. She was dark like her mother, but it was her sister he was interested in. His gaze shifted to the small child whose hand she clutched and whose hair she had been brushing moments earlier.

'Ana,' he began, talking to the middle child.

'That is not her,' the mother interrupted, before turning to the daughter who held the rice bowl. 'Fetch her.'

'Uncle Horz said —'

'Hush!'

'But Father won't —'

'Do it!' the mother ordered. They waited. 'How much?'

Lazar was taken aback by the harsh exchange between mother and daughter. Felluj's cold attitude also unsettled him. 'Er, we need to see her first.'

'Oh, she'll suit your purposes but I won't let her go cheaply.'

The two younger girls were weeping now to add to Lazar's discomfort, but the boy continued to run in small circles, chasing

53

insects and wholly oblivious to the transaction that was occurring.

The mother must have heard some movement because she called into the silence: 'Don't hide, Ana! Come here, girl.'

First came the eldest daughter, scowling, reluctantly pulling another girl who seemed unaffected by all the attention. Square shoulders tapered through a slender body. She looked like a young colt, with long legs beneath the loose-fitting sheath that clothed her. Despite the roomy garment there was the definite swell of a woman's body beneath. In truth, only Jumo noticed the rest of the child; all Lazar could focus on was her face, oval and framed by darkly golden hair that fell carelessly to her shoulders and seemed to absorb the very sunlight. But it was her eyes, flanked by long dark lashes that dragged him completely into her spell. Lazar could not register their colour even though he was staring right into them, for they seemed to dominate him, to own him. There was a sense of drowning in those defiant pools.

'Master?' Jumo urged quietly.

Lazar pulled himself free of his suddenly muddled thoughts and saw that the girl's eyes were a sea-green and that her mother was mocking him with her sly smile.

'Good enough?' she asked, unable to hide her sarcasm.

The Spur's mouth felt so dry that he could not trust himself to speak immediately and his gaze was already back to the child who stared unerringly back.

'How old is she?' he finally asked.

'I'm nearly fifteen summers,' Ana replied.

'She's ripe for your purposes,' the mother said matter-of-factly.

Lazar watched the eldest girl scowl again. 'What is your name?' he asked.

'I am Amys,' she answered sullenly. 'And my father will not agree to this.'

'Hush!' Felluj admonished. 'I will make the decision. Come, masters, let us talk in private over kerrosh.'

Lazar could not refuse. Hospitality was the way of the desert people. Even the poorest family would slaughter its last goat to entertain a visitor. The brewing of the bitter kerrosh was high tradition in Percheron and among the harem women it was nothing short of an art form.

'Where is your husband?' he asked the woman when they were seated in the hut.

'He is moving some of the goats. He has been away for several days.'

'Why is your older daughter worried about her uncle? She's also adamant that her father will object — is this true?' It seemed a stupid question even to him. Which father wouldn't object to losing his daughter to a stranger?

Again Jumo seemed to listen in on his doubts. 'The harem will take care of Ana and raise her in unrivalled splendour,' he assured the mother, although it sounded to Lazar as though Jumo was saying this more for him.

'She will be taught skills and she will read, write, dance. She will be given wealth and even status if she pleases her elders.'

'How much are you prepared to pay for her?' the mother demanded, ending Jumo's gracious explanation.

'You seem quite keen to be rid of Ana,' Lazar commented.

Felluj shrugged. 'She's not my child.' Lazar's eyebrow raised itself in query. 'She belongs to my husband,' the woman explained.

'She's his daughter?'

The woman laid three glasses on the scrubbed table.

'She's not his either. He found her.'

'Pardon?'

The woman poured a steaming glass of kerrosh before him. 'I've put in one ball,' she said, referring to the sticky mass of sugar favoured by most in the beverage.

'Thank you. Please continue.' He sipped his drink. It was good. Strong and sweet.

She passed Jumo his glass. 'My husband found Ana as a newborn on the northern ridges. It was a wild night previous. The Samazen had blown through and the next morning he went in search of the goats that had been pastured there. He'd lost his animals but found her instead. A useless exchange as far as I'm concerned. At least goats keep us fed, give us milk, provide yarn and skins.'

'A baby survived the storm?' Jumo voiced Lazar's silent incredulity.

Again the woman shrugged. 'I'm telling you what happened. You can believe me or not. He brought her home and raised her as his own. In truth, one more mouth didn't matter so much then, but we've had two more children since. I've never felt about Ana the way my husband does.'

'Your daughters show concern which you don't,' Lazar commented.

'Pah! They're just worried about their father's feelings, but I worry about how we will feed and clothe ourselves. She's another woman's daughter! I have no feelings for her at all. I'm glad to see the back of her.'

'Clearly,' Lazar muttered as if he were tasting something bad. 'This must be done properly, Felluj. I won't be accused of stealing a child.' There was derision in her laughter at these words and Lazar understood. Girls were often stolen from these tiny foothill families by bandits and sold into slavery.

'I am not others,' he qualified. 'Your husband must —'

She interrupted him. 'He will understand when he sees your coin.'

Lazar felt suddenly sickened by her attitude; it reminded him of Herezah. Two mothers, both using children to further their status. He knew what it was to live without a mother's love. Perhaps a life of luxurious imprisonment was better for Ana than what was on offer here.

'What price freedom?' Jumo said, as though responding to Lazar's silent thought.

'You tell me,' Felluj said, 'and then I'll tell you whether it's enough to appease my husband.'

'Twenty-five karels,' Lazar offered, which was low. He hated Felluj's greed.

She laughed. 'Fifty and you can have her.'

He drained his glass. 'Fifty?' He raised an eyebrow, waiting for her to capitulate and decrease her price.

'She's worth twice as much,' Felluj said, not at all intimidated.

'Not to us,' Lazar said and stood. 'Thank you for the kerrosh.'

She said nothing but he saw a slight hesitancy in her expression.

The children watched them wide-eyed as they emerged from the hut, squinting from the bright sun, and only Ana smiled. It was a spontaneous gesture. As she did so Lazar felt a sensation, one he hadn't felt in such a long time he thought he had forgotten what it was like. There was a connection so strong he felt the jolt of it catch in his throat; the warmth in her innocent expression reached into his chest and touched a cold heart that had not been warmed in years. How long had it been since he had felt anything for anyone? Oh, the friendship between himself and Jumo was indestructible, as was the curious affinity he felt for the strange dwarf, Pez; and he liked Boaz well enough. But love? Love was something Lazar did not possess in his life. Love had visited briefly in his youth and then been torn away. Since that time he had let no-one into his heart. Something about Ana's simple smile stirred thoughts long buried and wounds he had healed through detachment and determination. It made him feel weak to experience such an awakening.

'Farewell, sister,' he said deliberately — it was meant for Felluj but it was towards Ana's soft green gaze that he directed it.

No-one responded as the two men silently climbed onto their horses. Lazar gave one last look at Ana, who was now expressionless, and at her stepmother in whom he sensed growing disbelief. He turned his horse back towards the steep path and began counting. He would give it to fifty.

He had passed the count and was resigning himself to having read the situation wrongly when he heard a voice. It was Felluj; she had run swiftly up the incline at a sharper angle than they were traversing and was waiting for them at the top of the ridge. She was breathing hard and still looked defiant. There was no preamble or pretence at dealing with honoured guests now. There was a bargain to be made and goods to be negotiated. He had seen it often enough in the slave markets — this was no different. 'How much, then?' she demanded.

'I told you before,' he said coldly. 'Twenty-five.'

'That is too low, Lazar, sir,' she pleaded, her first display of courtesy since they had arrived, save the kerrosh.

'It is fair,' he replied and felt rather than saw Jumo's unease. They both knew Ana was worth three, maybe four times as much and even Lazar couldn't understand his reluctance to pay a premium for this stunning child.

'My husband will grieve for her. She is his favourite and she's not even of his own flesh.' Felluj spat into the sandy soil of the ridge where only the narla weeds and gerra grasses grew to sustain the goats.

Ana arrived, clambering up the ridge. Lazar could see in those long-lashed eyes that this girl knew no affection existed for her in her stepmother's heart. And it was this notion alone, this sense of pain on behalf of the girl — a pain he understood — that forced Lazar to relent.

'I shall give you forty karels. Ask no more, woman, for you shall get not a zeraf extra from me.'

'I shall take it,' she replied instantly, 'if you take her now. She has no possessions.'

'Will she not want to wish her family farewell?' Jumo asked.

'Take her, I say!' Felluj urged and pushed Ana towards them.

'Give her to Jumo,' Lazar ordered, reaching for a pouch at his side. He counted out the karels and said: 'Hold out your apron.'

She did so and he dropped the silver from a height, not even bothering to reach down. One karel bounced out and Felluj went scrabbling after it.

'I don't want to leave,' Ana said into the awkward silence as if she had only just grasped what was truly occurring here.

'Hush, child,' Jumo murmured. 'You must come with us now.'

She did not struggle but began to weep softly, looking behind to wave pitifully to her brother and sisters below. All the purchases of young girls had been hard on Lazar but this one touched his heart, for in truth the other girls had been seduced by the idea of wealth and luxury. Ana was by far the most beautiful but he sensed no amount of riches or pampering would appease her, though why he felt this way, he could not say.

They departed with the sound of forty pieces of silver jangling in Felluj's apron as she stomped back down the ridge to her family.

Soon Ana's home and even the ridge she lived below was out of sight.

'What do you want me for, sir?' she asked, reaching from Jumo's horse to tug at Lazar's sleeve.

'I do not want you for anything, Ana,' he said, more sorrowfully than he intended. 'You belong to the Zar now, his odalisque.'

∾ 6 ∾

Zafira lived in a tiny dwelling in the loft of the temple, reached by narrow stone stairs, and with a breathtaking view across the harbour. She shared it with doves mainly, who liked the high vantage of the eaves to roost amongst, but she made welcome the many small birds that came daily to her window for scraps and fresh water.

She had her back to that window and its sprawling vista right now and wondered again, as she stared into the steamy swirls rising from her cinnamon tea, about her recent visitor and his importance. The voices that haunted her dreams had told her to wait for him and to welcome him when he finally came. She had waited several years in vain, almost forgetting about it, and then suddenly two days ago the man they had spoken of had wandered into the temple. They had given her no description of him and yet she knew instinctively that the spur was the one. He was younger up close than she had expected, with rugged looks and a remote disposition. There was nothing soft about Lazar. In fact everything about him was hard. The angular planes to his face, the way he carried himself with such bristling strength beneath the loose robes, the determined stride, the glower he regarded her with, even the anger she sensed he repressed. His words, his attitude — all of him seemed hardened. But not cruel. No; secretive perhaps, determined, bitter even, but not cruel, for all that hard exterior.

Why was he important? Important to what? She could not guess.

Her present visitor interrupted her musings. 'I'll pay you for them,' he said.

She smiled. 'Mindless stuff, Pez, I promise,' she said and sipped. 'Is your quishtar all right?'

'Delicious and you know it,' he replied, 'no-one brews better than you, Zafira.'

'Perhaps that's what I'll be remembered for then,' she said, amused.

'More, I imagine,' Pez answered and there was something cryptic in his glance.

She left it alone. Pez was mysterious enough without reading into his words or second-guessing the strange machinations of his mind.

'How did you come to be here, Pez?' she asked suddenly, glad to move away from her confused thoughts.

'Like most of the foreigners here I was captured and sold as a slave. Except I was such an oddity there was really only one place for me.'

'How convenient then that you have such an amusing way.'

Pez eyed the priestess in that serious manner which very few were permitted to see. 'You know better than to goad me, Zafira.'

She took his admonishment in the gentle manner it was given. 'You're such an enigma, Pez. Why is everyone around me so mysterious?'

'Oh? Who else has you so baffled?'

'The Spur paid the temple a visit.'

Pez nodded as if he had expected this. 'Yes, well, he left the palace seething, I'm not surprised he came somewhere to calm himself. And where better than here?'

Her expression of query prompted an explanation from Pez and she learned of Lazar's special duties commanded by Herezah.

'Oh, I see,' she said. 'He did seem troubled.'

Pez's odd collection of features rearranged themselves into a smile and it did wonders for his face. 'Troubled is an understatement. I think it was a very good idea he left the city for a while.'

'Why to the temple first though?' she wondered aloud and then added, 'I've been having dreams, Pez.'

'Oh?' he said, unfazed by the sudden switch in topic. 'Can I help?'

'I don't think so. I don't even know why I'm telling you this.'

'Because we're friends, Zafira, and heaven knows there are few enough of those in this place.'

She nodded, understanding only too well. 'But why are we friends? Why have we chosen each other? How is it that I know you are perfectly sane whilst the palace believes you are the opposite?' she pressed.

'You question life too much, old woman,' he replied gently, cupping his deformed hands around the cooling bowl of half-drunk tea. 'You and I are both seeking the same thing — we recognise it in each other, it's why we are friends.'

'What is it we search for?' There was a plea in her voice.

Pez shrugged. 'We shall know it when it presents itself. And to answer your other question, I keep my sanity a secret because the semblance of madness keeps me safe. It is my only defence in a highly dangerous place.'

'I'm sorry, Pez. I don't know what's come over me today. I have this sense of . . .' She trailed off, shaking her head.

'A sense of what?

The priestess turned her hands palm upwards in bafflement. 'That something is in motion and somehow it involves me.'

'What do you mean?'

'Something important.'

'Go on.'

She gave a look of exasperation. 'I don't know, Pez. That's just it.'

'Is it connected with your dreams?'

She nodded. 'I'm sure of it but I can't really remember anything specific, other than I was told to expect a man and that he was important.'

'The voices you spoke of told you this?'

'Whispers really. But I can't tell you precisely what they say.'

'How do you know they meant Lazar?'

'I don't but I feel very sure it's him. Why I was told to expect this person I have no idea. Oh, Pez, I'm sorry to sound so vague.'

'Don't upset yourself, my friend. I myself feel I'm here for a reason but can't tell you why.' He smiled sadly.

'How long have you been in Percheron, Pez?' she asked.

He looked around and scratched his chin and Zafira was arrested by the notion that Pez looked like a bird. His nose reached so low it was almost a beak. It was the first time she had been struck by such a thought even though they had met like this many times. She tried not to smile at her silly notion. 'It must be past two decades now,' he answered.

'That long!'

'Must be. Boaz is fifteen and I was the Zar's jester for at least six summers before our new ruler was born.'

She smiled. 'And you've frustrated, exasperated and deliberately irritated Herezah for all that time, I'm sure.'

'Oh, that's the least I can do,' he replied, sharing her amusement. 'I hope you have no spies here, my friend, or our new Valide will have our heads on spikes before we pour another glass of tea.'

She stood to heat fresh water. 'Fret not, Pez. My doves here would warn me if anyone is around ... they coo at the slightest thing. I gather the changes have already begun at the palace. You'll have to watch yourself.'

'She hates me, that's clear, but mainly for the reason you speak of — that I frustrate her. I know she's using magical means to dig into my past, my mind.'

'How so?'

'Yozem.'

She made a sound of disgust. 'Evil woman, a curse to her kind.'

'She can find nothing on me,' he said softly.

Zafira was not prepared to let this comment be swallowed and forgotten with the fresh brew. 'Why not? Aren't people terrified of her because she can read anyone?'

Pez pulled an expression to suggest he was not bothered by it. 'Most don't even know whether she exists or not. She does, of course, holed up in the horrid crypt-like chambers beneath the palace. Either I'm impervious to her dark magicks or they don't exist and she's a fake. Whichever way it is, Herezah has nothing she can lay at my feet, and besides, Boaz loves me to bits. She will not win an argument for my death over the new Zar — trust me.'

'You're very confident, Pez.' Her tone suggested he should be more cautious.

'I am also very careful, my friend. Don't worry about me.'

'What about Tariq and that vile head eunuch?'

Pez nodded. 'With Herezah's influence and the power she will extend to them, I think we have a right to be worried. It's why Lazar's presence around the palace is important. He brings balance. Boaz worships Lazar, which is good fortune for us for he listens to what the Spur advises. I don't think our new Zar has much time for Tariq but he's still young. We cannot expect too much of Boaz too soon — he still has a very young man's notions and urges. In all truth I'm sure that he would rather ride and shoot, fish and play than think about political matters. This is what Herezah is counting on, of course. She'll fuel his pleasures, all the time usurping more and more power for herself and her sycophants.'

'A grim picture you paint,' Zafira said.

'Well, the assembling of a harem will keep all three of them busy for a while.'

Zafira nodded and they sat in comfortable silence for several moments as she poured a fresh bowl of tea for each and moved to the window. She sighed. 'So, I wonder what it is that we're both waiting for?' She stared out to sea and, as always, marvelled at the grandeur of the twins in the harbour. 'I feel we're like Beloch and Ezram out there, waiting for something to happen.'

'You might be right, old friend,' Pez answered.

Lazar seemed in no urgency to return to the city. They had made camp on a rocky outcrop and could clearly see the sparkling waters of the Faranel now and the glittering city spreading down to her edge. It was as if pastel lava had erupted from the hilltop where the palace stood and slid down to the natural harbour, hardening on its slow journey to form the superb architecture of Percheron.

It was Ana who made this observation, much to the silent delight of Lazar, quiet at the best of times but downright sullen this evening. 'And you've seen a mountain erupt and spill the earth's hot contents, have you?'

'In my dreams I have,' she said, frowning. 'I think they must exist somewhere across the lands and it was frightening, whereas Percheron lifts my heart.'

Lazar said nothing but was secretly thrilled by Ana's description of Percheron. Since first seeing the city he too had always felt . . . what was it? Restored?

'Well, I think it's a beautiful notion, Ana,' Jumo said, filling the silence, 'and shall always think of the city that way from now on.'

'Do you not like me, sir?' Ana asked, looking at the Spur in that direct way of hers.

'What makes you say that?' he growled, busying himself with stirring the glowing coals of their small fire.

'You glare a lot at me, sir. I don't know what I've done wrong.'

'You've done nothing wrong, Ana,' he answered.

'That's his happy face,' Jumo chimed in, and Ana giggled with him. It won a fresh scowl from Lazar.

'What are you sad about, then?' she persisted.

'I don't know,' Lazar answered and there was a wistfulness in his tone which puzzled Jumo. 'Here, eat,' he added, handing Ana a piece of the poultry they had cooked.

'I don't eat birds,' she said apologetically.

'This is chicken. Not a real bird,' Jumo put in.

'Because it doesn't fly you mean?' she said. He nodded. 'It has wings, Jumo. I think a chicken would fly if it could, which makes it a bird for me.'

'We'd all fly if we could,' Lazar grumbled.

Ana seemed to find this amusing and laughed again at the Spur. Jumo wondered about the last person who laughed at Lazar and where their head had ended up. And yet here he was allowing a young slip of a thing tease him. Wonders would never cease.

'Well, if you're not going to eat, let me suggest you sleep,' Lazar said to Ana. 'Tomorrow we'll ride all day and reach the city late. There won't be time to catch your breath even. Valide Zara will be keen to see you.'

'Who's Valide Zara?' she asked, all innocence.

Lazar frowned at the thought. 'She's your new mistress.'

'Is that who you're selling me to?'

'She has already bought you, Ana, not me. Your mother sold you to the harem.'

'Felluj is not my mother. I should prefer to stay with you and Jumo.'

The men glanced at one another. 'You will make friends, I promise.'

'Are you my friend, Lazar? Promise me you'll always be my friend.'

Jumo grinned privately. He had never seen his master so disconcerted.

'You have my word,' Lazar promised.

⌒ 7 ⌒

They arrived before sunset, a couple of hours earlier than Lazar had anticipated, so he decided to give Ana a brief tour of Percheron, knowing she might never be permitted to see this beautiful city again. By tomorrow morning Ana would know she was a prisoner with all those qualities that made her such an intriguing free spirit stamped out of her until she performed in the remote, rehearsed manner of all the harem women. He had heard tales of their personalities surfacing in the bathing rooms and behind closed doors, and he could believe it. Wanted to believe it. But to all intents and purposes, the women of the harem lost their rights to free expression. Perhaps even Herezah had been a carefree young thing once.

Herezah! The very thought of the woman made him want to linger as long as possible outside the palace itself with his precious cargo.

'Jumo, perhaps you could take the horses and our things back to the palace barracks?'

'Are you not coming, master?'

'I thought I'd show our guest a little of Percheron's sights before I deliver her to Salmeo.'

'Very good,' Jumo replied, but his warning glance said far more. 'Goodbye, Ana.' He helped the youngster from the horse they had shared.

67

She surprised him with a hug. 'Goodbye, friend Jumo. You won't forget me, will you?'

'Never. You will make us proud. One day I suspect Spur Lazar and I will have to bow before you.'

'I would never make you do that,' and she smiled softly.

Jumo straightened and took the reins of Lazar's horse. 'Be careful, master,' was all he would risk.

'I shall be back within a couple of hours at the most,' Lazar assured. 'Come, Ana, let me show you some of this beautiful city.' He turned his back on both of them and strode off.

'You'd better hurry, child,' Jumo urged. 'He waits for no-one.'

She spared a final glance for the tawny little man and then she was lost amongst the crowd of people pushing towards the main gates. It was not hard to spot Lazar towering erect over the shorter Percherese population. He had taken off his head covering and his dark hair had fallen loose to just above his shoulders. Ana reckoned it could do with a good wash and brushing. She imagined how this man's hair might feel if she was attending to it, and a warmth passed through her body. It felt good to be near Lazar yet if asked to explain why, she was not sure she could, particularly as he was so distant and grumpy, but there was something else. Her young mind could not wrap itself fully around it but she wondered if he was someone who could be badly hurt. A person who covered his weakness with his gruff manner. Despite that vulnerability, Ana sensed only intense power in the man. He was his own person. Although he might follow orders, she guessed that no-one told Lazar what to do; she knew in her heart she had a similar trait. This was obviously going to be difficult for her now that she had an 'owner' to answer to. Ana decided that she and Lazar were souls who were destined to meet, and as this notion gelled in her mind, she realised she had caught up with the man who claimed her thoughts. Ana startled him by taking his hand.

'I might lose you,' she said in answer to his surprised glare.

He nodded. 'Look at these creatures, will you?' he marvelled as they approached the city walls. 'Aren't they spectacular sculptures? They look so real.'

'They are beautiful,' she agreed, her eyes sparkling with equal wonder. 'But they are not sculptures, Lazar.'

'Oh?'

'They look alive because they were a long time ago.'

He snorted. 'They lived? What, that gryphon over there?'

She nodded seriously.

'How do you know? Are you that old that you have seen them?' he challenged with amusement in his tone.

'I think perhaps I am what they call an old soul.'

The huge gates of Percheron were supported by two monstrously large lions with jagged manes and huge wings that folded down their strong backs.

'Aren't they magnificent?' Lazar said, pausing to touch one. He always felt compelled to do so every time he passed.

'They are Crendel and Darso.'

'Oh, they have names too?' he said, irony lacing his tone now.

'Just like you and me,' she said, unaffected by the jest in his voice.

'I'm not even going to ask how you know,' he said, 'because I too can make up things, Ana, and I'm glad of your imagination.' He surprised himself by bending to pull her close and stare at her. 'Because it's your imagination that will save you. You will always have it to escape to.'

'Don't be sad, Lazar,' she said, stroking his lank hair.

Her touch was so innocent and yet so intimate it took his breath away. He was stunned to feel his heart melt as he stared at her large trusting eyes. He considered her bleak future as a plaything to a man. For a fleeting moment he considered running away with her. Taking her back to the foothills, or better, trying to find her true mother. Or he could just take her into his own home; he didn't actually live at the palace or in its barracks, so it could be done discreetly. Perhaps he could say he bought her at the slave market to help keep house for him. Then she would be safe. He would see to her education and he would help her make a good marriage. His mind raged and yet he knew in his heart he could do nothing of the sort. Herezah had demanded six girls of him. The men he had sent ahead already knew he and Jumo were last seen heading towards one of the families in the western foothills. The Valide was too cunning — she would learn of his new housekeeper. And Ana was far too beautiful to escape notice.

He looked away, resigned to her fate and hating himself that he had personally chosen her destiny. 'Let me show you some more,' he said, hoping his voice did not reflect the angst within. Silently he berated himself for his strange attitude these past couple of days. Suddenly he was an emotional liability; eyes misting without warning, feeling introspective, questioning his life and its meaning. And worst of all, allowing a young girl to add fuel to the fire of those insecurities.

Once again holding Ana's hand, he weaved her through the streets of Percheron as dusk descended and lamps were lit and the city clothed itself in its more salubrious mantle.

'You must be hungry?' he asked. She nodded. 'How about a sharva?'

'What's that?'

'I'll show you,' he said and his own mouth watered at the thought. 'I trust you eat meat?'

'I do. Just not birds,' and she smiled her apology. They wended a slow path into the markets, a warren of alleyways. People meandered around them, going about their business of buying everything from fresh meat to silver bracelets.

'I love it here,' Lazar admitted. 'Each narrow lane is known for a specific craft. Now this one that we're in specialises in the flat triangular sort of hats that the everyday Percherese favour. The hats for our esteemed citizens are made in another street. Now see that woman over there?' Ana nodded. 'She uses twelve needles to knit the yarn.'

'Ah yes, they do this in the foothills too.'

'Of course, you would have seen this.'

Ana smiled. 'It's knitted very wide and then they dye them and shrink the hats in the huge boiling bowls.'

'That's right. They call them the cauldrons. After drying them, they use a dry thistle to tease up the fibres, like this.' He pointed to another woman hard at her toil. 'And you end up with one of these beauties.' He put a red coriz, as it was known, on his head, its tassel dangling in his face.

She laughed. 'Another street?'

The next alleyway was devoted to rugs, and the one after that to fabulous cushions fashioned in velvet and silk, wool and skins in every size and shape imaginable. They made their way through the torch-lit alleys past shops selling fabrics and beautiful hanging lanterns, then exquisitely painted tiles and finally into the maze of lanes given over to the art of food.

Ana was drawn to the spice sellers where sacks of brightly coloured powders and seeds, beans and pods were displayed. She stood quietly and watched as women pointed to what they wanted and gave the amount. The man who sat cross-legged near a set of scales called to his helper — a tiny boy — who scampered around scooping up the wares into squares of fabric. The man would weigh them and almost always the boy was right, rarely having to return to the designated sack to fetch more of the spice or return some. Satisfied, man and customer would exchange money whilst the child expertly tied the bought produce into the square of fabric with a piece of silk.

'Tamara, caracan, alpse, vergun, zarakor,' Lazar listed, pointing to the various sacks. 'Smell this,' he said picking up a small pod and crushing it in his palm.

'Gezil?' she asked.

Lazar grinned. 'You're very clever, Ana. Do you know what it is used for?'

Ana shook her head. 'I know its fragrance because my father showed it to me once, growing on the long-leafed trees in the foothills. The berry hardens from red to this shiny black.'

Lazar nodded. 'They flavour custards with it, but if it is crushed before it hardens and rubbed on raw I'm told it's very good for toe sores,' and he pulled a face to make her laugh.

A man was roasting nuts over a small open fire. He beckoned to them. Ana looked up at Lazar expectantly — she hoped he'd say yes but she followed his gaze and saw another man in a tiny hole in the wall, slicing roasted meat from a spit.

'Sharva,' Lazar said theatrically and led Ana to the tiny booth. He put two fingers in the air and dug in his pockets for coins.

The man handed them each a folded flat bread, from which emanated a heavenly smell. Inside the folded bread Ana could see thin slivers of the flame-cooked meat, green leaves she had never seen before, rounds of something else green that looked like a fruit but not one she knew. She did recognise the fat chickpeas and translucent slices of onion, though. All of this was drenched with a thick, tangy white sauce that was soon running down their chins and her slim arms.

They sat down around a central stone fountain.

'Good?' he asked in between bites.

Ana's muffled response through her bulging mouthful made him laugh — it was obvious she was enjoying her meal. When they had finished, he bought her a small sherbet made from pulped fruit.

'This finishes it perfectly. It takes away the spiciness from your tongue and adds a cleansing tang. This sherbet is not as scrumptious as you'll eat in the palace, of course, and I'll let you discover why,' he said with a wink, handing her one half of a purple berren fruit, whose flesh had been scooped out and replaced with the cool sherbet.

She used the wafer he gave her to ladle the fruit pulp into her mouth and groaned her pleasure. 'I've never tasted anything like this before. I shall never forget it,' she said, laying a small hand on his wrist. Again she felt a pulse of warmth move through her as their skin touched. Lazar didn't say anything but she knew she had pleased him, adding, 'And I don't think even the palace sherbet could taste this good.'

'Why do you say that?' he asked.

'Because right now I'm free as I eat this. The next time I taste anything as good I shall be a slave — I'm sure that will make it taste very different.'

Lazar nodded seriously. For such a youngster, she could philosophise with the best of them. There was something rather unsettling about Ana's insights and yet, at the same time, they made him feel safe. As though he'd finally found a haven in someone else's mind.

They washed their hands and mouths in the small fountain.

'What's through there?' she asked, flicking water from her fingers.

'Aha, well now, beyond that bend are the lanes of gold. Would you like to see them?'

'Oh yes, I would.'

He guided her through. The sky overhead had deepened to black and the stars were bright and shiny like tiny jewels flickering amongst the inky cloak of night. Lazar realised he was having fun. He could not remember when he had last felt so carefree. Many people had recognised him, of course. The Spur was a distinctive man in Percheron, but it didn't matter tonight. Normally he hated the intrusion on his thoughts but tonight he nodded at the passers-by, accepting their acknowledgment and salutations, even smiling once — much to the surprise of the courteous person hurrying past.

In Gold Alley, as it was known, Ana watched the shopkeepers haggle over prices with their customers. It was a hive of activity and yet it seemed unhurried as people were absorbed in their transactions. Her gaze was drawn to one dark corner where she saw a tiny old woman, her face veiled, pulling what looked like a gold chain from beneath her robes, but she cupped it in her hand so quickly, Ana couldn't be sure what the jewellery actually was. The man she spoke with loomed above her, dirty, unshaven, clearly a street seller rather than a registered shopkeeper.

Ana mentioned it, pointing to the frail woman.

Lazar nodded. 'Yes, they're called alley cats here. They have no set spot; you'll see them roaming all the laneways, looking for people to buy and sell to. The shopkeepers hate them but it's not against the law so they continue, though I imagine it will be outlawed soon as there are just too many of them suddenly. They ask no questions, need no proof that the item you're selling is yours, give you no guarantee that the coin they pay or the gold they sell is genuine.'

'Then why does anyone do business with them?' she asked. 'Surely it would make more sense to deal with someone who must trade honestly?'

'Because the alley cats ask no questions. That woman probably needs the money so badly that she will deal with this person, even though she would prefer not to.'

'Can we not help her?'

'Why?'

'Because it's a good thing to do.'

He smiled at the earnestness in her expression. 'How, Ana?'

'You buy her gold.'

'What?' he laughed. 'I don't think so.'

'Please, Lazar. That man will try to steal it from her. She looks desperate so he'll not pay a fair price.'

'You're perceptive, Ana. That's surely what will happen but it's not for us to interfere.'

Her expression clouded, grew grave, determined. 'How much did you pay for me?'

'Pardon?' he said, taken aback by her directness although he knew he should be used to it by now.

'What was I worth to my stepmother?'

Lazar could see it was pointless trying to skirt this issue. 'Forty karels.'

'Offer the old woman the difference. I have no sense of value, Lazar, but I think you probably took advantage of Felluj's desperation to be rid of me — just as the alley cat is taking advantage of the old woman. You could see that our family was penniless and so you could offer what you wanted. What am I truly worth to the palace . . . twice as much?'

'Probably,' he admitted, compelled to be honest with this girl whose harsh words hurt deeply as she held him so painfully in her gaze. He felt the ache all the way to his heart.

'Then offer her the other forty — you can tell the Valide that I cost that much,' she begged.

Without giving Lazar another moment to consider, Ana rushed over to where the old woman was about to hand over her jewellery.

'Wait!' Ana cried. 'How much are you selling your gold for?'

The old woman — far older than he had first thought, Lazar noted — turned and smiled gently at Ana. 'Twenty karels, my girl.'

'I will give you forty for it!' Ana exclaimed.

'Hey!' the alley cat said angrily. 'Stay out of it, stupid girl. You don't look as though you have a zeraf to your name!'

Ana ignored him. 'Please,' she asked the old woman. 'Let me buy it.'

'Go!' the man yelled, pushing Ana, which was a mistake, for within a blink he felt his arm enclosed in a grip so hard he squealed.

'Don't touch her, scum,' Lazar said, squeezing harder, watching the man double over slowly. 'You're lucky I don't throw your kind into the pit, or worse.' He let go of the man.

'Spur,' he bowed. 'Forgive me, sir. But I was doing an honest trade with a customer.'

'Honest, my arse,' Lazar sneered. 'Go on, be glad I don't take it further.'

The man glared at Ana and the old woman but turned furiously and left without another word.

'It was honest by his standards anyway,' the old woman said generously from beneath the hood she seemed to hide under. Her voice was kind, with a soothing singsong quality to it.

Lazar retrieved his money pouch from his belt. 'Here, forty karels is the agreed price, is that right?'

'It is, I thank you, Spur Lazar,' the woman said and rather than holding out a hand, she opened a pocket, encouraging him to drop the coin into it, which he duly did. It occurred to him that this was odd but the thought was gone almost as soon as it arrived.

She turned to the child. 'And this is for you, Ana.' She handed the girl an exquisitely sculpted gold owl.

Lazar took a sharp intake of breath. It was a tiny statue of Iridor. He felt confused. He could have sworn it was a plain gold chain she had been selling, but even to his untrained eye it looked worth more than forty karels. However, something about her manner prevented him from saying so.

'Are you sure you can bear to part with this sculpture of Iridor?' Ana asked, stunned by the bird's beauty.

'Oh yes, and particularly to you.'

Ana smiled and the old woman reached out to hug her. Then she turned and tottered off. Lazar was still frowning; not only baffled by the gift itself, which had seemed to change shape before his eyes, but by Ana's knowledge of who it represented.

'I could have sworn she was selling a bracelet or necklace, not an ornament,' he said.

'I agree.' She hesitated before saying what was on her mind. 'And I never gave her my name and yet she knew it.'

Lazar swung around but the old woman had disappeared into the darkness of the alleys. 'She knew my name too, although I suppose I'm known in the city but not you.' He frowned again. 'Ana, how do you know the name of the bird that sculpture represents?'

'Everyone knows Iridor,' she said casually.

'Not everyone. Certainly not people your age.'

She shrugged as if to assure him it was of no importance, then added, 'I've always known him.'

He wanted to press further but Ana pushed the gold bird into his hand, taking him by surprise.

'It's yours,' she said, 'you paid for it.'

'Keep it, Ana. It was you who paid for it. You are worth ten times as much.'

She smiled up at him and the connection was true. He was not imagining the feeling of her warmth washing over and through him.

'They will not permit me to keep it, will they?' Ana asked.

He shook his head sadly. She was right, of course. 'I suspect not. It will go into the palace coffers and probably never be seen again or, worse, melted down. Iridor isn't exactly a friend to our people.'

'Pity he's seen that way,' she said sadly. 'He's always been our friend.'

Lazar was taken aback by her words. He felt himself slightly lost for his own.

Ana filled the awkward pause. 'No, you keep it for me. Let it remind you of me and of our friendship.'

Lazar pushed the bird into his pocket and took her hand. 'I shall keep it safe for you,' was all he would risk saying. 'Now, it's time I took you to your new home.'

'Lazar, don't just keep it safe. Keep it near.' She searched his face for some sort of confirmation that he understood her intensity.

All he could do was nod gravely and that seemed to satisfy her.

He hated every moment of the journey that brought them closer to the palace. With each step he felt that former sense of freedom, that release from the weight of his world, dissipate. With each stride he felt his shoulders hunch closer and his insides harden again once more, but this time it combined with a new sadness to ponder: Ana would be gone.

They arrived at the palace gates. He announced himself and his charge at the Moon Courtyard and now he experienced a terrible sense of loss. It was official. Ana had arrived and been registered by name at the palace. There was no turning away now.

She was palace property.

8

Pez found Boaz alone in his chambers. Joreb had long ago given permission for the dwarf to access all areas of the palace — he was the only person in the entire retinue who had absolute freedom. Thus the guards were used to seeing him come and go as he pleased, whether it be to the Zar's rooms or even the harem for that matter. He was the only intact male to visit the prized, most viciously protected place in the palace without any threat to his wellbeing.

'I thought I'd find you here,' he said. 'Would you prefer to be alone with your sorrow?'

'Do you know,' Boaz said, 'you're the only one who has even considered that I might be grieving for my father. Everyone else is treating me as though I should get over it and get on with taking on my new role. My mother's the worst. For her my grief is akin to a headache: something to sleep off with a mild soporific.' The last few words were uttered with such disgust that Pez remained quiet. The boy was angry and entitled to be. 'Don't they understand? My father has died! I loved him as any child loves their father.'

Pez moved deeper into the room. 'So how can we help you?'

'I just want to be left alone,' Boaz replied, sullen now. He had seated himself at a window and was gazing out across the harbour.

Pez looked at the Zar and realised suddenly how tall his young friend was, and lean — as his father had been. But that was where the physical similarities ended. In looks Boaz was all Herezah: dark hair and eyes, with smooth olive skin. He possessed her strong, beautiful bone structure, and Pez imagined how hearts must already be fluttering in girls' breasts at the thought of their new Zar.

'You know that cannot happen, Boaz,' Pez said gently. 'One of the major attributes that everyone will be looking for in you is strength of character —' He held his hand up to stop the Zar. 'I know you possess this but you need to show it to all the royal watchers who are waiting to pounce on your weaknesses and prey on them.'

'I don't want to be happy yet,' Boaz replied. His tone was haughty now. 'It's obscene to think I should sing and dance with my father's body barely cold.'

'I understand, truly I do, but you must demonstrate that you are strong. I don't suggest you make merry, Boaz, but you must participate in palace life. Don't withdraw. Be seen, be noticed. You don't have to smile or give pretence at happiness. In fact it would be all the more powerful if you were grave. It means you're taking your father's death seriously and that you're anything but a throne-hungry son. But let the palace see you around its halls and let the people know you are going about your duties stoically.'

There was silence for a minute.

'You're right, as usual,' Boaz said eventually. 'I'll make an effort.'

'I'm proud of you. Let your mother know you are equal to the task, and that this is your throne.'

'And not hers?' Boaz finished, turning around to regard the dwarf.

'I didn't say that.'

'You didn't have to.'

'I have no doubt that she can assist you immensely. But she can also undermine you.' He changed the subject, his voice turning bright. 'So, what have you been thinking about all alone in this grand new chamber?'

There was a silence and then Boaz sighed heavily. 'I've been staring out to sea all evening watching Beloch and Ezram.'

'Oh yes?'

'Do you know, Pez, it's the first time I've ever really paid attention to them. They've always been there so I suppose growing up I didn't take much notice.'

'I think most of the city folk suffer the same disease. One of Lazar's great gripes is that none of us appreciate the fine art all around us. Do you know their story?'

'Of the giants? No, we've never been taught the old legends — they think it's sacrilegious.'

'Of course they would! The priests fear a return to the old ways of worshipping the Mother.'

'You'll have to explain that, Pez,' the boy said, crossing his legs, knowing he was about to be told a story.

'How about I pour some wine first?' Pez poured two cups with watered sweet wine and waddled over to the window seat. The dwarf made himself comfortable and then cleared his throat.

Boaz gave a small grin, his first in days, and raised his glass. 'To a lighter heart,' he said. The two of them drank.

'Now, where to begin?'

'Tell me about the priestesses,' the young Zar suggested as he settled back into cushions.

'All right. Centuries ago, Percheron followed the ways of the Great Goddess whom we know simply as Mother, and worshipped female deities. The temples were inhabited by holy women. They were silent places, which is why you'll see so many of the sculptures in our temples with fingers to their lips.'

'What does it mean?'

'Silence represents the soundless womb that gave birth to the first gods. Some of the oldest writings teach that Silence was the mother to the Great Goddess herself.'

'But now they're noisy places. I don't often enjoy a visit to the temple.'

Pez nodded. 'The priests changed everything. Now the temple is a gathering place. Prayer blends with socialising. Moneylenders, as you know, now set up their stalls outside the temples because these are places where lots of people meet.'

'So temples were once quiet places of prayer and overseen by women?'

'Yes, indeed. The holiest of our people were women. Lots of the symbols you see around you, Boaz, have female connotations.'

'Oh?'

'Over here.' Pez pointed to a recurring motif on a painted frieze on one wall of the chamber. 'You see this. What do we call it?'

'Wait,' Boaz said, screwing his eyes tight and concentrating. 'It's known as the universal life charm.'

'Good, your scholars teach you well, even though they don't explain much. Did they teach you that it's also known as the Cross of Life and that it represents the union of the female and male?' Boaz shook his head. 'The oval shape on the top of the cross is female. The cross itself is male. And there's more if you look for them.' The dwarf paused and took a sip of wine. 'Think of the decoration of the great feasting hall in the palace. What symbol comes to mind first?'

'Er, the one which looks like a shell that you can hold to your ear and hear the sea in.'

Pez smiled. 'Right again. That shell is called a cowrie.'

'I know that.'

'Do you know what it symbolises though?'

'No. Tell me.'

'It's the female sex and was often used to represent the Goddess.'

Boaz opened his mouth in wonder and Pez grinned at the boy's eyes sparkling with enlightenment. 'But the cowrie symbol is everywhere in Percheron — in our homes, our paintings, on our porcelain ...'

'Everywhere,' Pez echoed. 'This land celebrated women once; it prayed to the Mother Goddess and it revered its holy priestesses.'

'But ...'

'But now they are nothing,' Pez finished for him. 'Yes, people have forgotten and your generation isn't even taught Percheron's spiritual history. It's the smug priests who run the temples and the few remaining holy women are ridiculed.'

Boaz looked out to sea and digested what he had heard. Minutes passed and Pez sat comfortably in the silence. Finally Boaz turned back to his friend. 'So, in truth, the Zar's harem is a mockery of what we formerly worshipped and held dear. Women are no longer revered in the same way; they are slaves to men's needs and whims.'

Pez had not expected the youngster to make this connection so swiftly. Perhaps there was hope for Percheron with this intelligent, perceptive young man so quickly growing into his throne.

'One might look at it that way, Boaz, yes. The women of the harem are powerless, and the luxury and decadence in their lives all but makes them pointless. They have no role to play other than to serve men. The priests of yesteryear encouraged it for that reason and now in a twisted way the palace harem is all but sacred.'

'When did this happen?' Boaz asked.

'Oh, a very long time ago. At some point the holy men became jealous of the power of their female counterparts and decided to do something about it. I simplify it, of course, but only to make it easier to understand. I hadn't planned on giving you a lecture in history tonight.' He smiled crookedly.

'But it's all so fascinating. My father's women were happy, of course,' he said. 'Well, until the harem was disbanded.'

'Were they happy, Boaz? Do you think they would choose their bored, decadent, sometimes debauched existence over freedom, the right to choose their mate and have children who won't be slaughtered simply because they might threaten a throne?'

'I did not order murder,' the boy bristled.

'Nor did I say you did. We come full circle. Your mother did what was right for today's times. She did the only thing she could to protect the security of the Chosen's throne. Every one of the other women would have done the same and yet that doesn't make it sit any easier in the mind, does it?'

Boaz shook his head. 'I have nightmares about it. I'm not just grieving for my father, Pez, I'm trying to come to terms with the loss of my brothers ... my friends.'

'I know, child, and we must respect that.'

'Isn't the position of Valide Zara a contradiction, then, to the way you say we now live? Surely my mother's power harks back to the days of the Goddess when a woman was powerful?'

'Not really. You see, your mother is powerless without you, Boaz. Never overlook that. You are her power; your position nourishes her influence. She has none in her own right. If something were to happen to you her title would be stripped and she would be nothing again ... cast to the streets as she cast her rivals not so long ago.'

Boaz frowned. 'I've never looked at it like this.'

Pez said no more about it. Enough seeds had been planted in the boy's mind tonight. 'So now, Beloch and Ezram, our magnificent giants you asked me about.'

'Oh yes, I'd forgotten.'

'Some people believe, myself included, that giants once roamed the land and that these two were the most powerful warriors amongst their race.'

'This is a myth, surely?'

'No myth,' Pez said gravely. 'Beloch and Ezram worshipped the Goddess and it is said that the warlock Maliz — aided by the god

Zarab — founded the new movement to dislodge holy women from their pedestal. Through Maliz, Zarab fuelled the jealousies, weaved magicks upon his followers to overthrow the priestesses and install the new era of the priest.'

'The giants?'

'They were a threat to Maliz. Not only them but the rest of their kind and all the strange statues you see around the city. They were once beasts who revered the Goddess. They gave her power.'

'So?'

'Maliz made a bargain with the god, Zarab, and turned them to stone.'

Boaz clapped his hands, enjoying the tale. 'What happened to Maliz?'

'No-one knows. His is a murky history. The old stories say he was turned into a demon. Some believe he works still through others.'

'What, today?' the Zar asked, incredulous.

The dwarf nodded. 'They say he never died. He just moves from one body to another. His spirit lives on.'

Boaz grinned, impressed. 'That sounds rather terrifying.'

'Believe me, it is.'

'How did he do this?'

'Maliz practised the Art Noir — have you heard of this?' Boaz shook his head. 'Well, suffice to say it is an unpleasant pastime. His bargain gave him everlasting life.'

'And Zarab? What did he get out of the pact?'

'The destruction of the religion of the Mother Goddess. Now Percheron prays to Zarab.'

'Oh, I see. How very neat.'

Pez ignored the flippant remark. 'There's a catch, though. Zarab knew the Goddess would rise again, so Maliz's everlasting life was inextricably linked to her.'

Boaz frowned. 'I don't understand.'

'Well, it is because of this link that Maliz can continue to live. It is said that he moves through bodies awaiting the coming of the Goddess, watching and studying who it might be. There will be signs of course — Iridor for instance — and then once again they will battle it out.'

'Iridor?'

'Surely you've seen all the images of the owl around our city?'

'Of course. And this is Iridor from the old stories?'

'From Percheron's history,' Pez corrected, wondering if his tale was falling on deaf ears.

Boaz's eyes shone. 'A brilliant story.'

'It's so many centuries old, it feels like folklore,' Pez cautioned.

'I still see priestesses, though.'

'Indeed they exist, but very few. They remain powerless, though always believing that the Mother will rise again. They are tolerated because most in Percheron hardly know the history and don't care about the women who keep to themselves and keep the ancient unused temples in good order ... for posterity.'

'So do you believe Maliz exists, Pez?'

The dwarf hesitated. 'Yes,' he answered truthfully. 'I think he is always watching, waiting.'

'You believe he continues to reincarnate himself so that he can watch for the Goddess?'

'He doesn't reincarnate himself, Boaz. He simply claims a fresh body as his old one begins to perish or become too frail for his needs. He is unnecessary as long as she is powerless. As her power increases, so does his.'

'So they cancel each other out?'

'Not really. Each has helpers of a sort to assist them to outwit the other.'

'Oh?'

'The Goddess, for example, has Iridor. He, too, only comes into fleshly being as a herald of her arrival. He is her messenger, and as Iridor gets closer to incarnation Maliz gains strength and

goes looking for his new body, new victims to pull into his web ...
onto his side, you might say. But he and Lyana are linked to each
other.'

The mention of claiming bodies had pricked Boaz's intrigue
further. 'Can Maliz be anyone, then?'

'Presumably,' Pez said carefully.

'Me?'

The dwarf frowned and it struck Boaz that the question made
him uncomfortable. 'I would know if you were,' he finally replied.

'Why?'

Pez shook his head. He began to hum to himself. 'I just would,'
he said in a singsong voice.

Boaz ignored Pez's antics. 'So he's always alive then. Always
looking for the next victim?'

'You could say that.'

Boaz didn't mean to tease but very few opportunities ever
arose when Pez seemed in the slightest ruffled. 'Could he be you?'

Boaz had meant it playfully, to stop Pez from being so reticent
all of a sudden, but the dwarf looked up, alarmed, the mask gone
for a moment. The young Zar felt as though he saw his curious
friend emotionally naked for the first time. Then, within a blink,
the vulnerability was gone and Pez was laughing. 'No, child. I am
too stupid-looking for Maliz to want this body.' Pez suddenly
became conspiratorial and surprised his companion by radically
changing the subject. 'Boaz, do you know your mother is
welcoming forty-two of the girls from which she hopes one day
you'll select your wives?'

Boaz scowled. 'I'm not ready to, er ... you know.'

Pez laid a reassuring squat hand on the boy's good arm. 'I
know. But she must prepare them for the day when you are ready,
so they're brought in very young and taught everything they need
to know about palace etiquette and you. Some girls will be
marked as special and they will learn their letters and language,
dance and poetry.'

'I'm not sure I'm interested in girls,' Boaz replied glumly.

'I suspect you will be soon. Shall we spy on them?' Pez said, a glint of wickedness in those strange yellow eyes of his.

'What?'

'I know a hiding place. We can watch the girls being presented to your mother. No-one need know. Perhaps we can pick out a couple of beauties for you.' Pez nudged the Zar who laughed but not convincingly

'You're mad, Pez.'

'Apparently I am,' and he gave the grin of a lunatic.

Each man who had secured his quota of girls was required to present them to the Valide. Lazar stomped gloomily through the corridors wrought in marble sculpture. Snatches of torch-lit gardens and tiny, exquisite courtyards could be glimpsed through the latticed walkways; the sounds of cicadas singing and fountains gently gurgling permeated the heavy evening air scented with jasmine and honeysuckle. But the Spur was blind to the beauty of the palace tonight.

His mind was filled with worry for the future of Ana, wondering how he might help ease her into palace life, the prison sentence he had committed her to.

There was no way out for her now. Ana had been whisked away by guards before Lazar could say goodbye. The young woman had turned solemnly as she was led away and her sad gaze had held him as though she could actually touch the deep pool of sorrow he thought he hid so well. She seemed to know him in those final moments and he knew her. Even in the first delicious throes of love in his youth, Lazar had never experienced such a sense of belonging. It was as if Ana could see into his secretive soul, had somehow trapped it into her own heart and now she owned him.

Bah! he to himself. *What you need, Lazar, is a soft bed, a good woman for the night and several carafes of wine. No better way to*

drown your sorrows. But the words sounded as hollow in his mind as the click of his boots on the marble floor.

He was the first to arrive at the Choosing Room because he was the only man sent out to find suitable girls who had the run of the palace. Like Pez, Zar Joreb had granted Lazar open access to everywhere but in the Spur's case it was everywhere except the harem. The others would probably be gathered in the Moon Courtyard, the first entry point into the palace proper, awaiting their escort of eunuch guards.

The Choosing Room was the chamber where all the new odalisques were brought to be looked upon and judged whether they were suitable for the next inspection ... a far more intrusive and disturbing experience for the successful girls. But not this evening. The chamber had been opened only once in the last few decades and Lazar could tell that a veritable army of slaves had been sent in to air, clean and freshen the room. Now all the shutters were open and the glass lanterns were clean and lit; formal seating had been arranged, including a throne-like set-up, presumably so Herezah could play at being a queen and forget that she too had once been brought here as a young slave.

He could feel the bitterness welling up again, knew he must get a grip on it before proceedings began or it would not bode well for him or young Ana.

He emptied his mind — something Jumo had taught him to do — and focused on the ancient, intricately painted friezes around the walls. He had never visited this room before, and although he recognised the pattern as being common enough in Percheron, now that he was concentrating on it he realised it wasn't just an abstract shape but in fact was the curve of a cowrie shell. It was beautiful. Painted in soft hues, the design rolled elegantly around the walls, framing arches and windows, small recesses and the great doors that had guided him into the chamber. And now that he looked at them with studied pleasure he noticed that the doors themselves had the same sweeping curves of the shell hammered out of the bronze they were fashioned from. The walls were washed in shell pink and the floors were a pinkish marble — all in all a thoroughly feminine hall, Lazar decided, impressed.

His pleasure was interrupted by the swish of silks and a voice he knew and despised. Suddenly he was back to reality and Jumo's clever trick would no longer work for him.

'Ah, Spur Lazar,' Salmeo lisped. 'I hope you've found our boy some beauties to bed.'

'Not so fast, Grand Master Eunuch, Boaz will choose his time.'

The eunuch licked his lips and Lazar hated the way his pink tongue flicked through the gap in his teeth. There was something quietly obscene in the gesture. 'I noticed you admiring the decor,' the eunuch said. 'It signifies the female form, did you know that, Spur?'

Lazar shook his head and strolled away as if his interest had been caught by something.

'Ah yes,' the huge man continued, following him, 'this chamber is dedicated to women. It is where they are formally given into the care of the harem; their last contact with men in general.' He giggled and covered his grin with his huge hand. 'But of course they've known no men,' he added as if in self-admonishment.

Lazar made a soft growling sound of disgust at this sudden affectation. He'd heard enough stories to know the chief eunuch took his own cruel form of pleasure at the expense of the harem women, except there were no longer any women in the harem; they were still essentially children, who needed protecting and nurturing. He wanted to laugh at himself for his own ridiculous sentiment — it was so ironic that he was one of the perpetrators who had brought children to the palace, whilst still making mewling sounds of complaint. He moved further away, not wanting to smell the fragrance of violets that Salmeo habitually blew over all those he spoke with. It seemed like a grim parody that someone so vile would breathe such sickly sweet breath.

'Spur, Salmeo.'

Lazar turned to find Tariq bubbling over with self-importance.

'Are you required here, Vizier?' Lazar asked, his tone as casual as he could achieve. 'Surely your expertise is needed elsewhere?'

The man swelled with pride. 'You're right, of course, Spur. But the Valide is keen for me to see all aspects of the palace workings. Establishing a harem is fundamental to the smooth running of the new Zar's reign. She believed it was worthwhile that I be present.' He shrugged, feigning gentle modesty at her order.

The jewels on his split beard were now accompanied by tiny bells which tinkled as he moved and Lazar was reminded of another reason why he wanted to be gone from the palace. What would happen to Percheron in the hands of Herezah and this supercilious fool? He forced a smile to cover his disgust, gave a short bow and excused himself from these two vulgar partners of the Valide Zara.

A gong was sounding somewhere close and served to distract his companions' attention.

'The Elim comes,' Salmeo said.

Footsteps sounded louder, and low murmuring voices of men could be heard. Six spotters, as Herezah called them, were led in, flanked by twelve guards, all distinctive by their loose, pristine red uniforms. Each guard had his head shaved — there was no mistaking the Elim. The spotters themselves were mainly merchants, and among them was a man Lazar was acquainted with. Bosh could supply almost anything anyone could ever want, legal or illegal. Finding young girls for a harem would have been easy for him. Lazar had had his run-ins with him over the years, thanks to the man's natural tendency towards breaking laws, but Bosh was good-natured enough and Lazar would rather deal with ten or even twenty of his kind than one of Salmeo's or Tariq's.

'Why the blindfolds?' Tariq asked.

Lazar refused to answer the mindless question but Salmeo was more enlightening. 'Although the Choosing Room is not technically within the borders of the harem, it remains close enough that traditional precautions are still taken. These men have no idea where they are right now and they will never find out. The blindfolds will be removed once the great doors are shut and returned just before they open and the six are escorted back out.' Salmeo smiled and Lazar was reminded of a predator. 'You are most fortunate that we did not provide similar treatment for you, Vizier.' The words were harmless enough but the intent was all too clear.

Salmeo gave a sign and the great doors were closed with a deep clang. The blindfolds were removed and the spotters blinked, got their bearings; Bosh saw Lazar immediately and nodded.

'Welcome, brothers,' the Grand Master Eunuch said. 'May we offer you some refreshment?'

Curtains at the back of the room were pulled apart and a small stream of servants — all male — flowed smoothly into the room and around the newcomers. Each held golden trays upon which sat great goblets, dewy on their sides from the iciness of the beverage.

Bosh sidled over to Lazar. 'Do you know they lug blocks of ice and sometimes snow from the Azareems, across thousands of leagues, just to chill the palace beverages,' he declared in wonder.

'So I've heard,' Lazar replied in a voice to deaden all awe.

The wealthy trader raised his goblet. 'To the new harem, then. Zorash!'

Lazar couldn't bring himself to toast the very thing that was making him feel so disturbed. 'To beautiful women,' he offered instead and Bosh drank with him, winking as he did so.

'I'm surprised you were asked to get involved in this task, Spur,' the man commented.

'So was I. Excuse me.' Lazar nodded and moved away.

Bosh was not upset by the Spur's abrupt manner. Everyone in Percheron knew him to be a difficult man, who rarely involved himself in anything deeper than cursory conversation. The man shrugged, approached another of the merchants and was soon comparing notes on the quality of the girls.

Lazar wondered where Ana was, wished again he could change everything that had happened since arriving on that ridge in the foothills. He should have left the tranquil scene as he found it; listened to his heart and turned for home.

He had a vague feeling of impending danger. A sense of something dark building, gathering, forming itself. And somehow he seemed to be at its centre.

9

Pez led Boaz through a maze of corridors the boy was sure he had not travelled previously. Now that he thought about it, his world was so small. Life in the palace might well be grand but everything about his existence was controlled by his mother. It was Herezah who authorised all the people who would be responsible for his getting up and going to bed, being bathed, fed, educated, even down to choosing where and with whom he played, when younger.

He and Pez were thumbing their nose at traditional rules and Boaz knew he had agreed to this lunacy only because he was angry with his mother and it felt satisfying to act so independently and without worrying about the consequences. He was the Zar after all.

Mind you, now that they were here — in the most dangerous part of the whole of Percheron to be seen if you were an intact male — he didn't feel quite so keen to snub authority or risk the certain wrath should anyone, not just his mother, find out. He wanted to say as much but as he opened his mouth to speak, his friend hissed a warning.

'Now silence, Boaz,' Pez urged. 'We're about to enter the realm of the harem.'

Boaz looked suddenly fearful. 'It's forbidden, Pez.'

'Not forbidden to me,' the little man said and grinned wickedly. 'And let's not forget who you are.'

'Nevertheless,' Boaz said, grabbing his friend's short arm. 'I cannot. My mother would —'

'What? Kill you? I think not. Not when you are the source of her status.'

'Well, she'd never forgive me.'

'What if I told you I could ensure that you were never seen?'

'I should not believe you.' Boaz laughed.

'Then you must trust me. I will not lead you into trouble, Boaz. I am leading you towards enlightenment.'

Before the Zar could reply, a boy of about Boaz's age rounded the corner.

'Zar!' he exclaimed, cringing instantly into a bow.

Pez sighed. That was that then. Lucky they hadn't actually crossed the official, invisible line that separated harem from general palace.

'Hello, Kett,' Boaz said good-naturedly, recovering from the shock of discovery but only barely. 'I'm escaping my tutors and keepers, guardians and mother. Everyone in fact. Do you know Pez, my jester?'

Pez began to pick his nose and render a small jig.

Kett, a servant to the eunuchs, shook his head dumbly, looking from the Zar to the clown, who was now examining the contents from his nostrils.

Boaz winced. 'He has some awful habits. Don't mind him. I haven't seen you in ages.'

'Forgive me, High One. Since turning fourteen they think I'm ready to take on more duties. They keep me busy, Majesty,' he said, bobbing another bow. 'But I miss our fun.'

'Kett was a playmate of mine for a while,' the Zar explained to Pez, who pretended to pay no attention to anything but digging at his ear. 'His mother served my mother when she first came to the palace. Kett was allowed to join in some of my games until my mother felt we were becoming too close. She separated us.' He looked back to the boy whose black face had not lost its expressiveness with the added years. 'How many years ago was that, Kett?'

'Four, Majesty. My humble prayers for your father but I admit I rejoiced to hear that you were our next Zar.'

'Thanks, Kett. So what are you doing?' Boaz was keen to lose the royal tag for just one evening. He pulled the dwarf's hand away from his nose. Pez began to sing instead.

'Is he always like this, High One?' Kett asked.

'I'm afraid so. He can be very amusing, though.'

Kett looked dubious but remembered his manners. 'I've finished for the night, Majesty. I was on my way back to my quarters. I'm not allowed anywhere near the harem, of course, but some of us use this corridor as a short cut to our dormitories.'

'Oh, of course. I guess you would get into trouble if you were seen in the harem.'

Kett grinned. 'I don't want to follow in my superiors' footsteps and be a eunuch — I think I like girls too much. I want to be one of the Spur's men if they'll let me. My mother's connection to yours might help, now that your mother is Valide Zara.'

'Good for you, Kett. I hope you get what you want.'

The boy nodded. 'Is there anything I can do for you, High One?' he asked. 'I hope you don't mind me mentioning that you shouldn't be here either.'

'No, you're right. We were just larking around. Pez's silly singing and dancing led us here.'

'Let me guide you from here, Majesty,' Kett offered.

'Do you like to see naked girls?' Pez asked, a question that brought polite conversation to a halt. The two boys stared at one another. Then both stifled embarrassed laughter. 'Because I know a hiding spot where we can see them, tra-la-la.' He began to dance again, a dullard's grin on his face.

'Is he mad?' Kett asked.

'Completely,' Boaz confirmed.

The dwarf slid through a doorway hung with black velvet.

'What's he doing?' Kett asked, alarmed. 'That's forbidden!'

'Not to him. Pez has royal permission to go wherever he likes, including the harem's hallways and chambers.'

Pez stuck his head out of the curtains. 'And so do you, Zar Boaz. You *are* the royal authority. There is no higher authority in the land than yours.'

'What's he talking about?'

Boaz sighed. 'He's daring me to go into the forbidden halls of the harem.'

'No, High One. You cannot,' Kett begged. 'Come, I shall take you from here.'

Boaz looked between the two, but the challenge in Pez's expression won out. Boaz knew he was essentially someone who craved peace, quiet, study and reflection. Oh, he loved to play boisterous games but he didn't like getting hurt and he didn't like hurting others. In truth Boaz would prefer to rule with compassion rather than the dictatorial approach his father had taken and his father before him. However, he understood that this was the way of the Zars of Percheron and that strength and discipline were the foundation of the rule. If he could, he'd run away to one of the desert monasteries Lazar had once told him of, but that was the child in him. He must dig deep and turn quickly into the man his father had chosen him to be — firm, decisive, ruthless.

'Come, Boaz,' Pez urged in a whisper. 'You must see what your mother is planning for you.'

'Come with us, Kett,' Boaz offered, on a whim.

'Cannot protect the servant boy,' Pez muttered in a singsong voice but Boaz ignored him.

'You said you liked girls.'

'I do. Not enough to be beheaded for them.'

'I won't allow that. You forget I am Zar,' Boaz answered haughtily. Surprised at his own courage, Boaz grabbed Kett's arm and dragged him between the curtains.

Kett yelled but Boaz pushed a hand across the boy's mouth. 'Hush now!'

'Can't protect him,' Pez sang softly as he waddled deeper into the dark corridor.

'You hush too,' Boaz growled to Pez. 'This is your fault. Now lead on!'

The three adventurers moved in silence. This particular passageway remained black, draped with fabric. Finally they emerged into a dimly lit opening from which several corridors led.

Pez put his finger to his lips and Boaz felt a tingling fear crawl up his spine. Zar or not, this was fraught with a danger he didn't want to meet.

'Where we need to be is still on the fringe of the harem,' Pez whispered. 'Follow me,' and the boys dutifully followed the little man, hoping to the gods that no-one was coming the other way.

Pez appeared to read their thoughts. 'Everyone will have been banished from these hallways for the duration of the Choosing Ceremony. Fret not, we are alone. But from now on we must remain silent as mice.'

They nodded, spectral in the murkiness where tiny flames in hanging lanterns cast a thin, ghostly light.

They twisted and turned down various corridors until finally Pez slowed and gave them a look of dire warning. Boaz could see a new intensity of light ahead and nodded to his friend. They had arrived.

Moving forwards tentatively they held their breath until they reached some latticework, which offered thin protection between themselves and a gathering of people in a decorative chamber. They were men, drinking, socialising. Their noise drowned out anything the three interlopers might say.

'This is called the Choosing Room. It's where a selection of girls will be presented to the Valide Zara. It is from this range of lovelies that you will eventually choose your wives, Boaz,' Pez whispered.

'Do I get any say in the matter?' he muttered.

Pez grinned. 'Of course. But your mother makes the initial selection. She is seeing forty-two girls today.'

'Where is she?'

'Arriving any moment now, I'd suggest.' Pez glanced at Kett, could see the strain of terror on his face, wished deeply that Boaz had not invited this boy along. He was a danger to all of them and yet, that thought aside, there was something else about Kett which nagged at Pez. Something important. He didn't know the boy but he felt as if he should. There was a connection between them, which it seemed only he felt. He berated himself for not being able to see it more clearly, or understanding why he felt sudden sorrow for the child.

But it was too late to turn back. Guards would have been posted now that the Valide Zara was on her way. They were trapped and would have to remain here, silent until Herezah had left the chamber and returned to her own rooms.

He thought about what had driven him to this madness. The voice of the old woman had urged him. He had no idea who she was or why she spoke to him. She had told him many years ago that he had a task — a critical one — and it concerned what she had called the Return. It was too abstract even for Pez's clever mind. He often thought he dreamed the voice but he obeyed it nonetheless.

He came out of his worried thoughts to concentrate on peering through the latticework. The old woman wanted him to see something — he was not sure yet who or what. The woman told him his heart would tell him; the same heart that was hammering now with anticipation.

A herald sounded loudly from the surrounding balustrade, calling everyone to order. The men hushed. The Valide Zara was announced and Herezah swept into the chamber from a secret entrance that obviously connected to the harem proper. Lazar

99

noted she was following strict protocol in being covered head to foot but there was nothing modest about the way she presented herself. Dressed in brilliant emerald silks, only her eyes showed and they were dark and dangerous. She had expressive eyes and even from this distance Lazar could read the excitement in them.

She shimmered as she moved, the lantern light catching the tones weaved into the silk, one moment violet, the next deep emerald and then a hint of a dark pink. There was no question that Herezah could silence a room with her dark beauty — even veiled she commanded attention.

Everyone bowed low to acknowledge the Valide's arrival. Then Tariq and Salmeo moved forwards to join her on the special plinth erected for this evening's proceedings. Both seemed to be basking in her bright glory. Oh yes, Lazar thought, Herezah would find willing servants in these two. And again a gloom settled about him as he considered just how Ana would cope with these cruel, ambitious people controlling her life.

'Hail, Valide Zara,' Salmeo called and everyone responded.

'Thank you, brothers, for your rousing welcome.' There was a playfulness in Herezah's tone tonight. She was enjoying herself; this was surely a moment she had dreamed about.

Herezah continued. 'We are gathered this night for you to present suitable girls for inclusion in Zar Boaz's harem. I thank you for helping us to find the raw material from which he will select his wives and thus future heirs for Percheron, and we will be glad to pay handsomely for each of the girls deemed suitable.' She nodded towards Salmeo, who beamed in response and stepped forward as she moved to sit on her throne.

It was Salmeo's turn. 'I would like to clarify on behalf of the palace how the choosing of the Zar's harem works. Firstly, you have brought between you forty or so girls aged between ten and fifteen. We thank you for this. As agreed we will pay twenty-five karels per child, no matter whether they are chosen or not. The girls we accept will attract a further fifty karels paid to you as your finding fee. Those we do not select you may sell in the market for your personal gain or keep to do with as you wish.' His tongue flicked between his teeth and his lips shone with the moistening. All but Lazar laughed at his innuendo. Permission to rape a child had effectively just been granted under royal authority. He felt a desperate surge of hope that Herezah would reject Ana for some reason — he didn't care what — and then he could keep her from this evil trio's touch. No-one in their right mind could resist her, of course; Lazar knew he was clutching at the thinnest of straws.

Salmeo was still speaking. '... Vizier Tariq will see to payment, yes,' he answered someone. 'Which brings me to the point that the entire fee will not be settled for the girls chosen this evening until they have completed the Test of Virtue.' He allowed this seemingly innocuous statement to hang for a moment. 'I'm sure you understand, brothers,' he added lasciviously.

If he had not heard his name called first, Lazar was sure he would have found a reason to leave the chamber.

'Spur Lazar kindly agreed to help us with the quota of girls and I'm sure none of you will mind if he presents his selection first. He's a busy man, as you know, and no doubt is eager to return to his duties having been away. Spur?'

Lazar ignored Salmeo and cleared his throat. 'Valide Zara, please forgive my dusty appearance, I have not had time since returning from the foothills to change into something more appropriate for your company,' he said, as he approached the plinth. In truth he could not care less about his appearance, especially where she was concerned, but it was something to say into the silence and it played to her vanity, particularly with what he was planning over the next few minutes.

Herezah nodded. 'Worry not, Spur, I'm sure most men would give an eye to look as good as you do even in dirty garments.'

The men around him sniggered, mostly out of jealousy, but Lazar deliberately kept his expression blank, his eyes firmly fixed on the Valide. But then Herezah knew precisely how to provoke a reaction from him, how to tease or embarrass him. So far she'd never won the anger she so craved from him. He would not give it now even though it simmered inside.

'Thank you, Valide, for your generosity.' Lazar moved quickly to business. He wanted to be gone as soon as possible. 'I present six applicants for your consideration.'

A bell sounded, another set of curtains was pulled back and a line of girls were led in, all naked save a gauzy sheath which gave them a sense of modesty although it hid nothing. He ignored all the others and looked only at Ana. He hated that the other men in the room were enjoying the sight of this girl's body, just ripening into womanhood.

'Come, girls.' Salmeo shooed them into position in front of Herezah and began the introductions. 'This is Fajel, she is ten and as you can see is straight-limbed with a tendency towards being tall, I would suggest ...' Lazar forced his mind to drift. He did not want to listen to this.

He fixed his own stare onto Herezah, to give the impression that he was paying close attention, but gave nothing of himself to her. He knew she watched him more closely than the child and he deliberately blanked his face, knowing how much it irritated her. She got bored with trying to win any flicker of interest from him and returned to the job at hand.

'Can you sing something for us, Fajel?' she asked and the girl nodded. 'Go ahead, then.'

A sweet sound broke across the mainly silent room, interrupted only by shuffles or coughs. There was no more socialising now. Each man wanted his six chosen above all others.

The girl finished her song. 'That was very nice,' Herezah said, condescendingly. 'Turn around for me, child.'

Salmeo aided the spinning of the girl so the Valide could see her from all angles. 'This one will stay slim, Valide Zara,' he hazarded.

'Yes, we'll take her,' Herezah said, sounding slightly bored. 'Next.'

It continued. Lazar was not involved in any of the choosing but he was required to stand alongside the line and he was pleased that Ana was last and he was able to be next to her as the line dwindled. He could feel the heat from her body radiating to where the back of his hand barely touched the thin gauze that separated his skin from hers. He wished he could hold her hand once more and offer reassurance. It would be hollow, though — it would be a lie and Ana would know it, he was sure.

Finally it was her turn and he took a deep, steadying breath, hoping nothing of the turmoil he was feeling was given away on his face.

Salmeo continued. 'Valide Zara, this is Ana, found in Shanar. She is almost fifteen and already a dazzling beauty if I might say so. I would urge that this girl is the pick of the forty-two on offer this evening. I understand the Spur paid a premium for her.'

'Indeed, Salmeo, and rightly so.' Herezah stood. Lazar knew her interest had been piqued by the presentation of Ana. It was everything he had hoped would not happen. 'She's from the foothills, you say?'

Lazar took a moment to realise Herezah was addressing him. 'Er, yes, Valide, from the west. She belongs to a goatherd's family, but she was originally an orphan, adopted by them.'

'That hair!' Herezah said, unable to hide her excitement. 'Where does one find a child of this colouring in the foothills?'

Lazar shrugged, feigning boredom. 'I'm told by the stepmother that she was found after the Samazen had passed through. She was newborn. Presumably her family perished. As for the colour, I suspect she is from the far, far west, probably merchants.' He had been pondering the same questions himself since buying her. The story was too thin and yet that had been the only time that Felluj had seemed to be completely genuine with them. The child had been found and adopted — there was nothing else to discover and her real family was probably dead and was almost certainly from a country no-one in this room, save himself, had ever seen.

'Oh yes, yes,' Herezah was saying over his thoughts, 'spin, child, let me feast my eyes upon you.'

Ana obeyed and for the first time Lazar looked too. He felt the tug in his heart — the pinprick of pain he had experienced at her smile. She was perfect. He had been wrong to think her coltish; he had been fooled by the baggy clothing her stepmother had forced on her and the square shoulders. Beneath Ana's transparent shift was a nubile body rounding into the fullness of womanhood. Her belly was taut, flat; her curves still gentle but filled with promise. Her breasts were already full and high.

Herezah stepped down from the plinth and shocked everyone by reaching out and pinching one of Ana's nipples. To her credit, Ana did not flinch.

Herezah laughed with pleasure. 'Oh yes, watch them rise strong and ready to the touch. This one is more than wanted; this one is desired. Boaz will love her. Congratulations, Lazar.' Herezah looked directly at Ana now. 'You're very beautiful, my dear, do you know it? Will you use it in the right way, I wonder?'

'I am how I am, Valide,' Ana said levelly, taking everyone by surprise. Herezah's question was rhetorical and no-one had anticipated a response. When it came it silenced those gathered, including the Valide. Salmeo glared at the child.

'And headstrong too, I see,' Herezah continued. 'That we shall need to work upon.' She looked towards the chief eunuch. 'Salmeo.'

'Yes, Valide,' he lisped enthusiastically.

'I may even take this one on myself.'

Lazar's heart sank. How much worse could it get for Ana?

'Who better to prepare her for Boaz than the person who knows him the best?' the Valide asked no-one in particular and laughed beneath her veils.

'That is a high compliment to the girl, Valide,' Salmeo admitted. 'You are fortunate, child,' he said to Ana, still glowering at her audacious comment earlier.

'Ana, you are now odalisque of the harem of Zar Boaz, King of Kings, Mightiest of the Mighties.' Then Herezah smiled. 'And I am your mistress now.'

Ana said nothing this time, even though everyone now anticipated some response. It was Lazar who filled the pause.

'Valide?'

'Oh yes, Spur, you will be paid handsomely for this find.'

'That is not my query, Valide Zara. There were conditions with Ana's purchase.' He wondered whether he could pull this off.

'Conditions?' she said in the quiet voice he knew well. Herezah had learned long ago not to fall into the trap of screeching as other women might, or raising her voice when she disagreed. She had taught herself to harness the emotion into a deadly calm.

Lazar, however, was ready for her. 'Yes, that's right. It's unusual, I agree.' He contrived a tone of embarrassment. 'Valide, this girl was too special to pass up. I thought you might be prepared to make an exception. But I understand if you'd take umbrage at being dictated to by a mere peasant.' He did his best to insult her politely, hoping against hope she'd rise to his bait and banish both him and the girl. 'In fact, if you are offended — and I would not blame you if you were — I shall stand by the rules you have made.'

'Which are?' she asked.

'That the money I spent on her is my loss and I must make it up as best I can.'

'I see,' Herezah said and he knew he had not won the gamble. Her interest in the girl was too strong, and he knew how she loved to trade words with him.

'So what are these "conditions"?' She laced the final word with grim humour and he could hear the men muttering behind him, could imagine the wry smiles on their faces.

'The mother insisted that Ana be permitted freedom one day each month.'

'Preposterous!' Tariq cried on behalf of the Valide, his beard jewels flashing in harmony with his anger.

Herezah raised a hand. She looked towards Salmeo, a question in her eyes.

'Never permitted previously, Valide Zara,' the eunuch replied, equally outraged.

She nodded and returned her dark gaze to Lazar who refused to squirm beneath it.

'I understand,' he said, beginning to bow, hoping to remove himself.

'Not so fast, Spur,' she said softly. 'The girl is young. What sort of freedom did her mother have in mind for her daughter? Perhaps if we could send Salmeo to escort her. She would be veiled completely, of course, at all times.'

Now he did squirm. 'Er, well, Valide, I think she rather had in mind something less constricting.'

'Oh?'

'Her mother impressed upon me that Ana is startlingly intelligent. She had hopes that we might be able to encourage learning language, culture —'

'Yes, of course,' Herezah interrupted, 'she would no doubt get all of that and more if she shows talent.'

'I'm not explaining myself well, Valide. Perhaps it's because I feel extremely awkward about the full extent of the mother's conditions.'

Herezah's patience was wearing thin now. 'Why don't you lay out the full extent of the conditions, Spur, so I can make a firm decision.'

'She required me to be her escort,' he said firmly.

'You!' Her voice was soft but as angry as he could recall.

He nodded. 'My apologies, Valide. Felluj entrusted this most precious child of hers to me personally. She charged me with Ana's safety and education. She understood me to be a soldier and decided that I was the most appropriate ... um ... guardian, for want of a better word.'

The pause — and what wasn't being said in the dread silence

that followed his words — was so palpable and heavy, Lazar felt quite sure it could be cut up, served on a platter and forced down his gullet. He had played his hand.

'And if I did not choose Ana, Spur, what would you do with her? Make her your own?'

'I would sell her, Valide,' he said, adding an undertone of insult to his voice. 'I have no need for a child in my life.'

The eyes sparkled in between the slit of the veil. She was loving watching him bristle.

'But you want to be her guardian, is that right?'

He deliberately took a controlled but audible breath to suggest he was getting tired of this line of questioning. 'The promise under which she was sold demanded that I agree to this condition on your behalf. I knew I had no right to do this, Valide Zara, but I believed the girl was worth it. She is special, I'm sure we all agree on this, and someone to match minds with Boaz, who is something of a scholar. Ana has the potential to be a fulfilling mate for him, rather than just a plaything. I'm sure you above most would understand such a thing.' His words couched insult with compliment, deliberately done. Certainly his final line was meant to remind her that Joreb had chosen her for Absolute Favourite not only because of her beauty and prowess as a lover but because she had a bright, quick mind to match his own.

'One day a month you say?'

'That's right. She would be in my care for that full day.'

'She would be veiled fully. No-one may look upon her.'

'Of course,' he said indignantly.

'Let me think on this, Spur. Ana must pass her Test of Virtue. Present yourself at the palace for my answer in the late evening tomorrow. We shall take supper together and discuss it. Until then, you are dismissed.'

He bristled silently, hating the position he found himself in, being ordered around by this woman. Supper! Allad save him, he thought, calling upon his homeland god. 'Thank you, Valide

Zara.' He bowed and as he did so a loud sneeze exploded from nearby. It wasn't someone in the room.

Salmeo looked thunderstruck, and with a single signal, men began to swarm.

'You fool, Kett,' Boaz hissed, terrified.

'I … I couldn't help it, Zar. I will not let them know you were here,' the youngster beseeched, scared that he might bring down the wrath of the harem on the Zar. 'Run!'

Pez had to admire the young servant's courage. 'No use running. There would be guards at every point since Herezah left her chambers.'

'What can we do?' Boaz asked, head swivelling this way and that looking for an escape.

'There is no escape. We must wait.' They could hear men's voices, footsteps.

'Wait!' Boaz somehow managed to convey a yell in his whisper.

Pez noted how calm Kett appeared, his only show of anxiety the way he shifted his weight from foot to foot.

The dwarf spoke in a voice Boaz had not heard before. 'Boaz, stand close to me.' The Zar began to splutter noises of hesitation but Pez ignored him. 'Do it now! There is no more time.'

'What can this possibly do?' Boaz asked, putting his arms around the shoulders of the dwarf who leaned back against the Zar.

'Hush, Boaz, not a sound!' Pez commanded. 'Forgive me, Kett,' he added in a whisper. 'I cannot protect you as I warned, but you and I will see each other again.'

'Who are you?' Kett asked, frightened but remaining stoic as the voices got louder.

'Wait for me,' Pez said, remembering something the old woman had whispered to him. 'Betray me not.'

It was all he had time to say before the guards were upon them.

They descended on Kett; the boy made no protest. Boaz couldn't understand it; they were standing so close to him, it was obvious — surely — that they would be seen as well. Yet the guards' gazes appeared to slide past them. He wanted to shout at them but in truth his mouth was too dry to utter a sound. He felt as though the light shining through the latticework had lit them up like the trees they decorated for the Festival of Light, but no, the guards ignored the Zar and Pez and simply manhandled Kett away down the corridor.

They were left alone, the voices and footsteps dissipating as the confusion in the Choosing Room increased.

'Pez,' he whispered, quite sure his bowels had turned to water. 'What just happened?'

The dwarf sighed. Boaz was too intelligent to trick and he needed the boy to know that this was all for a reason.

'I told you I could protect us, not him.'

Boaz broke away from his friend, spinning the small man around. 'What do you mean by that? The guards were as close as I am to you and they didn't see us!'

'Hush, High One, or they'll be back.'

'You tell me how it can be that they saw Kett but not us.'

'Another one of my tricks, Your Majesty,' Pez answered.

'No!' the boy hissed. 'That was nothing like pulling kerchiefs from your nose or doves from your hat. That was much, much more.'

'Boaz, I have asked you to trust me and I'm going to ask you to indulge me a little longer.'

'It's impossible what just occurred,' the Zar moaned. He was prevented from saying any more with the arrival of Kett into the Choosing Room, hanging between the grip of two guards. The Zar's attention was diverted but he gave Pez a warning glare that their conversation was not done with yet.

'Is this who was snooping?' Herezah demanded.

'We caught him in one the corridors behind this chamber, Valide Zara,' one of the Elim answered. He bowed and Kett was dropped between them. He kept his head lowered.

Herezah looked to Salmeo who moved, his huge bulk surprisingly light of tread, over to the cringing boy.

'Look at me,' he commanded and there was no mistaking the power of this man. 'What were you doing in the corridor in a restricted area?'

'Grand Master Eunuch, I was lost,' Kett said, and it sounded pitiful. 'I was hurrying about my duties, I took the wrong entrance — I'm so sorry, sir — I found myself on the other side of the room and knew I shouldn't be there and I became too frightened to move or make a sound.'

'You weren't very successful, were you?' Tariq piped up. He looked around, waiting for someone to snicker at his sarcastic jest.

'Forgive me, Grand Master. I tried so hard to stifle my sneeze but that only made it worse.'

Lazar grimaced. He sensed it would get ugly for this child. Salmeo was too cruel to let such an insult to his authority pass, particularly such a public one. He glanced behind him to Ana. She was still in the chamber; her minders had not had the opportunity to leave since the interruption.

Ana returned the look, her expression fearful.

'What is your name, boy?'

'I am Kett, Grand Master Eunuch. I run errands for some of your men, although I hope to join the palace guard when I reach a suitable age. I am the son of Shelah Mohab.' He hoped the mentioning of his mother's name might help his perilous situation.

'Shelah?' Herezah enquired. 'My old servant?' She stood beside Salmeo in front of the boy.

Kett bowed low again on his knees, his head touching the pale marble floor. 'Valide,' he whispered. 'Yes, you were her mistress.'

'I see.' Herezah glanced at Salmeo.

Not to be outdone, the Vizier sidled up beside the Valide and the Grand Master Eunuch. 'The penalty is death, surely?'

Salmeo turned to address Herezah, although everyone could hear him. 'The Vizier speaks true. It is death to anyone unauthorised who sees the girls of the harem. Guards!'

Lazar could not permit this. 'Valide, if I may be permitted?' He even bowed. Whatever pleased her, this boy's life must not be taken.

'What is it, Spur?' she said, feigning irritation.

'Thank you, Valide Zara. I don't believe this boy's life should be forfeit.'

'How dare you!' the Vizier began.

'Why do you say that, Lazar?' Herezah said from behind her veil. A laziness to the tone. He knew it well — it was seductive and dangerous.

'This boy — and let's not forget that this is all he is — is innocent of anything sinister, Valide. He has told you that he was lost and it would be generous of you to spare his life.'

Lazar could see the Vizier fuming visibly; Salmeo, as angry, was not nearly so obvious. The lids of his eyes had closed slightly, shading the windows into his thoughts.

'He must be punished,' the eunuch said softly.

'And I agree,' Herezah added. 'Innocent of intent or otherwise, this boy was where he knew he must not be. It is forbidden.'

'But, Valide, he did not realise until it was too late that he was somewhere he shouldn't be. He is a child. If he were a man I would agree he should know better. If he must be punished, so be it, but not death. If I may be so bold, perhaps you might start your son's reign with a show of mercy, Valide. The palace will learn soon enough of your magnanimous gesture.'

He was daring her into doing something generous which her two sidekicks would abhor. They used their positions as a club with which to beat their subordinates into submission. Herezah was no stranger to this concept either, but he was counting on her vanity to win out. He held his breath as she watched him intently.

It was at this moment that someone else joined the debate; someone so unexpected that it made Lazar draw in his breath sharply. The situation he had almost won had turned suddenly, exquisitely, dangerous.

'Valide, High One,' Ana said, sliding in on her knees next to Kett, head bowed to the ground, her creamy back exposed through the transparent sheath.

Salmeo signalled angrily to the eunuchs who had allowed her to escape their care.

Herezah smiled and there was a slyness to it. 'No, wait. Let's hear what this girl has to say. Ana?'

'Spare him his life, Majesty,' she said, using all the wrong terminology to address Herezah, not that it offended the woman who gloated above her. She was not looking at Ana of course, but watching the Spur of Percheron who stared at the prone figure beneath him, aghast.

'Why should I, Ana?' she continued.

'Because you can. You are all-powerful, Valide, and because, High One, I will exchange something precious for Kett's life.'

At this Herezah gave a tinkling, affected laugh. 'Oh my dear, what can you possibly have that I would want?'

'My freedom, Valide Zara. I relinquish all of it. If I pass the Test of Virtue, I will give up the condition my mother placed upon the Spur. I will remain in the palace for —'

'No!' Lazar interrupted, unable to help himself. It had taken all of his wits to negotiate the release of Ana into his care and she was casting that freedom to the wind. He admired her courage in placing herself at the mercy of people who could order her death too, for nothing more than insubordination. But his despair was a selfish one. He wanted to see Ana again, not see her absorbed into the harem so fully he might never hear the musical lilt in her voice or watch her beauty settle into full womanhood. 'This cannot be permitted, Valide.'

'Why not?' She was relishing every moment of his discomfort. 'Ana makes a gracious plea for Kett. Surely you admire it?'

There was little he could say to that. 'I made a promise,' he said helplessly.

'And you saw it through to its conclusion. I had already decided to grant Ana the condition you argued for so eloquently. It is Ana's freedom and so it is hers to give back to me if she so wishes.'

He had not hated Herezah so much in all the time he'd known her as he did at this moment. Clever Herezah had seen through his guise. She knew how to read men and she had read him like an open page. She could tell that he wanted Ana, and no matter how noble his intentions were, she intended to deny him. And why, he asked himself. Because he would not give himself willingly to her. He would give his time and affection to a girl, but not to her and so Herezah had found a new way to punish him.

Young Ana could not appreciate all of these undercurrents swirling around her. She asked her innocent question. 'Will you spare his life, then, Valide Zara?'

'Yes. I will take the precious exchange you offer, Ana,' the Valide said, loading the word 'precious' with sarcasm. 'This boy will not be executed,' Herezah added, to the audible disappointment of the Vizier and the relief of all the others who were audience to this theatre. Salmeo was unreadable.

'He will of course be punished,' Herezah said and Lazar heard the viciousness in her voice.

She addressed the boy now, who was still bent in obeisance. 'Kett.'

'Yes, Valide Zara?'

'Ana here has bought your life with her own freedom. You will not be executed as protocol calls but I fear you must now join the very place you have trespassed upon.'

Kett looked at her, confused.

Salmeo understood, however. 'Call the priests,' he said to his guard.

'Valide,' Lazar started.

'Enough, Spur. We have indulged you. Please step back,' she said and the Vizier gave a triumphant glare at Lazar, who had no choice but to do as he was ordered.

'This will not take long, brothers,' Salmeo assured.

'I am going to ask you to step outside for a short while,' Herezah warned those gathered. She glanced Lazar's way and he knew she was smiling beneath the veil.

10

'Quick, we must leave now,' Pez urged.

'Wait, what will happen to Kett?'

'You heard. He is to be punished. Let's go.'

'Shouldn't we stay?'

'It won't be pretty,' Pez said. 'Trust me, you don't want to witness it.'

Boaz followed his friend, his mind in confusion. 'Aren't there guards?'

'They've gone to fetch the priests. I know a way we can get out if all the corridors are not heavily watched. Hold my hand.'

'Why?'

'Do it!'

Boaz assumed that they were fortunate and that the excitement of the proceedings had made some of the guards sloppy enough not to notice them. Pez knew otherwise. He guided them expertly through various twisting walkways until Boaz found himself coming out by the Lion Fountain.

'Here? How?'

'I told you, I know my way around. Now come, we are still in danger.'

They arrived breathlessly back at the Zar's quarters, Pez affecting a wild laugh and somersaulting down the main hallway to Boaz's huge doors. The two Elim bowed to their Zar and then laughed. They knew the lad well enough to share a joke with him.

'Where does he get the energy?' one asked.

Boaz shrugged and pushed the dwarf into the main chamber.

Inside, the Zar ignored protocol and, with difficulty due to his injured arm, poured them both a goblet of wine. He handed it to his friend with a shaky hand. 'Now, tell me.' Boaz sipped his wine to calm his frayed nerves and rising temper.

The little man sighed and all amusement died in his eyes. 'It's called shepherding.'

'What does that mean?'

'I can, temporarily at least, block people.'

'Block them?' Boaz frowned.

'You know,' Pez said awkwardly, 'steer them away — you could say — as the shepherd steers his sheep.'

'You mean, stop them seeing you?'

The dwarf nodded. 'Not for long.'

Boaz suddenly understood. 'You have the Lore?' His tone was leaden with fright.

Again Pez nodded, his expression grave. This was not something he had wished to reveal.

'And do you use it often?'

'No. I have little need for it.'

'So what are you? Some sort of sorcerer?' Boaz asked, aghast.

'No. I possess such a tiny sense, I wield no real power.' He crafted a lie now. It was necessary. 'A throwback from my great-grandmother who was sentient. For the most part she kept her power a secret.' He watched Boaz's eyes widen at the discovery of this knowledge — all a lie, of course. 'It's nothing, Boaz. I have only a touch. Something only slightly more impressive than my silly tricks.'

'Why have you not mentioned it to me before?'

Pez shrugged. 'It didn't seem important — as I said, I haven't used it since I came here. I'm the Zar's idiot. It wouldn't do to be casting spells.'

'What is the extent of your magic?' the boy persisted.

'That's it,' Pez replied diffidently. 'I can shepherd and that takes so much out of me I usually need to sleep for a whole day. In fact I feel quite ill now.' He blinked slowly. 'I couldn't risk you being found there or I would never have used it.'

The boy continued to watch him with new curiosity. 'I shall have to think on what you've told me.'

'Our secret?'

'I have no reason to reveal you, Pez. You're my friend, aren't you?'

'I am. More than you can know.'

The Zar was suddenly apprehensive. 'Why did they call for the priests?'

'There is to be a ceremony.'

'Oh? I didn't understand what my mother meant by welcoming him to the place he had trespassed upon.'

'She is formally making him a member of the harem, Zar,' Pez replied.

Boaz considered this. 'But how can she when he's ...' His face drained of colour. 'He's to become a eunuch?'

Pez nodded. 'She will be taking his manhood as we speak.'

Kett, in his fear and confusion, seemed to be the last person in the chamber to understand what was about to happen. Even Ana had grasped what was unfolding and tried to squirm away through the legs of her captors.

Herezah was having none of it. 'She must bear witness. It was she whose body he watched. She who has caused his downfall, you could say.'

'Valide, I really must object,' Lazar began but he was cut off again, this time aggressively.

'Don't ever object to me, Spur. Remember your place. The girl will bear witness, as will you.'

Salmeo whispered something to her and she nodded.

'Guards, please show our guests into the chamber across the hall. In there is a courtyard — you can take some fresh air and we shall serve refreshments. We shall not keep you long.'

Muttered whispers of concern, confusion and relief broke out amongst the guests.

Salmeo took over. 'Elim, the Spur and the girl are to remain. Vizier, my humblest apologies, but I must ask you to leave also.'

The Vizier swelled like a rooster about to unleash a tirade of protestations when Herezah used her quiet voice to still him. 'Thank you, Tariq, I know how careful you are to observe the traditions of the harem. Perhaps you can keep our guests entertained on my behalf. We shan't be long.'

The stooped thin man pursed his lips and had no choice but to take what was clearly an order in the same gracious manner in which she had delivered it.

The priest arrived with a trio of helpers in tow. He'd obviously been informed of what must occur for he carried a small velvet roll and they carried towels, pails of steaming water and various other instruments of their ritual.

They bowed to Herezah. 'Valide Zara,' the priest said and she nodded. He turned immediately to Salmeo. 'Grand Master Eunuch, this is most unusual.' There was a slight waver of worry in his voice.

Salmeo gave a gesture of helplessness. 'These are unusual circumstances.' They both looked down at the trembling Kett. An assistant, known as a knifer, was lighting small wax candles and placing them in a crescent around the boy; another was dousing some of the lanterns around the chamber. Kett was being thrown into a small pool of light as the rest of the people around him were cast into shadows.

Herezah, who had never witnessed such a thing as the making of a eunuch, felt a thrill of excitement. 'How long will this take?' she asked.

'We shall be swift, Valide,' was all the priest could offer. He wasted no further time, giving whispered orders to his assistants.

Lazar moved back to lean against the wall. He knew its solidity would be a welcome friend within a few minutes. The Spur was hardly a squeamish man but this was one ceremony he was glad was a secret ritual. He cast a careful glance towards Ana; she looked desperately pale and frightened. Ana turned as if hearing his thoughts and they shared a long searching look. The depth of sorrow in her eyes awakened a fierce yearning in him. He wanted to own her. He wanted her to be his and now she was lost to him, offering herself up in exchange for the black servant. Kett would hardly thank her for it, Lazar thought grimly, believing he himself would rather die than go through this barbaric procedure and, worse, live with it for the rest of his life.

Salmeo began to speak quietly as the preparations were made. Kett began to whimper, catching sight of a small curved blade now being studiously sharpened by the priest.

'What you are about to witness is one of the most secretive of rituals preserved in the harem. It is not to be spoken about outside the harem walls. In this rare instance it is being used as punishment, but Kett will appreciate in time to come that he is privileged. It is a high honour to serve in this way.' Salmeo stopped abruptly and turned to the priest, also a eunuch. No doubt both men were remembering their own terrifying rite of passage. Lazar held his breath and prayed the next few minutes would pass quickly.

'Ready?' Salmeo asked.

The priest glanced at his helpers, each of whom nodded solemnly. 'We are.'

'Kett,' Salmeo began. 'Be brave now. Your blood is spared and you are entering a new way of life. A new form of service. The most secret and privileged of slaves.' His voice was so cloyingly gentle that Lazar had to look away from Kett's trusting face. The boy knew something terrifying was about to occur but Lazar could see that he also grasped that he had no power to prevent it. It was easier to co-operate and, like Lazar, pray to the gods that it end quickly.

The assistants undressed Kett and laid him down on his back. His head and shoulders were framed by the flickering candles. The priest threw something into the flames, which sparkled and crackled. It seemed to signify the commencement of the ritual. Two of the assistants flanked Kett to hold the boy down when the struggle began. The third man used long strips of white linen to bind the area tightly beneath Kett's belly button. They did the same to the high part of his thighs. Kett began to moan. He understood now. Curiously, he turned his head and searched for Ana who locked her gaze with his. Lazar watched the two youngsters share something. Sympathy? Fright? He didn't know, but with adults in the chamber perpetrating this horror, it was little wonder that they sought solace in each other.

'The bandages prevent excessive bleeding,' Salmeo explained softly to Herezah.

'Can he die from this?' she whispered.

'Oh yes. Many do in fact. Zarab will choose.'

'Drink this,' the priest said, handing Kett a small cup and helping him to sit up and drink it!

Herezah was intrigued. 'Is that for pain?'

'A dulling concoction to prevent panic,' Salmeo answered.

A prayer was murmured over Kett, the priest and his assistants holding hands above the child. An assistant reached for a bowl. Another prayer was cast before a sponge was dipped into the bowl and squeezed out.

'What's that grey liquid they're smearing on him?'

'That's boiled water-of-pepper and juniper. It is made by the priest who casts prayers to purify it and to purify the boy. He must do this three times in between praying for Kett's life to be preserved and for his own hand to be guided for the cut.'

Kett squirmed under the heat of the liquid around such a tender area. Lazar could see steam rising from the boy's body, wanted to close his eyes but kept them open to honour the slave who was showing more courage than he felt sure he could under the same circumstances. He was moaning, yes, but no words, no pitiful cries, or begging for mercy. Why? And all the time his head was turned towards Ana, watching her whisper her prayers.

'What is it supposed to do?' Herezah asked as they watched the priest complete the third bathing. Salmeo kept his voice low but Lazar could hear the words plainly enough, which meant they were sparing Kett none of the grisly details. 'It simply bathes the area. Makes it as sterile as possible, Valide.'

'I see. And you, Salmeo, went through this precise procedure?'

'Yes, Valide, to a point.' His timing was perfect for the priest had just positioned himself between Kett's legs. He reached for the sickle-shaped knife. 'And now we must choose,' Salmeo finished.

'Choose what?'

'What type of emasculation you wish for Kett.'

Lazar fancied that he saw Herezah tremble at the eunuch's words. 'Choose?' she repeated in a smoky voice. 'Explain the options to me again.'

'Yes, Valide.' He knew she would ask this of him, understood her need for theatre and the cruel streak that demanded she make the boy suffer a little longer. 'There is the clean-shaven or the Varen. All of the sexual organs are removed in a single cut. Or, there is the Yerzah — this fellow loses only the shaft. Perhaps the worst of the three, Valide.'

'Oh? Why do you say that?'

Salmeo shrugged. 'Well,' and somehow everyone in the room knew the Grand Master Eunuch was Yerzah, 'he has the ability to procreate, he just doesn't have the equipment.'

'Why is that hardest of all?' Herezah persisted.

Salmeo's lids lowered slightly and Lazar noticed the rope scar twitch. 'Because he doesn't lose the desire to copulate, Valide. He cannot satisfy a woman by traditional means and he cannot satisfy himself by any means.'

'I see,' she said, smiling beneath the veil, storing away another treasured item of information about the Grand Master. 'And the third method?'

'Is called Xarob. This eunuch is rendered sexless by the damage, often removal, of the testicles.'

'How do you damage them?'

Salmeo looked at Kett; the boy needed to be cut before all blood was strangled by the tight bandaging. 'We must hurry now,' he said softly, adding, 'damage can be achieved by twisting the testicles, searing them, bruising them or bandaging very tightly as one might an animal who is to be castrated.'

'Thank you, Salmeo. I think Kett is best served by becoming Varen.'

'Clean-shaven?' the priest repeated, to be sure.

'Yes,' Herezah affirmed. 'Proceed.'

The priest nodded at the assistants who flanked Kett and they immediately held down his arms. He did not struggle. He was frozen in fear, refusing to look at anyone but Ana. Two of the assistants placed a knee across his bandaged thighs. They could not risk him jerking when the blade was doing its work.

When both were satisfied they had the boy effectively pinned, they nodded. The priest carefully grasped Kett's genitals, ensuring he had them in a firm grip before he pulled them away from the boy's body, and in a single motion cut through skin and tissue until everything formerly attached came away in his hand.

Kett screamed and mercifully blanked out, as did Ana, who hung limply between the arms of her guards. Lazar was helpless to aid her and was working hard at damping down his own bile.

The bloodied mass in the priest's hand was reverently placed in a white porcelain bowl.

'They will preserve that for him. Most of us like to keep the removed flesh,' Salmeo said.

Herezah had not so much as blinked at the ghoulish procedure. 'How generous,' she commented. 'Actually, I should like them.'

Salmeo looked sharply at her. 'That is not traditional, Valide.'

'Nevertheless,' she said and left it at that.

The priest and his assistants worked fast now, taking advantage of Kett's swoon.

'They are placing a wide needle into the tube at the root of the shaft,' Salmeo said. 'It is made of pewter and will keep that tube of flesh open but plugged until Kett heals.'

Lazar watched as the wound was dressed with saturated papers dipped in chilled water. Then it was bandaged. The priest sighed and nodded.

'It is done,' he said.

'And?' Salmeo asked.

The priest stood, wincing as he straightened. 'He will live. He's young, he'll heal fast. It is a clean wound. Now he must be walked.'

Salmeo looked at the Valide. 'Kett will be kept conscious now and mobile for the next four hours. Only then will he be permitted to rest.'

'Can you do the walking somewhere else?' Herezah asked, her callousness impacting so hard on Lazar he nearly shouted in protest. He balled his fists instead and stared at his feet, counting slowly in his mind, using the hard, guttural Galinsean numbers which felt more aggressive.

The priest nodded. 'Who will be looking after him?'

'I shall arrange for helpers,' Salmeo said.

'Thank you. You know the routine, Grand Master, nothing — absolutely nothing, not even a sip of water — must pass his lips for three days.'

'I remember,' Salmeo said and Lazar heard the anger — or was it pain — in his tone.

'He will be in agony of course, and he will beg for relief from feeling parched. He will want to pass water but he must not, under any circumstances.' Salmeo nodded. 'I will return in three days to remove the spigot.'

'What happens when that occurs?' Herezah was clearly fascinated.

The priest answered: 'When the needle which has plugged the hole is removed, a fountain of bodily fluid is spurted from the opening. Kett will feel immense relief when this occurs and it will signal that he is out of danger and he can begin his healing.'

'And if not?' Herezah asked.

'If he cannot pass water, then he is doomed to a slow, agonising death. I would suggest it would be easier to put him out of his misery in this instance.'

Kett groaned, was coming back to consciousness. Tears leaked out of his closed eyes and his body trembled. Ana was still slumped between her captors.

Lazar could no longer bear it. 'Valide,' he began.

'Yes, you are dismissed, Spur. Don't forget our appointment tomorrow — I do not like to be kept waiting.' She turned to Salmeo. 'Let's get this all cleared up. The merchants will be eager to complete their business.'

It was as if the whole process with Kett was nothing but an intriguing interlude that had now lost its novelty.

It was all Lazar could do to affect a terse bow before he stormed from the chamber.

Lazar ranged swiftly through the palace until he emerged into the Moon Courtyard and the balmy evening. He dragged in a lungful of air to quell his mounting rage.

Furious with himself for showing his feelings to Herezah, he was also torn apart by the loss of Ana. Thinking about Kett made him value his own body and the fact that it was whole. Perhaps what he needed was that jug of wine and a willing woman to ease his despair. He thought that was what he was going to do to finish this night but Lazar did not head into the Carafar district.

No, he was drawn elsewhere for solace, to where a woman who could not speak might offer some comfort.

❦ 11 ❧

Tariq sat alone on the balcony of his home and seethed. Not even the soft moonlight glinting off the calm harbour could ease his anger — not that anyone would know he was in this mood. Vizier Tariq was a master of hiding his thoughts, although he deliberately played a dangerous game within the palace. He knew they all thought he was a shallow fool and desperately ambitious. He permitted the Valide — and to some extent the fat black eunuch — to trample him because for now it suited his purpose. Unlike the old Zar, who though disliking him sought his assistance, they didn't take him seriously, although his position required them to make pretence at doing so. And no doubt the Valide could see the value of being seen to have the Vizier on side. He hoped she might consider him even more valuable in time to come.

Oh yes, he could see all of this. But they could not see him. And they did not know him or what he might have the power to do.

The harsh voice invaded his thoughts. *All alone, Tariq?* When it spoke it sounded like boulders chafing against one another.

As you find me, he answered carefully. Although the shock of its invasion had dissipated, its intimidation had not. He felt intensely frightened by it and hoped the voice — whoever it belonged to — could not see into his thoughts as easily as it seemed to enter his mind.

Your jewels glitter in the moonlight. When they do that it means your beard is trembling. And when your beard trembles, Vizier Tariq, I know you are angry and no doubt plotting.

Is that so? Tariq was impressed and terrified. He closed his eyes to steady himself for there was no way to rid himself of the voice. It came as it chose and he had no control, no power to block it, and something in that deep, almost ancient tone suggested he not attempt to banish it. *Am I that easy to gauge? Perhaps I should rid myself of the beard if it so easily reveals me.* Tariq was proud of himself for feigning such a relaxed approach.

Perhaps you should. It's an affectation only. The time is drawing close when you will need none of those things.

You speak as if you know me, yet this is only the third time we have spoken.

I do know you, Tariq. I know you better than anyone.

May I ask some questions?

Why not?

Do you talk with others?

Few.

Do you visit other people as you visit me?

Now?

Yes.

No.

But you have?

Over time.

The Vizier repeated that cryptic answer in his mind. What could it mean? *Where are you?*

Close.

In Percheron?

Yes, but time, usually my friend, is now my enemy.

Tariq found some spine. *Do not push me.* He held his breath, then added: *What you ask is complicated*, and he heard the plea in his own voice — was ashamed of himself.

There was a silence in his mind. He waited.

What is the basis of your reluctance? the voice asked.

Tariq sensed it was less sure of itself and was pleased. It felt good to sow some doubt in its arrogant mind. *I'm just not sure, that's all.*

I have watched you for years. I have smelled your ambition, tasted your desires, felt your anguish at those who think you stupid. I admire your resolve and the way you have disguised your true self, beguiled the new Valide, tricked the black eunuch. The cunning in the voice was back and the compliments worked.

Tariq couldn't help but swell with pride. He briefly wondered whether his intruder was inhuman. He had a sense of it being some sort of creature, but how could that be? Nevertheless, he was secretly pleased it knew how crafty he was *Why do you know all this?*

Because I have chosen you.

Chosen me? he repeated and then took a risk despite his fear. *What if I don't care to be chosen? What if I am happy as I am?*

Now the sinister voice boomed laughter in his head. It sounded like mountains of granite shifting. *Content? I think not, Vizier. Consider that I bring all of my knowledge to you. Imagine it! Centuries of information. I can tell you anything you want to know about our history — even where the Zar Fasha's famed treasures are buried.* Tariq's beard quivered and the thing laughed again in his head. *You thought it was only legend, didn't you? It is truth. He buried it with all of his wives and his heirs. He was quite mad.*

The Vizier shrouded his thoughts as best he could, uncertain of how successful his attempt was. *So, you can offer me riches, what else?*

Isn't that enough? Isn't that what you want, Tariq? To be wealthy beyond imagination?

Oh, I have a vast imagination.

Again amusement rumbled through his mind. *What else can I tempt you with?*

What else can you offer? Tariq tried to sound casual, hardly believing he was having this conversation.

The voice had arrived the evening before the Zar died. It had come to him as he was now, relaxing on his balcony, taking the night air. He had been startled, dropped his wine. Fright had taken hold until the voice calmed him, told him Joreb would be dead before noon the following day and that he, Tariq, was in a perfect position to stamp his claim as premier counsel to the new power entering the palace, the Valide Zara. The Vizier woke before dawn the following day thinking he had simply dreamed the episode. But as his mind cleared, so did his memory and by the time the sunlight had shyly stolen across the sky, Tariq knew he had experienced some sort of premonition and hurriedly made his way to the palace to tell Herezah. It was only his insistence that this was an emergency that had persuaded the First Wife and Absolute Favourite of Zar Joreb to agree, irritated, to meet with him before her grooming was done. Heavily veiled, she greeted the news with disdain, particularly as the physicians had tentatively hazarded that Joreb could recover and be back on his horse by the next moon.

When the news of the Zar's decline through the night was delivered to Herezah, she instantly resummoned the Vizier. His confidence restored, he smiled at her, throwing caution to the wind and his fate in with hers.

'If he dies, I shall need the right men in the right places, Vizier Tariq,' she said with a new level of respect in her tone.

'*When* he dies, Favourite Herezah, you will need me alone.'

He noted the flash of contempt which sparked in her eyes and imagined the soft scowl behind the veil at his audacious claim, but then Herezah did not know about his visitor. Tariq had realised with the news of the Zar's worsening health that the voice was real and it spoke truth.

It interrupted his thoughts now. *I offer you power.*

I am already Vizier.

You are nothing, Tariq. You have a title but no real power.

Then you must explain this power. What you want of me is significant. The return for my generosity must be equal in measure. The voice had a way of firing his imagination and greed. He wanted power. That was his true desire. He wanted Herezah and that fat slave to know the truth. They would no longer dismiss him from the chambers where they whispered. He wanted to be Grand Vizier, to see fear in their eyes, to have the pair defer to him. *Now who is reluctant?* he gibed.

Anger this time. Controlled but certainly there. *I will bring you real power, Vizier, of the sort you cannot attain alone.*

Tariq persisted. *As Vizier, I have authority over the whole of Percheron.*

This time the voice sounded more like a growl. *Pitiful! That is not the sort of power I speak about, you fool. I'm talking about sentience and sorcery . . . the power of the gods!*

Tariq felt his skin prickle with excitement and fear. This claim was far darker, far more frightening than the Vizier could possibly have dreamed. Sorcery ... power of the gods. What could he mean? Who was he? The intruder had so disturbed him that he had not once had the presence of mind to ask for a name. He surely had one?

Tariq felt his heartbeat accelerate. With magic he truly would have power of the sort he could only dream of. Old Yozem and her blood-tellings would be cast into the streets. Herezah would have no need for the crone now. She would have him, Tariq, and need no-one else. *Tell me how,* he asked, glad he did not have to use his voice to speak, or the visitor would surely know how nervous he was and how dry his throat had suddenly become.

I have said enough. I offer power of a nature you have never known and can never know without me.

And all I must do is temporarily surrender my body to you?

Yes, the voice answered. *A small gift by comparison.*

What will you do with it?

I need a body, Tariq. That is all.

In order to do what?

Nothing that will affect your lifestyle or pleasures. You will be rich, you will be empowered, and you will be indispensable to the ambitious Valide Zara. How much more could you want?

What more indeed, Tariq privately reasoned. The bargain was more than just tempting. *Can you give me youth again?*

You'd look rather obvious as a young man, the voice baited. *Don't you think someone might notice?*

Tariq gritted his teeth. *Can you make me feel younger, appear less aged?*

Like the Spur? The voice knew his weaknesses too well and used them in cunning fashion.

What do you mean by that? he blustered.

I told you; I know you, Tariq. I know your desires as well as I know my own and I feel your envy for the man Lazar. He is the most handsome man in Percheron. Every woman's heart flutters when his glance meets theirs. Is this what you want?

I hate him!

I know. If I gave you such a dashing appearance you would suffer a notoriety that your more secretive side would not appreciate. I imagine the Spur does not care much for the attention he wins from the fair sex.

He's a fool!

Because he doesn't lie with every woman who throws herself at him?

Tariq chose not to answer.

Yes, I can make you appear younger, more charismatic and thus attractive to women. Does this satisfy?

I shall give you my answer tomorrow.

I want it now.

I need to think it through. You are not in a position to demand anything.

You are right. The voice's amusement was back. *Tomorrow then.*

What is your name?

What does it matter?

I must know who you are, what you are. Silence made his head feel suddenly hollow. He tried to be patient, tried to out-think the person who demanded his body. But he could not wait. 'I must know,' he whispered in a croaky voice.

I am called Maliz.

~ 12 ~

As Tariq was haggling over the darkest of bargains that night, Lazar strode — he believed aimlessly — with only his deeply disturbed thoughts for company. He felt numb. The evening's events had unfolded so rapidly and into such an ugly scenario that he could hardly believe he had participated.

One minute he had negotiated the monthly release of Ana into his care and the next she was a prisoner for life. He knew he would never see the girl again and he could not bear it. Could not bear it! Not again. He was convinced that his heart had taken too many years to recover from the adolescent sickness of being in love and having it ripped away; it had healed over the years but badly, and it remained fragile. He had never allowed himself to open up to any woman again. Oh, he enjoyed them well enough, and he knew they responded with great fondness to his temporary affections, but that was all it was. Affection. He rarely permitted himself to see a woman more than a few times. Lazar wanted no attachments, no heartbreak for her or for himself. But Ana! How could he have let down his guard so recklessly and allow her in?

He could hardly be in love with Ana he reasoned through his distress, and yet he felt deeply attached to her. Was that love? He was fifteen summers her senior, almost old enough to be her father. Talking of love sounded somehow obscene even when it was safely hidden amongst his private thoughts. But he wanted her close. His heart demanded they be allowed to see each other and it had been permitted. Royal sanction. But Ana gave it up for the life of a stranger — a black slave. A child. He loved her all the more for her sacrifice. He felt nothing but admiration that she would act so selflessly whilst he could not.

As he acknowledged this, he looked up expecting to find himself entering the Carafar neighbourhood and realised that he was standing on the steps of the tiny temple again. He shook his head in wonder, with no idea what he was doing here and the realisation that he had been walking with no purpose for a couple of hours. It was late.

He ran up the stairs, two at a time, and bent to pass through the entrance into the serene peace. The temple was illuminated softly by a tiny rose-coloured bowl of oil that hung from the ceiling. It threw long shadows across the altar and lit a glow around the statue of the beautiful woman with birds flitting around her skirts. The owl regarded him. He felt sure there was a hint of amusement in its gaze — as if it knew some great secret. He looked at the woman and again her soft smile seemed as though it was just for him. He approached and stood before her, staring. Something compelled him to touch her and he reached for her smile, expecting to feel the cool lips of the marble she was sculpted from. Except they weren't chill to the touch. Lazar could swear that the woman's lips were warm beneath his fingertips. And now he was convinced there was a blush to her face, the lips flooding with life. His shock was interrupted by a voice and he stepped back, startled. When he glanced at the statue again it was ghostly white in the soft glow. His mind was playing tricks.

'Welcome back, Spur. I thought I heard a sound.'

Lazar knew he had entered quietly. 'You have superb hearing, Zafira.' He bowed courteously.

'Once again I interrupt you. Forgive me.'

'No, I just had nowhere better to go on this eve. I took a walk to clear my head and found myself here.'

'As good a reason as any. Come, will you take some quishtar with me?'

'It is near midnight.'

'No matter.'

'I would be delighted.'

He followed the tiny priestess to the back of the temple and up some stairs, finding himself in the small but airy space where she lived.

'It's adequate,' she said, noting how his eyes moved swiftly around the room.

'The view is worth the climb,' he said and she smiled at his compliment.

'Make yourself comfortable, Spur.'

'Call me Lazar, please.'

'Thank you.'

He looked at her living space: the tiny cot neatly made; a shelf with a few items, hardly valuable but no doubt precious to her — an old vase, a tiny painted tile, some delicate glass. The furniture was sparse and battered and yet it looked lived in, appreciated. The single cushioned chair was threadbare but it too appeared comfortable, moulded to her shape. A few scattered cushions looked as though they had been embroidered by her own hand.

Zafira spoke as she worked. 'I prefer the dried husk of the wilder desert cherry myself. Makes for a more delicate infusion than its city or foothill cousins.'

'Can you tell the difference?'

'Oh yes, Lazar, you should pay more attention. Quishtar has many flavours depending on its region. It's part of our life's fabric — far more than a mere beverage. It promotes fellowship, it calms, it loosens the tongue,' and she smiled knowingly at him.

After the water had boiled, he watched her pour the delicately golden infusion from a spouted metal jug, deftly lengthening the stream between the spout and the bowl-like porcelain cups she aimed for. He had seen this done in the marketplace but it was a pleasure to watch it being effected with such care for his benefit alone.

'Is that just for theatre?' he asked. 'Where I come from, we just pour our drinks.'

'And where is home for you, Lazar?'

He felt the weight of his secret as he reached for the lie. 'Merlinea.'

'Ah, and yet your angular features scream Galinsea.'

'Galinseans have yellow hair. Have you met any?'

She studied him. 'A few. Your colouring is certainly all wrong for a Galinsean, I admit.'

'But I am typical of a Merlinean.'

'Except for those eyes. Who gave you those?' she enquired, a sparkle in her own eyes.

'My mother. She's from the far north-west. A land called Dromaine.'

Zafira must have guessed he did not enjoy speaking of his background and she deftly returned to their original conversation thread. 'Everything in the making of quishtar has a purpose. Quishtar needs to breathe as it arrives into the drinking bowl. I always like to think that it's sampling the air it is being exposed to. Then it knows what to reveal when it's drunk.'

He laughed. 'You make it sound alive.'

Zafira tapped the large cup she pushed towards him three times with a single finger. 'An old custom. Seals friendship,' she added and there was the soft amusement on her lips again.

Although he hardly knew the old girl, Lazar already liked her very much, and he was not known for making friends easily. There was something about her. He was surprised he had told her as much as he had. For now he was glad of her uncomplicated company and the diversion of her chatter about the customs of Percheron.

'. . . or you'll burn yourself,' she finished.

'Forgive me,' he said, shrugging with a helpless expression on his face.

'Pay attention, Lazar,' she warned gently. 'I said use the linen or you'll burn yourself.'

He nodded, understanding immediately. 'You know I've lived here for almost as many years as I did in Merlinea, and yet I tend to take kerrosh rather than quishtar.'

'Then you are in for a treat.' She chuckled. 'Enjoy its fragrance first. What can you smell?'

'Spice, although I can't say which one.'

'Good.'

He smelled again. 'Um, faint citrus?'

'Yes.'

'The roasted aroma is not there as I'd expected.'

'Excellent, Lazar. It is not meant to be in the higher-quality infusions. Anything else?'

'Yes, but I don't know how to describe it. Vaguely floral, somehow earthy.'

She smiled. 'You have a good nose. This means you have keen taste.'

'Explain it to me.'

'Well, quishtar has no taste as such. It is not bitter. It has no sweetness, no sourness. Obviously nothing salty about it. It is not savoury. It has no flavour at all.'

'I don't understand.'

'Quishtar is all about fragrance. Your nose does the tasting for you, which is why you were able to pick out the flavours from the fragrance. So drink, my friend, and tell me what you taste.'

He sipped and instinctively closed his eyes. 'All that we listed before. Spicy, citrus, something vaguely floral and earthy.'

Zafira enjoyed regarding him whilst his eyes were shut. He was, by nature, watchful and to have him so relaxed changed his whole demeanour. Gone was the caution and tension. She noticed the gentle lines that ran either side of his aquiline nose to his mouth. When he smiled, they deepened, only adding to his handsome face. 'You see?' she said. 'You are tasting what you smell. But this only happens with the best infusion.'

He opened his eyes. 'How intriguing.'

'Life can be like this drink, Lazar,' she said, eyeing him closely over the rim of her bowl.

'How so?' He felt himself relaxing.

'It can fool you.' His glance flicked away from the freshly scented steaming vapours and into her rheumy gaze. 'Not everything is as it seems,' she added.

He sensed she was conveying a message to him that she was deliberately clouding. 'Let me pour another bowl for you.' When he didn't decline she took his cup and went through the same motions as before — in comfortable silence this time — and set it down before him.

'Aren't you going to tap the bowl three times?'

'No, we are friends now.'

There was something final about that comment. As though something secret had passed between them.

'Why do I feel like talking,' he wondered aloud, 'when I should be going?'

'Are you in a hurry?'

'Only to escape.'

'What are you running from?'

He sighed. 'My life.' And then for no reason he could explain, Lazar began to tell her about Ana. It seemed to pour out of him, as the quishtar had poured out of Zafira's spouted jug. He spoke at length, running his fingers through his long dark hair as he concluded '... they made her watch it all.'

The priestess took an audible breath, hissing it through her aged teeth. 'Cruel,' she whispered. 'And so your bargain is nullified?'

He nodded, feeling intense sorrow at admitting it openly.

'The child has a curious background,' Zafira mused.

'She has no background that I know of.'

'The fact that any baby can survive the Samazen, whilst goats could not, makes her special in my eyes.'

He shrugged. 'She was fortunate ... born lucky perhaps.' The old woman said nothing, allowed him to continue. 'She is special, though, for many reasons.'

'Be careful, Lazar. She belongs to the harem now.'

'Yes,' he said, hearing the hateful resignation in his voice. 'Untouchable.'

'Of course Pez is in the palace,' she said, the merest hint of cunning in her tone.

'You know him?' He looked up in surprise.

'I do.'

'How can that be?'

'Why should I not?' Lazar had no answer for her. 'Because he's considered a halfwit, you mean?' He nodded. 'Oh come now, Lazar, we both know he is no such thing.'

The Spur suddenly found himself on unsteady territory. Pez's sanity was unknown to almost everyone. Only he and Boaz knew the truth. Pez had sworn both independently to secrecy. Lazar had shared that knowledge with no-one, not even Jumo in the early years, and he never discussed it with Boaz, for they were rarely alone to talk about anything so private.

'Relax, my friend. He has revealed himself to me,' Zafira assured, although she could see that the Spur was not prepared to confirm or deny. Good. He was true, then.

'You have not answered my question,' he began. 'How do you know Pez?'

'He visits now and then.'

'Here?'

'Where else?'

'When was the last time?'

'Yesterday. We shared quishtar.'

'And what else?'

'If I'm being truthful I'd say we also shared confusion.' Now she looked hard at him.

'Over what?'

'Why we both feel we have been brought together. That there is some purpose to our existence in Percheron.'

Lazar snorted. It was an attempt at derision he wasn't truly feeling. 'Everyone has purpose.'

'Do they? What's yours? Why are you here and not in Merlinea? What keeps you here? There is anger in you tonight, and rightfully so, but nothing prevents you from walking away. Yet you stay. No-one invited you to the temple yet you came. Not once in all the years you've lived here ... and now twice in a few days.'

Her observations prompted a strange new sense of disturbance in his world. The world he thought was so straight, so balanced, so controlled, suddenly felt out of kilter.

'I think I'm the one now confused.'

'Don't be. Just don't shut possibility out.'

'What possibility?'

'That there is a reason for Pez revealing himself to you and me; that you have felt compelled over the last few days to visit the temple; that a baby survives the Samazen and you find her some fourteen or fifteen years later.'

'You think there is a link between us all?' he asked, frowning.

'Who's to say?' she answered, irritating him slightly by the sudden sidestep. She had deliberately led him through this conversation and now she seemed to be pulling away.

He wanted answers. 'Why won't you be frank with me?'

She put her bowl down, taking a few moments to fold the linen napkin. 'You think I am evasive?'

'There's something you're either frightened of or not prepared to share.'

Now it was the priestess's turn to shrug. 'Forgive me. I don't mean to make you feel uncomfortable.'

'You don't,' he replied.

A silence stretched between them, both measuring each other, knowing whatever was said next would likely change what had begun as a casual acquaintance into something more intense.

It was Zafira who began. 'I have had the feeling for a long time now that there is a force at work. I cannot explain it. It is just something my instinct tells me. Recently it has become more insistent. It speaks of danger and yet it also speaks of deliverance. I don't understand it myself.'

'And this feeling relates to you?'

'Yes, but to others too.'

'Who?' She didn't answer. 'Am I now making you feel uncomfortable?' he asked.

A soft laugh. 'Yes, as a matter of fact. I feel as though I'm talking nonsense and to such a new friend.'

'It's interesting that you've called me friend twice now.'

'Aren't we?'

'We hardly know one another.'

'We've shared quishtar. It's enough.' And her words felt true to him. 'But what binds us, Lazar?' she suddenly asked. 'What compels you here? What makes me know that it is you who approaches even when I can't see you? What do we have in common?'

He hesitated, 'I can tell you what attracts me, Zafira, if that would help.'

'Please,' she replied, 'go on.'

'I think I came to see the statue again. The one in the temple.'

'Lyana.'

He nodded. 'I have never seen anything as beautiful, and Percheron is filled with beautiful art.'

'And you like beautiful things, Lazar. It is why you like this odalisque so much perhaps?'

'How odd that you mention her in the same breath. At times I do feel about Ana the same way I do about the statue. I want to gaze at them for their beauty, it is so arresting, but I want to protect them from those who would do them harm. I want to communicate with them. I think I came here tonight looking for an answer.'

'And have you found it?'

'I don't know. I wanted my mind to be eased and that has certainly been done in talking to you.'

The edges of Zafira's eyes crinkled as the smile lit her face. 'That is a high compliment, Spur.'

'Isn't that what friends do for one another? They comfort.'

'Indeed they do.'

'And does Pez come for comfort?'

'No. He comes and stirs me up.' They shared a moment's amusement. 'It's a strange thing, Lazar, but there are times when I feel that Pez knows so much more than he lets on. There is wisdom in that curiously deformed face of his. Has it ever struck you that he looks like a bird?'

'No!' he laughed. 'But I shall certainly study him now you say so. Oh,' he said, and reached into his pocket. 'That reminds me. The most curious thing happened around sunset. Ana spotted this old woman in the bazaar — you know, in gold alley?'

Zafira nodded absently. She began clearing away the bowls. 'Go on, I'm listening.'

'Well, the old girl was bargaining, selling some gold. I could have sworn it was a chain ...' He frowned to himself as he recalled the scene. 'Anyway, she was negotiating with an alley cat.'

Zafira, her back to him, made a sound of disgust. 'At her age she should know better.'

'Yes, it's what I thought too. But before the alley cat could close the deal, Ana leapt in and begged the old woman to let her buy from her instead.'

'Why?' the priestess said, retrieving the jug and emptying its contents into a pot plant outside one of the small windows.

'You know, I'm not sure. She said it was because she felt the bargain would not be fair. But there was more to it than that.'

He heard Zafira chuckle quietly by the sink of water where she cleaned the bowls. 'I suppose you bought it, did you, Lazar?'

'I did,' he admitted, sheepish.

She turned with a look of soft admonishment, as though he should not spoil the child so. That expression froze when she looked at what he held out in his hand.

'Where did you get that?' she asked in a harsh whisper, dropping the bowl in her hand. It shattered on the floor at her feet.

He was taken aback. The small gold owl sat small but heavy on his palm, warming against his skin. He could swear the jewels in its eyes glinted with a light of their own. 'This is what Ana bought.'

'Lazar . . .' Zafira said, her tone filled with fear.

'Yes?'

'Hide it!'

'What?'

'Put it away, now!'

Alarmed, he slipped it back into his pocket. 'What's wrong?' Zafira was breathing heavily and she groaned, leaning against the sideboard. 'Do you need a healer?' he asked, uncertainly.

'No,' she assured him briskly. She took several deep breaths. 'That's Iridor you hold in your hand . . . or at least his image.'

'Yes, I know. So?'

Zafira sighed and turned to extinguish two of the three lamps burning, the shattered bowl forgotten. She took a taper and lit it from the remaining lamp then sat down at the table and lit a half-burned candle. The flame instantly threw a glow onto their faces. Lazar felt as though he was being drawn into a secret.

'How much do you know about the owl?'

He shrugged. 'As much as the next person, although I should admit I'm rather fond of him. He was the first of the graven images I saw on entering the city . . . I regard him as . . . well, as an old friend.'

'I see,' Zafira nodded gently. 'Another coincidence or is it part of the web that binds us?'

He looked at her quizzically.

'Let me tell you what I know. Iridor,' she began, 'is as old as time itself. He is a demigod who takes the shape of an owl. The owl works for the Goddess. He is her messenger.'

'And why are you scared by him?'

'Not by him, Lazar. By those who would see him dead.'

Lazar leaned back and regarded her. Battling with his intrigue was scepticism; she could see that.

'Come with me,' she said.

Downstairs she led him again to the statue. 'Do you see now, Lazar?'

'Iridor,' he murmured, looking at the owl on the woman's shoulder, with its somewhat bemused expression.

'What does he say to you?'

'I don't understand.'

'He is a messenger. What does this sculpture of him say to you?'

Lazar was as honest as he could be. 'He has a secret.'

'Ah,' she replied. 'Does he wish to share it with you?'

He looked again at the owl. 'Yes, I believe he does. He seems faintly amused. Isn't that how he strikes you?'

She shook her head slightly. 'He looks extremely sombre to me.'

'No smirk?'

'Not at all. He has only grave tidings to give to me.'

'Surely not?' the Spur said, disbelieving. 'We are both looking at the same image.'

'That's the way of Iridor. He brings different tidings to each; he is one thing to one person and something else to another.'

'And he belongs to her.' Lazar reached again to lift the golden statue from his pocket. The eyes did not glow now, although curiously the gold felt warm. He felt Zafira flinch as it emerged. 'I haven't told you the whole story yet.'

'I would hear it but first put that owl away, Lazar, and promise me this, that you will never tell anyone of this possession.'

He regarded her intently, baffled by the fright he read in her eyes. 'Ana knows of it. It is hers. She asked me to keep it for her.'

'Then she is supposed to know of him and she was right to ask this of you. It would be confiscated at the palace anyway.'

'Yes, that's what she believed. She …' He hesitated. 'When I said I would look after it for her she insisted that I not just keep it but that I keep it close. I have no idea why.'

Something registered in the priestess's eyes. It was like a flare of knowledge but it passed so quickly that Lazar convinced himself he had imagined it. 'Zafira,' he said, 'there is another confusing aspect to our meeting with the hooded old woman.'

She looked again at the statue of Iridor and he obediently secreted it again. 'Tell me,' she said.

'She was a stranger to me, and as Ana had only entered the city an hour or so previous, it was impossible that the woman could know of her. The girl has never been anywhere beyond her dwelling in the foothills.'

'So?'

'So how come this woman called Ana by name?'

They stared at one another, said nothing for a moment. The wick sputtered in the oil lamp and the harbour sloshed gently outside. Otherwise there was silence and it thickened around them.

'Are you sure Ana did not introduce herself at any time?'

'Quite sure. It was Ana who picked up on the fact that the woman named us.'

'Would you recognise this woman again?'

He shook his head, not releasing her gaze. She knew something, or at least suspected something, but he could not read her. 'She was hooded.'

He saw how her lips thinned and her hands trembled slightly. They had been sure and steady when pouring the quishtar — now Zafira was nervous … or was she scared?

'Describe what you remember,' she asked in a somewhat choked whisper.

'Tiny figure, hooded, dressed in dark clothes — black, I think. Gentle of voice — a beautiful voice, in fact, and if not for that recognisable quality it could be any frail old woman of Percheron.'

'Not any. Not carrying a statue of Iridor,' Zafira assured.

'What are you not telling me, priestess? What is scaring you? What does your life have to do with mine or Ana's or Pez's? You are hiding something.'

She shook her head sadly. 'I hide nothing. I am as confused as you sound, Spur. But I have knowledge and that can be frightening.'

'What do you know, then?'

She raised her eyes once again to him and they regarded him fiercely.

Her voice was hard when she finally replied. 'I know only this. With the coming of Iridor, the cycle will turn. The demon is remaking himself.'

Lazar had no comprehension of what she meant and yet her words made his blood feel cold.

'So what now?' he asked, lost on this strange path she was leading him.

'We wait.'

'For what?'

'The rising of Iridor.'

~ 13 ~

Pez felt unsettled having left a still somewhat perplexed young Zar on the pretext that he was fatigued and feeling ill.

He roamed the palace imagining he was on some sort of slippery slope, grabbing for purchase but failing, falling fast into an abyss. He couldn't pinpoint what it was that was disturbing him. He needed quiet to think it through.

People were used to seeing the dwarf moving through the hallways at all hours, often giggling to himself or suddenly sitting down in a corner or sliding down the banister of a staircase. He almost always appeared distracted, but tonight he needed no artfulness.

Pez's mind was working overtime. Was it Kett? The young black slave had been the first surprise, he had to admit, and the girl had been the second.

But then this all came afterwards.

The sense of destiny had been niggling at him for a while now. The first inclination that danger was headed his way was the arrival of the old woman into his life. He frowned. Yes, it all began there.

He pushed aside heavy curtains to enter a darkened room. Moonlight filtered through shutters and as his eyes adjusted to the depths he could see now it was a reception chamber. It looked as though it hadn't been used in an age. No-one would come in here tonight. Still he took the precaution of hiding in the inky shadows before he allowed his memories of that strange event to filter back into his consciousness.

It was almost four moons ago, when Joreb was still healthy on his throne and the harem had been bustling with the activities of women and their idle chatter. It was an ordinary day, nothing different about it; no omens or warnings. He had been in the harem at the time, awaiting the Bundle Women who brought goods into the protected place. Each had been hand-picked by Salmeo and was required to show proof of his authority — his seal on a small parchment — permitting them to trade within the harem. The Bundle Women's arrival always caused a stir; anything to break the tedium of another day of bathing, dressing, resting and eating. The women of the harem wanted for nothing — except freedom — but still they bartered furiously for the cheap, gaudy fabrics and silly trinkets these purveyors brought to them. Serious purchases of silks and jewellery were all handled by Salmeo. The Bundle Women were a diversion, nothing more.

One particular woman, younger and sweeter than most, had arrived to peddle ribbons. No-one seemed at all interested in her goods that morning. And so she turned to Pez of all people, a simple bystander — there for amusement and not much else — and offered him a red ribbon. He had looped it around his ear and danced energetically, weaving amongst the wives and odalisques who were rummaging through the displayed goods, making a few laugh, and then shook his head sadly and returned the ribbon to her.

As their fingers touched, she grabbed his hand. 'I must speak with you, Pez,' she whispered.

Naturally Pez was taken aback, not just by the nature of her message but by the fact she named him and spoke to him as though he was of sound mind.

'Come,' was all he said and he led her to the back of the room. No-one paid any attention but he was glad that Salmeo was not present, for the Grand Master Eunuch missed very little.

The young woman followed, bringing with her several ribbons. 'Look as though you're considering them,' she suggested, although it sounded to him more of a command.

And when he looked up in response he saw that this was no young woman. Before him stood a crone. He was not imagining it — she appeared older than the oldest person he knew. He was also not imagining that she had appeared young only moments earlier. It terrified him, for Pez, although empowered with the Lore since childhood, deliberately shrouded his talent and hid behind his deformity. If he was honest with himself he would admit that he had never really understood why. His natural abilities with the Lore could make him rich, powerful. But Pez was not seduced by either. Since he had been old enough to appreciate the extent of his skills, he had instinctively kept it secret. He could not explain why. It was as though an inner voice guided him in this decision.

Until the crone had pulled away his sanctuary of secretiveness, no-one, not even Lazar whom he felt he could trust with his life, knew of his Lore skills.

He remembered now, as he sat in the dark, how some of the women glanced over and their gazes slid back to their own negotiations. No-one could see the truth. The crone looked young and desperate to them, trying to get a fool to buy her wares. He saw differently; could see skin stretched as thin as a veil across her skull. It appeared translucent. He could see the marks of age on it and the tiny veins beneath. Her features, although he had stared at them, he could not readily bring to mind now. Her colouring had been ghostly pale and he recalled how he had found himself breathing shallowly from the fright of discovery.

'Don't be frightened of me, Pez,' she said in the kindest voice, handing him a green ribbon. 'Forgive my guile. I am your friend. We have always been friends.'

'Who are you?'

'That is not important. What is important is who you are.'

His expression turned to one of confused query. He did not know what she meant. Had she not just named him, knew who he was?

She seemed to read his thoughts. 'You are Pez for this battle, yes. But you must know who you truly are. There is so little time. We must gather ourselves. It begins. He is remaking himself.'

'What begins?'

'Listen to me,' she said, her urgency infectious. She looked over and saw that the Bundle Women were packing up their wares. 'They are leaving and I with them. You must discover yourself.'

She turned to leave but he grabbed her arm, confusion warring with irritation on his face. 'Who is remaking himself?'

The crone only said one word but it was enough to freeze him to the spot.

He had still not moved even minutes after the departure of the Bundle Women and the harem atmosphere had died back to one of bored quiet. Some of the girls had called for their pipes. Soon they would be in an opium haze of oblivion. No-one took notice of Pez, probably thinking he was off on one of his fanciful voyages in his head.

Finally he found the courage to repeat in his mind the word she had spoken.

Maliz.

Since that name was uttered Pez had committed himself to learning all that he could of the demon, once a warlock, who had given Percheron its famous stone creatures. And he had learned much.

He had learned nothing of himself, though, and that bothered him. Why had she told him to go in search of himself? What did she mean that he had another name?

Kett's appearance and the beautiful girl presented before Herezah had for some strange reason prompted him to recall the old woman's warning. But why?

He sat in the dark and teased at his problem. What did he know? He had spent many hours in secret wandering through the great library of the palace, which had some of the oldest tomes in Percheron. No-one else seemed to visit the library, although an old fellow by the name of Halib seemed to know his way around and didn't appear to mind that the Zar's jester was wandering through the silent rows of books.

And so over the past months he had learned that Maliz, originally a mortal and a warlock, had supposedly begun the campaign to topple the might of the Goddess to ensure the priestesses of Percheron — who had held such quiet power — were reduced to nothing more than a memory. His reward was immortality as a demon — perhaps the most powerful demon. Now the priestesses, like Zafira, practised their faith very privately and humbly. Today they were no longer persecuted, for it had all happened so many centuries ago and those who pursued the faith of the Mother Goddess were so few and scattered they were considered harmless, reclusive. The Goddess' followers had been rendered so impotent that most of today's parents, ignorant of the history, believed the Sisterhood of Lyana was a good place to send wayward girls and unencumber themselves from ugly daughters who might never make a good marriage. More as a place of retreat than anything else.

Pez was surprised to learn that Maliz was inextricably linked with the Goddess. She was not just a passing whim of his. She was his nemesis. And, so the writing told, he remade himself — whatever that meant — when all the signs were right for her to rise again.

It was written in the tales of legend that Maliz had beaten her back thrice, but on each occasion, over many centuries, she rose stronger. It was predicted privately by those in the faith that her next return would be her final one and that Percheron would once again worship Lyana.

Pez thought about that now. The crone's visit suggested that he was being somehow drawn into that struggle. Why? It brought him back to the same question. Who was he? Why was he important? She had told him to find himself but so far nothing had surfaced to give him a clue. It was intriguing but unsettling. Perhaps she had sensed his magicks but until this evening with Boaz he had not wielded them. Nor would he again, he hoped. Once was dangerous enough and now Boaz appeared mistrustful and even hurt that his friend had this secret.

Thinking of Boaz gave a prick of regret for the young black boy.

He had felt an instant connection to Kett but no inclination why. He did not know the family; had never come across the child before. Perhaps that was a good place to start. Pez stirred from his shadowy spot, fixed a vacant expression on his face, and emerged into the corridor of the harem. He knew they would still be walking Kett around, keeping him conscious, and he went in search of the knifers whom he hoped would save the boy's life.

Following the Spur's dismissal by Herezah, Ana had been removed to a waiting chamber. She had had to be carried from the Choosing Room after witnessing Kett's savaging but she had noticed the Valide's intent gaze following her and she had seen the expression of despair on Lazar. Would he ever forgive her, she wondered.

Shortly Salmeo had come for her. The Choosing ceremony had obviously concluded. 'Are you recovered, child?'

She nodded. 'I am well but not recovered. Never will I recover from what I witnessed.'

His scar moved in tandem with his knowledgeable smile. 'Come, my dear,' he said, voice gentle, taking her hand. 'There is something we must do together.'

Ana instantly recoiled. The huge eunuch was frightening but not because of his appearance. It was his manner; her instincts suggested that intimidation was always his intention despite his avuncular tone. He was the Grand Master Eunuch and she had seen enough in the Choosing Room to know that within this man lay power, driven by a hunger she was not mature enough to understand but could certainly detect.

'Ana, you must do as we say now,' he continued, more firmly, not perturbed by her reluctance. He had seen it many times, knew the reaction he could provoke simply by his presence. He loved that he could do this and it mattered not to him that it was a fourteen-year-old child cowering. Fear was power.

'I don't want to,' she answered.

Brave, he thought, most would not challenge again. No doubt that courage would manifest itself as feistiness in future years. She was just another in a line of rebellious youngsters, including Herezah, who believed they might fight the system in the harem. But soon enough they learned the way. There was no resistance. His word was law.

'Must I have you carried?' He spoke in a patrician tone but it was all threat.

'No,' she fired back, 'I shall walk.'

Yes, indeed, this one would be a challenge, and he smiled at her. She did not return it. 'Where are we going?'

'You are already here, Ana. You are home now. We are simply moving to another part of your home.'

'This is not my home. This is my prison.'

He made a soft sound of admonishment. 'That attitude will not help you, child. You must work hard and learn your duties and then perhaps you will come to the notice of the right people.'

'I already have,' she said.

He knew she was right and felt a thrill that this one's spirit would be fun to break. The feisty ones always were. For now he was content to continue with the charade of kindness. By tomorrow she would understand that he was never to be challenged again.

'You are now in a part of the harem where no man may trespass, Ana. Eunuch slaves alone are permitted to walk these hallways amongst the women.' She touched a painted frieze as she walked alongside him.

'Beautiful, isn't it?'

'It is the mark of the Goddess.'

'Hush, we do not speak of that here.' He wondered how a peasant girl might know such things.

'Why? Does it frighten you?'

'No. It is irrelevant, that's all.'

'Not at all, Grand Master Eunuch Salmeo. It is extremely relevant, considering you only move amongst women and men who are more feminine than male.'

He recognised the direct insult, quietly again admired her composure in one so young. It would desert her shortly when she understood what was about to occur. He had the patience of a crocodile. He would punish her in oh so many ways for her provocation.

They moved in silence through a series of dim hallways. Salmeo was relishing the privilege of knowledge and the fact the silent walk would aid in building tension for this youngster who would be taught her second lesson tonight. Her first had been visceral but she had been an observer. Her second would be far more personal.

They reached an arched opening, and as they stepped through, two eunuchs straightened at the sight of their chief. Both reached to push open the double doors which led Salmeo and Ana into a sparsely furnished room warmed gently by a small brazier. Arched windows were latticed and only two candles burned, flickering in a soft draught.

'This room is very private, Ana. It is attached to my suite.' She did not respond. 'We are surrounded by a walled garden; all eyes are turned away, child. It is just us now.'

She found her voice. 'I thought I was being taken to my sleeping quarters.'

'No.'

'But it is so late.'

'This will not take long.'

'You have told me where I am. Why am I here?'

'You have been chosen by the Valide Zara as a suitable mate for her son, Zar Boaz.' He watched carefully as her gaze darkened slightly. Good, she was nervous. There was no other giveaway sign, which only served to intrigue Salmeo more.

He waited and when she said no more but fixed him with a stare instead, he continued. 'I must check that you are a virgin, Ana.'

'Reminding you of my young age is not enough, presumably.'

He almost clapped at that. He did appreciate her spirit. Most of the girls usually broke down at this point.

'No,' he answered. 'It is not enough. It must be personally verified by myself.'

'Or what?'

'Or you cannot join the harem.'

'That's perfectly acceptable to me.'

Now Salmeo did allow the broad smile to break across his wide face and reveal the cavernous gap in his front teeth. His tongue flicked into and out of the hole like a snake tasting vibrations in the air.

He saw the girl's flinch of disgust, fed on it.

'Ana, pay attention,' he warned softly. 'You cannot break the promise that has been made to the Valide. Money has exchanged hands, agreements have been reached, and you yourself have made a bargain with the Zar's mother. There is no higher commitment you could make.'

'Other than with the Zar himself,' she qualified.

And he nodded, impressed by her steadfast manner. 'Yes,' he agreed. 'But this means you cannot leave the harem —'

'But you just said that unless you affirm my virginity I cannot join the harem, which suggests there is a lawful way to leave it,' she argued.

He put his meaty hand to his lips to stifle the chuckle. 'You did not let me finish, child. There is most certainly a legitimate way — as you describe — to leave the harem before you join it.' He paused before saying quietly: 'You may leave it dead. Your throat slit or your head severed or perhaps you prefer drowning, which is certainly the less messy but presumably more uncomfortable method available for our use on the women. You may most definitely leave the harem in a velvet death sack.'

'I see,' she answered and held his gaze. 'Then proceed.'

'Good.' He clapped his hands and seated himself behind an ornate desk. A side door opened and a small man entered carrying a salver of water. Another followed bearing a tiny jar of oil, a pot of soap paste and linens. In silence the Grand Master Eunuch allowed his hands to be washed. It was done with reverence by the first slave after the second had tipped some oil into the water. His hands were then lathered with the soap paste and rinsed before Salmeo held them out to be meticulously dried.

They bowed and departed having not uttered a word. To their backs the chief said, 'Send in the ferris.'

Now Ana watched a third person enter. He was a tall slave bearing a tray set with a small clay bowl.

'Undress now, Ana,' Salmeo began, saw her open her mouth to contradict and added, 'or he will do it for you.' Salmeo nodded at the slave.

She didn't look at the man but regarded Salmeo instead, their glares locking. The Grand Master Eunuch felt disquieted that it was he who capitulated first. 'Assist her!' he barked.

'Don't touch me,' Ana cautioned. 'I shall do it.'

She lifted the sheath over her head and stood naked before Salmeo, defiance in her glare, hate in her heart and fear tingling through her body as she watched him dig into the pot. When he withdrew his finger she noticed that it contained a thick, sticky substance.

'This sap of ferris will make it easier on you,' he said, and he took his time smearing the gluey white paste over a couple of his pudgy fingers.

Fright took hold within Ana. She could guess where those hideous fingers would probe. She glanced at the hand with the long nail painted red and wondered what that signified, but her thoughts fled back immediately to what was to come.

The Grand Master Eunuch sighed and slowly lifted himself to his full, intimidating height.

'Ana,' he began and noted by the scowl how she despised hearing her name uttered by him. 'I know this sounds difficult but you will make it far easier on yourself if you can relax.'

She could not. Her body began to shiver involuntarily as he approached.

He could see her fear at last and although it made him gloat inside, he masked his expression into one of concern, ignoring the pulsating sensation that rushed through his body towards his groin and lay there as an angry, bitter, unanswered need. 'You must trust me. It will be over quickly if you do not struggle.'

Ana backed away only to feel the unyielding body of the slave who had moved behind her. Now there was nowhere to flee.

The Grand Master Eunuch would normally have the girls held down by another but he wanted Ana all to himself. Wanted to feel the heat of her through his silks, experience her fear as her trembling body touched his, see the anger nonetheless in those clear, bright eyes. He wanted her humiliation to be complete and provoked by his touch alone.

He arranged himself opposite her on a cushioned bench, his glistening fingers held in the air. 'Lay her across me,' he ordered the slave, who proceeded to lift Ana without much effort.

Salmeo expected the usual screams and pleas, wanted them, but all he got was a groan, deep and angry but one resigned to its fate. He smiled inwardly. This girl was definitely going to give

Herezah some grief. He couldn't wait for the sparks that would fly when these two spirited personalities clashed.

The long-limbed girl was laid across his expansive lap. 'Go now,' he dismissed the slave. He turned his attention back to the girl. 'Now remember what I said. This goes much easier if you find a way to loosen all the tension in your body, especially here,' he said, touching the rise of her pubis. 'Open your legs, child,' he added firmly.

'I hate you, Salmeo.'

'Everyone does,' he said, and grinned as he pushed his finger into Ana, feeling for the hymen that he already knew would be intact.

Pez found the knifers with Kett's seemingly limp body hung between them. The boy's toes trailed now and then, but with their whispered encouragement he found the wherewithal to stagger in a slow circle.

Pez skipped into the room and circled the strange trio. He cackled, pointing towards the bulk of bandage between the boy's legs and then holding his own crotch in mock sympathy. He continued his merry way around the perimeter of the room, singing now. He did a somersault or two before arriving to stare deeply into the stricken, exhausted face of Kett. Pez moved backwards in time with the trio's rhythmic pace forwards.

'Will he die?' he chirped in a singsong voice.

One of the men shook his head. 'He will survive now that he's endured this far, I'm sure.'

'Hsst!' the other warned. 'Not until he makes water must we assume.'

'Kett, Kett, Kett,' the dwarf sang into the boy's face and then worked the name into a strange rhyme. All the time he stared hard, waiting for the slave to register.

Finally, painfully, Kett opened his eyes to slits. They were bloodshot, as were his lips, which were bloody from biting them hard when the cut was made.

'The drug is wearing off,' one of the knifers whispered. 'He'll start to cry out soon.'

The other nodded. 'How long to go?'

'Another fifty revolutions of the chamber at least, or until we hear the third bell.'

'Leave us, Pez, you're not helping him,' one said.

'But I like him,' Pez replied. They both looked at the dwarf, baffled, and then ignored him again, vaguely irritated by his presence as he waddled backwards in time with their steps. 'We are friends aren't we, Kett?' he said into the boy's face.

The boy winced and then muttered something neither of the supporters heard but the dwarf did and it frightened him.

'I am the raven,' Kett slurred, then his eyes closed and he returned to his dazed stumble.

∾ 14 ∾

Jumo was relieved to see the familiar figure and distinctive lope of Lazar arrive at the Spur's house in the early hours of the morning. The man he had waited for all night arrived tired and distracted.

There was no greeting. 'You shouldn't have waited up, Jumo. You know you don't have to wait on me.'

'I have left a carafe of wine on the verandah.'

Jumo left the Spur to brood alone staring out to the Faranel and presumed he would remain there for what was left of this night. He was right; the next morning he found the chair empty but with a discarded blanket lying across it and a second carafe of undiluted wine nearby.

Lazar emerged minutes later looking freshened and clean-shaven but drawn as if sleep had eluded him. His eyes possessed a haunted quality too that Jumo had not seen before. Something was brewing. He had known this man too long not to be able to read the signs. It would be best, then, to give him the news now.

'A messenger arrived not long ago, master.'

'New orders?'

Jumo heard hope in his friend's voice and he knew how much Lazar must want to escape Percheron. 'He was sent from the palace … from the Grand Master Eunuch's office.' He watched Lazar's temple pulse. Knew that sign well.

'And?'

Nothing to be gained by hedging. 'It's Ana. She has gone.'

'Gone?'

Jumo nodded. 'Through the night.'

Lazar looked at him, pain fleeting across his face. It seemed such an impossible claim. No-one escaped the harem. The palace would expect him to find her, of course, not just because he had brought her to the harem but because he was the Spur and in charge of all security. 'Any clues?'

'They think she slipped away disguised as a black eunuch.'

Lazar, turning to move away, swung around now and regarded Jumo with a hint of bemusement. 'They jest!'

'Apparently not,' and Jumo couldn't help a small smirk himself. 'They believe she wore a black jamoosh and blacked the area around her eyes with ash from a brazier.'

Lazar couldn't help but admire Ana all the more for her wonderful defiance of the most sacred rules, but the amusement died quickly when he grasped the import of her rash actions. 'They'll punish her, of course.'

Jumo nodded. 'I would say so. The Valide will want to for the spectacle of it and Salmeo will have to in order to reinforce his authority.'

'We must find her first.'

The Valide had spent a restless night. She had slipped between her silken sheets with a sense of triumph the previous evening. Everything, she decided, was coming together nicely. She had both the fat eunuch and the fool Vizier eating out of her hands. She was confident that Boaz's harem would be one of the finest ever assembled and the goatherd's adopted daughter was a prize jewel amongst a veritable collection of precious gems. The girls were stunning but there was something extraordinary about this one. She felt sure Ana would be one of those who would produce an heir; Boaz would pick her as soon as he was ready to lie with a woman, for Ana's looks were too startling to ignore. However, she would have to be careful that this one did not steal her son's heart entirely. Herezah wasn't ready for a power struggle.

Boaz was going to need careful handling. She needed to find challenging diversions for him so he would feel important, useful whilst not meddling with the day-to-day running of what was clearly now her realm.

'I've waited too long for this,' she had muttered as she sipped on the citrus infusion she insisted on taking every morning. A lot of the other women had allowed themselves to run to fat in the harem, especially those who had never caught the attention of Joreb. He may have lain with them once or twice, but he soon sorted his favourites from those he was not interested in, and although these estranged women remained pampered and primped they were largely ignored. With no future other than slothfulness available to them, it wasn't long before their lives diminished into a continuing indulgence of food and mind-altering confections to dull their frustrations.

Herezah had not had cause for the same frustrations and thus she took great care with her body's appearance — no, her frustrations were born out of ambition and impatience. Now that she had in her grasp what she had dreamed of for so long, she was not going to let it go — not even to the son who made it all possible. Boaz was young, he had plenty of wild oats to sow and energy to burn off in playful pursuits. He did not need the serious burden of running a realm she could so easily handle for him. She was going to make everything as easy as possible for him, and she reasoned that this new era in their lives was going to give them a wonderful new and close relationship.

After her tea she rose, her mind still battling with the question of Ana and what to do with her. She decided that the best way to handle the child was to put her own claim on her. Mark her as the Valide's own slave. Then she could break and control the girl before she became available for the Zar's needs. How clever that she might turn the new odalisque into one of her own agents.

Herezah could spy on Boaz via Ana, plant ideas into his mind through his favourite lover, control him fully, especially if he chose Ana to be one of his wives. She hugged herself. What a good day this was.

Before she could take her morning exercise the news had come, delivered personally by Salmeo. When he was announced she knew it had to be something of importance. She had him admitted but did not offer him a seat — he was interrupting her morning routine after all.

'Speak,' she commanded, more than enjoying her new authority over the one who had inflicted humiliation upon her in years gone by.

'Valide,' he began as she reached for her steaming cup of kerrosh, which she took in its most bitter form. No sweetening for Herezah. 'One of the new acquisitions has escaped the harem during the night.'

If he thought the Zar's mother might overreact he was very wrong. In wonder he watched Herezah's unveiled face display no outward signs of anger. She paused in her sipping of the kerrosh and then delicately reached her long arm to place the porcelain cup back on the tray. Herezah, for all her failings, was a naturally elegant woman. It was little wonder that Joreb, a lover of the finer things in life, had fallen for her dark beauty and exceptional grace.

'Ana?' she asked, almost as though she were expecting this news.

He nodded and his scar appeared more livid for the shame he was obviously feeling.

She spoke chillingly softly. 'How can this happen, Salmeo? I belong to the harem. I know that what you're suggesting is impossible.'

'Nothing's impossible, Valide,' he tried but at her instantly furious glare sighed. 'Normally, yes. We are, however, not dealing with a normal child, if you'll permit my saying so, Valide.'

'How so?'

'She has intelligence and, I might add, defiance enough for ten odalisques.'

Herezah smirked. 'I think you're right. How did she escape?' She was intrigued that any girl could find a way out of the harem; almost jealous in fact.

This was not difficult to answer but it was horribly embarrassing for him. He tried to hold the Valide's keen gaze but he soon found himself looking elsewhere. 'After completing her Test of Virtue, she was left alone momentarily to gather her composure and reclothe herself. She took that opportunity to steal some garments and blacken her face. We discovered a jamoosh was missing and the grate of the brazier had fallen to the ground. She used ash on herself apparently.' He shrugged. 'There were black smudges on my walls and she had thrown ...' He hesitated.

'Thrown what?'

'She had smashed the clay pot of ferris and placed it into the burning embers.'

Herezah gave a gurgle of laughter. 'Oh, such spirit. She hates you early, Salmeo.'

'I am used to it, Valide,' he said softly and fought the urge this time to look away from her sardonic smile. 'She loosened some fretwork and escaped through my courtyard.'

'Why wasn't I informed immediately?'

Again he hesitated. 'I thought she would be found more swiftly, Valide.'

'So what do we do?'

'I sent a message to the Spur at dawn.'

Her eyes flashed at his name 'Why, because she was his bargain?'

'Because he argued for her release. I think the Spur is fond of the child. He looked bereft when she relinquished her freedom for the slave's life.' He enjoyed making her lips thin at the mention that Lazar may yet feel affection ... and for someone else.

She did not rise to the bait. 'I saw it too. What does it mean, Salmeo?'

He moved his huge shoulders in a shrug. 'I cannot tell,' he lied. 'The Spur has always been one so devoid of connection to others that I can't reason this link.'

'Can you not?' He shook his great head. 'I would say that our young odalisque has touched the man of ice, warmed his frozen heart.'

His tongue flicked out to moisten his lips. 'Do you know this for sure?'

'Call it female intuition. He argued too passionately not to be involved with the girl somehow.'

Salmeo was impressed with Herezah, for it obviously grieved her to admit this. 'You are perceptive, Valide.'

She dismissed the compliment with a wave of her hand. 'So what of the child?'

'She will be found within the hour, I promise. She could not get far at night — she was barefoot, I believe. She is too recognisable and, I suspect, tired, hungry and already regretting her wild adventure.'

Herezah didn't necessarily agree with his summary but she understood he needed to regain some face. 'You must ensure word of this does not get about. We must not allow our girls to have any notion that escape will be tolerated. It was not even dared in my time,' she said, quietly irritated that she had not thought to try.

'No-one will know, Valide.'

'She must be punished, of course.'

'I agree,' he said, again relieved. 'May I make a suggestion?'

'Go ahead,' Herezah said, knowing how his cruel mind worked. She stood and took her half-finished cup of kerrosh to the window.

'She should be flogged.'

Herezah did not turn from the idyllic view of gardens stretching before her. 'And break that beautiful skin?'

'It will heal, she's young enough that it won't scar if we use an expert. Anything less would be a compromise, I fear, Valide.'

Now she laughed, deep and sly. 'A compromise to your position, you mean. I understand, Salmeo, better than you know. But it's fine with me. I want a physician's opinion before it's done, though. She must not mark.' She turned now to emphasise her instructions and fixed him with a stare.

He nodded. 'As you command, Valide.'

'And her virginity?'

'Intact.'

'As we knew. Did she weep when you did it?'

'Not even a tear,' he confirmed, recalling only too well how Herezah had cried hysterically when it had been her turn many years previous. He watched the disappointment dance briefly across her face but she masked her expression in a moment. *Good,* he thought, *I can still hurt you.*

'Find her!' she ordered.

Lazar and Jumo had started from the palace and agreed to work out in a broad sweeping arc — Jumo heading away from the city and Lazar moving deeper into it, towards the bazaar.

'We were there together, she might head for the familiar spots I showed her.'

Jumo had nodded agreement. 'I shall meet you by the People's Fountain by fourth bell.'

They now stood worriedly side by side, having met as planned but with no good news.

'Where would a child go?' Jumo wondered aloud. 'With her looks she would be an instant target.'

This comment only served to frustrate Lazar further and he punched the marble of the fountain. It hurt but rather than showing it he plunged his aching fist into the pocket of the long white formal jamoosh he wore.

And felt the warmth of gold. 'Iridor,' he muttered.

Jumo turned in query. 'Master?'

'Iridor! Of course.' He began hurrying away. 'Keep looking through the bazaar,' he called back. 'I have a hunch where she might be.'

Lazar suddenly felt sure he knew where Ana would have ended up. He arrived at the tiny temple having weaved his way at full pelt through the harbour streets and out onto the peninsula. He had to lean against the white wall of the holy building and suck in long, deep breaths before he bent and entered the hallowed space.

It was cool and dark as usual, except this time, kneeling next to Zafira, was another, engulfed in a black jamoosh which was far too big for her.

'Ana,' he said and his voice sounded loud and coarse in the silence.

Zafira opened her eyes from prayer first and turned, putting a finger to her lips. Then she stood, awkwardly, grimacing from old aches in her back and knees before she approached Lazar, a look of understanding on her kindly face. 'As you see, another visitor,' she whispered. 'Troubled, like you.'

'They'll be turning Percheron upside down for her, Zafira.'

She nodded. 'Give her a few more moments. She is as taken by the sculpture of Lyana as you are.'

Lazar grimaced at the delay.

'How did you know to find her here?' Zafira asked softly.

He shrugged. 'I didn't. I've just looked everywhere else,' he lied. He did not want to bring Iridor into the conversation again, knowing how it had affected the priestess last time.

'She's been here since the early hours.'

'How did she find it?'

'I thought you might have told her about the temple.' He shook his head. 'Well, she told me all about you and how kind you've been.'

'Kind?' he mocked. 'I sold her to the harem.'

'And she forgives you, Lazar.'

He grunted. He did not want forgiveness. He wanted control again. 'I have to take her.'

'Will they punish her?'

Even though he did not reply, he could not hide the truth from the old woman.

'You must protect her from this,' she urged, clasping the hard muscle of his arm.

'I have done all I can,' he replied, his anguish obvious.

'There is still more you can do, Spur Lazar,' she argued and her gaze suggested she had just said something prophetic.

He shook his head. This was all spiralling out of control. 'I am honour-bound to the Zar and by my position in Percheron. I must take her back to the palace,' he replied, his voice hard. 'I'm sorry, Zafira.'

'So am I,' she said, just as cold.

And it was with those words that Lazar decided he would follow through on his vague plans made during the night. He walked over to Ana and lifted her. She permitted him without a struggle but her eyes were filled with a sorrow that broke his heart.

'I'm sorry,' she whispered.

'I know.' He so wanted to kiss her golden hair and tell her he would make everything right again. Instead he stalked out of the temple with her. He did not look back but then Zafira did not expect him to.

The priestess's words rang in his ears. She had insisted he could do more. *What?*

'Take me away, Lazar,' Ana moaned as he set her down.

His jaw ached from the way he was grinding it. 'Ana, my duty is to the Crown of Percheron.' For lack of anything remotely comforting he quoted an old Percherese military saying: 'A man without honour is a man lost.'

Ana gave a wan smile. 'My uncle said that once.'

'Ana, I —'

'Please, I know I have to go back, Lazar. It's all right. Ah, there's Jumo,' she said, using Lazar's companion as an excuse to end their awkward conversation.

'Ana.' Jumo moved quickly to hug her, relief in his eyes when he stepped back. 'You frightened us.'

'I knew you would come and that Lazar would find me,' she answered. 'Thank you, friend Jumo, it is precious that I can see you again.' She kissed both of his weathered cheeks.

He glanced at Lazar. 'Do we have to take her back immediately?'

The Spur sighed. Wretched Jumo could always read his thoughts, and worse, Jumo got to hug Ana and be kissed by her. It annoyed him that he was himself so reluctant to show her even the slightest amount of the affection he felt. 'No,' he said, running a hand through his unkempt hair. 'We can at least share a kerrosh together.'

They walked with Ana between them to a shop they knew sold the best morning kerrosh in the bazaar.

'Find a spot,' Lazar suggested to Jumo, having noticed the long queue. 'I'll get them,' he added, knowing one of the advantages of being Spur meant a small crowd such as this simply parted at the sight of him. 'Thank you,' he uttered to those who bowed and moved aside to allow him through to the counter.

'Spur Lazar,' the owner acknowledged, grinning to show the few teeth in his head. He expertly poured hot frothing milk from a long-handled jug into another. Years of practice meant he didn't even have to look at the motion — it all happened through sense, touch and skill. The milk turned a burnt golden colour once combined with the hot kerrosh and the smell of it made Lazar's belly grumble. 'Three and give me that plate of skazza.'

'Hungry today?' the shopkeeper said, still grinning as he reached for the heated glasses to fill.

Soon Lazar was shouldering his way back with a tray of steaming kerrosh and pastries oozing with honey.

Ana's eyes lit. 'Our mother never offered it with milk!'

'Paradise in a glass,' Lazar said, trying hard to lighten the gloom that had settled around their tiny table.

Jumo raised his glass. 'Recovery for the troubled soul.' He looked hard at his friend.

'Ana,' Lazar began gently, pushing the plate towards her. 'Eat.' She took one of the sticky pastries. 'Did you run away because of Kett or because they scared you afterwards?'

'Doesn't Salmeo deliberately scare everyone?' she asked.

Lazar felt her quip bite at where he was hurting the most. What was in his mind to have given her over to that evil man? He watched her chew on the pastry, the syrup oozing over her lips, glazing them to a high shine. He stared at them, feeling a stirring in his bleak heart, and momentarily hated her for doing this to him, for making him care.

She pulled a strand of hair from her face with sticky fingers. 'Salmeo did an inspection of my body,' Ana said matter-of-factly. 'Inside my body.'

Lazar's cup slammed down onto the table. He didn't flinch at the scald of the hot milky drink that spilled over his sunburned hand.

'I gave him no satisfaction. That eunuch will never break me, although I can tell that's his intention.'

Lazar had no chance to reply for a group of Salmeo's Elim arrived, their distinctive red jamooshes giving them away instantly.

'You have found her, my lord Spur,' one said, as all in the group bowed low.

'Only moments ago,' he answered.

'My lord Spur,' the first repeated, 'we have orders to —'

Lazar held a hand up. 'Yes, I imagine you do … er?'

'Farz,' the man answered.

'Thank you, Farz. I found the child cold and hungry. I am seeing to her wellbeing immediately and then, as requested by your master, I shall return her to the palace.'

'May we not relieve you of this burden, lord Spur?'

The man was persistent. Jumo could see the pulse at his master's temple throb again, a sure indication that the Spur had run out of patience. It never took very long.

Jumo spoke quickly into the thick silence. 'No, Farz. You go on. Return to the palace and inform your master that Ana has been located. The Spur will bring the girl as soon as she has been nourished. You can see she is appropriately covered. There is no insult to the harem.'

The men looked between themselves, clearly confused. They did not want to act without courtesy to the Spur and yet each knew Salmeo would cut their throats just as soon as reward them, depending on how they pleased him. It would not please him if they returned empty-handed.

Lazar understood this. 'Take a kerrosh — put it on my slate. Then you can escort us back to the palace if that is easier.'

The men looked uncertain.

'Come, let me order with you, I need another.' Jumo stood, shooing the men deeper into the shop. He shot a wink at Lazar as he herded them towards the counter and saw his friend give a sad smile of thanks. Both knew Jumo had bought Lazar and Ana some precious private minutes together.

Lazar turned back to Ana, who was staring solemnly into the dregs of her glass. 'You must promise me that you'll never attempt anything like an escape again.'

'I cannot promise you that, Lazar.'

'Ana, I will not always be around to save you.'

'There is no need. Your responsibility ended when you presented me to the Valide and collected your gold.'

Oh, how her words hurt. She shook her head, frowning to herself. 'I'm sorry, Lazar,' she said, contrite. 'Zafira told you I'd forgiven you for selling me to the harem. And I have. Please ignore my accusations. I am tired.'

'You've made me extend my commitment to you,' he said carefully.

She eyed him gravely. 'I don't recall how.'

'By insisting I keep the owl statue close.'

Recognition dawned. 'And have you kept him close?' He lifted the gold statue out of his pocket. A soft smile played at her lips. 'As beautiful as I remember him. Lovely Iridor.'

Lazar sat back in his chair, astonished. 'Ana, where have you heard this name? Did Zafira mention it?'

She shook her head gently. 'Iridor is my friend,' she said, a faraway look in her eye. 'Take me back now, Lazar. I don't want anyone to get into further trouble on my account. It was wrong of me to leave as I did. I knew I could never escape, in truth. I was upset over Kett and then the Test of Virtue. It was so easy but I wasn't thinking clearly and once I was out I felt compelled to find the temple.' Her voice trailed off.

He had no time to ask how she knew the temple existed because he could see Jumo approaching, an expression of helplessness on his face. Presumably the Elim had knocked back their kerrosh so fast it had hardly touched the sides of their throats. They were taking no chances with their own lives. He understood — Salmeo could be hideously cruel. 'Come then, Ana,' was all he said, hating himself for not having an answer to this dilemma. She rose soundlessly as he pocketed the owl.

It was a strange troupe wending its way back to the palace and certain punishment.

∾ 15 ∾

'How is your arm this morning, my lion?' Herezah asked, reaching to run her hand through Boaz's hair. She had come to her son directly after meeting with Salmeo and was relieved to note he didn't pull away from her touch. She had made a silent promise that she was going to find again that affection they had shared in his early childhood — and Herezah knew it was up to her. Boaz would not give it willingly because he felt deserted by her. He had learned to live without her and now she was going to have to turn that all around.

'It hurts still but the new physician says I will heal fast because I am young and it was a clean break.'

'I never understood how it happened.'

He shrugged, pretended to put a book back on the shelf so she would not see the lie in his eyes. 'I fell awkwardly.'

'Because I frightened you, my darling?'

'Yes. But I am stronger now.'

'I know you are,' Herezah cooed, 'and I'm impressed.' He was taller than her now. One more summer perhaps and he would be a man. 'Boaz, it is vital that you show that same strength now to those around you.'

'It's a little early to impress myself on the people, Mother. Father's only been dead a short while.'

She heard the bitterness. 'Nevertheless,' she persisted, following him to the window. 'Here, sit with me a moment.' She took his hand and pulled him down beside her 'Precious Light, I don't mean the people of Percheron as such — not yet anyway. I mean that the people in this palace need to know you as a strong leader. It's their idle chatter that will pass through the city like wildfire. What they see they won't hesitate to gossip about, whether good or bad. But you must always remember, no-one is your friend, Boaz, except me. I'm the only person who has your absolute best interests at heart.'

He tried not to show his disdain. 'Pez is my friend.'

'He's a fool,' she replied briskly. She softened her tone again. 'I know you like the dwarf but you don't want people thinking your only companion is an idiot.'

She was right, of course, but then she didn't know the truth of Pez and never would if he had his way. 'I have many friends in the palace,' he said.

'Oh? Name one for me?'

'My tutor —' he began.

'Whom I've specifically appointed. No, Boaz, name me someone who is a true friend to you, who is not paid to attend you and owes you nothing.'

He hated the way she always needed to be right; never allowed him credit or even the room to make the simplest of decisions. Here she was again all but humiliating him in trying to make her point. There was only one other true friend and it was a name he knew would stick in her craw, for even Boaz could see how his mother craved the attention of this person. 'Lazar is my friend.' He watched her pause, take a slow breath.

'How true.' She forced a smile and took his hand between hers. 'But apart from the Spur, who is not in the palace often enough to be relied upon, you have no real friends.'

'What is your point, Mother? Does any Zar have any real friends? He is the ruler and by his very position is envied or despised or feared.' He removed his hand.

'That is my very point, son, which is why you must count on me and trust me. I am your flesh. I want what is best for you.'

He sighed. 'What is it you want of me, Mother?'

'I want you to be more visible.'

'To whom?'

'To those who count; those in authority who influence others.'

He smirked. 'The Vizier and the eunuch, you mean.'

She ignored his barb. 'You're going to have to attend dinners, meetings, a lot of tedious gatherings.' She paused. 'Some of these events are going to be harder than others.'

'What do you mean?'

'Well,' she said, playing with the sash of her gown. 'Your brothers —'

'Mother! We have been through this. I was injured!'

'I know, my lion. I know. But you were not present for Joreb's funeral or the festival to commemorate his life. It was noticed.'

'I was still very upset at his death.'

'And I wasn't?' Herezah challenged. His defiant gaze faltered. 'No matter what's happening in here,' she pointed to his heart and then to his head, 'you must always do your duty and look strong.'

They were interrupted by a knock at the door. She looked to him to give permission but knew she had won today's battle.

'Enter,' Boaz said, distracted.

His private servant stepped in, a young man called Bin, and bowed. 'Your High One, Valide Zara.' They both nodded. 'I'm sorry to disturb you, Zar Boaz, but the Grand Master Eunuch wishes to speak with the Valide. He says it is urgent.'

'Show him in,' Boaz ordered. After the servant had disappeared again he looked quizzically at his mother. 'Trouble?'

She had no time to answer. Salmeo entered. He too bowed and acknowledged both his superiors. 'Forgive my interruption, High One. The Valide Zara asked for this news immediately it was available.'

'Ah, the girl,' Herezah said. 'She's been found?'

'Yes, Valide. At the bazaar.'

'By the Spur?' she asked eagerly.

'Yes. They were sharing a kerrosh.'

'Oh?' she replied, stung. 'How cosy.'

'She was cold, we're assured. The Spur felt it was necessary to offer some nourishment. They shared pastries too.' Salmeo gave nothing away in his bland expression that he was enjoying baiting Herezah.

'So thoughtful of him,' she said in a contrived tone of boredom. 'Where are they now?'

'Awaiting you, Valide Zara.'

'Dismiss the Spur. Leave Ana in the harem. She can suffer the wait a little longer at my pleasure.'

'As you command, Valide.' He bowed and departed, relishing the chance to send the arrogant Spur packing.

'Mother, what is this about?'

'Oh, nothing that I can't handle,' she said, not meaning to sound dismissive and realising all too soon her mistake.

Boaz recalled the dwarf's warning that it was vital he begin to impress upon his mother whose throne she served. His tone bristled. 'If you want me to be more visible then I demand to be included on all matters relating to the palace, Mother. Is that clear?'

She turned at his sharp tone. This, she had not anticipated. 'Why, yes of course.' She felt her own anger stoke but pulled it back just in time. 'Forgive me, son, I just didn't think it was of importance.'

'I will be the judge of what is important. Tell me what this is about.'

'There is a girl —'

'I gathered,' he said.

For the first time Herezah saw Boaz for the rival he was. This journey was obviously going to take longer than she'd thought.

She tempered her tone. 'I'm sorry, darling. Let me start from the beginning. Last night we made the selection of young women who will form the new harem.' She could not know how he held his breath, relieved beyond belief that she could never know he had been present. 'And there was one particular girl called Ana — quite a remarkable child in looks and composure — who obviously hasn't taken to our hospitality.' She chuckled.

'She ran away?' he asked, incredulous.

'Yes, silly girl. Disguised herself with a eunuch jamoosh, blacked up her face with ash and somehow sneaked out of the palace.'

She noticed how her tale fired his imagination — wonder was reflected in those dark, intelligent eyes.

'How ingenious,' he said. 'I should like to meet this Ana.'

Time to get her own back. She knew how squeamish Boaz could be. 'Well, now, that's a fine idea, Boaz. I shall include you in her interview.'

'For what?'

'For punishment later today,' she said and smiled demurely at her son as she took her leave.

Lazar seethed silently, glowering at the all-too-polite Elim guard who reassured him that the Grand Master Eunuch would not keep him long. Jumo, of course, had not been invited into the waiting chamber, and Ana had been whisked away by the red-draped guards who insisted it was their role to escort her into the harem. His only consolation was that Herezah was not here to gloat.

Salmeo must have dropped in on his thoughts, for the Grand Master Eunuch entered at that moment and smiled condescendingly, the smell of violets wafting about him. 'Sorry to keep you, Spur.' It had already been two bells since they had arrived, which meant the big black slave had kept him waiting an hour.

Lazar glared at him.

'This is a delicate matter for the harem, Spur. You must show patience.'

'I think I have.'

'Indeed,' Salmeo replied dismissively. 'We have kept you from your duty long enough, which is why we no longer require your presence.'

Lazar could hardly believe what he'd heard. 'What sort of jest is this, eunuch?'

'Grand Master Eunuch if you please,' the huge man corrected in a slightly effeminate manner, which only served to infuriate Lazar further. 'No jest, Spur. The Valide's orders.'

'Orders? I wish to see her.'

Salmeo closed his eyes and shook his head. 'Impossible. She is not seeing anyone today.'

'Then I shall speak with the Zar.'

'He is unavailable,' Salmeo replied curtly.

'This will not do.' Lazar forced back his wrath.

'Spur, if you please, this is no longer a matter for your consideration. The girl is returned — we thank you for aiding in that but she is the property of the Zar ... she belongs to the harem and the harem alone will decide her fate.'

'Fate? What are you talking about?' although he already knew.

'She is to be punished. It will be private. You have exchanged the girl for gold. Your business here on this matter is concluded. We shall look forward to welcoming you to the palace on your other official duties, Spur, but now I would ask you to leave. My men of the Elim will —'

'Don't bother.' Herezah had put Salmeo up to this, Lazar was sure. He could see her delight flashing in the man's triumphant gaze. 'You may tell the Valide, when she is available, that I wish to speak with her about my position as Spur.'

'I shall do that,' the Grand Master Eunuch said and watched the Spur depart.

Lazar found Jumo waiting in an open-air walkway that led out to the Moon Courtyard.

'I see it went badly,' Jumo said, hurrying to keep up with the Spur's long, angry strides.

'That fat lump of dung!' Lazar muttered.

'Where are you going?' Jumo asked as his companion swung down a hallway.

'To find Pez,' was the gruff reply.

The dwarf was singing to himself in the library, turning pages of books far too quickly to be reading them. Lazar noticed, however, that Pez was not looking at the book he held but one on the floor.

'Pez!' he hissed.

The little man looked at him with a mixture of surprise and amusement. 'Yellow?'

'Don't play with me. This is important.'

'Well keep your voice lower then.'

Lazar crouched by Pez on the floor, between dusty books and two vast rows of tomes rearing up towards the ceiling. 'I need your help.'

'What can I do?' the dwarf whispered, eyes watchful for Habib, who was in charge of all the books.

'Don't worry, Jumo's keeping watch.'

Pez nodded. 'Let us speak plainly then. What's wrong?'

'There's a girl called Ana who joined the harem last night.'

'Yes, a very special child.'

'You know her?'

'Only by what I gleaned from eavesdropping.'

'Where?'

'Hidden in the corridor during the presentation ceremony.'

'You were there!'

Pez nodded. 'So was Boaz.'

'What?'

'They caught the slave, Kett. We escaped.'

It occurred to Lazar to ask how the guards had missed the peeping Zar and his jester, but he had more pressing things on his mind. 'That savoury episode aside, Ana took fright and escaped last night.' He was pleased that the dwarf didn't bother with asking how she had done such a thing.

'And Salmeo wants blood?'

'Herezah, of course, is pulling his strings.'

'Of course. How can I help?'

'Just speak to Ana if you can. I don't think they'll hurt her. They'll try to frighten her more than anything. But let her know she has a friend in you. I've been banished. They want me nowhere near her.'

'Until you sleep with Herezah this persecution will continue.'

'Let it!' Lazar growled. 'I must go.'

'I shall see if I can find Ana now,' Pez assured. 'Boaz is smitten, I'm sure. He hasn't said much but he'll get around to talking about it soon enough.'

Lazar didn't know if this pleased him or not, but at least it protected Ana. 'Good, perhaps he can offer her the sanctuary I couldn't. Thank you, Pez.'

'Don't mention it. I've needed an excuse to meet this fascinating creature. Now go, or you'll get us both into trouble. I'll send word, I promise.'

'I shall be leaving the city in a few days,' Lazar warned as he left.

Pez adopted his vacant expression and went in search of the child at the centre of the harem's controversy. He found a group of girls crying as they were led out of one of the main chambers behind two eunuchs. Another pair of the men brought up the rear.

He deliberately skipped past the line, twirling and whistling. It didn't do much to improve the girls' mood but it cracked a smile on the faces of the lead eunuchs.

'Where do you go?' Pez sang, although he could not see the child he sought amongst them.

'Even you won't cheer this lot, Pez,' one man answered. 'This is the second group for their Test of Virtue.'

Pez reeled away rhyming the word virtue with all manner of odd words including shoe and view, clue and stew. The girls did not laugh and he couldn't blame them. He weaved his way amongst the halls of the harem hoping the girl wasn't bathing, the water pavilion being the one place where he was excluded. It seemed strange to be roaming this area, normally full of whispering or excited giggling, plotting or sighing, now so devoid of noise. He found Ana alone in a room of divans, curled up in a window seat and staring out through the lattices.

He sang her name into the silence and when she turned he saw that she had been weeping.

'Who are you?' she asked, not at all perturbed by his appearance.

He skipped up to join her, hefting his short body onto the seat. 'I'm the court idiot. Are we completely alone?' She nodded. 'I belong to the Zar. Do you know his name?'

'Boaz?'

'Good girl. Well I am a friend of Boaz but I am also a friend of yours.'

'Why are we whispering?'

'Because I cannot risk anyone knowing that I am not a fool.'

'Oh.' Her eyes shone. 'No-one knows?'

He put fingers in the air as he said the names of those who shared the knowledge, hoping that anyone looking in would think he was telling her all the insect names he knew or something similarly pointless. He wore a manic grin as he did so. 'The Spur, his shadow Jumo, the Zar and a priestess called Zafira. No-one else except you now.'

'Why can't people know?'

'Too dangerous,' he mouthed and suddenly leapt up to spin around the room.

She couldn't help but grin at him. 'And you trust me with such a secret. How is that? You don't know me. I don't even know your name.'

'I am Pez. I trust you because of Lazar. He trusts no-one, of course, but he seems to care about you.'

She looked suddenly awkward, shy. 'Did he send you?'

'Yes.'

'Why is it dangerous for anyone to know about you, Pez?'

'Because it is. You have to trust me but you must trust no-one else in the harem itself. None of its odalisques, none of the eunuchs or other slaves. Do you understand?'

She nodded, wide-eyed. 'You'd better do another twirl around the room.'

'Has anyone said anything to you since you were returned to the harem?' he asked as he returned to her.

Ana sighed. 'They've told me nothing. The eunuchs who wear red asked me to wait here. Why are there none of the other girls?'

'I met some of them in the halls. They were facing their Test of Virtue.' He watched her defiant expression falter and understood she must have already undergone this humiliating ritual.

'The Grand Master Eunuch is detestable.'

'That's his intention. He wants you to loathe him. It makes him more powerful.'

'He wants to frighten me.'

'And did he, Ana?'

She shook her head. The defiance was back. 'No, I just hate him, that's all.'

'In truth you would all have had to face this unpleasant test anyway.'

'Except it would be done by a trusted woman, and only when we were facing marriage. Not done by some fat, sweaty eunuch who has the desire but nothing save his groping finger to satisfy it.'

He was silent, fully sympathising with the horror of such a thing being perpetrated on anyone.

'I don't like men,' she suddenly said.

'Don't you like me?'

'Except you,' and as she touched his arm, Pez felt a thrill of something pass through him. He had no idea what it was but it felt good. The sensation — for he had no other way to describe it — made him feel suddenly safe.

'And Jumo. Surely you liked him?' he continued.

'Oh I do. Jumo is lovely.'

'Lazar? I admit he's hard to like. In fact —'

'Yes,' she cut across his words. 'I do like Lazar ... very much. I'm just not sure if he likes me sometimes.'

'Take no notice. He usually kills those he doesn't like and those he can't kill he simply ignores.'

She exploded into laughter.

'You have a wonderful laugh, Ana. It's like birdsong and sunshine, a sea breeze and the scent of peryse, all thrown into one delicious sound.'

'How can a laugh have a smell, Pez?' she said, enjoying his imagery. She loved the delicate peryse blooms that only flowered briefly in spring for a short burst of spectacular colour and their soft yet somehow intense fragrance.

'Well, your laugh conjures an image of a field of peryse flowers.'

'Everyone else is right, you know; you're definitely mad.'

He leapt from the seat and began to dance again.

'Do you know what they're going to do with me, Pez?' Ana asked, suddenly sounding nervous.

And he too became serious. 'They will need to punish you, Ana, as a warning to the other girls. No-one to my knowledge has ever escaped the harem before, so they'll use you as an example.'

'They'll hurt me then?'

Pez was not one to lie to those he trusted. 'Not to the point of marking you. Something brief and scary for the others but transient, I imagine. Lazar asked me to tell you to be of stout heart. He will see what can be done.'

'He can't save me this.'

'From what I hear he's already stuck his neck out for you, child. He won't stop now. Lazar is one of the most intense people I know and the most driven. I imagine when Lazar loves, he loves hard and in a single-minded fashion.'

She blushed furiously. 'Are you saying he loves me?'

'I'm saying he will never allow someone he considers a friend to suffer if he can help it. Not very much stands in his way if he wants something.'

'Except Herezah,' she said, remembering the previous night and the way the Valide's eyes so often glanced towards him.

'Be careful, Ana. The Valide is more dangerous than you can imagine. You must ingratiate yourself with that one — far more than Salmeo even.'

She didn't reply but nodded.

'And now I must go,' he said.

'Must you? Can't you keep me company?'

'I want to check on Kett.'

'The slave boy?'

'Yes.'

'Can I come?'

'No, you must —' Pez heard footsteps and he immediately began cartwheeling.

Three Elim arrived.

'Miss Ana?' one said politely and bowed slightly.

'Yes?'

'We have come to fetch you.'

'Anything to save me from this fool,' she said, pointing to the spinning dwarf.

Pez felt his heart lurch for the girl. She sounded so brave and yet he knew she must be terrified. She had understood the pact between them and was already protecting his secret.

'Where does little Ana go?' he sang at the men, darting in front of them and pulling their sashes.

'Not now, Pez,' the leader said.

'I must know or I shall start to screech.' He'd done this once before and the Elim would never wish another similar scene again.

The man instantly capitulated. 'She is to be flogged. Valide's orders.'

Flogged? Ana could only mouth the word to herself in shock.

'Then take her away,' he sang, his heart racing with fear for her as he twirled out of the room and hit the hallway running at full pelt.

He had to find Lazar.

'It's Pez, master. He says it's urgent.'

'Bring him in.' Lazar turned to step inside from the balcony and saw Pez was already present. No salutation. 'What?' he asked, his gut twisting with worry.

'They're going to flog her,' Pez said, still breathing deeply from running to the Spur's formal abode.

Lazar, never one for wasting words, looked to his manservant. 'A horse, Jumo.' The dark man turned and hurried from the room. 'How much time have I got?' Lazar urged Pez.

'Little. The Elim fetched her whilst she and I were talking.'

'Knowing Herezah she'll want to turn it into a spectacle.'

'In which case, you can still make it before they begin.'

Lazar crossed the vast chamber in six strong strides. 'Will you be all right?' he asked, looking over his shoulder to his friend.

'Don't worry about me. Just get to Ana and think of something quickly, Lazar.'

The pain deepened on the Spur's face. 'That's just it, I have no idea how to save her. I've been racking my mind all morning.' His voice sounded hollow.

'Get a message to Boaz,' Pez said. 'You could claim the Right of Protectorship!'

His words turned the agony on the hardened features of the Spur to dawning relief. 'Thank you,' was all he said.

It seemed to Pez the Spur felt more for this young woman than he cared to admit, probably even to himself, if he were willing to offer such a sacrifice as this plan would require. The dwarf shook his head, for if he was truthful there was something about Ana that compelled him too. When she had touched him earlier it had felt as though she had ignited his soul; it was as though they were linked spiritually, and yet how could they be?

Jumo returned to disrupt his curious thoughts. 'What's he planning? He wouldn't say.'

'Right of Protectorship for Ana.'

'May Zarab save us,' Jumo said, touching hand to lip in a calling to the great god. He looked so fearful, it sent a fresh wave of guilt through Pez for suggesting such an idea. 'Herezah will love it.'

Pez nodded.

'Come, let me take you back in the cart,' Jumo offered. 'He's going to need all the help we can give.'

Lazar reached the palace in minutes, leaping from his horse and throwing the reins at his own men who stepped aside and allowed their chief to run across the main courtyard. Patrolling soldiers saluted, fist on head then heart, but he didn't acknowledge any of them.

Once inside he ran directly to the office of the Vizier. Tariq kept a suite of rooms at the palace for official duties. It was a stroke of luck that the bejewelled peacock of a man happened to step out of his chamber the moment Lazar barged into the suite.

'Tariq, I must speak with you urgently,' he bellowed.

'My, my, Spur. This is most unusual. Can we not set an appointment?' His oily manner never failed to stoke the embers of anger that always glowed within Lazar.

'No we cannot! It is important. Do you think I would come to you like this otherwise?' He controlled his wrath — it would get him nowhere. 'I would appreciate your help, Vizier,' he added contritely.

'I see, come in.' Tariq's tone was bland and disinterested but he was clearly relishing the humility of the Spur.

Lazar stalked past the surprised assistant and closed the door of the exquisitely appointed chamber he rarely found himself in. He remembered now why he hated to speak with the Vizier in his rooms. The man's choice in furnishings and décor was ostentatious to say the least. Everything about him was contrived. And besides, he knew how much Tariq disliked him. It had never bothered him but it made their dealings tense. With Joreb in power it had been easier for Lazar to work with virtual autonomy, but with Herezah now pulling Boaz's strings that would be impossible. Lazar suddenly felt revolted by the notion that he was now somehow beholden to this fool of a Vizier who had the ear of the Valide and thus the Zar. He forced himself to be polite.

'I must speak with the Zar.'

Tariq made an irritating noise of condescension, as if scolding a child. 'This is not possible, Spur. He is taking some quiet time in reflection and study.'

'I wouldn't make such a request if it was not important.'

'So you say. But so is the enrichment of the Zar's knowledge. Could anything be more important in fact, hmm?' he asked, jewels twinkling in the shaft of sunlight that he had deliberately chosen to position himself in.

Lazar knew it was pointless to argue this. 'Then will you get a note to him on my behalf?' he said, then added, 'Please, Tariq.'

The man quivered slightly, presumably at the humble tone in Lazar's voice.

'I shall do my best.' He pointed. 'There is a tablet of paper, use what you will and ink in that pot — I shall order a runner.'

'Thank you,' and Lazar wasted not another moment in scribbling out a rushed message to the Zar. He folded it and placed it into the small silken purse the Vizier indicated. 'One more thing. I now need to speak with the Valide Zara.' He saw the Vizier open his mouth to say the obvious but Lazar cut him off. 'Don't tell me this is impossible. I am the Spur of Percheron and require access to our most senior person in the palace. Without the ability to speak with the Zar personally, my rank demands I be given an audience with the Valide.' And then he added: 'I would not ask if it was not critical.'

'Spur, this is not the way we —' There was a soft knock at the door. 'Enter.'

A servant arrived. He bowed and Lazar felt relieved to see the silken purse put into the man's hands. Now that the message was on its way he could be more forceful.

'Hurry please,' he added to Tariq's instructions and the servant nodded and left promptly. He turned back to the man, no longer in sunlight and looking decidedly gaunt and old too. It was hard to age the Vizier because he hid behind so much decoration, but perhaps for the first time Lazar realised that this was Tariq's last chance to stamp his mark on Percheron. He would not survive another shift in power. It was the moment to play on the man's fears. 'I know this is not usual. But the circumstances are not usual either. I've told you it's important, and if you ignore this request, Tariq, then I will use all of my status to make this go badly for you.'

'How dare you threaten me!' The Vizier fairly shook with indignation.

'That is not my intention. I'm trying to impress upon you how important it is that I see the Valide.'

'And you will not share with me this important matter?'

'Tariq, you are more than welcome to join the meeting but if you don't organise an immediate audience, I will make my own way to the Valide's suite right now.'

It was an audacious threat considering Lazar had no permission to enter the harem. The Vizier looked horrified by the suggestion but he knew not to challenge the Spur to defy palace rules. The man was a law unto himself. May Zarab rot his soul! And what if his news really was important? The Valide would be furious if he didn't allow it to be passed on. Unless he ingratiated himself fully with her, he would remain her puppet. Or she might choose to crush him and leave him nothing, not even his life perhaps. And she a slave! He himself came from a fine family with a proud lineage. This woman was bought in a slave market where a representative of the harem had dug his finger into her mouth and checked her teeth whilst she stood naked and humiliated with countless numbers drifting by and watching. Now she ruled the country!

Wasn't getting rid of powerful women the way of Maliz? The demon's name slipped into his mind so easily now. Oh yes, Maliz's mission had been to undermine and destroy the power of the priestesses, to prevent Percheron from worshipping the Goddess and to replace her with gods, like Maliz's own master, Zarab, whom everyone called upon now.

Maliz's whispered promises made Tariq feel as though he too could be like Lazar, showing disdain for rules and taking the attitude that he knew best and was in control of his own destiny. And what if he could look younger, more handsome and be more like the Spur? Perhaps Maliz could help rid Tariq of Herezah as well and he could take her role as chief adviser to the Zar. The demon was still waiting for his answer. In truth Tariq was terrified of him and still had not come to terms with the fact that the demon had sought him out; that something he had always considered only folklore was suddenly so real.

He realised the Spur was glaring at him and waiting for an answer. Oh how he longed to make that man suffer!

And you will if you say yes, the familiar voice whispered, obviously eavesdropping on his thoughts. *I will help you to do just that . . . but not yet. Give him what he seeks. I promise you will have the last laugh.*

I must capitulate? Tariq answered, aghast. *What good is that to me?*

Wait and see. And then the voice of Maliz laughed deeply in his mind.

'I'm waiting, Tariq,' Lazar reminded, tiring of the long time the Vizier was taking to consider his request.

The Spur's voice jolted him from his thoughts. He was torn. Follow his own instincts or follow Maliz's? The demon seemed to know something. If he took Maliz's advice it would be a signal that he was ready to take the next step. Was he ready to give Maliz what he wanted?

Lazar made a sound of impatience.

'All right, Spur!' Tariq replied, angered. 'I shall organise it. Wait outside if you please.'

'I don't have time to —'

Perhaps it was Maliz's laugh that gave him spine. 'Do as I say. Sit outside and wait until I can contact the Valide Zara and get permission. That is the best I can do.' He was even able to hold the Spur's steely gaze without flinching or backing down.

Lazar sighed. 'Thank you. You might as well call the Grand Master Eunuch into the meeting. It concerns him too,' and he turned away.

Tariq stood before Herezah in one of the palace salons, quietly fuming that Salmeo, who had been summoned by the Vizier's staff, had somehow sidled his huge bulk to stand beside the Valide Zara, thus giving the impression that they were both in authority and Tariq a mere servant delivering a message. When he bowed to the Valide, it felt to him as though he was also bowing to the eunuch. This was not lost on Salmeo, of course, who wore a soft smirk along with the brightly coloured voluminous silks today.

'Well, the Grand Master Eunuch is here now. Vizier, what is it that you had to say to us?' Herezah asked from behind her veil, her tone conveying her annoyance at being interrupted.

'I do apologise, Valide Zara, at disrupting your day.'

'Tariq,' she began again testily, 'why *am* I being disturbed?'

No opportunity to string this conversation out and make himself feel important. 'The Spur is here, Valide. He insists on being permitted an audience with you. I requested that the Chief Master Eunuch be present only because the Spur asked.' He allowed a brief smile to touch his own lips, glad that he had made it clear he did not consider Salmeo important enough to be called into meetings as a matter of course.

He was irritated to see a glance pass between the hateful eunuch and the Valide. They knew something. They knew why Lazar was here!

Of course they do, Maliz breathed into his mind.

'And what does the Spur want, Vizier? Have you established that much?' Salmeo asked, all sweetness.

Tariq felt his gut twist. The eunuch was doing this deliberately to alienate him. How could the Valide allow the black slave to usurp her authority by speaking for her?

He ignored Salmeo and directed his answer to Herezah. 'He asked me to be present too, Valide. This obviously concerns all of us.'

'Not really, Vizier, but we might as well hear him out. Send him in.'

Normally Tariq would have bowed and turned to do her bidding but he had taken the precaution of bringing his secretary with him. He looked to the man who lurked at the very end of the chamber and gave him a signal, intensely pleased that he was not required to bow again.

Why don't you ask them? Maliz suggested. *It's about a girl. The one presented by the Spur who caused such a fuss. She went missing through last night after Salmeo had left her. It's his fault.*

Tariq felt a sharp spike of pleasure course through him. Maliz had his advantages. 'Valide, may I ask if this has anything to do with the girl, Ana? I hear she went missing last night; slipped the Elim and mocked the Grand Master Eunuch ...' He watched the rope of a scar twitch on Salmeo's face and his eyes become hooded with suppressed outrage.

Ah, the fat one didn't like that, Maliz cackled. *Hurt him more. Go on!*

'If the Grand Master Eunuch needs assistance in policing these children, I'm more than happy to organise a higher level of guard around the harem, Valide,' he offered, all innocence.

Maliz laughed. *Good.*

Salmeo didn't wait for the Valide to answer. His voice came sharp, each word a dagger. 'That will not be necessary, Vizier. It was a momentary lapse. It will never occur again.'

Tariq raised an eyebrow. 'If a mere child can slip through your net—'

'Zarab strike you —'

'Stop!' Herezah admonished. 'Perhaps it is a good idea to intensify the Elim guard around the harem. These girls are far too assured.'

Tariq bowed to her authority, feeling he had won the battle of words today. Salmeo uttered nothing but his body language said more than enough.

Oh he's going to make you pay for that, Maliz observed, full of glee.

He can try, Tariq replied, feeling surprisingly charged with confidence from the barbed discussion.

That's the spirit, Vizier, and with my help and presence, you will prevail over the fat eunuch. Think about it. I shall expect your answer by this evening. Then he was gone.

Herezah had moved to sit on a simple bench although she looked as though she had set herself on a throne such was her regal bearing. 'Where have you planned that the flogging will take place, Salmeo?'

'We agreed to keep it private. I thought it best to conduct Ana's punishment in the Courtyard of Sorrows.'

'Very good.'

Tariq asked for no explanation. He could work this out for himself.

The Spur was shown in. 'Valide,' he said and bowed briefly. 'Thank you for seeing me.'

'You are head of Percheron's guard and her security, Spur, why should I refuse you?' she replied, then added: 'Ever.'

He ignored her couched invitation. 'I am here today about Ana, the girl I brought to Percheron.'

'The girl you sold to the harem,' Salmeo qualified.

Lazar ignored him. 'Valide, as you know, I returned her to the harem after her escape last night. Frankly, I'm as horrified as anyone else but I'd like to know what terrified her so much.' He glared at Salmeo.

'Lazar,' Herezah began softly, naming him to ensure she gave the impression they were friends. 'Ana may be remarkable in looks and spirit but she cannot be treated any differently to the other odalisques, not until she can claim status as favourite or wife.' Then in a more condescending manner, but still laced with gentle concern: 'You do understand don't you, Spur?'

Lazar felt his limbs stiffen with aggression at being so belittled but he made himself appear at ease. 'Of course, Valide. I would not suggest otherwise. It's just that ...'

'You see,' she interrupted, 'the Test of Virtue is never a pleasant event for any girl, but we must all face it during our lives. It was simply Ana's turn last night.'

'I am aware of this, Valide. I came here today not to argue that case but to find out what your plan is for Ana.'

'My plan?' she repeated, a hint of derision creeping into her voice.

He humbled himself. He had to. 'Yes, Valide. You see, I never took any gold in exchange for Ana so I feel I do still have a small claim as her charge.'

'Do you indeed?' Herezah was angry now. 'Is this right?' she asked Salmeo.

'Valide, I have no such knowledge. I can check this, of course, but the Spur turning down the gold offered is hardly the harem reneging. It is his choice, surely?'

'That's right,' Lazar chimed in. 'I am not making any claim on Ana, I am simply making an inquiry as to your position on her lack of foresight last night. Her immaturity, the newness of her surrounds, the strangeness of Percheron — and let's not forget the cutting of the slave would have heightened her emotion, made her unstable. She is, after all, still young.'

'I was far younger than Ana when I had to face the test, Spur, and I did not flee.'

'Perhaps it did not occur to you, Valide. Perhaps the werewithal to do such a thing was not available to you. Presumably the Grand Master Eunuch failed in his supervision of this child. I am assuming she was left alone with access to her disguise?' He watched the huge eunuch bristle. 'Perhaps it is the Master of the Eunuchs who deserves the reprimand here, Valide, not the girl.'

Herezah did not so much as blink. 'You could be right, Spur. And I will consider such a measure, but Ana must bear the consequences of her own actions. As you say, she is young, but of an age when we can all be responsible — you might consider that my own son rules Percheron at fifteen. I was already a wife at this same age — a mother in fact. It may be a tender age but it is not an immature one, Spur. Ana made a very unwise decision and one, I'm sure, given her intelligence, she understood would have repercussions.'

As Herezah staked out her position Lazar already knew he had lost this argument. He could not talk Ana free of punishment. It was obvious they intended to press ahead and that meeting with him was purely for diplomatic reasons. He took a steadying breath, knowing what he was about to put in place would cost him dearly. He felt a buzzing near his leg as Herezah finished her speech. He reached into the pocket of his loose robe and felt the warmth of Iridor. It gave him courage. 'May I ask what her punishment is to be?'

'I suppose it is of no consequence to tell you.' Herezah looked towards Salmeo to do the honours — it was a small crumb of revenge for him after the battering he had just taken beneath the cutting words of the Spur.

'It is the decision of the harem, which will always mete punishment to its own, that the Odalisque Ana will be flogged — thirty lashes.'

Lazar blanched. 'Valide! She is a child, she cannot withstand such a thing,' he beseeched and watched how his plea sent a shiver of delight through the veiled woman.

'And if she flags during her punishment,' Salmeo continued firmly, 'she will be permitted a day's recovery before she completes the remaining lashes.'

It made little difference to Lazar, who didn't even spare the eunuch a glance as he spoke. His own gaze was locked on Herezah's. The dark eyes sparkled with triumph. She knew she had him right where she wanted him.

'In that case, Valide,' Lazar said, bowing low, 'I must invoke the Right of Protectorship.'

The words hung in the air amid a shocked silence. Such a thing had not been claimed in living memory but they all knew full well what it meant. It was enmeshed in the tapestry of the harem's existence. Odalisques had no powerful protector, which is why they schemed and made alliances. It was the only way to stay out of trouble. 'I'm sorry, do you know what that involves?' Lazar asked as condescendingly as he could.

'We know,' Tariq observed. 'You will take the punishment on behalf of the girl.'

'That's right. Valide, the law says —'

'I know what the law states, Spur,' she shot back. 'But you forget, you need the sanction of the Zar first.'

'He has it,' Boaz announced, entering the room somewhat theatrically. Lazar felt his insides loosen with relief as he dropped a bow to the presence of their ruler, as did everyone else in the chamber.

'Mother, frankly I cannot condone the lashing of one so young. I find it, well ... distasteful, to say the least.'

'Mighty One,' Salmeo began, bowing again for good measure, 'the harem has a right to punish its own without the Zar's ... interference.'

'I understand that, Grand Master Eunuch.' Boaz's tone was measured. 'But the Spur here has the right to make the claim. The girl was his find. This is also the law of the harem, is it not?'.

'It is, Zar,' Salmeo grudgingly admitted.

'And I for one would rather a man is flogged, than a young woman. I'm sure Lazar can handle thirty lashes of the Sparrow's Tongue,' Boaz said.

Herezah smirked coldly behind her veil. 'Except, son, the method of flogging is purely the choice of the harem and this is something in which even your status cannot interfere.' Herezah's tone was so icy the atmosphere in the chamber became brittle.

'What do you mean?' Boaz queried, faltering for the first time.

'She means that the Elim will choose what to whip me with,' Lazar said, a bitter smile turning up the corners of his mouth. He had eyes only for Herezah and she him, both duelling, both determined to hurt each other.

'Is this right?' Boaz demanded, looking at the Vizier.

The Vizier nodded. 'Yes. The Elim alone make the choice of weapon.'

Boaz looked beaten. Lazar could not have the boy crushed like this, not when he was just beginning to flex his authority.

'Your High One,' he said, bowing, 'I accept. Thank you for giving me your sanction to claim the Right of Protectorship.'

'Zarab be merciful upon you,' Boaz replied, knowing he could do no more. 'Where is this Ana? I would speak with her.'

'She is not yet ready, son,' Herezah said.

'Ready enough to take your punishments, Mother,' he said firmly, knowing she would despise being spoken to with such disdain in front of these men, particularly Lazar. 'She's therefore more than ready enough to meet her Zar. Have her prepared, Salmeo.' Salmeo looked towards Herezah. 'Is there a problem, Grand Master Eunuch, in taking an order from your Zar? Do you need sanction from the Valide as well?'

'No, High One,' the huge man replied, admonished, 'I shall see to it immediately. What about the Spur?'

'I'm not going anywhere.' Lazar's voice was caustic. 'Just tell me where you want me to be.'

'The Courtyard of Sorrows,' Herezah said, wresting back some authority as Boaz stalked away. 'Ana must be present. She will understand what she has perpetrated this day. ' She nodded to Salmeo. 'See to it.'

The Elim had been given strict instructions. Ana was to be bathed and dressed in a particular white robe, which could be slipped off her shoulders to reveal her back for the flogging, but new orders arrived as the slaves were hurriedly tying up her hair. She could not hear what was being said but she could tell that the eunuch in charge of proceedings was filled with consternation. He stepped into the small bathing chamber after the Elim had left and whispered to the senior slave. Then he too departed, leaving her alone with the two women preparing her.

'What's happening?' she begged.

'You are to be dressed in a different gown. Step out of that one, please, Miss Ana.'

'Why?'

'You are not to be flogged.'

'Tell me, please, what has occurred?' she begged the middle-aged slave, who was pulling the white gown from her shoulders.

'I have no information, Miss Ana, other than to dress you in more formal clothes.'

She got nothing further from the woman. Ana obliged, climbing into soft silk trousers and allowing a long silk jamoosh of pale blue to be draped over her until only her eyes showed.

'You must wait now, my lady, in the adjoining chamber. The Elim will come for you.'

Ana was led next door. She had not been in the same room twice since arriving at the palace and could only wonder at how many hallways and palatial rooms the harem consisted of. She sat alone on a divan, her head bowed and the doors guarded. Although frightening, it had seemed somehow easier to accept the flogging rather than the unknown. Now she had no idea of what was ahead.

Butterflies fluttered in her belly, and as if on cue there was a sudden activity at the main doors and the dwarf came bounding through.

'Pez!' she cried, never so relieved to see anyone as she was at that moment.

He was pulling silk handkerchiefs from his sleeves, his nose, his mouth, his ears and muttering about wishing he were a fish who could swim the oceans. He ignored her for a minute at least, jumping and singing and then ranting that the kerrosh was too hot and the iced sherbets too cold. Then he lay on the floor and stared up at the painted ceiling. 'Are they watching?' he whispered.

She glanced towards the guards and shook her head. 'How come you got past them?'

'I'm mad, remember. No-one cares about me.'

'Do you know what's happening?'

'It's Lazar. He's claimed the Right of Protectorship for you.'

'What does that mean? They've told me I won't be whipped today.' From the divan where she sat looking down upon the dwarf she sensed something grave had occurred.

'That is because Lazar will take the flogging on your behalf.'

'Oh no!' she cried, standing up. The guards looked around but didn't care that she was upset. Any number of things could upset a girl, including a dwarf saying frightening things. They smirked and turned away again.

Pez hurried to reassure her. 'Ana, hush. Lazar will be fine. He is a toughened soldier.'

'How was he allowed to do this?'

Pez sat up but turned his back on the men so they could not see his lips moving and Ana took his hint and did the same.

Pez explained. 'The Right of Protectorship stretches back centuries and it was only because of an ancient yet infamous instant of it being invoked that it remains in the history books today. A wife of the Zar had made him cuckold to a eunuch.'

'How can that be?' she interrupted.

'The eunuch's cutting had not been done properly and he had hidden this fact, managing to continue carnal relations whilst living among the eunuch community. He would have got away with his sexual activities if not for falling in love with one of the wives. She became pregnant and the Grand Master Eunuch at the time knew it was not possible that she was pregnant to the Zar. The girl refused to reveal her lover, such was her devotion to him, and so the Zar, incensed, proclaimed her death. The smitten eunuch stepped forward and claimed the right to be executed on her behalf, invoking one of the oldest laws of Percheron that a person can escape punishment if another accepts it instead.'

'Oh, so this is custom?'

'In Percheron, yes. I don't know of anywhere else where such a law exists. The eunuch was immediately ganched, a hideously slow and painful death involving being thrown onto hooks. Wherever on the body those cruel hooks snag is where the victim is suspended, eventually to die.'

She flinched. 'And I just get a whipping,' she muttered.

'You have not cuckolded the Zar. There is no greater treachery within the harem.'

'Do they still ganche people today?'

'Oh yes. There hasn't been one in a long time — I suspect we're due.'

'How is Lazar?'

'Determined, aloof, angry as always.'

'How can I thank him? How do I repay him?'

'By staying out of trouble, Ana. They have you marked now as rebellious. You must conform as best you can if you are to survive in this place. I imagine Salmeo has been deeply humiliated by this event and now you're escaping his punishment.' He made a tutting sound of soft despair.

'You think he'll want revenge?'

'I do, so you must not make it easy for him to take it. Stay out of his sights, Ana. Blend into the harem with the other girls and be dutiful. Learn all that they want you to and perform your tasks diligently. Survive.'

She nodded. 'Can you take a message to Lazar for me?'

'Of course.'

'Will you tell him that he is free of me? He is no longer beholden in any way. I am alone now and I accept this. I will be a dutiful odalisque as you suggest. I bear no ill will towards him and that I am ...' she hesitated, 'happier for knowing him.'

Pez said nothing. He didn't have to. They sat in sad silence for a few minutes and then the Elim arrived to disrupt their quiet.

'It is time, Miss Ana,' one said. 'Be off with you, Pez,' he added, pulling a face of disgust at the way the dwarf was picking his nose, humming tunelessly to himself. 'You will have to get used to the dwarf, Miss Ana,' the man said more kindly. 'He has the run of the harem. We cannot stop him from being here.'

'He doesn't trouble me,' she answered as sweetly as she could. 'He doesn't even talk to me — he just seems to murmur nonsense all the time.'

'He's been like this for years but he belongs to the Zar and is untouchable. Now if you'll come with us.'

Pez pushed himself to his feet and groped his crotch and then pointed to Ana. 'This one will please the Zar,' he said and giggled maniacally before running out of the door.

～ 16 ～

Salmeo's heart was pumping hard and it was not only blood it was pushing around his body. Anger throbbed in tandem. The eunuch hated to reveal when his emotions were being stirred; he preferred that no-one knew what he was thinking or how he was reacting to a situation. But the peacock Vizier and the arrogant Spur had belittled him before the Valide — just when he had begun to win her trust and complicity.

He banged the marble in rage. Even though his eyes were open he saw nothing, for his thoughts and boiling blood blurred everything. What he wanted was revenge and the Valide had given him the means.

A knock at the door brought him out of his angry thoughts. 'Enter,' he boomed.

His trusted and most senior Elim stepped inside and bowed low. 'Master,' he said, not straightening until his superior gave him permission to do so by speaking.

'Horz. You have heard what we do today in the Courtyard of Sorrows?'

The man stood up. 'Yes, master. I have been informed that we do not punish the odalisque but the Spur.'

'Indeed we do. Who had you earmarked to perform the whipping on the girl?'

'Someone very experienced, master, who knows how to lash softly without marking.'

'Change him. I want one of the apprentices to do this one.'

'Master?' Horz was confused. An apprentice meant it would almost certainly be badly done.

'The Spur is to be hurt, Horz. Must I say it more plainly for you?' The Elim shook his head. 'The Spur has called the Elim into question today. He mocked me in front of the Valide. He believes it will be a simple case of taking the child's punishment. I choose otherwise.'

Horz could feel the hate emanating from the Grand Master Eunuch. Even the words of his master's preamble sounded chilling. Whatever was coming was clearly going to be dangerous.

Salmeo continued. 'I want the Viper's Nest to be used on him.'

Horz heard himself gabbling. The whip Salmeo spoke of was only traditionally used to kill or as a preamble to death by other means. 'Master, please —'

'Do as I command you, Horz. The Snake it is and make sure whoever wields it has no idea how to use it. I repeat, I do not want the Spur softened, I want him hurt. And should he die . . .'

Die? Horz could barely speak. 'Yes, master?' he managed to choke out.

'We shall not be held responsible. I will see to it.'

Horz bowed, expecting to be dismissed.

'I am not finished yet,' Salmeo said, a slyness in his tone that told Horz he was yet to hear the worst of his master's plan. 'I want the tongues of each viper to be dipped in drezden.'

The Elim could not speak. His lips had gone numb.

'Have I made myself perfectly clear, Horz?' There was a threat in the question.

'Yes, master,' came the strained reply.

'Good, because it's your life and those of your brother and his family in the foothills if my orders are not followed to the letter.

I suggest you apply the drezden yourself. Oh, and Horz — no-one knows of this but the two of us ... I suggest we keep it that way.'

Lazar had been staring into space, his mind empty of thoughts for the first time in as long as he could remember. He wasn't sure whether it was the dulling sense of anxious anticipation or the fear of what he planned to do beyond today. He had discussed the latter with no-one yet — not even Jumo. It seemed to be the only decision he could take to rid himself of this asphyxiating sense of dread — that he was somehow connected to something far bigger than his own tightly kept world of Percheron. It was the statue of Lyana in the tiny temple that kept returning to his thoughts and unsettling him. Something in her gaze called to him — no, implored him — but he didn't know what it was she wanted of him. That effect had not waned over the days since first sighting her — if he was truthful, he would admit it had only intensified. And yet for so many years Lazar had felt completely assured of himself and his position in Percheron. Lazar rarely let himself think about his homeland for fear of those thoughts damaging the fragile, precious veil of secrecy he had built around himself. It was his protection.

Now he no longer cared. Was this feeling of unsettlement the power of the statue? The surge of Herezah into such a position of authority and her relentless intention to make him dance to her chosen tune was sickening enough. However, Herezah paled to invisible in comparison to the frightening sense of loss regarding Ana. Was everything linked? He tried every possible approach to convince himself that Ana was not important. She was a naive girl, he told himself, but the truth was she might be young, but her soul was old. He accused her of being cunning, deliberately pulling at his heartstrings, but he failed here too. There was nothing conniving in Ana — she was true; true to herself, true to him, and true to those she dealt with. He even tried to convince himself that she would not remember his name after a year in the

202

harem and that she was like all women in that brood — simply trying to better themselves.

Finally he had to accept that Ana had so profoundly affected him that he could no longer think in the neat, straight way he was used to. Life felt suddenly disordered, routine was smashed, his secure, private existence in Percheron was over. And still he could not target precisely what it was about this youngster that could have such an effect.

He was reacting towards her as if she was of a similar age to himself and, heaven forbid, eligible. He did not want his heart touched, yet she had done just that with a single look. Then she had proceeded to break that fragile heart by turning down his offer of regular escape from the suffocating dullness of the harem.

Lazar knew he would never stomach being so close to Ana and yet so far.

This was why he was planning on leaving Percheron. He had only to get through today and then he would be gone — fleeing from all that was suddenly so unsettling.

He laid his head back against the cool marble of the wall and closed his eyes to await his friend. He was sure Jumo would find him prior to the flogging.

He was right.

Jumo had arrived at the palace and with Pez's guidance had found where his friend had been asked to wait. Granite-faced members of the Elim greeted the former slave and would not have permitted him access but for the presence of Pez.

'We're here to see the Protector!' the dwarf repeated over and again, spinning in frantic circles.

When the Elim began suggesting that Pez would be allowed in but not Jumo, the dwarf stamped his feet and grabbed Jumo's hand. 'He's my friend,' he howled, then growled and bared his teeth at the Elim, who were more than used to the small man's antics and thoroughly capricious ways.

One sighed and said, 'What would it hurt?' and Pez began dancing, fingers in each ear, which never failed to amuse.

Once inside the chamber the dwarf became serious. 'They obviously agreed to it,' he said to Lazar.

The Spur nodded. 'They could hardly refuse. Thank you for suggesting it.'

'I don't think you'll be thanking me soon, Lazar,' Pez answered. He sighed and his expression begged their indulgence as he began to jump around and make a noise so that the Elim outside would not wonder why Pez had gone quiet.

The same notion that Pez had aired was rushing through his companions' minds. Salmeo would make the Spur pay a heavy price for this humiliation. Lazar had been taken in the direction of the barracks but then, as if looping back on themselves, the Elim had brought him to a wing of the palace he had never explored.

'This is not part of the harem,' Jumo muttered.

'No. This is the Hall of Sorrows,' Pez answered, becoming still again. 'It's where prisoners of the royals are brought to wait before they face their punishment.'

'I've only seen it from the other side,' Lazar commented absently. 'It's a very pretty courtyard, with birds as sentries, I think, around the edge of the walls.'

'They're ravens,' Pez replied. 'The bird of sorrows,' and a thought nagged at him.

Lazar nodded. 'Fitting.'

Jumo knew not to say too much. Lazar had made a decision and he was never one to go back on his word. 'Master, I doubt very much that they will use the same whip as they would on the child.' There, it was out — what they were all secretly worrying about.

Pez nodded sagely. 'The Elim confer with the Inflictors to choose, as I understand it.'

'Yes, so I've been informed,' Lazar confirmed. 'I think we can stake our lives on it that Salmeo will select something vicious.'

'Are you frightened?' Jumo asked tentatively.

'My only worry is for Ana,' Lazar said. 'I have a feeling they'll make her watch.'

'I think you can count on it,' Pez answered. 'She's an incredibly assured young woman, my friend. I don't think you should fret too hard about her. She will survive this. Just consider yourself now.'

Lazar shrugged. 'There is little to consider. They'll do what they will and I must bear it.'

Jumo felt his stomach roll at the thought of what cruel fate would befall his friend. His grim thoughts were silenced by the sudden movement of Pez doing a handstand against the wall and beginning what was known affectionately amongst the ranks of soldiers as his jibber-jabber.

The dwarf had sensitive hearing for within moments the door had opened and four of the Elim stepped inside and another two remained outside.

'Spur, if you please,' Horz, the most senior, said courteously.

Jumo couldn't imagine anyone amongst the Elim was too happy about their role today. The Elim were subject to the whims of their commander, the Grand Master Eunuch, and they were fearsome fighters, all of them. No-one should ever imagine that because they'd been rendered sexless by the blade that they lacked the passion or courage that went with manhood. Most of the Elim proved their bravery by entering the service of the eunuchs as adults. The other eunuchs of the harem, those never permitted to wear the red robe, were mostly cut when they were still in childhood and unable to understand, beyond the pain and fear, what was being given up.

The Elim expected to be rewarded in Heaven, as promised by Zarab, whom they worshipped vigorously.

Jumo stepped in front of Lazar. 'I am his second.'

Horz nodded. 'We gathered,' he said. 'This is acceptable.'

They had to talk above the din of Pez who was making quite a show of himself.

Horz turned and bowed to Lazar. 'I'm sorry, Spur, about the dwarf's interference but the Zar rules . . .'

'I know,' Lazar replied. 'I take no notice of him at the best of times.'

'Can you tell me how this is all to be handled?' Jumo asked, determined to know exactly what they were up against.

Again the senior Elim nodded calmly. 'The Spur is to be flogged.'

That much was obvious. Jumo kept his face expressionless. 'By whom?'

'I do not know the Inflictor.'

'You mean you don't know the man himself or you don't know which of the Inflictors has been chosen?' Jumo persisted.

The Elim's hesitation was telling. As he opened his mouth to answer, Lazar cut him off. 'Leave it, Jumo. It's going to be done, and frankly I don't care by whom.'

Pez began chanting: 'Don't hurt him, Horz, or he'll get angry.' No-one took any notice.

'If you'll follow us, Spur,' Horz said and glanced at Jumo. There was something in that single look to make Jumo's heart sink further. Something was up — he could feel it in the tension of the Elim.

'Thank you, Horz,' Lazar muttered.

The Elim were ruthless enough when required but he understood how none would be looking forward to today's event. He grudgingly accepted that they would probably have preferred to whip the girl rather than humiliate, probably injure, a fellow warrior who was clearly innocent. That said, he could sense their quiet admiration that he had offered himself up instead.

This was the way of the Elim. It was the very basis of their own creed. They offered themselves to their god and made a costly sacrifice on his behalf. They were respected and feared whenever they were seen outside of the harem, and inside they had complete control. Not even Herezah would risk offending the

Elim. It was a finely tuned balancing act. The Elim needed the harem to exist, whilst the harem needed the Elim to keep discipline and to keep it safe.

He fell into step between the six Elim, each as tall as him, and decided he would give Herezah no satisfaction this day.

The six men and the victim stepped out into the sharp afternoon sunlight. Jumo unhappily followed and slunk into the shadow cast by the minaret outside the walls. His presence here was permitted merely as a servant to carry, if necessary, the body of Lazar from this place. Pez came behind Jumo, all but catapulting himself from the doorway into the Courtyard of Sorrows and tumbling into a series of manic somersaults aimed purely to irritate Herezah and her sycophants. He succeeded brilliantly by rolling to a halt atop a man's foot. Only one he knew wore jewelled slippers during the day and outside — he couldn't have planned it better.

'Curse you, Pez!' the Vizier said, kicking at the dwarf with his free foot.

Pez rolled away in mock agony, ensuring he made a loud to-do. Two of the Elim hurried up to help him; one of them was Horz.

'Vizier!' the Elim admonished. 'Pez has the highest sanction in all of Percheron. You must —'

'I know, thank you, Horz,' Tariq interrupted testily, angry with himself for such a blatant error but he detested the dwarf. He especially despised that Pez had such a free rein throughout the palace and indeed the harem. Today had been trying and now the dwarf's antics, which never failed to embarrass the Vizier, had allowed the tension he was feeling to boil over.

He half expected the demon to speak now but Maliz had been strangely silent since the meeting this morning. He watched Horz pick up the still-writhing dwarf and carry him aside and he noticed Pez grinning back, mocking him. Oh, how he hated that fool. If he knew he was anything but a halfwit he would contrive the idiot's death. It was this single spume of bile within that helped Tariq to make his final decision. Yes! he would accept Maliz's offer. He wanted power, he wanted riches, he wanted freedom from the shackles of people less than himself. He would no longer answer to any of these pitiful folk, least of all a deranged dwarf. He grimaced with pleasure at the thought. It was only a temporary arrangement and what did it matter if the demon had use of his body for this period. The rewards more than outweighed the brief inconvenience. He had no idea how it was all going to come about but his wrath gave him the impetus to place his faith in Maliz.

He felt a fierce joy at reaching a decision but his elation was interrupted by a short fanfare to herald the arrival of the Zar, looking tall and suddenly proud.

Boaz was accompanied by his mother. She was fully veiled but nevertheless dazzling in a deep blue robe. They stepped out onto the balcony that overlooked the Courtyard of Sorrows. Everyone bowed to the royal couple.

And then another door opened and Ana was escorted by two burly Elim to stand in the courtyard itself. She too was fully veiled and Lazar hated that her beautiful face was covered from him.

Nevertheless the softest of smiles seemed to touch her eyes and he knew it was just for him. His heart felt as though it was shattering into countless pieces and with that deeply despairing pain came understanding. His decision to take her place might be confusing for everyone else but not for him. It was for the oldest, most simple of reasons that drove men and women to do courageous, often ridiculously dangerous things. And that reason was love.

He loved Ana.

At this moment of realisation he felt the warmth of Iridor burning next to his leg. He placed his hand against the tiny statue and felt its comforting heat. With that warmth came a sense of peace. He had made the right decision to do this; Iridor was telling him as much. And he realised it was best he leave Ana to her new life whilst at the same time not punishing himself by remaining in Percheron. To his homeland he must return and face the consequences. He would start life anew and she would build hers amongst the halls of the harem. If Pez was right and Boaz had already had his interest triggered in this girl, then she had a future.

Salmeo's voice broke into his thoughts as the eunuch began explaining what had occurred to create this situation. None of it needed explanation, of course, for everyone around was well aware what had transpired. This was purely protocol.

'... and so it is with respect that we now inflict the punishment on Spur Lazar who has claimed Right of Protectorship upon Odalisque Ana, property of Zar Boaz. The slave's transgression is considered extremely grave and by no higher authority than the Zar himself ...

'... it is out of veneration to our Zar and to our way of life in the harem that we insist this punishment is taken seriously.'

In spite of his determination not to give anyone the slightest satisfaction, Lazar felt a stone hit the pit of his stomach. Salmeo clearly had something special in store. Lazar tore his gaze from Ana to stare at the timber that he would be tied against. He had seen many floggings, knew what to expect, grasped that Ana's punishment would be symbolic, whereas his on her behalf would be more stringent and he understood that some days of healing would be required before he would be able to move with ease.

The post and cross-timbers that they would tie him to looked intently sinister now. It was not to be a simple lashing.

'... It has been decided that the Spur will be given thirty lashes from the Viper's Nest.' A murmur buzzed across the balcony as Boaz turned to his mother, presumably to share his concern. She whispered something but it was hardly a long enough conversation to resemble anything close to a discussion. Poor Boaz — he was in for a harsh lesson this afternoon.

Lazar glanced towards Jumo and saw the fear written across his friend's face. How he wished he could spare his companion this trial. As for himself, there was no escape and Lazar had always been of a philosophical nature when up against any sort of foe. You either win or you die trying, was his favourite mantra. He intended to win, although, recalling the Viper's Nest, he knew it was the most vicious of weapons against skin and quite capable of killing.

He looked at Pez whose face had drained of colour. The dwarf also knew what this meant and without further ado was skipping around the courtyard, apparently accidentally treading on the toes of the silent Vizier before careering through the door and away from the Courtyard of Sorrows.

Lazar knew that wherever he was headed, Pez was already putting things in place to help when the flogging was done.

'Let us proceed,' Salmeo said.

Before any move could be made, Ana, no doubt gathering that the Viper's Nest was no simple whip, began to struggle and cry. 'No, this is my punishment,' she wept.

'Hush the girl!' Salmeo ordered

'I demand to take my own punishment!' she yelled now, looking directly at the Zar. 'Your Majesty, overturn this, I beg you.'

Boaz stepped forwards and placed his hands on the balcony's stone railing. Everyone fell silent. Salmeo closed his eyes beseeching Zarab that the Zar would not acquiesce to the girl's plea. They saw the Valide lean slightly towards the boy — no doubt she had whispered something to him from behind that veil, for Tariq noticed how the Zar's body tensed. There was anger there. They would not have him under their collective thumb for very much longer if they all did not give him more credit. They would need to occupy the new Zar, shower him with diversions, pander to his whims and free him from all responsibility if they were going to take over complete control of Percheron.

Boaz took a calming breath. 'Odalisque Ana,' he called into the courtyard. 'You have visited this despair upon yourself by your flouting of the harem's strictest law — the law of discipline. Did you know that this crime could be punishable by death?'

She shook her head, dumbfounded.

'It is I who will not permit such a thing. It is I who have also permitted that your brave protector, our own revered Spur of Percheron, might take a commuted sentence on your behalf. Please do not beseech my generosity further, Odalisque Ana, for I fear my kindness to the women in my harem is being tested today. I am a friend of the Spur' — he spoke to everyone now — 'and I abhor what he is about to endure. But I admire him and respect him only more for his courage in protecting someone whom I should have protected from herself.' He looked back to Ana. 'You may be excused if you wish not to witness your own punishment being inflicted.'

Lazar loved Boaz for what he had just done. By reprimanding Ana so publicly it would save her further torment from her superiors. Now that the Zar had spoken, no-one would be permitted to add to his censure. Ana was naive and could not yet know that not even the Zar himself could overturn certain rulings within the harem. Boaz had offered his own form of protection through his personal admonishment and now he was offering Ana a chance to escape the trauma of watching the flogging take place. The young man was becoming more canny by the day.

They all waited for Ana's response. She bowed to her Zar and then eyed him defiantly. 'I will bear witness, Your Majesty, so I never again have any misunderstanding of the barbaric dwelling in which I'm forced to live.'

Salmeo, Tariq and Herezah gasped at her brazenness. Lazar could feel the anger at Ana emanating from the three most powerful people in Percheron, beneath the Zar. He had to pray that Boaz's personal fire had indeed been lit by Ana, for he was all that stood between her and a life of misery.

Boaz spoke again. 'Bring the Odalisque Ana to my chambers this evening. I wish a private audience.' His tone was harsh and the trio who wanted to rule him breathed with relief that not only was he taking charge over such insult but it appeared that he would be seeking his own private retribution later.

Tariq secretly thought Boaz should rape the girl, viciously breaking that precious hymen in his anger at being so publicly rebuked. Then kill her even. No-one in any authority would care. They would all help cover up such a death.

Good, Tariq. It's fascinating to hear your angry thoughts, Maliz said suddenly.

I thought you'd deserted me.

How touching. I like to be missed. Someone will need to take control of the Zar for I fear he is taking full control himself. I trust you've reached your decision, Vizier.

I have made my decision.

And?

There are conditions.

I make no further bargains.

This is just a temporary arrangement. Will you confirm that?

I will leave your body the moment I'm done with it.

The demon's reply was a lie so gossamer in texture the ambiguity of the words was not detected by the eager Vizier. *Then I accept.*

There was a moment's silence in his head and then deep laughter. *I shall see you tonight. Go to the bazaar — pass the slaughterhouse — I shall give you directions from there. Now I truly go. Preparations must be made.*

Maliz —

No! Not now. Come tonight, late. I shall explain all.

And the demon was gone. Tariq, as if snapped from a sleep, focused again and watched the famously handsome Spur of Percheron being led to the scaffold where, if the Vizier had his way, the man would be flogged to death.

❧ 17 ❧

A heavy silence fell upon the crowded courtyard. Yet another door opened and a stranger stepped into the arena. He was young and looked unsure of himself. Behind him came an even younger bearer, carrying a white linen cloth upon which lay the fierce Viper's Nest. It was so called because the whip comprised six leather thongs, which currently curled around each other somewhat harmlessly but when unleashed could snap against a man's back so fast and viciously they were akin to the movement of a viper. The cruel instrument was nicknamed the Snake; each thong forked into two, like a serpent's tongue, and on the tip of each tongue was a tiny silver bead, sharp-edged and crafted deliberately to break skin.

Lazar swallowed hard, but to the onlookers he seemed unmoved by the arrival of the weapon. He had never seen the Snake used but he had heard of the intense injuries it could inflict. No wonder Salmeo was all but shivering in anticipation. Well, he would put on a good show for them and he would bleed hard but he would not cry out for mercy — he would sooner bite out his own tongue than vent a plea to these mongers of pain. He raised his head to look around the rim of the courtyard at the birds of sorrow which lined the high wall. They seemed to mock him but he cared not.

'Welcome, Inflictor,' Salmeo said. He bowed to Boaz again. 'Your High One, this is Shaz.'

'This man looks young to be an Inflictor,' Boaz said, estimating Shaz was no more than a summer or two older than he was.

Salmeo dipped his head in mock humility. 'Yes, Great One. Our Inflictor is away in the far north. I'm sorry to say his deputy is indisposed today — very unwell in fact — with a high fever.'

'So who is Shaz?' the Zar persisted, sensing a ruse. He glanced towards his mother, wondering if any of this might have been her idea. Herezah gave nothing away in her dark gaze but shook her head slightly, as if this was all news to her. Boaz knew his mother well enough to know when she had been taken by surprise. Shaz had nothing to do with her, then.

'He is an apprentice, Your Majesty,' the Grand Master Eunuch replied.

'An apprentice!'

Salmeo shrugged innocently. 'Your High One, what can I do? The sentence has been proclaimed. The rules of the harem demand that the flogging be carried out immediately. We had no idea that the Spur would choose this path or perhaps better arrangements could have been made. I would have insisted, in fact. But my understanding was that a member of the harem was to be whipped. Shaz is more than capable of lashing the Odalisque Ana expertly.'

'And the Spur?' Boaz demanded.

'Shaz's superior has indicated that he is the most talented apprentice in years,' he lied.

Boaz bristled. Growing up in the harem had prepared him for the subtleties of Salmeo. 'Then because of the harem's incompetence in being unable to provide a senior Inflictor, I am using my authority to commute this sentence.'

Salmeo trembled with anger. 'Zar Boaz, I must pro—'

'No, Grand Master Eunuch, it is I who protest. This is being handled badly. I accept that the Odalisque Ana has committed a serious crime and I accept that she must be punished. We all accept, because it is written in our laws, that the Spur can claim the Right of Protectorship and take the flogging on her behalf. Finally, we all understand the law of the harem that the Grand Elim alone decides on the method of punishment. But, Salmeo, my word is the law of our land and I have the power to reduce this sentence, if not the way it is carried out.' Even without the fully deepened voice of manhood Boaz's tone brooked no argument. He was stirred by the cruelty that was about to unfold here and against someone he admired. He offered the only protection his status could, glad now that he had paid attention to the tedious lessons in the Law of the Zar.

'Lazar will receive ten less than the proposed number of lashes because of the bumbling manner in which this serious event is unfolding.' He took a deep breath. 'If I could, Salmeo ...' Boaz deliberately used the eunuch's name rather than his title in order to reinforce his personal authority over the man, 'I would postpone it until someone experienced could deal the blows. I know I cannot.' He didn't wait for a response from the Grand Master Eunuch, looking instead to the uncertain young man who awaited the order to proceed. 'Shaz.'

'Yes, Your Majesty,' the young man said, confused and startled.

'Twenty lashes only. Do you understand?'

He bowed low. 'Yes, High One.' He hesitated as if to add something, but caught the sharp shake of the head from Horz. So did Lazar.

This was all planned then, Lazar realised. Salmeo must have contrived all of this in a couple of hours. Impressive. Poor Shaz. He was being set up to make a complete mess of a man's body and Lazar understood he would have to steel himself not just against the lick of metal against skin but the certainty of incompetence.

There was nothing he could do. Horz was already indicating that his robes were to be removed. As Shaz unrolled the Snake, Lazar quietly undressed, wishing this could have been a private debacle rather than having so many witnesses. He stripped down until he stood only in his white trousers and boots, his dark hair shining against the bronzed body.

On the balcony, behind her veil, Herezah took a long, steadying breath. She had pictured Lazar naked many times in her life; she had dreamed of him moving rhythmically above her, his expression filled with the ecstasy of riding her body. But no imagination could make up for the reality that was Lazar. He was, to her despair, so much more desirable in life than in her dreams. He stood boldly before them, his broad chest visibly moving now with the deep breaths of anticipation. She took in the sight of his strong arms, shaped by hard muscle, which he usually hid beneath floaty robes. His light-eyed gaze was distant. He had left everyone here, she realised, and he was disappearing to a new place where perhaps he might escape the shock of what was coming. She felt mild distress that this beautiful body was about to be damaged before she could enjoy it, but then she had no idea of how serious the injury might be. From the distance of the balcony where she and Boaz stood, it was to all intents a normal whip. They could not yet make out the number of thongs on the curled weapon nor the beaded tips.

There was nothing she could do to help Lazar — even for cynical reasons of her own pleasure. All she could do was relish this opportunity to see him bared and humbled. After all, what were a few lashes to a strong man? She hoped he would groan from the pain and give her satisfaction for all the years of private groaning she had done on his behalf.

Herezah felt a soft shiver of pleasure ripple through her body as Lazar lifted his eyes and looked at her. Oh the exquisite defiance in that glower. She wished she could drag him off and bed him now — nothing would give her greater release than to take him when he was so flagrantly thumbing his nose at those around him.

Was he scared? Surely just a little, for the whip looked suddenly fearsome as the young man, Shaz, unfurled it and cracked it in a couple of practice lashes. Zarab's Breath! but it was more complex than she had imagined — so many whips within the one weapon. It snapped loudly around the courtyard and she noticed Ana flinch. Good! She wanted to ensure Ana knew what she was responsible for. And he, poor fool, blinded by honour, would shed blood today for a girl who would forget his very existence within a few months.

She was dragged from her cruel musings by the movement of Lazar towards the post. She looked at his broad back now as his arms were raised and tied firmly to the crossbeam. The muscles which striped his body showed themselves as they tensed in readiness and Herezah held her breath awaiting the sound of the Snake's first bite.

Pez was running as hard as his stumpy legs could carry him. People laughed and some who knew him called out to the dwarf but he heeded no-one. And as he ran he felt a burning sensation. He thought he was getting warm from his exertion but it was not that sort of heat. It was not on his skin but in his mind and deep within his body. He felt suddenly connected … but to what? It was calling him. Compelling him. Where to? He reached out for the answer as he careered closer to the waterfront.

Shaz nervously flicked the Snake. He had not understood why the Deputy Inflictor had suddenly summoned him to his chamber barely an hour ago and given him instructions that made his hair stand on end.

'You will be inflicting a flogging today,' Rah had said flatly.

'Sir? Is this a practice on the dummies?'

'No, Shaz. This will be on a real man.'

The youngster was understandably shocked. 'I am not ready, sir, only yesterday you said —'

Rah's eyes appeared shrouded. He sounded awkward and his tone angry. 'I know what I said. I have been given orders.'

'Sir, have I offended?'

'No. Just follow your orders.'

Shaz risked his superior's ire still further. 'You cannot leave me to this, sir, when I can't —'

Again the man interrupted his apprentice. 'We have no say in this! It comes from the highest authority. You have been chosen to do the whipping. Do your best. Remember all that we have taught you. If anyone asks, I have been taken unwell. Do not let your own down.'

Shaz had felt the panic taking over. 'But I am not ready.'

'No. But you also have no choice. This is what you've trained for — it's simply happening earlier than we or you would like.'

'But I know I will injure him. He may not recover.'

Rah felt pity but there was no way out of this for the lad. 'Take a deep breath between lashes. See the place where you intend the whip to hit, visualise the tip on the spot of skin you are looking at, take aim and snap the whip cleanly, as you've been taught. You know what to do — do the best with the skills you have, Shaz.'

'What if I hurt him too much?'

And then his superior looked down, beaten himself. 'That is their intention, I imagine.'

It all fell into place for Shaz. He was merely a pawn in a much bigger game played by far more important people who did not respect the work he and his superiors did, the pride they took in doing it properly. 'They're sending you away deliberately so that your apprentice makes a fool of himself and a mess of some victim's back?' he asked, stunned.

'But it is far worse than I have indicated, Shaz. You are instructed to use the Snake.'

At this Shaz quailed. 'No sir, I cannot do it. I have never yet touched the Viper's Nest. I am not ready to wield it.'

'That's what they're looking forward to, son.'

'Who is the victim?' he asked, unable to imagine which poor sod had so offended the Grand Master Eunuch to be earning this level of punishment.

'This is the very worst of it. It is the Spur of Percheron whose back you will draw blood from today. I am sorry for you, Shaz. Zarab guide your fist.'

And so here he now stood, trembling, terrified, the Snake lying limp in his clenched, sweaty hand after two practice cracks, waiting to be fully awakened and unleashed mercilessly at the Spur. He had always admired the Spur; watched his long stride around the palace grounds, been impressed by the way his loyal men had leapt to his bidding, had even gladly taken advice once when Lazar had caught him practising his craft on the dummies.

'Remember that's a man, Shaz,' the Spur had cautioned. 'You must respect his body, as you would your own. Keep mindful that he needs to be able to walk away from this post with a little bit of his pride intact. If you whip him too low too often he won't be able to walk, and if you concentrate the lashes too high he won't be able to lift his arms. Men have work, families, lives. They must be able to return to them. Whippings are punishment only for a transgression — you are not trying to maim or kill the man.'

And Shaz had tried not to forget that guidance. Now he was supposed to remember it as he stared at the broad, unblemished torso of that same man who had given the advice.

'Spur,' Salmeo addressed Lazar, 'are you ready?'

'Get on with it, curse you!' Lazar snarled.

'I am obliged to ask whether you would like something to bite on,' Salmeo offered politely, keen to prolong the high drama of this moment.

'No!' Lazar spat.

'Thank you. Please position the Odalisque Ana behind the flogging post.'

'What?' Lazar roared now, pulling against his bonds as Ana was led by Horz and one other to stand in front of the Spur.

'Forgive us, Spur, but this is part of the tradition when protectorship is claimed,' Salmeo answered. 'The true victim must share the pain of the protector.'

'You barbarian, Salmeo.'

The eunuch could not help a small smile. 'Shaz, you may proceed.'

As the young Inflictor took a deep breath and flicked the Snake backwards in preparation for his first lash, Boaz turned to his mother. 'I shall never forgive those involved for this.'

'It is the Spur's choice,' she replied, voice hard and as sparkling as a diamond. 'You can only admire him for it. I do.'

As she turned back, the Snake struck for the first time.

❃ 18 ❃

Lazar had thought about closing his eyes to Ana but they seemed to have a will of their own. He saw her eyes water and he shook his head softly, willing her to be strong. They both felt the beauty of that moment, entirely connected, only the pair of them — no-one else mattered. Ana shook her shoulder free of Horz's curiously protective hand and wiped at her tears quickly, mouthing something to Lazar he would never see for the veil covered her mouth.

It was just as well for it would have undone him.

The first bite of the Snake struck wildly across his shoulders and Ana watched Lazar open his mouth in a wide grimace but no sound came out. She would never admit to the smiling eunuch, who was watching her and not the Spur, that she would rather be here focused on Lazar's face than having to confront the damage at his back. Ana glanced towards Jumo whose expression was blank but she could read beneath it to the horror and the fear. He blinked as the whip was flicked back again for the second strike and she returned her attention to Lazar who was breathing hard, his only way of steeling himself against the burning pain. The Snake bit again, and this time Ana saw its forked tongues curling around Lazar's chest, ripping savagely through flesh as blood rushed to the open wounds and ran down his body.

She heard a sound of awe mixed with horror. She was not sure who gave it and hoped it was Herezah. Perhaps from that height, the royals had not realised the deadly nature of this weapon.

Lazar closed his eyes now, squeezing them tight, but still no sound issued. Ana felt her heart racing — eighteen more to go — and this time she risked a glance up at Herezah. Ana saw only hunger in those dark, cruel eyes.

The third strike was clearly off target, some of the beads, with their sharply razed edges, raking through Lazar's hair, tearing the flesh of his scalp as Shaz inexpertly flicked the whip backwards. Ana noticed how horrified the young Inflictor looked. She could not see any of the damage, bar the wounds on Lazar's side, but she could see the lifeblood coursing from the injuries and could imagine how ugly it must already appear from the Inflictor's perspective. Shaz faltered as he drew a shaking hand to wipe the sweat from his face. And still Lazar gave no sound.

The fourth stroke whipped cruelly around to his belly as Shaz desperately tried to adjust the height of his lashing to avoid the victim's head. Again skin tore and yielded bright blood, keen to drench Lazar's white cotton trousers. Blood was running down his face too, joining with the sweat won from pain. Lazar's freshly washed hair, once shiny in the afternoon sun, was now damp and clumped with the liquid of life.

The fifth lash of the Snake won a groan — short and guttural. Salmeo smiled — he had obviously been waiting for it. The Vizier was less obvious. He looked towards his bejewelled sandals but there was satisfaction nonetheless, Ana noticed. After the next five strokes, Lazar's body gave little resistance and although he gave no further sound, he began to slump against the pull of the bonds that once held him upright.

Halfway.

Ana saw that Shaz was panting, perspiration sheening his body. He cracked the whip again, his expression anguished. And as he dragged it back, his assistant handed him a cup of water, which he gratefully drained with a shaking hand.

No-one offered Lazar anything but silent love or hate, depending on who Ana looked at.

He had counted each shocking bite of the Snake and with the mounting toll he felt his strength being leached away with the blood that ran so freely now. By the eleventh, he was losing the will to fight. He adjusted his original notion that a flogging was not designed to kill or maim. Lazar felt that one or both would occur. He could no longer open his eyes and his throat was parched, his lips too dry and cracked to let much sound out even if he could. His touchstone, Ana, the reason he had been able to withstand this vicious punishment for half the number of strokes, was gone for him now. He knew she was there, willing him to stay strong, urging him silently to prevail, but he could no longer see her through the blur of the blood and the intense, searing pain.

Something else. He wasn't sure, for never having been flogged before he had no idea if the numbness he was experiencing was the body's own weapon against the shock. But it felt like a death creeping through him, as if his very veins were running with a killing liquid rather than life itself. Lights, incandescent and of all colours, were flashing behind his eyelids ... was this death beckoning? It would be so easy to give in to it. Should he? Was that the fourteenth lash? He could no longer tell, could no longer count, could no longer hear anything around him. He wasn't sure he would ever open his eyes to look on her fair eyes once again and bid her farewell. Sweet Ana. He had not meant to give his life but if he had to then he was glad it was for her. He loved her and could not help himself in this. Oh he knew she was too young to be loved in the way his treacherous mind tormented him. And he knew, deep within his fractured heart, that she loved him too and he did not care that it was a childish love from her, for a first love is always the sweetest, the most intense and pure.

How odd that he could remember it so well. Lazar thought he had buried the memory of Shara so deep he could never lift it free again. Loving Shara had been so easy — youth made it easy and carefree and filled with such brightness that he never imagined it could be tarnished. But life had taught him that even the most radiant of treasures could be dulled. And life was teaching him that same harsh lesson once again.

He envisaged his legs giving way, unsure of whether this had in fact occurred, for he no longer felt connected to himself. The pain remained unfortunately, sharp and vivid, but it was the sense of weakness that frightened him. Had he called out? He had no idea. He was no longer in control of his wits. Lazar wanted to believe he was still standing rigidly against the post taking the punishment, but he suspected his stance was not nearly so proud.

He began to tremble, became aware of it because his teeth began to chatter, jarring him into a sense of wakefulness but only enough to reinforce that he was sure he was dying. A rush of anger blazed at the notion that his death would give Salmeo, and no doubt, Tariq, such satisfaction. His anger brought a measure of clarity to his dulled mind, allowing him to hear the murmur of Shaz counting his seventeenth stroke. He had almost made it but death was whispering gleefully to him. The Valide would not be so smug about his passing. She might be enjoying his suffering but she would not be smiling when he died, for who would protect Percheron?

Lazar felt himself withdrawing fully within himself. He was suddenly tiny, retracting into his soul, which he must now relinquish to the gods.

It was time. *Give in, Lazar*, he heard himself beg inwardly. *Let go*.

And then a new voice, cutting shrilly through the pain and despair. *Lazar! You must live. Fight it. For her . . . for Ana, if not for yourself. Live, damn you.* He could not tell whether it was a man or woman who spoke.

Who? It was all he could muster in response but wasn't sure he had formed or even spoken the word.

'Last stroke!' he vaguely heard in the distance. Again he had no idea whose voice had called it. He could no longer remember the name of the Inflictor.

I am Iridor, said the intruder. *You are done, Lazar. They have finished with you but we have not. We need you. Promise me you will live. Swear on Ana's life!*

I swear it, he thought he might have replied as he slipped into the void of unconsciousness.

Jumo had watched, traitorous tears betraying his usual stoicism as his master — his great friend — sagged so far it was only the bonds around his wrists that prevented him from slumping fully to the ground. He had watched as Lazar's knees had buckled by the thirteenth vicious stroke and then Lazar had called out Ana's name on the sixteenth lash. Jumo saw all tension leave Lazar's body by the final bite of the Snake as he surely yielded his life.

Jumo looked deliberately towards Salmeo, who sought permission from the Zar. Boaz, white-lipped, nodded and then stomped away, acknowledging no-one, leaving his mother in his wake. It didn't matter to her, Jumo noticed, for she could not tear her eyes from the ruin of the blood-soaked man.

He gave a glance at Ana. The terror in her eyes pained him but there was nothing more he could do for her as she was hurried away from the carnage, blood spattering the veil she wore.

'You may remove the Spur,' Salmeo said carefully. 'Thank you, Inflictor,' he added, tossing a purse at the feet of the trembling Shaz.

Everyone retreated from the courtyard in silence, leaving Jumo alone with only Shaz and his younger, equally shocked assistant to look upon the mess.

'Have I killed him?' Shaz asked, barely able to speak.

'He breathes,' Jumo said with an intense relief that lasted only a moment. The Spur looked as if he would not last much longer. 'Water!' Jumo commanded and the younger boy rushed away as Shaz approached, crouching and then falling to his knees beside the man whose flesh he had all but flayed. They could see bright bone through the mess.

'Will he survive?' Shaz begged Jumo.

Jumo shook his head. 'I cannot see how.' He spoke in a monotone, not wanting to share the depth of his hurt with anyone.

Shaz began to wail softly, rocking backwards and forwards on his knees. 'I told them I wasn't ready. I begged them not to force me do it but Rah made me.'

'Rah?'

'The Deputy Inflictor — he was told to claim illness.'

'When?'

'This morning, after he told me of this flogging. Felz, our superior, is away.'

'Ah,' Jumo replied. It all fell into place. 'Salmeo suggested Rah be sick, you mean?' Shaz nodded through his haze of tears. 'Help me cut him down,' Jumo said, suppressing his fury. It was not the boy's fault.

Before they could cut Lazar free, the assistant arrived with a bowl of water and rags. Using his fingers, Jumo dripped water through the cracked lips of his unconscious friend, praying silently to his god that this life would be spared. Lazar coughed weakly but it was the gladdest sound Jumo had ever heard.

'Lay those wet rags against his back,' Jumo directed, checking again that Lazar breathed. 'There is nothing we can do for him here. He will need a physic's attention.' The two young men set to. 'Do it gently,' Jumo cautioned unnecessarily.

Shaz's eyes widened. 'Sir, look,' he said nodding towards Lazar's wounds.

Jumo returned his attention to Lazar's back. 'What? I know they're bad.'

'No, look,' Shaz said, more fear in his voice now. 'There,' he said pointing, wiping blood from Lazar's neck.

Jumo said nothing as his mind raced to understand what the strange bright streaks were that traversed Lazar's neck, despite it being relatively unscathed by the Snake.

'What could it be?' Shaz thought aloud.

Jumo blinked slowly with resignation. So the palace had not intended for the Spur to survive. 'There is only one thing that leaves livid marks like that,' he whispered, his voice filled with rage. He looked up at Shaz. 'Poison.'

The young man shook his head in desperate denial. 'No, sir, not me. I did not do this.'

Jumo's eyes narrowed. 'Who then, Shaz?'

Again the youngster baulked. 'I don't know, sir. I swear it. I was given no instructions. No-one tampered with the whip to my knowledge.'

Jumo watched a new shiver overtake Lazar's body. He was not cold, he was already past shock and he was dying. There was no time for recriminations if the Spur was to have even the slightest chance to live. 'Pick him up,' he ordered and both obeyed wordlessly, carefully lifting by his arms. 'Lay him over my back!' Jumo commanded, bending slightly.

Shaz nodded. 'How will you manage?'

'Don't worry about me, Inflictor, worry about yourself and whether your head will still be connected to your body after the Zar hears of this,' he growled. Then, without a farewell, he left the Courtyard of Sorrows and its stench of blood and betrayal.

For a thin man, Jumo was deceptively strong. He was all hard muscle and tough sinew and this was not the first time he had carried his master in this fashion. That previous mercy dash had saved Lazar's life. Let it be so again, he prayed. He hoped his legs would stay loyal and not buckle as he began to run with his heavy burden.

At first he hardly recognised that it was Pez shouting to him. Jumo was so focused on his feet moving forwards that he didn't even hear his own name being called. The dwarf had to grab him before he drew to a halt.

'Quick! I have a cart,' Pez said, 'I know where to take him.'

Jumo wore the expression of man in deep shock. 'He's been poisoned,' he declared.

Pez's face had never looked more grave. 'I figured as much. Come, time is against us.'

Jumo laid Lazar on his belly in the back of the cart. 'He breathes,' he noted in a faraway voice.

Pez squeezed the loyal man's arm. 'He's strong of heart, mind, body. If anyone can, he can survive this.'

Jumo tried to nod but instead gave a dry sob. Odd questions roamed through his mind as they travelled, him guiding the donkey as if from memory, for he was certainly not concentrating, and Pez squealing in the front and throwing nuts at the people they passed.

Jumo hardly heard but found his voice. 'Why do you suggest the Sea Temple?'

'We'll have help there. Hurry, Jumo.'

They said nothing else as they weaved an exasperatingly slow path through the afternoon crowds. They had covered Lazar fully so he remained anonymous, but many passers-by still glanced into the back of the cart and saw the shape of a man beneath the light linen. Pez began to whistle tunelessly and made faces at onlookers; Jumo ignored everything but the hammering of his heart, willing the donkey to go faster through the throng. Finally they were out into more open pathways and the beast could make quicker progress.

Standing on the steps of the Sea Temple was the priestess he had seen only once on the first occasion Lazar had visited. She was shading her eyes against the glare of the sun, waiting for them anxiously.

'Quickly,' she urged. 'Lay him down by the altar just inside. Let Lyana look upon him.'

Jumo grimaced. How many more gods would they call upon today to save Lazar? He hefted his friend once again over his shoulders and felt intense relief to hear the man groan softly. The climb up the flight of steps felt like a mountain with the weight on his body and the suffocating crush of fear within himself. Inside it was cool and serene; the silence and darkness calmed him slightly as Zafira fretted, pointing to the altar.

'Over there please,' she insisted.

'A bed surely?' Jumo suggested, angry at her.

'Do as Zafira says,' Pez said gently.

Jumo knelt and then rolled Lazar as carefully as he could off his shoulders with Pez and Zafira guiding Lazar onto his belly once again. The linen covering fell away and Zafira's hands flew like startled birds to her mouth, covering the cry of wretchedness at the sight of the Spur's injuries.

'Oh, Mother,' she wept. 'Help this soul, guide us in this.'

Jumo gritted his teeth. His part was done for the time being and he suddenly felt helpless. 'The poison will kill him before the wounds,' he growled.

'Do we know what type of poison?' Pez's question snapped the priestess out of her stupefaction. They heard her knees protest as she lowered herself beside Lazar. Fresh water and linens were already prepared and waiting. She squeezed out the first linen and began her gentle toil.

Jumo shook his head. 'I don't, but I think Shaz is innocent of treachery.'

Pez sighed. 'I think we can assume that Salmeo is behind this. I wonder who else.'

'Not Herezah,' Jumo offered sombrely. 'Are you aware of her fascination for Lazar?'

Pez kneeled too. 'I'd have to be blind and deaf as well as daft not to be. You're right, she would not have sanctioned this.

Lazar's too important to the realm anyway. Herezah might be ambitious and wicked but she's far from stupid.'

'The Vizier?' Jumo offered as they watched Zafira gently cleanse Lazar's back.

'Give him this,' Zafira said softly to Pez.

'What is it?'

'It will bring a small measure of comfort. I can't risk putting him to sleep until we know more about the drug used on him. Jumo, help me clean away the blood — I need to see him more clearly.'

'Tariq does not have access to the Inflictors or their weapons,' Pez continued. 'No, if this hasn't come from Herezah, and I think you're right in that, then this is all Salmeo's work. He alone can give such a command.'

'Shaz seemed to know nothing of it.'

Pez shrugged as he dribbled the concoction into Lazar's barely parted lips, grimacing as most of it ran down the side of his mouth. 'Why would he? He is simply the fellow who will take the blame. I imagine even his superiors are pawns in this.'

Lazar's back was cleaned of old blood. Now his wounds seeped bright, fresh lifeblood from the new attention.

'Most would perish from this alone,' Zafira muttered to herself and her companions knew she spoke the truth. She gently traced the livid tracks of the poison. 'It moves very slowly. I have no idea what it is.'

'So what do we do?' Jumo asked, frightened all over again. Why he had thought an old priestess and a dwarf could save Lazar's life he didn't know. It all felt suddenly useless.

As he hung his head a shadow darkened the entrance. He didn't notice but Zafira and Pez did.

'I'm sorry,' Zafira said from the ground where she knelt. 'You've come at a trying time, as you can see.'

'I do see.' It was a woman. She was softly spoken and her voice had a musical quality as she asked: 'May I come in? Perhaps I might help?'

Jumo watched the hooded figure step out of the doorway, where she was encircled by the light of the sun, and into the shadows. Their visitor was petite yet her presence seemed to pulse with an aura of authority. Somehow none of them could deny her access to Lazar.

She knelt beside him, making a soft sound of concern. She pushed back her hood and Jumo noticed first her white hair, which must have been golden when she was young. As she turned to face him he saw that the woman was indeed older, somehow familiar, skin like beautiful ivory parchment, unblemished except for the handsome lines of time. The deep kindness she conveyed in that look eased his despair even though her words did not. 'He will slip beyond us within hours,' she said to him but it was meant for all of them.

Jumo wasn't sure what to make of such a comment. 'Can you help him?'

'He is very close to death. I should have seen something like this coming.' This last she said beneath her breath but Pez's sharp hearing caught it, and he frowned, wondering what she could mean.

He glanced towards Zafira who gave an expression of bafflement. They both snatched a look at Jumo but he was concentrating deeply, his focus given entirely over to the old woman.

'There is poison,' he confirmed and she nodded.

The old woman leant close to Lazar's back and sniffed. Then she nodded again, deep in thought. 'I think this is drezden. A nasty, debilitating concoction. Normally it would be administered to a healthy person orally and death would follow within hours. It has a distinctive spicy smell, reminiscent of clove ... can you detect it?' They shook their heads dumbly. 'You've all been a bit preoccupied,' she offered kindly. 'The drezden in this instance has been administered topically via the weapon used to flog him. It is not an effective way to deliver the poison but, as you can see by the tracks, it is working, but slowly. This is our single hope.'

'He can beat it?' Jumo asked hopefully.

'Unlikely, and his horrific injuries will probably kill him first.' She gave him a look of genuine sorrow. 'I'm sorry, Jumo.'

Pez was the sharpest, noticing how she used Jumo's name, making a friend of him. He also noted that both Zafira and Jumo seemed overawed by the stranger's presence. 'Do we know you?'

'In a way,' she said, indicating that they should lay the wet linens back in place. 'Those will need to be kept constantly damp.'

'I have never met you before,' Pez said, a soft challenge in his tone.

'Ah, but you have, friend Pez. Remember a red silk ribbon?'

His initial intrigue curdled to shock. The Bundle Woman! She looked different and yet, now he thought about it, somehow the same. She was not as old as she had originally appeared to him.

'How do you know my name?' Jumo asked, suddenly focused again.

'I know all of your names. You are Jumo, this is Pez and,' she bowed her head slightly, 'this is a sister, Zafira.'

'You are a priestess?' Zafira exclaimed, obvious delight in her voice.

The old woman smiled but said nothing until she looked down upon their patient. 'And this is Lazar, whom we shall probably lose but not without a fight.' Her words reassured Jumo, even though he could almost hear the death knell for a man he loved.

'What have you given him?' the woman continued.

'The root of calzen,' Zafira answered, 'to ease his pain, not that it can really deaden this sort of pain. I couldn't risk a soporific.'

'The right decision,' the woman said. 'I cannot do anything here. We have to move him.'

'Is it safe to?' Pez enquired, fascinated but also suspicious of the old girl who had still not mentioned her own name.

'Lazar is dying, Pez. Nothing we do can make much of a difference until I can get him to the Isle of Stars.'

Now they all stared at her.

'The leper colony?' Jumo said it for them.

She shrugged. 'It's safe and no-one comes there.'

'You live there?' Zafira asked, unable to mask her incredulity.

'Now and then.'

'Who are you?' Pez tried, determined.

'Questions, questions!' She smiled and the warmth made their hearts feel instantly lighter. 'I will answer them all but I have a precious man's life in the balance. Please, help me get him to the island, although I suspect, Pez, that you should return to the palace.'

'Yes but —'

'Go, brother Pez. You cannot help Lazar any more than you have. I promise we shall get word to you and besides, I gather I have some questions to answer for you.' Again the gentle smile that prevented him from pushing further.

Pez knew he would be missed at the palace and that was courting danger. He touched Lazar gently on his blood-streaked face and then was moved to bend close and kiss him. 'I shall see you again, my friend,' he whispered, and with one sad glance towards the others, he departed the temple.

As he wended his way back to the palace Pez pondered — amongst many confusing aspects of today — the few moments where he was sure he lost consciousness. One moment he was dashing at high speed from the temple to find Jumo again, and the next he was out cold on the roadside. No-one bothered with him and he had regained his wits slowly, uninterrupted by curious passers-by. He could not account for the fainting spell but he was convinced he had seen himself urging Lazar to hold on, to not give his life to this attempted execution.

And now the Bundle Woman returning to his life. She had manipulated all of them, convinced Jumo of Lazar's inevitable death even though their friend still breathed, still clung to life. But she had soothed them all too. What skill. He looked forward to learning more about her.

Pez was deeply confused and anxious, but no-one back at the palace so much as noticed. It was what they were used to.

∽ 19 ∾

Ana was hurried away from the Courtyard of Sorrows and taken directly to a sleeping chamber, which she realised, she must be sharing with three other girls. The four beds being tidied by a slave suggested as much. The Elim passed Ana into the care of an older woman who had presumably been waiting for her.

'She's in shock,' the woman commented, looking at her.

Horz, who had accompanied Ana and tried to soothe her, had been ignored by the odalisque, blamed by him in fact for what had befallen Lazar. He spoke quietly to the slave. 'She will need your care — perhaps something gentle to help her rest. As you know, she has been out all night and this afternoon she has witnessed something no child should see. It has been difficult for her.' He said no more. The slave nodded and urged Ana to come with her, which Ana gratefully did, glad to be rid of the eunuchs.

'Does he live?' she demanded of them before they left.

'I doubt it,' Horz said softly and again Ana refused the sympathy she saw in his unhappy eyes. 'No-one could survive that.'

'Come, child. Let me take that bloodied veil off you,' the woman said kindly. 'I am Elza.'

'My name is Ana,' she replied, glaring again at the Head of the Elim. Horz's presence seemed to distress her and Elza glanced sharply at him to suggest the Elim should leave. They did so silently.

234

Ana relaxed slightly once they had departed. 'I want to keep this,' she said suddenly, rolling the veil into a ball, as if by doing so she could stifle the pain of Lazar's potential death within it. She could not think on such a grievous outcome right now.

'What?' the woman exclaimed. 'This messy thing? Whatever for?'

Ana decided to lie. She had no desire to let anyone know that the blood of Lazar meant more to her than anything else in her life. To cast the veil away — her only physical connection with him — would feel like casting him away. The droplets of his blood were ghoulish, she knew this, but it was all she had. No more tears would she shed over this man. She hardly understood it herself but she believed she loved Lazar — would never love anyone with the same depth of feeling she felt for him.

Ana had chided herself the previous night that her heart was deceiving her. She was so young and she guessed Lazar was a man of almost thirty, maybe older. It was a ludicrous situation, but control of her longing heart that thumped so rapidly every time this man was near was no longer hers. They had not spent much time together but she could re-create the feel of her hand in his, the smile she worked so hard to win on his face, the softening of his expression when their eyes met. She could bring to life in her mind the rich timbre of his voice with its foreign lilt. And the warmth of his body standing next to her the night before in the Choosing Room; it felt to her as if a furnace had burned between them. She had risked leaning closer to him — in front of Herezah — just to feel that hardness of his body.

Ana had wondered long and deep, as she prayed to Lyana in the temple, whether it was wrong of her to desire Lazar. She was so young in comparison to him. But Ana felt powerless where Lazar was concerned. Where Salmeo's touch caused her entire being to clamp shut, just a glance from Lazar achieved the opposite. It niggled at her to do something with the flood of desire.

235

Lazar, she appreciated, had not once in their brief encounters behaved in anything but a formal, seemingly detached manner. The only time he might have let his guard down slightly was in the bazaar when he seemed momentarily carefree, but his treatment of her was dignified. In her moments of sensibility, she had to question this relationship and perhaps accept she was reading far too much into it. And yet this afternoon, in the Courtyard of Sorrows, she had felt their bond as a tangible link and she knew it was true. She was not lying to herself. She knew now in her heart that there was love there in return, but whether it was the type of love she wanted from him — that, she couldn't tell. He might see her as an uncle might view a favourite niece, but she couldn't believe that. And as he had borne her punishment she had heard him whisper her name. He had spoken to her alone and he had been prepared to give his life for her — it was too much, more than she deserved. He had looked dead by the end of it but she forced herself to believe otherwise.

She cast a prayer to Lyana, made a bargain with the Goddess: *Let him survive and I make no further claim on him. I will not pursue him and I will not encourage him. I will remain steadfast to my duty and cold to his entreaties, should he give them.*

She looked at the veil and realised Elza was waiting for an answer. Pez's warning to trust no-one resonated loudly in her thoughts. 'This was my first formal occasion for the harem. It's a special keepsake for me.'

'How grim of you, child. Very well — put it away and don't frighten the other girls with it. That's your bed over there.'

'By the window?' Ana was surprised. 'I would have thought that one would be taken already.'

'Pez — the Zar's mad jester — came and slept on it last night. He refused to leave it until the girls got tired of asking.'

'Oh?'

'And then he said he'd put a curse on the bed and the others got so frightened I had to shoo that terrible dwarf away. Have you seen him yet?' She didn't wait for Ana to answer. 'He's such a fool. But the young Zar loves him as much as his father before him did. I don't see the charm, myself. I think Pez is a nuisance and I'm sorry you're left with a cursed bed.'

'I have seen him,' Ana replied carefully. 'How did the women before us like him?'

'Oh, well enough. He entertained them. He's harmless, I suppose, but he disrupted those children so much they could hardly settle.'

Ana had to suppress a smile. She knew Pez had chosen that bed just for her and loved him for it. It was easily in the best position in the whole chamber. 'Well, I'm not afraid of any curse.'

'That's the spirit,' Elza said, not really paying much attention. Ana stood naked before her. 'You've had your Test of Virtue, haven't you?'

Ana nodded.

'Good. Let's get you into a warm bath. Put this robe on and come with me. You're in for a special experience.'

Ana slipped into the silken robe, feeling the soft touch of it against her skin, and then begged a moment to tuck Lazar's Veil — as she thought of it — beneath her pillow.

He would always sleep close to her now.

They had rowed in silence so far through the late afternoon. Jumo worked the oars whilst Zafira fussed over the unconscious Spur; the stranger sat with her back to the rest of them, chanting beneath her breath as if in prayer.

She spoke suddenly, interrupting their thoughts. 'Can you row close to Beloch?'

'The waves might dash us against the giant,' Jumo warned even though the sea wasn't rough today, but amazed that she could make such an odd request when time was so against them.

'Beloch will not hurt us.'

Jumo mumbled something but steered them closer to the giant who loomed massive now that their tiny boat was up close.

'Why must you do this?'

'I want to speak to him,' she answered and she did just that, balancing herself precariously as the boat rocked perilously. None of her companions understood what she said to the giant.

Jumo scowled. 'We'll all drown.'

The old woman smiled serenely at him. 'Thank you, it meant a lot to me that I could do this.'

'Do you speak to the giant each time you go to the island?' he asked.

'No,' she said, her voice suddenly detached, as if her thoughts were far away from them. 'I have never rowed to the island before.'

Jumo didn't say any more — the situation was turning too strange.

'We require no refreshment,' Zar Boaz said to Bin, dismissing the servant but also displaying that none of his wrath has dissipated. He knew he must learn to disguise it if he was to emulate his father.

Salmeo and Tariq stood before him and bowed again to show they were waiting on his every command.

Boaz did not acknowledge their courtesy. He reined in his anger and steadied his voice. 'Have we heard any more?'

The Grand Master Eunuch adopted a look of concern. 'No, Majesty. I dealt with the pig Inflictor,' he lied, 'who had no skill at all for his chosen career.'

Boaz nodded. 'Where were the senior Inflictors — Shaz cannot be all that we have in the palace?'

Salmeo shook his head, his frown deepening. 'No, Great One, that's right, but we had no option but to use Shaz. Would you like me to have him punished?'

'Not especially. I would prefer you to punish his seniors who were not present. We cannot have the head and his deputy both unavailable. It is unforgivable!'

Boaz instantly regretted calling this meeting whilst his emotions were still raw. Seeing his friend so broken had sickened him sufficiently that when he had strode from the balcony he had actually lost his morning's meal into the bushes not far from his chambers. Mercifully, with no guards on the balcony with them, no-one but his mother was privy to this show of weakness and she had sensibly said nothing, simply offered him a linen to wipe his mouth.

'I'm retiring for the day, Boaz,' were her only words and he heard the slight quaver in her voice and knew that Herezah was as sickened as he. She had learned to control her physical reactions and he made a promise to take a leaf out of his mother's book. Once again he privately acknowledged that no matter how much she frustrated him, she still had plenty to teach him and his father had been politically astute to choose her as his Favourite. At her words he had nodded but first risked taking and squeezing her hand in thanks for he knew she would share with no-one his embarrassing show of distress. It was obvious she was taking this new partnership of theirs seriously and it was time he stopped fighting her and used all of her knowledge and political skills instead.

Salmeo cleared his throat and Boaz was returned from his thoughts. 'Shall I punish them, High One?'

'What do you mean?' Boaz had been too distracted. He privately admonished himself as he watched Salmeo's eyes narrow. Boaz felt he was being tested by the Grand Master Eunuch.

'How far would this punishment extend, Majesty?' Salmeo replied carefully. 'Are you calling for death?'

Boaz took a deep breath. 'If the Spur does not survive the flogging, Grand Master Eunuch, then you will choose one of the Inflictors to pay for their collective failing with their own life.'

'The choice is mine — is that what you're saying, High One?'

Boaz hated Salmeo in that moment. He fixed him with a stare, reminiscent of his father — one he'd seen the old Zar give many times when his ire was up 'We're both speaking Percherese, Grand Master Eunuch. I'm sure you understand my order.'

Salmeo bowed, disturbed by the Zar's sudden sense of power. 'As you command, Majesty.'

'Where has the Spur been taken? Tariq, I wish my personal doctors to attend him.'

Tariq's jewels glinted on the ends of his quivering beard. This was not really a task he should be given but anything which ingratiated him to the Zar he was happy to see to. 'Of course, High One, I will seek that information for you. Is there anything else I can do, Your Majesty?' Tariq all but felt Salmeo's sneer.

'That will be sufficient. Where is Odalisque Ana?'

'As I understand it her clothes were bloodied. The Elim escorted her to her chambers to bathe and rest after her night's adventures.'

Boaz agreed but he couldn't back down now. 'Bring her to my private study. Immediately.'

'Yes, High One,' Salmeo bowed. 'Should I inform the Valide of —'

'My mother,' Boaz began, unable to control his rising temper now, 'has absolutely nothing to do with this. You would be well advised, Grand Master Eunuch, to learn to do my bidding without questioning it. I will not warn you again. I might be young, Salmeo, but I am the highest authority in this realm, or are you already placing your loyalty in the wrong place?'

The huge man's flabby face wobbled with the effort of holding back his own rage. 'No, my Zar. I just thought it right to caution against —'

Boaz laced his next words with as much contempt as he could load into them. 'Don't think, Salmeo. When the command comes from me, just do it! And don't ever caution me again. Is that clear?'

Salmeo bowed to hide his own disgust at being spoken to publicly in this manner. 'Yes, Majesty,' he managed.

It was Tariq's turn to stifle a sneer.

'I'm afraid I can't give you the treat I promised, Odalisque Ana,'
Elza said, returning to her from taking a whispered message. 'We
have to bathe you quickly in a tub.'

'Why?'

'The Zar wishes to see you.'

'Boaz?'

The slave looked at her aghast. 'Hush, child! Never speak his
name unless he alone gives you the authority. Haven't they
taught you anything yet?'

'I've spent only a few hours in the palace, how could they?'
Ana replied tartly.

'You'll do well to curb that defiance in your tone, Miss Ana. Take
my advice, for your haughtiness will not be tolerated. Rule number
one,' she began, leading Ana to a new chamber, a small one, filled
with single cubicles, 'is you never speak the Zar's name. He is Your
Majesty, High One, Mightiest of the Mighties, or similar.'

Ana nodded. She remembered Pez's warning that she must
blend into the community of the harem or risk Salmeo's
attention.

'Rule number two: bathing daily is part of harem life,' Elza
pointed towards the cubicle. 'We use these rarely. From now on
you will use the main pavilion and spend the entire morning
there on your grooming.'

'What a waste,' Ana murmured.

Elza heard and smirked. 'You'd better start getting used to
boredom, Miss Ana, for you'll spend your whole life getting ready
and hoping the Zar will wish to share even a few words with you.'

'Looks like I haven't very long to wait, doesn't it?' Ana replied,
wearily.

'Oh child, you are in for a very rough time of it if you keep
that attitude for much longer.' Elza sighed. 'Now hurry, slip out of
your robe. I have to get you washed and dressed.'

So much for a rest, Ana thought, dreading what the Zar would want with her after his public admonishment.

Jumo insisted on carrying Lazar on his back again. Their host led the way surprisingly briskly up broad, mercifully shallow steps cut into the cliff face. Zafira climbed slowly next to him.

'What are we doing here?' Jumo muttered to her.

'I don't know but it feels right, don't you think? It's too much of a coincidence that she came along just when we needed help. She said she'd answer our questions — we must be patient.'

At the top of their climb they saw a cottage set back from the cliff edge, a small copse encircling its back.

'Here we are,' the old woman said. 'The lepers are housed a long way from here. There are only six of them left anyway, and I rarely see them. Jumo, can you manage?'

'Yes, let's just hurry. His breathing has changed.' It was true; Lazar was suddenly struggling for breath.

Once inside, the old girl took command again. 'Lay him on the pallet and light some candles from that lantern, Jumo. We shall be busy and the sun will set without us knowing. Zafira, perhaps you would make us some quishtar?' The priestess was happy to busy her hands and immediately set to finding the utensils and materials she needed.

Their host returned her attention to the man on the bed and his anxious friend, who was placing lit candles nearby. 'Are you afraid of snakes, Jumo?' He shook his head, not looking at either of the women, but focused on the grey pallor of Lazar's complexion and the rapid heaving of his chest. 'Good. In the cellar is a heavy-lidded jar. Inside are two snakes. The yellow-bellied one is harmless. The one with the striped back is deadly. He is the one we need. Have you handled a snake before?'

'I have,' Jumo replied, not able to hide his irritation at her lack of anxiety and his growing terror that Lazar would die today. 'What does this have to do with Lazar?'

'Drezden is made from the poison of the drezia snake. It's favoured by assassins who want to be gone well before the death occurs. Drezia venom is deadly but slow, if not given orally. On its passage to the heart it simply numbs. Once it reaches the heart, however, it paralyses and death is instant.'

'You want me to milk the snake?' he asked, deliberately rushing her to save Lazar's life rather than giving lengthy explanations.

'Precisely,' she replied. 'Here, straight into this,' she said, pointing Jumo to a small porcelain cup.

'How does this help Lazar?'

And at last he heard through her mild manner to the concern she had worked to disguise. 'Do it now, Jumo, my brother. He is too important to risk. I will explain once we're all set.' He followed where she gestured and found the entrance to the cellar. 'Be careful. If it bites you I have no medicine that will stop the poison killing you.'

'Very reassuring,' he muttered, as he began to descend.

'His breathing sounds very shallow,' Zafira noted again.

'Not a good sign,' their host replied, Jumo already forgotten and left to his fate. 'But that's to be expected. My name is Ellyana. Forgive my poor manners.'

Zafira nodded. 'Shall I take off the linens?' She pointed towards Lazar's back.

'Yes, please.' They heard a small scuffle from below. 'Jumo?' Ellyana called and there was an element of fright in her tone.

'I'm all right,' came a muffled voice and the two women glanced at each other with relief.

He emerged a few moments later with a clear liquid — barely enough to cover the bottom of the cup it was contained in.

'It is enough,' Ellyana said, answering his look of worry. 'Now, let me explain. I promise to be brief. I have seen this sort of poisoning before and delivered in a similar style. It can be beaten. However, if Lazar survives, you need to know that he will never be whole again.'

She paused so her listeners could digest that dark news. Neither spoke so she continued. 'Jumo, your master will always need the poison of the drezia snake close. He and it are now bound together, forever, like lovers — even though they are enemies.'

'What occurs?' Zafira asked for Jumo's sake; the man was so stunned by the news that he seemed unable to speak for himself.

'There will be no warning. A trembling, wasting fever will strike. Very debilitating. The only temporary cure is more of the venom in its purest form and in tiny quantities ... far less than we have here. Right now though we have to flush the poison from his body. We need lots of quishtar and my own brew. There will be pain — severe — and you will both need to be strong for him. He is going to suffer badly if he is to recover.'

'Will he recover?' Jumo dared to ask.

'If I'm frank — and I fear I should be with you — then I would say he will most likely perish. Too much time has elapsed, his wounds are frighteningly dangerous. The poison aside, those injuries alone have the capacity to kill him,' she said gently, and he hated the sympathy evident in her expression. 'We will try but I think you must be prepared to lose him, Jumo.'

'He is strong,' Jumo countered.

Her tone was even more tender when she risked closing a hand over his arm. 'I know. And you will be equally strong for your friend.'

Jumo ferociously blinked the tears rushing to betray him. 'What about his wounds?'

'We will need to clean them thoroughly and then sew the deeper ones to close them against infection. For the rest we shall have to rely on this salve,' she said, indicating a stone jar. 'Could someone help me with that, it's very heavy.' Jumo obliged, grimacing at its weight, and slid off the lid at her nod. 'It smells bad but it is a wonder ointment,' she continued. 'Perhaps you wouldn't mind smearing that onto some of the less vicious wounds right now. It will seal them from the air, from disease.'

'They're all vicious,' Jumo said, shaking his head at the state of Lazar's body but taking the jar to him anyway.

'Zafira, do you have steady hands?'

'I suppose, why?'

'You will need to do the sewing, my sister.' Ellyana held up her own shaking fingers. 'Part of growing old,' and her sad smile was only for the priestess.

Zafira looked worried. 'I'm not sure I can —'

'I will help you,' Ellyana assured, not giving the priestess another chance to protest. 'We must all wash our fingers with this special soap paste,' she warned, pointing to a pot. 'It will burn your skin but it will ensure your fingers are very clean and we will not infect Lazar's wounds as we treat them.' They both nodded. 'Right, let's clean our hands and then we begin. We have a long night ahead of us.'

As if in response, Lazar groaned weakly.

'What do you mean, you can't find any trace of him?' Boaz demanded.

Tariq's lips pursed. He had failed the Zar in the first task assigned him. 'Forgive me, High One. I have sent runners to the Spur's house, to the barracks, even to the city temples, where I thought he might be laid out by the priests for medical help. No-one has any information to give us.'

'Well, someone must have seen him depart. Where is Shaz? Perhaps he has some notion.'

'No, High One. Apparently Shaz and his assistant handed the Spur's body to that fellow called Jumo, Lazar's second, and the man departed the Courtyard of Sorrows. One would assume he'd take him straight back to the Spur's house for care from a physic, but apparently not.'

Boaz frowned. 'Send out word into the city. Someone must have seen something. I want information from you and your spies by the end of the day, Vizier.'

Tariq bowed, wondering what had risen up in Boaz. It was as though the boy had aged five years since the afternoon flogging. The Vizier felt he was being ordered around like a slave by a lad whose voice had barely broken. 'Immediately, Your Majesty,' he said, through clenched teeth hidden by his beard.

A soft gong sounded, saving him further conversation with the young Zar.

'Go about your business, Vizier. I'll await your news,' Boaz said wearily. 'Enter!' he called over Tariq's head. Bin emerged into the chamber as the Vizier departed. 'Yes?'

'High One, the Grand Master Eunuch and Odalisque Ana await you in the antechamber of your study.'

'Ah, good. I wish to change. Can you send in my dresser.'

'Of course. I will bring your visitor into the study when you are ready.'

Boaz returned to his bedchamber and within moments his dresser arrived. After changing into loose linens — all white with a charcoal grey waistcoat — he asked the servant to order refreshments.

'Some frozen sherbets and a flask of chirro,' he suggested. The man bowed and departed.

Boaz stepped from his chamber into a small reception room that led to his private study, smaller and more intimate than the one where he normally received people. He was paying Ana a high compliment in permitting her to visit him in this room. He knew he was risking the wrath of all the people vying for his loyalty in doing so and this pleased him greatly. Once inside he took a deep breath before reaching to pull a chord that sounded a bell outside.

The double doors were opened and Bin ushered in a slim, veiled figure dwarfed by a sour-looking Grand Master Eunuch. Boaz realised he was actually holding his breath with nervousness. He let it out slowly as the oddly matched pair stepped into the middle of the room and Ana, well prepared by Salmeo, immediately sank to her knees and then prostrated herself as was required. Bin closed the doors.

Salmeo took the lead. 'Your High One, this is most unusual to break harem protocol. The girls are not yet acquainted with all of the rules and we haven't even enjoyed the ceremony of the handkerchiefs.' Although the words were polite enough the tone was acid. 'Perhaps I should remain here with the Odalisque Ana whilst —'

'That will not be necessary.' Boaz was going to add thank you and stopped himself at the last instant. It was time he got used to giving commands. 'I am changing some rules, Salmeo.' He did not allow Salmeo the moment he needed to offer his caution at such a suggestion. 'The first is that it is to be my choice as to when and how I meet with the members of the harem. I think the handkerchief ceremony is romantic but trite for these modern days. If I'm old enough to rule, I'm certainly old enough to be in the company of a female my own age, in the middle of the afternoon and without a chaperone, and certainly without all the trials and innuendo which apparently had to be ploughed through in my father's day.'

Salmeo's feelings, normally so well disguised, were plainly written over his aghast expression. 'But, Your High One, I —'

Boaz feigned dismay. 'I trust you're not about to caution me?' he said, amazed that his voice was so steady, the tone so condescending. It felt suddenly wonderful to wield a power that could have a man such as this gabbling before him. He pressed his point. 'I'm not bedding her, Grand Master Eunuch, I simply wish to talk with her. You're very welcome to remain whilst we speak.' He paused only briefly to take a breath before adding: 'So long as you remain outside. I desire a private conversation with Odalisque Ana.'

The huge black man again opened his mouth to speak but nothing came out. He glared at the prone figure of Ana — who had not moved since her arrival — and then into the simmering expression of the Zar.

He could not win this one but he knew who could. 'I shall do that, High One,' he answered as humbly as he could manage. Then he bowed and left, hurrying to seek an audience with the Valide.

Boaz looked at the figure on the ground. 'Please, Odalisque Ana, rise.' When she was standing before him, her eyes still cast to the floor as presumably she'd been instructed, he gestured towards some comfortable divans by the grand windows. 'Join me.'

'I thought you were angry with me, Zar Boaz.'

He sighed softly. 'I am. Lazar has suffered pointlessly today because of your headstrong ways, but I made my rebuke public for entirely different reasons than you think. I think the Spur will have understood, so be assured I haven't asked you here to make you suffer more. I'm sure you're suffering enough.'

She bit her lip hard in order to force back the tears. 'I have never felt more lost than I do right now ... or bereft. If I could change what happened today, if I could take back my actions, I hope you know I would, Zar Boaz.'

Sincerely done, he thought. 'You'll have to forgive the décor,' he said brightly. 'This is my father's choice. I haven't the heart to change it, even though the Valide suggests I impose my own style.'

'You loved your father,' she spoke from behind the gauzy pale blue veil, eyes still downcast.

'You may remove your veil, Odalisque Ana. It is not required in my private presence, and I allow you to look upon me.' She raised her eyes and he was pleased to see the directness with which she held his gaze now that permission was hers. She took off her veil slowly, careful not to disturb her hair that had been brushed with a hundred strokes, Elza counting each and smearing an oil into it to make it shine even brighter. As her face was revealed to him once again, and this time at such close proximity, he felt his breath catch at the sight of her. He had thought this girl beautiful from a distance, but Ana, he now discovered, was infinitely more fetching this close. Her skin was smooth and unblemished but slightly burnished from the sun. He remembered how the harem women worked hard to keep their complexions as pale as possible but on Ana this golden colouring was like a glow from within ... sun-kissed.

'I did love my father very much. I miss him,' he said.

'I love my father too, Zar Boaz. I miss him as deeply as you miss yours.'

'Please, sit down with me.' He watched her glide to the divans and carefully seat herself opposite him. 'Where is your family from?'

'West. The foothills. My father is a goatherd.'

'Is he proud that his daughter now lives in the palace? It must be a far cry from what he is used to.' He had considered this a fair question, one designed to encourage her to talk about the family she had left behind. He was not ready for the quiet rebuke.

'My father is a simple man, Your High One. He has no conception of palace life. He also had no say in my being brought here. If it were left to him I think he would be proud for me to have remained as a goatherd's daughter.' She lifted her chin and as her eyes met his he instantly recognised a kindred spirit; both of them too young to be on the paths they were, both wishing they could be pursuing the lives they wanted rather than the ones they were being forced to follow.

'Forgive me, Ana, I meant no insult.'

'None taken, Majesty,' she said smoothly.

Boaz was already fascinated by her, but still felt relieved when their somewhat strained conversation was interrupted by a gentle knock. 'Come,' he answered. A servant entered bearing a tray. 'Ah, I took the liberty of organising some refreshments,' he said to fill the silence as the man laid out the food and wine. 'I hope you won't say you don't eat sherbert.'

'Oh no, I do,' she replied and Boaz heard the girl in her for the first time. 'I tasted it in the bazaar,' she gushed.

Boaz grinned. 'I heard about your adventure. It's why I wanted to meet you.'

Boaz watched, disappointed, as her green eyes, brilliant as gems, clouded. 'I've seen the error of my ways, High One.'

'Ana, I wasn't going to reprimand you. I was going to congratulate you.' She held his gaze, not believing what she'd heard. 'Zarab knows I yearn for some freedom myself.'

'But surely you have that as Zar?'

'I think I am as much a prisoner of my own palace as you are. I wish I had your reckless spirit. Truly. It must have taken real courage to spit in the eye of Salmeo. I know I shouldn't say this to you but I felt elated when I heard.' He all but whispered his words for fear the fat man could hear through walls.

'You mean that?' Her eyes glittered again.

He touched his hand to his forehead and then his lips in the region's manner of communicating that he spoke the truth. 'Our secret, though.'

It was her first reason to smile since she had hugged Jumo the previous day. Thinking about Jumo made her think of Lazar, and a familiar pain squeezed at her heart. 'You were there this morning,' she said flatly. 'I can't derive any pleasure from my courage — as you call it — after what the Spur went through on my behalf.'

'He must think very highly of you, Ana.'

He watched her face darken, tried to imagine what thoughts she hid. 'I think he feels responsible because it was he who bartered for me.'

Boaz sensed she was not being completely honest. 'He took no gold in exchange for you, I hear.'

She nodded sadly. 'I have not been given any information as to how he is.'

Boaz knew he shouldn't be sharing so much information but it felt so long since he'd been around someone his own age. 'I have been trying to find out more. Rumour has it that he won't live past this day.' He watched shock hit that lovely face as effectively as if he'd leaned across and slapped it.

'That can't be so, High One! Please, don't say this to me.'

'But you saw the pitiful state he was left in. Even from my more distant spot I could see his back opened to the bone. None of us should be surprised if he's already dead but we should all be ashamed.'

'I couldn't see the damage, I could only see his honourable face and how much it took for him to bear his injuries without sharing the pain with all of us.'

Boaz whistled low under his breath. 'I don't think anyone there would have thought less of him if he'd screamed with each lash.'

'I suspect screaming is not Lazar's way,' she said softly. 'He would consider it an intolerable weakness in himself.'

'You seem to understand him intimately despite the short term of your relationship.' Boaz saw her frown at his words. 'Er, I mean that you seem to know him very well.' She did not respond and the young Zar struggled to win back her trust. 'I have sent runners out all over the city. We shall have news of the Spur soon.' Now her eyes raised again to regard him and he could see the hope reflected in them. 'I shall get word to you, I promise.'

Ana studied him a moment longer. 'You know Salmeo will be telling your mother about this meeting.'

Boaz bristled. 'I am the Zar, Ana, or do you, like the Grand Master Eunuch, forget this?'

'No, High One. It is my turn to apologise, I meant no offence. I am only concerned that I have been marked as a troublemaker and do not wish you to get into any bother on my account.'

He laughed. 'I am the Zar,' he repeated. 'No-one has any authority over me.' Boaz stood, feeling taller, stronger suddenly. 'Thank you for making me remind myself of that.'

'High One?'

'Well, I think I too had overlooked just how powerful a person I am now. My father tried to tell me on his deathbed. He urged me to remember that I was the Chosen One. He selected me above all of his other sons to rule after him. Rule I will and I will not be cowed by an ambitious eunuch ... or my mother.'

She appreciated his fighting words. Felt much the same herself but also knew how helpless she was. 'I hardly know more than your name and age, Your Majesty, but I hope you don't feel it is forward of me to say how proud you make me feel. You speak to my own heart in what you say. Slave I might be considered but only by others. I too will not be humbled by Salmeo ... or —' She stopped, realising she might be about to make a grave mistake.

'My mother ... you may say it,' Boaz encouraged. He reached for his goblet of wine and drank, moving to sit by her now. The sherbets melted into a fusion of colour within their silver dishes, untouched on the tray. 'You may speak of her before me.'

He saw how carefully she watched him and guessed she had been warned, probably by Lazar, to trust few, if any, in the harem. 'Ana, I am not your enemy. You may speak freely.'

'I think not, High One,' she said finally, disappointing him further. He had not won her trust, then. 'I must not speak out of turn. It is probably wise if I keep my thoughts to myself.'

'You don't understand. I thought we might be friends.'

'You have many new friends now, Zar. There are forty-one other girls, as I understand it. All pretty, all picked carefully to suit your needs.'

'And I'll bet none of them as feisty as you, Ana.'

'I don't know that word, High One.'

'It means that you are spirited.'

'Ah, I have a lot to learn it seems.'

'Let me teach you.'

'A Zar teaching a slave.' It wasn't a question and he could hear the note of wonder in her tone as if she couldn't conceive of such a thing.

'Why not? How do you think my mother rose to her station, Ana? Don't be fooled by all of the grandeur. Every Zar ever born is the product of a slave. My father and his father before him, and his father before that mated with slaves and sired the next Mightiest of the Mighty.'

She nodded, frowning as if seriously considering his words. 'Well, now you put it that way . . .' she trailed off, not prepared to say much more.

Boaz pressed his point. 'My mother was taught extensively by the harem's tutors, but my father was also extremely generous to her and shared much of his knowledge. I shall see you get the education your intelligence deserves.'

'Your High One, may I ask a boon of you?'

'So soon, Odalisque Ana?' She looked back at him, chastened. 'A jest,' he added quickly. 'Ask me.'

It came out in a rush. 'Please don't single me out, Majesty.'

He wasn't sure what he had expected but he certainly hadn't anticipated this. 'What do you mean by that?'

'I have been warned to keep my head down. I have been marked as trouble by powerful people. I have no choice but to live this life of an odalisque, but perhaps I can live quietly and not create more ripples to reach the Valide or the Grand Master Eunuch.'

He nodded, understanding perfectly. 'I can get around this situation, Ana.'

'I don't see how.'

'That's because you don't understand the ways of the harem yet. Will you trust me, even though I suspect you've been warned to do the opposite?' He watched her blush and saw that he had guessed rightly. 'Trust that I wish you no harm and that I would appreciate your friendship for now, nothing more.'

'Of course — I can hardly refuse you, Zar Boaz.'

He smiled sadly. She had been cautioned well. 'I shall not allow anyone to object when I seek out your company.'

'Will you be fair to everyone?' she implored.

'If I enjoy some of the others, yes, I will spend time with them. I cannot guarantee it. My father once told me that a beautiful woman can be just as vapid or dull as a plain one. Beauty is no guarantee of intelligence or charming company. I am only now beginning to grasp what that meant and I understand why he chose my mother. She was always ambitious but she was also quick of mind and wit — this appealed to him.'

'Is this why you pursue me, High One?'

Boaz laughed. 'I think you're wonderfully daring. Something I'm not. If I didn't like you so much already, Ana, I'd urge you to keep following your spirited path and do everything you can to irritate and exasperate Salmeo.'

'You will keep your promise and let me know what you might discover?'

'I shall, for it gives me an excuse to see you again,' he said brightly.

'The Grand Master Eunuch said it is not usual to —'

Boaz was quick to interrupt her. 'Salmeo can say what he wishes, Ana. He is not the Zar. Things are going to change. My father chose me because he believed in me.'

'And your mother?' she risked.

'Is Valide only because of me.' Saying that made him think of Pez, and now that he did he realised he hadn't seen the dwarf since the flogging. He returned his attention to Ana. 'She will not give me too much grief. The first thing I shall do is introduce a picnic at each full moon.'

Her eyes shone at the mention of it. 'Outside the palace?'

He enjoyed seeing her pleasure. A jolt of desire coursed through him, startling him. 'Of course. I too feel cooped up here. I know when I was younger and lived amongst the harem women that they always complained of how dull their lives were. For all the luxuriousness of their existence, each day was the same for them. It never impacted on me — I was too young, perhaps too indulged as an heir to consider what their complaints meant. Well, I can change that. I can organise for all of you to get out of the palace.'

'You are wonderful, Your Majesty. I know I thank you for it and I feel sure the other girls will too.'

He beamed, enjoying her praise, wanting to see that glitter in her eyes often and feel that spark of desire surge. 'I'm sorry about the sherbet,' he said, eyeing the rainbow-coloured mess on the tray.

'You're the Zar, order it again!' she suggested airily, emboldened by his words of power.

$\backsim$ 20 $\backsim$

Pez fretted that he should not have left Lazar to the ministrations of a stranger. He should have stayed, kept vigil, urged his friend to hold onto life. Why did he have such a sense of doom? The only reassurance he could derive was that Jumo was present. Jumo would sooner die himself than lose Lazar. Pez knew Lazar's companion would send news shortly whether the fight had been won or lost.

Lost? He couldn't imagine Percheron without Lazar striding around it. How odd that he saw them as intricately joined, as if man and city belonged to one another. Surely he couldn't die as a result of the city's own punishment system?

The notion of Lazar's mortality put Pez into a bleak state of mind. Instead of feigning his normal ridiculous moods, he plunged into a sombre one. He began counting backwards in another language. Any scholar would recognise it as Haslin but that didn't matter. It sounded strange to the lay ear and that's what he needed. So long as he maintained an air of distraction, even disturbance, no-one at the palace would bat an eyelid that he wasn't cavorting as usual. The numbers he muttered managed to keep him focused as he plunged deeper into the halls towards the harem. He intended to find Ana but as he approached the forbidden entrance he turned away. Suddenly the thought of seeing Ana made him feel even more guilty. She would look at him with large, trusting eyes and hope to hear good news. He had none to give — no news at all, in fact, other than the grave observance that it was most likely Lazar would not survive.

Instead, he waddled down a different series of corridors that took him towards the chambers of the eunuchs. This area half encircled the harem so that the eunuch slaves had easy access to the women they served.

He deliberately began to mutter to himself. 'Where is Kett, must find Kett, how is Kett, our new pet.'

Someone passing heard him. 'Hello, Pez.'

'Kett?' he asked, forcing a dazed expression and then he picked his nose.

The slave stepped back. 'Is that the new boy?'

Pez hopped around, not answering. 'Poor Kett. Lost his flesh. The knifers took it.'

The slave nodded. 'He's being attended to now. They're going to remove the stent early, I think. You'll find them —'

Pez didn't linger; everyone was used to the dwarf doing everything except observing good manners. He belched instead and skipped backwards down the corridor. After the man had gone by, shaking his head, Pez doubled back. He didn't need to be told that the priest and his knifers would be in the Hall of the Precious. It sounded huge but was in fact just a large, airy chamber with a glass-domed roof and a central table upon which the victim was laid for the unravelling of his bandages. It seemed to Pez to be premature to be doing this, but he was not in a position to question the wisdom of their actions.

In the hall, he found a prone Kett, groaning in the middle of the room. The marble table was slightly tilted and had grooves in its sides with a drain at the bottom. It had been used for centuries for this procedure.

Salmeo, of course, presided over the event. 'Ah, Pez,' he lisped. 'We wondered where you'd got to. Proceed,' the Grand Master Eunuch ordered.

Pez hummed distractedly but focused on Kett, who seemed to have lost so much weight and yet his belly bulged obscenely. He began to giggle, pointing at the boy's enlarged abdomen.

Salmeo hissed at him. 'Have respect, dwarf!' Then he turned back to the priest. 'Are you sure about this?'

'Do you care?' the man said somewhat testily.

Salmeo leant forward, the air between priest and himself suffused with the scent of violet. 'I don't. But I think the Valide would prefer to know her old friend's child and the former playmate to her son survives.'

'In that case I think this is our only choice,' the priest said unflinchingly, directing the careful unwrapping of the bandages. 'See how he perspires and trembles. His body is being poisoned by itself. We must release the fluid and hope he is strong enough. Normally I would only do this after three whole days have passed, but the swelling of his body is a dangerous sign.'

The Grand Master Eunuch nodded. 'Do it.'

'If no liquid is passed when we remove the stent, then he is as good as dead.' Now he spoke in a whisper to the eunuch out of respect for the patient. 'It would be best to help him along should that occur.'

'I understand.'

The horrific wound inflicted by the sharp curved blade was revealed, the pewter tube looking insanely odd as it poked upwards from the mess of the boy's groin.

The men attending to him and even those observing became so silent and still that Pez was sure they must all look like a painting. He presumed all the men around him were remembering their own similarly traumatic experiences.

'He is young,' Salmeo muttered softly as if to reassure himself as the priest, reciting a prayer, reached for the pewter stick.

As the man pulled on the stent, Kett screamed.

'Pah! It is stuck,' the priest admitted. 'Quick, warm water and oil to ease the flesh back. Hurry!' he urged the helpers.

The area was bathed and although Pez presumed this was done gently it did not sound as though the effects were gentle. Kett continued to writhe pathetically against the strong arms that pinned him to the cool marble. They did not soften his protest, though, and he sang it loudly, cursing the very mothers who bore them, losing vital strength with each insult.

The priest pulled again sharply on the tube and it gave. Behind it gushed a torrent of bloodied water and the relief in Kett's anguished sighs was obvious. The flow continued with force for several seconds and then dwindled but didn't stop, not for a long time, and Pez noted now how well designed that marble table was for its purpose, draining the waste efficiently, cooling the slightly fevered body.

Salmeo looked expectantly at the priest, who nodded. 'He will live,' he pronounced. 'The water is running clear.'

'I shall tell the Valide,' Salmeo said, his shoulders relaxing as he departed, ignoring Pez who danced away from beneath the approaching bulk.

Pez approached. 'Can he hear me if I sing?'

'He is conscious,' the priest answered as if he was replying to someone sane.

'And what if I whispered?' He grinned insanely.

The priest rolled his eyes in exasperation. 'Don't upset him, Pez,' he warned.

That was the last thing Pez intended but he smiled indolently all the same, knowing no-one present could deny him anything he chose to do, such was the Zar's law. Pez leaned close to Kett's head.

'Kett, it's Pez. You've made it.'

The boy said nothing, although his groans continued. 'I'm going to make a suggestion for your work and you're going to accept it the moment it's offered. Understand? Don't say anything just take my hand,' he said, his hand already hovering nonchalantly over Kett's. He felt a soft squeeze. 'Good boy,' he whispered. 'Just trust me now. You get stronger — work hard to heal. Now cry out as if I've antagonised you.'

Kett gave a weak yell.

Pez giggled.

'Begone, Pez,' the priest said wearily. 'Isn't it enough that this boy nearly lost his life?' He knew it was a pointless accusation for the dwarf hardly understood anything anyone said to him.

Pez began to sing nonsense, dancing his way to the door. Kett was safe. Now he had to find Boaz.

Lazar was semiconscious now and raging. The very mild sedative, which was all Ellyana could risk, had worn off and it was taking all of Jumo's strength to hold him still whilst Zafira finished dressing his wounds.

'His back looks like a bad piece of child's practice sewing,' she commented, embarrassed by her work.

'Such beautiful skin he has too,' Ellyana said softly from behind.

'Lazar! Hush!' Jumo cried. 'We are tending to you.'

'He can't help it, Jumo, and he cannot hear you, I suspect,' Ellyana advised in her quiet manner. 'It's the poison. It makes him angry.' Jumo saw some dark humour in her comment. 'You are amused?' she asked.

'He's always angry,' Jumo replied dryly. 'But I presume this is a good omen, him being angry enough to fight us?'

Once again his hopes were dashed. 'The opposite. It means the poison is winning.'

'I'm done,' Zafira said wearily, stretching. 'His wounds are sewn — as best I can — the salve is on and I've dressed all of his back.'

As if the demons within had suddenly lost energy at her words Lazar slumped against the mattress, silent. In fact he became so still that Jumo had to look carefully to convince himself that his friend still breathed.

'They will need to be changed twice daily,' Ellyana warned.

Both listeners nodded absently, lost in dire thoughts.

'Are we losing him?' Jumo asked.

She stared into his earnest expression, desperately wanting to lie and ease his pain but she couldn't. 'I won't tell untruths for comfort's sake. He's dying, Jumo. This is the final stage before the venom works on the heart. I think perhaps we were too late.'

'No!' She laid a hand on him and he shook it away. 'We have to save him. You brought us here, you made him make that journey across the water and up the cliff side.' His voice broke. 'You save him,' he demanded. He glanced towards Zafira through a mist of tears he refused to spill and he could see the hopelessness in her gaze. So she too understood that Lazar was as good as lost, even after all her work.

'Jumo,' Ellyana began.

'Don't placate me,' he warned. 'You wouldn't have come here if you didn't have a vested interest in him. I don't know what that interest is, and to be honest I don't care. I just want you to try, even if you think you're wasting your time.'

'No waste to save this man's life,' she uttered softly. 'I want him to live too but I want you to understand that it's not within my power to give him life.'

'But you can try to save it!'

'Yes,' she nodded, resignation in the soft sigh that followed. 'I will try for you.' She picked up the cooled pot of liquid she had made. 'This special tea we've brewed is from the rare circad. It is the only thing I've discovered that can act aggressively against snake poison and it is especially effective against drezden … if administered quickly enough.'

'How often do we give him the tea?' Jumo asked.

'As often as he will tolerate it. It is unpleasantly bitter. The more we get into him, the better his chances of healing. He will bring it back up but we just have to persevere.'

'Then I will persevere,' he echoed firmly. .

Ellyana smiled sadly. 'Jumo, leave this to the women. You have done all you can.'

'What?' Jumo could barely think beyond his commitment to Lazar — the fear of leaving him alone in such a perilous state showed itself in a rare angry frown.

'Go back to the city,' she replied calmly. 'Wait for news.'

'But why not —' he began, but was stilled by the sad smile on the face of the old woman and the way she calmly lifted a finger to quieten him.

'Jumo, we now know that Lazar has enemies within the palace who feel sufficiently threatened by him to make a very determined attempt on his life. We are presuming it is the Grand Master Eunuch at work but we are not certain. The Vizier could be involved, the Valide might have a hand in it, even the Zar if he's been compromised in some way.'

'Never,' Jumo whispered, further angered by the suggestion, for Lazar had such faith in Boaz.

'We cannot be sure, is all I'm saying and we shouldn't risk our tiny chance at reviving him by letting anyone know where he is.'

Bitterness laced his tone. 'What do you want me to do?'

'Return to Lazar's house and await information. If he lives, you can spread the good news and be our eyes. Watch for who reacts positively but mostly for who does not. Pez will be a great help in this. But you can keep your ear to the ground around the city and listen to what the people are saying. We need to know that Salmeo and his cohorts aren't spreading rumours about the Spur. We must be informed of Lazar's position before he sets foot back in the city.'

'You speak as if you believe he will live,' Jumo observed.

'If he dies, Jumo, then you and Pez can still be of more use to Lazar in Percheron proper than here. You can see who relishes the news of his death, react quickly. Either way you are serving your master best by being close to the palace.'

Jumo shook his head. 'I would prefer to be with him ... to the end if necessary. I don't want this man dying alone.'

'He won't be alone,' she countered firmly. 'Zafira and I will be at his side for every minute that he breathes.'

'I can't leave him,' he beseeched. 'I couldn't live with myself if anything should happen.'

Ellyana took his hand in hers. 'I will give every bit of myself towards saving him — so will Zafira. It doesn't need three of us and Lazar can benefit from your presence elsewhere.'

Jumo closed his eyes with frustration. 'But the very moment I return to his home I will be besieged with enquiries. What am I to tell them? They will find out where he is anyway, so how am I protecting him?'

'Quite simply, friend Jumo, because you will not tell the truth. Our aim is to keep his antagonists well away from him until we know he's strong enough again.' She shrugged. 'So, without knowing who his enemies are, we must treat all of them as foe. You must lie. You will tell anyone who asks after Lazar that following your arrival at the Sea Temple, where he requested you take him, he fell deathly ill. The priestess said she would do what she could for him and suggested you leave him with her for a while until she could assess the extent of his injuries.'

'No-one will believe this,' he said.

She continued as if he hadn't spoken. 'You can say you were so shocked by Lazar's condition that you weren't thinking straight. She gave you a drink and you had no idea that it was drugged with a sedative. When you woke Lazar was gone and you've been searching ever since and found no sign of him.'

His incredulity deepened. 'You think they'll accept any of it?'

'Yes, because there is no word of him. There is no sign of him. No-one saw us leave with him, and no-one must see you return. You will have to go in disguise.'

'And how do I explain my absence for so long?'

It was Zafira who came up with the idea in the end. 'You could legitimately claim that you were so overcome with grief that you found the nearest drinking hole and drank yourself into oblivion.

You'd need to buy off the silence of the mosha-man, of course, but that won't be hard.'

'I don't drink in mosha houses,' Jumo complained, knowing it was a hollow attempt to thwart the idea.

'Then throw the liquor over yourself. You only have to smell of it to convince anyone listening to your torrid tale.'

'She's right,' Ellyana agreed. 'It's a good plan.'

'It makes Zafira out to be a villain though.'

Zafira snorted gently. 'As if that frightens me, dear Jumo. We who worship the Goddess have lived as outcasts and villains for the entirety of my lifetime and well before that. I have my faith, it is all I need. What people think of me in my dotage is of no concern.'

Ellyana pushed harder. 'Jumo, can't you see that we are helping Lazar not punishing you?'

'Yes, of course I can,' he snapped. 'But you don't understand how much we've been through together.' He looked at the face of the man he loved. It was devoid of expression. His lips were a pale smudge on the once-bronzed skin that now looked leached of all colour.

'It is best that you leave now — getting this tea down him is going to be ugly,' Ellyana warned.

Jumo turned to her again. 'What do you mean?'

'He'll rail against it with the little strength he has left and that exertion alone could cost him his life. It will be a gentle balance between forcing him to drink whilst not making him fight us as well as the poison. Leave us now, Jumo. Use the boat and row yourself back to the harbour. I promise we'll get word within the next day or so.'

Jumo turned helplessly to Zafira for support but her expression was implacable. She agreed with Ellyana, that much was clear. He raised a finger in warning. 'Be sure you do and be sure you save him, or so help me, Ellyana, I shall come looking for you.'

∾ 21 ∾

It was humid in Percheron, the air stifling within the confines of the city. Despite the heat, the bazaar hummed with its usual activity as traders encouraged the evening's stream of humanity to buy everything from freshly baked honey puffs to painted tiles.

As usual Gold Alley was the most congested area; the Percherese did not rush into the purchase of gold but loved to roam the small corridors of glittering stalls at leisure. Many would pay close attention to the changing prices over days, often weeks, before investing. Others just liked to sit down with the traders and enjoy touching the seductive metal long before they were ready to pay good cash. There was never any hurry. The merchants gave time to each customer, often sending their subordinates to fetch tea that arrived in colourful glasses on small trays. Tea meant hospitality and fellowship. It prompted conversation and ultimately sales.

Tariq saw none of this, however, as he hurried through the sloping streets. The colour and ritual of Gold Alley was lost on him, his eyes fixed ahead on the next corner, his mind enmeshed in visions of power and wealth. He didn't stop to help or even apologise to the youngster whose elbow he clipped, sending a tray of dark golden tea clattering to the ground as cranberry-coloured glass, edged in gold, smashed in a hail of tinkling shards. It was fortunate no-one recognised him, for the Vizier's forked and bejewelled beard alone normally marked him for who he was. But Tariq had taken measures this night to disguise himself. The tea boy would later blame an ignorant woman, tall and fully veiled in the jamoosh.

Tariq pressed on, his mind a whirl of possibilities mingled with fear. Was he doing the right thing? It was only temporary, he reminded himself, and then he'd be set up with unimaginable wealth for what was left of his life. He wasn't so old, in truth; he was simply worn down, and if he were fully honest it was the riches that attracted him more than power. Power was for a younger man. If Maliz had visited him ten or fifteen years earlier then Tariq might envisage himself as contriving to be the second most powerful person in the realm, but since this afternoon he had decided he was tired of the palace, wearied of the political manoeuvrings, unhappy that he now served a Zar who was still too young to grow a beard.

He'd never had a good relationship with Joreb — this much was true, or he would already be Grand Vizier. But to be back at the beginning, having to prime and grow a new relationship with someone who was already so untrusting of him was draining. Joreb had not cared much for Tariq but they had forged a working relationship; however, Tariq suspected Boaz was going to make changes to the old ways. So perhaps in the end Maliz's offer of extraordinary wealth was the ultimate reason for agreeing to his terms. Tariq could see himself retiring and living the decadent life he'd always dreamed of. That kind of wealth was power in itself anyway.

He would no longer be a servant to the royals but one of the people they entertained.

He enjoyed this thought.

Maliz had come to him briefly this evening and reminded the Vizier of his decision. Tariq had hesitated and the demon chose against filling the silence with his usual urgings. This time there was no chatter. Perhaps it was the emptiness of noise in his mind that caused Tariq to agree. He wanted all the things that Maliz promised and the demon knew it so he had simply waited patiently for the capitulation.

You will never regret it, Maliz had replied, his tone slightly mocking. He had given the Vizier directions and disappeared swiftly.

And so Tariq had disguised himself as a woman beneath the veil, the only way he could think of to hide his instantly recognisable beard. Now he was hurrying through the streets, the spilled tea long forgotten as he made his way towards the harbour and an area known as the Ditch.

There were fewer lanterns here so the shadows were deeper, and the salty tang in the air became stronger. People were dressed more roughly but nobody gave the tall woman a second glance. A new smell permeated his senses — fragrant and strong, layering itself across the almost permanently fishy odour that hung predictably around the foreshore. His nose told him he was close to the main spice market as the mix of seeds and powders, fresh herbs and spices clamoured for his attention.

Tariq felt safer in the bazaar, not only because there was so much more activity beneath the lanes of brightly coloured wares but also because women shopped. Fewer were veiling themselves, he noticed with interest — it had been a long time since he'd wandered the streets of the common people. Full veiling of women had once been a national tradition but that had begun to die out over the last century as more liberal attitudes prevailed. Now only high-caste families preferred that their women remain veiled outside their homes. And royalty of course.

Tariq forced himself to stop at several stalls and consider the wares on offer. He figured it was more natural for him to weave his way towards the western part if he looked like a genuine shopper. It would turn no heads, he decided, and attention was the last thing he needed.

With a forced casualness he dawdled by a stall selling hot spices, picking up cloves and cardamom seeds and smelling them, turning over chillies to check colour and freshness, before moving on. This time he stopped by a store selling only variations of pepper, fascinated by the colours and choice on offer. Finally he strolled down the middle of the main thoroughfare, turning towards the western gate and maintaining his casual meander, pretending to be absorbed in the produce until his eye caught the sign that read 'Beloch's Table'.

It was every bit as vulgar as he'd imagined. A fat man with a dirty apron grinned at him, a calon hanging from one lip and smoking itself, it seemed, by the length of ash still clinging on.

'My sister, can we serve you today? Quishtar perhaps or a plate of yemshi?' he offered.

The cockroach crawling across the owner's foot was indication enough of how he ran the establishment.

The cheek of it, the Vizier thought, simmering beneath the veil, *using the name of one of the city's great icons to herald this tawdry little eatery.*

He passed over the karel he had readied. 'I've been told to give you this. You have no memory of my being here,' he said. If the grubby owner was surprised to hear a man's voice from behind the jamoosh, there was no outward sign. 'I wish to use your back door.'

'Be my guest, er ... sister,' he said, pocketing the karel as expertly as the best thief might. No-one had seen the coin change hands and the tall woman was instantly forgotten as the owner began soliciting new customers.

The Vizier moved quickly to the back of the eatery, pushing past servers and the two cooks until he spotted the open door and the lane beyond. He turned as instructed and could make out the small green doorway at the end of the alley, courtesy of a single lantern. It was dim, though, and deserted. Few sounds escaped to this seemingly derelict part of the Ditch. A rat scurried by, leaping over his foot and causing him to let out a small shriek of disgust. He could feel his own heart pounding now. Was this such a good idea after all? He told himself that he could still back out. Maliz would be angry but what could he do to him? He was only a voice, and even if he was more, the demon must be relatively helpless at this stage or he wouldn't be seeking a new body to cohabit with.

He stopped, now only a dozen or so steps from the door. This was it. If he was going to flee it would have to be now. As if on cue an amused voice filled his head.

Welcome to my abode, Tariq. Please, come in.

Too late, he thought, there was no choice any more. 'Where are you?' he called tentatively. Speaking aloud made him feel only marginally more secure.

Step inside. There are a few of us but you'll know me soon enough.

Tariq found himself facing the green door. He reached for the handle, taking a deep breath. He had never been so scared in his life.

Pez turned on his usual antics for the men before knocking theatrically on the Zar's door. At night Boaz was waited on by guards on both sides of the door to his sleeping chamber, so Pez was greeted by a grim-faced man who obviously didn't appreciate the late-night arrival.

'Oh, it's you,' he said, a hint of disgust in his voice. 'We're to permit you even if he's sleeping so I suppose you'd better come in.'

'Do you like custard?' Pez asked earnestly.

'Not particularly,' the guard replied. 'I'm not keen to wake His Majesty.'

'Oh, His Majesty loves custard. I prefer dolphins. What about slugs, do you like them? They sing rather oddly.'

The man raised his eyes in frustration. The hour was weary enough without this nonsense. He turned on his heel and left Pez standing by the door.

Pez hesitated. He had made a curious decision to be not altogether truthful with Boaz, and although he couldn't quite recall why, he was sure a voice had whispered this strange suggestion to him.

He knocked gently at the bedchamber door, wondering what in Lyana's name he was going to say to the boy about his whereabouts these past hours. From behind the door he heard mumbling and risked opening it.

'Purple flowers smell strange,' Pez muttered.

The door was pulled back fully. 'Where have you been?' Boaz demanded and Pez was taken aback by the vehemence. He looked around to see where the guards were, an excuse rushing to form itself when Boaz continued. 'I've been worried sick about you.'

Pez turned back, relieved. 'I'm sorry, High One,' he replied. 'I can explain.'

'Come on in. I couldn't sleep anyway. There's hardly a breath of air.'

'It's worse in the city.'

'Is that where you've been?'

'Yes,' he lied.

'Good. I figured you'd been with Lazar. Now tell me where he is and that he's recovering. I shall send my own physics immediately. He must have the best attention.' The Zar shook his head. 'I haven't been able to think straight all evening.' He was going to say more when he noticed his friend's grave expression.

'I can't help, High One,' Pez replied solemnly. 'I have no idea where he is.'

'What? You too?'

'Me too?'

'Pez, no-one can tell me where the Spur is. I've had the city combed and there's no word on the street of his whereabouts. How can a man who looked half dead and yet so recognisable disappear like this without help?'

Pez's voice was hard when it came. 'He didn't only *look* half dead, Majesty. He was dying.' The dwarf confirmed the Zar's worst fears.

'Please tell me you're jesting and that you're now going to give me the truth,' Boaz tried, his heart filled with dread.

'I lie not. It's true that I accompanied Lazar and Jumo to the Sea Temple. If they're not there now, then I have no idea where they are,' he said, hating himself for the fabrication.

The boy studied him. 'But you and Lazar are such good friends. Surely you would have stayed with him?'

'I don't care to be abroad in the city too often or for long periods, my Zar. I was no help anyway. Lazar was unconscious and his wounds were so horrific that both Jumo and I were helpless.'

He watched Boaz force control over himself. It would have been easy for the boy to fall apart at this moment but Pez felt a gentle pride that the young Zar was rising to his station.

'Why the Sea Temple? No-one goes there,' Boaz queried.

Pez shrugged. 'Jumo tells me it is a place Lazar discovered very recently. He liked its peace and the fact that it is deserted, save for an old priestess.'

'So he asked to go there?'

'I don't know, Your Majesty,' Pez lied. 'I imagine not, for he was unconscious, as I said. I think in his panic Jumo took him to the quietest place he could think of.'

'But there's no care there,' Boaz groaned. 'It doesn't make sense. Even from my distant vantage it was obvious he was seriously injured.'

'You have no idea of the extent of it,' Pez murmured.

Boaz strode to the door, opened it and waited, presumably for a guard. The Zar muttered some angry orders before slamming the door. 'I've sent some runners down to the Sea Temple.'

Pez nodded. He knew they would find it empty, but for some reason he chose to keep this to himself. He was reminded of the whispering voice that urged him to do this and he felt a crawling tendril of fear pass through him. What was happening to him? Who was talking to him?

'It was a shocking outcome, Great One,' he risked. 'You know Salmeo designed it to turn out the way it did.'

'Of course I do! When it comes to the harem, however, I don't have as much say in it as everyone seems to think. Salmeo and the Valide *are* the King and Queen of the harem. I am merely whom it services.' He grimaced.

'How did your mother react?'

'To be honest I believe it was as much a shock for her as it was for myself.'

'Really?' Pez didn't sound convinced.

'I asked her directly whether she had any involvement and she denied it. I know my mother well enough, Pez.'

The dwarf remained silent, duly reprimanded. So far he had not mentioned the use of poison. 'Tariq?'

Boaz shook his head. 'No, this is all Salmeo's work. It has his cruelty stamped all over it. As for the Inflictors, someone will swing for this if I don't have news of Lazar soon.'

'It was not the boy's fault, High One. He looked more terrified than anyone.'

'I don't care,' Boaz snapped. 'Woe betide if I receive bad news about Lazar. I think you all forget that he was my friend — one of so few I have in this place.' He slumped down on a sofa and stared out of his window. 'I met with the Odalisque Ana today,' he said, as if he wanted to change the subject.

'Oh? That's unusual. Must have delighted Salmeo.'

Boaz found a small but wicked smile. 'He hated it. Went rushing off to my mother, who apparently told him to obey his Zar and not run to her with complaints. No doubt she has come to the same conclusion as us, that this was Salmeo's doing. She is not pleased.'

'How was Ana?'

'Devastated, although I think my company was good for her, and I would be lying if I said the outcome wasn't mutual.'

'So you like her?'

Boaz turned his gaze from the window to the dwarf. 'You knew I would. That's why you risked so much that night of her presentation to the Valide. What are you up to, Pez?'

Pez leapt onto a seat. 'Nothing, High One. I had seen her beauty and heard from Lazar of her intelligence,' he lied. 'I thought she might be someone who could offer you honest friendship as much as pleasant company. I'm just glad you liked her,' Pez said quietly. 'May I ask a boon?'

'You will whether I give permission or not,' Boaz said but not unkindly.

'I sense Ana is about to be elevated to a status beyond simple slave and I'm wondering if you would be generous enough to appoint one solely to serve her.'

'What? She's only been here a few days. My mother would object fiercely.' Boaz shook his head as if the whims of his mother were beyond him.

Pez answered instead. 'I'll tell you why she might, if I may be so bold?' The boy nodded. 'It's because of Lazar. Your mother's interest in Lazar is hardly a secret. His obvious sense of commitment to Ana, so brilliantly and rather sadly displayed by today's theatre, has piqued your mother's curiosity. She wants to know what's behind it, what drives it ...' His voice trailed away at the sound of a knock at the door.

'Come,' Boaz answered.

It was the head guard. 'Your High One.' He bowed low and long.

'Do you have news of the Spur?'

The man straightened. 'Majesty, the Sea Temple is deserted, although we did find bloodstains in front of the altar.'

'And no-one knows of the Spur's whereabouts?' Boaz persisted, knowing it was a pointless query.

'I had men ranging throughout the harbour for any news. A child thought she saw a man being loaded into a boat but the mother was scared of us asking questions and the little one clammed up. When we tried again she denied it and claimed she had dreamed it.'

'What sort of boat?'

'A rowboat she said,' the man replied doubtfully, 'but there is nowhere to go to, Majesty, that is close enough to row to or where help can be sought.'

'What's that island not so far away?'

Pez held his breath as the guard frowned and then brightened. 'There is the Isle of Stars, High One, but that's a leper colony.'

Pez belched. 'And who'd go there?' he murmured.

'All right, Briz, keep trying with your men. He must be found.'

'There's fifteen of them still hunting down anything they can.'

'Wake me if you hear anything at all.'

'Yes, High One.' He touched hand to his heart and took his leave.

'Take some rest, Boaz,' Pez suggested after the guard had gone.

'What were you going to ask me about Ana?'

Pez sighed. 'The newly made eunuch,' he began.

'Kett.'

'Yes. He would make a good servant for Ana.'

Boaz nodded. 'I share your guilt, Pez. But now is not the time to be singling Ana out for special status. She has begged me to treat her the same as the other odalisques and because of my mother's interest I'm inclined to acquiesce.'

'We should help him,' Pez persisted, again unsure why, but somehow certain that there was more to Kett; the boy claimed to be the black bird, whatever that meant. And yet when he said those words it touched a nerve somewhere deep inside Pez.

'Leave it with me. I will not see him badly done by — perhaps in time we can consider the position you have suggested.'

Pez nodded. It would have to be enough for now.

'You never did tell me where you've been all this time,' Boaz replied and Pez realised he was not going to be let off the hook that lightly.

Tariq stepped gingerly through the doorway to be confronted by several people in various stages of decomposition. That's the only way he could describe it. Most were old — or at least that's how they appeared — and each was filthy, dressed in rags. All were ravaged from starvation. He knew these to be members of the city's lost, which was how people with a conscience referred to them. Most called them the Sewer Rats. These were people wholly forgotten and ignored by all but the Vizier and his council who wanted them removed. The word removed was broadly used. Tariq himself meant it as 'removed from the earth' rather than just removed from society. He would have gladly signed their death warrants, but more conservative council members were still arguing as to whether the Isle of Stars — already designated as a place for the unwanted — could be used as a convenient spot where these undesirables could waste away. Tariq was fearful that Boaz would demand that Percheron take better care of its lost people. The Vizier wanted no drain on the city's budget for these fools who were, in his opinion, too lazy or useless to lead a productive life. The city was far better off without them.

He grimaced as one toothless hag staggered towards him; fortunately for Tariq the old girl was almost blind with cataracts and he pushed her aside. Another he kicked.

'Maliz!' he called, emboldened by his power over the wretches around him. He avoided a third of the damned, dropping his shoulder and callously shoving the helpless fellow into a wall, sending him spinning into the shadows. Tariq sneered. 'Demon! I seek you.'

And I hear you, came a familiar voice in his head.

I can't see you.

Come closer, Vizier.

Now Tariq felt the spike of fear he had held at bay take full hold. Perspiration broke out beneath his robes and he threw off the jamoosh as much to see more easily as cool himself. 'Where?' he whispered into the darkness.

Not far.

The voice might be coming from behind him, he thought. He swung around wildly, leaping back at the same time, but there was no-one new, save the same pathetic souls he'd already dealt with.

'I ... I have no idea where you are,' he called, far less confidently. 'Show me.' He smelled first rather than heard or saw the tiny figure that seemed to have crept out of the darkness to stand before him.

'Do you see me now?' said a frail voice.

He did, dismayed to be confronted by a feeble old man who seemed to be wasting away.

'You?' he asked, incredulous.

The figure nodded. 'Don't be fooled, Tariq,' it said in the old man's wispy voice. 'I am who you feared meeting.'

Tariq stepped back. His arrogance returned. 'Who could be scared of you?'

'Are you testing me?' Maliz asked evenly, his fetid breath making Tariq wince. 'I'd advise against it. You are beguiled by appearance alone, Vizier, and that is a mistake. You should keep in mind that I choose to walk in this form.'

'Why?' Tariq asked, trying to avoid breathing through his nose.

'It suits my purposes,' replied the frail man. 'Who would think to find the Demon Maliz here amid Percheron's unfortunates.'

'Who indeed?' echoed Tariq, with sarcasm.

Suddenly the more familiar voice boomed in his head. *You are the one who is pathetic, Vizier. You look at me as if you could snap me in half and be done with it. Why bother? Go back to your life, Tariq. Return to the palace and be abused by Herezah and upstaged by Salmeo and treated like a filthy servant by the Zar. You are nothing in their eyes. Nothing! An inferior, ageing politician with nothing much to contribute to any of their goals, save being a useful punching bag ...*

Maliz continued the stream of insults but Tariq didn't hear any more. His anger was roused as the truth of the demon's words exploded in his mind. He *was* nothing. They *did* all treat him as though he were dirt on their shoes.

'Enough!' he roared and the old man gave a black-toothed, diseased smile.

'Does the truth hurt, Vizier? I can make it all so different for you.'

'Prove it, show me your powers, show me riches, give me unequivocal proof that you are who you say you are.'

The old man sighed. Maliz's deep and ancient voice said in his head. *If I'm to show you things, you will need to leave your body here.*

Tariq baulked. 'No!'

Fret not, you will still own it, still belong to it but I can take you to places that only your dreams have imagined previously.

'And I will not die by leaving my body?'

No.

'What, can't you just steal it?'

Maliz laughed but there was no humour in it. *I can't. I am not permitted by Zarab. You must offer me your body before I'm permitted to enter it as anything other than a voice.*

Tariq heard the truth in Maliz's confession. 'Do it, then. Show me all that you can to convince me to utter the invitation you so desire.'

The Vizier closed his eyes instinctively and felt a mighty push, as though all the breath was being squeezed out of him.

See for yourself, said Maliz.

Tariq had the sensation of trembling with fear — or was it anticipation — yet could not feel himself shaking. And similarly he told himself to open his eyes but there was no physical movement, he could simply suddenly see.

Herezah? he exclaimed.

I thought you'd like to look in on the person whose attention you crave most.

I'm in the harem!

Not physically, Tariq.

Herezah was taking a late-night tea infusion alone but Tariq could see she wasn't sipping from her cup. She looked maudlin and disinterested. Sadly she was clothed — he would like to have seen her naked.

I can give you that too, Maliz breathed into his mind.

Tariq ignored the way the demon read his mind. *Why so moody tonight?*

Think! You want to be Grand Vizier yet you ask the simplest of questions that perhaps even that fool, Pez, could work out and he has none of his faculties as far as I can tell. The Vizier felt the sting of criticism. *You are aware of why she is angry, depressed tonight, I promise you. Work it out,* Maliz encouraged. *There is rarely more than this reason for any woman to be so low of mood.*

A man.

Which one?

Tariq was nervous. *Boaz?*

Maliz growled his disappointment. *Don't be naive, Tariq, Herezah plays her game better than any other. Try again.*

Lazar.

Yes! Of course Lazar. There is no other man that interests her sexually.

She's maudlin because of his flogging?

Because of his apparent death, I should think. It isn't looking good for the Spur.

Do you know everything, Maliz?

Sadly, no. I know only what I see or eavesdrop, and everything I see or hear is open to interpretation. Fortunately I am sharp enough to get it right most times. She is not so short-sighted by the way. A lot more is at stake.

She's worried about Percheron's security without the Spur.

Correct.

I see. Of course I hate Lazar, I hope he is dead, Tariq surprised himself.

I know this. I know everything about you, Tariq.

Show me more.

What do you want to see now?

The harem proper. The girls.

Tsk-tsk, Vizier, Maliz admonished. *Look,* he said.

And Tariq was moving through the empty halls of the harem. *It's beautiful,* he gushed.

Always the best is hidden, Maliz said and laughed. *The girls are asleep.*

Except one, Tariq replied as he spotted Odalisque Ana sitting in the bench of a window. *Can you eavesdrop her thoughts?*

I have not tried. I can if you wish, but not everyone is as open to me as you have been.

No, show me the Zar instead, Tariq demanded.

He was instantly privy to Boaz, also slumped at a window in his suite. Nearby sat the dwarf.

Another person I hate is Pez.

He is no-one.

They watched Pez suddenly cock his large head to one side.

As usual he's not paying attention. The Zar is talking to him. This is so typical of the ingrate.

Now they watched Pez stand, his body tensed.

'Now what's wrong?' they heard the Zar ask.

The dwarf began to leap around the furniture singing.

'Pez, stop,' Boaz urged. 'No-one is —'

Pez's sudden high-pitched squeal shocked the young Zar into silence.

'Must write, must write!' Pez began to moan.

'Write what?'

Boaz and his two invisible visitors watched the dwarf scrawl something onto a tablet of paper. Then he coughed at it, repeatedly. He sat on it and farted.

Tariq groaned. *I truly despise Joreb for bringing this troll into our lives.*

He's harmless but I take your point. It's a pity that the son thinks so highly of him. Maliz watched Pez suddenly rise again, lift the crumpled sheet of paper and fling it at the astounded Zar.

'The birds are pecking me,' he shrieked at Boaz. 'My flesh is burning,' he howled and ran out of the door.

I just hope he has a seizure and dies some time soon, Tariq said caustically.

Maliz said nothing, watched Boaz read the note absently and then do the curious thing of setting it alight from a nearby candle. The parchment burned and the Zar watched it disintegrate to ash. They both observed how he suddenly looked angry and strode to the door, flinging it open and demanding one of the guards enter.

'Yes, High One?' the man said, bowing and straightening with a concerned frown.

'You tell Pez that if he ever writes such obscenity to me again, I will bar him from entering my rooms. Make it clear to him, will you?'

The man nodded, stunned a little by the outburst. 'He never takes any notice, Great One.'

'Tell him anyway,' Boaz ordered and flung the door closed behind the retreating guard.

Oh that's interesting, Tariq said. *Perhaps a falling out between our Zar and the fool. Maybe the halfwit went too far this time.*

It appears so, Maliz admitted. *I'd love to know what he wrote that so upset the Zar.*

Finally, show me riches, Maliz, Tariq said, no longer interested in eavesdropping on the royal apartments.

As you wish. Is this our final journey?

Yes. You have convinced me of your magical power. All I need now is to see some of the treasures you've promised and we will seal our bargain.

Boaz found Pez, as instructed, in the Golden Garden. This was a private courtyard that no-one but the Zar himself could use.

280

Sometimes it was used to entertain one of his Favourites or to impress a new odalisque, but in the main it was a place for peace and reflection away from the palace life.

'What was that all about?' Boaz hissed.

'Forgive me, Boaz,' Pez said and he sounded rattled. 'I had to get us away from there.'

'What in Zarab's name happened?'

The dwarf shook his large head. 'I don't really know, in truth, but something chilled me.'

'I don't understand.'

'No neither do I, but something or someone was with us in your chamber.'

'You jest.'

'Do I look like I'm trying to entertain?' Pez snarled.

'No, you look frightened. I've never seen you like this. You think someone was eavesdropping? But where? There aren't many places to hide in that particular room.'

'No, I don't mean like that. I mean someone was with us in spirit.'

Boaz raised his eyebrows in mock defeat. 'Oh I see. An invisible eavesdropper.'

'Don't mock me, Boaz. I did what I did for our own protection. Someone was listening, I tell you. I don't know who it was or why or even how they were doing it, but my Lore skills picked it up instantly.'

Boaz looked chastened. 'Sorry, Pez. I don't mean to make fun. It's just so hard to stomach.'

'Zar Boaz, you witnessed and experienced first-hand the power of the Lore. You must trust me when I use it as protection for us.'

'I do trust you.'

'Then know whoever it was listening to our conversation was not friendly. There was something dark and malevolent in its presence.'

'This is getting worse,' Boaz said, standing from the fountain edge he'd been sitting on. 'What do you expect me to do?'

'Nothing! Just don't ignore my warnings or devalue them by not taking them seriously. Someone who is not your friend visited you today, Boaz, and it was done using the Lore. From now on we must be on our guard.'

'Well if I can't see or hear them, how will I know?'

'You won't but I will. If I should behave as I did tonight, yelling something about the moon, you'll know I am warning you.'

'All right ... but we're safe here presumably.'

'I no longer feel we're safe anywhere,' Pez admitted. 'I shall have to be much more watchful.'

'So this is an enemy? Who could have sent this person?'

'I have no idea. But it's very dangerous. If I'm discovered —'

'What would it matter, in truth, to anyone in the palace?' Boaz challenged but not aggressively. 'What could anyone do if it was revealed that you have your wits about you and this has been a trick you've pulled for years?'

'It's not the people of the palace I worry about, my Zar,' Pez said cryptically. 'Come, the feeling of being observed is gone. You can return to your chambers to sleep.'

Boaz sighed. 'I won't be doing much sleeping until I hear about Lazar.' But he followed Pez anyway who had decided to crawl out of the Golden Garden making braying noises like a donkey.

'All right, how?' Tariq demanded, his mind still reeling from the riches he had seen. Maliz had shown him the hidden treasure of the idiosyncratic Zar Fasha from a previous century, who had insisted on his corpse being entombed in the desert along with his fabulous wealth and entire harem. Except the people from the harem, unlike their Zar, had been very much alive when entombed and their twisted skeletons with jaws opened in agony were testimony to the desperate way in which they'd perished, screaming to be let out of their deep prison beneath the sands. None of this troubled Tariq — all he could focus on was the treasure itself and the decadent way he would soon be living once he had accessed it. 'Although I've never understood what it is that you mean to do,' he added carefully.

Maliz was back in his wizened guise of the near-toothless man. 'I have explained enough. You want what I can give you. Now either you take what I'm offering or you leave and never come back. I can find another.'

Another what? Tariq wondered, his mind racing to make a final decision. *Another fool?*

Another host, came the deep-voiced reply in his mind. *Let me be your guest,* he offered, more gently now. *And I will teach you and show you all that you have desired these years gone. I will keep my promise.*

Have you always used another?

Yes. When I am dormant I deliberately seek old, unremarkable bodies to live within. They don't require much effort from me and they can move around without drawing too much attention to themselves. This one is my favourite so far. He laughed nastily.

'What do mean, dormant?'

Maliz gave a despairing sigh and spoke in the old man's voice again. 'Must I explain it all? Surely you know your history. I rise when Iridor does.'

'Iridor?' Tariq clearly had no understanding of the old world.

'The Messenger.'

'Whose messenger?'

'Hers! The Goddess ... Lyana!'

Tariq couldn't help the nervous laugh that escaped. 'Lyana? Are you mad? I know Maliz was a great sorcerer once and that legend says he made some terrible bargain with Zarab, but Lyana is just someone the priestesses of old fabricated to win favour.'

'You are the one fooled. Lyana is as real as I am! I sense her coming and I know Iridor has returned — he always comes first but he is cunning. He can hide himself better than she can. I must find them and destroy them. It is my reason for being.'

'Is that your bargain with Zarab? Everlasting life?'

The old man nodded and gave his vile grin. 'Life everlasting has its advantages, Vizier. You can be part of it.'

'How do you mean?'

Someone groaned in the background but they ignored it. 'Youth. I can provide it along with all the other promises I've made.'

'I can be younger not just look younger?' Tariq asked, astonished.

'You can be anything I want you to be. You just have to tell me,' Maliz answered, his tone seductive. 'We are a partnership. You lend me your body — for a while. I bring all of your dreams true. I am not interested in your pursuits, Tariq. I have my own mission and the two don't have to conflict. We just help each other achieve our desires.'

'As simple as that,' Tariq said flatly.

'It need not be any more complicated.'

'And then you will leave my body ... when you have achieved your dreams?'

'Of course,' Maliz said truthfully. 'I have no need of it beyond such time.'

It was more tempting than ever. 'Why don't you just enter a young man's body, then?'

Maliz's patience was running out. 'You can only make a bargain with someone who wants what you're offering. You were an easy choice.' He did not add that his senses told him Iridor was near the royals so he was an obvious choice, particularly as he was so easily corrupted and desperate. 'I need someone with intelligence, with some wisdom of years and with a desire to help me as much as I can help him.' Tariq nodded, close to giving in now. 'I find the young too selfish, self-absorbed. They don't aim high enough these days. They want it all given to them. They are lazy. Not like you, Vizier. You've worked hard to make something of yourself and it's fitting that your efforts are recognised. You are everything I have searched for. Will you not invite me in, brother?'

'All right, Maliz. I give you permission,' Tariq said, hardly daring to breathe now that he'd uttered the words.

Tariq could not know that Maliz was feeling similarly tense, sensing himself so close to his prize now. 'You must say this: Maliz, come into me. Take my soul.'

If Tariq had thought through the careful phrasing he might have sensed the trap, but his thoughts were swollen with notions of power and grandeur.

He repeated the phrase dutifully without thinking.

And felt the spine-tingling entry of Maliz into his being and heard the cold, malevolent laugh of the demon as he betrayed Tariq. At the end, the person who had been the Vizier didn't even have the strength to make a fight of it. It was probably the shock of discovering what a traitor Maliz was, and all the lies that had been spun simply to have the Vizier's body for his own, that left him unable to do anything but capitulate to the mighty force that was the Demon Maliz.

He gave a sad scream of impotent rage as his soul was shredded and spat out through his own mouth in a red mist of surrender.

Maliz smiled with Tariq's mouth. The demon had risen.

～ 22 ～

Pez's hopes were answered the following morning. He'd spent most of the night talking with the Zar, who was clearly too fretful to sleep. And when the young ruler had drifted off in the early hours, Pez was too anxious to take any rest himself. The previous evening's intrusion had frightened him — it still did. Pez had never experienced anything like it before and as much as he tried to convince himself that the visitor — or whatever it was that had caused his blood to chill with fear — was somehow spying on the Zar, he could not shake off the notion that the intruder was watching him, not Boaz.

By sunrise, none of the sense of dread had left him and Pez was convinced that the invisible watcher meant only harm and he would now have to be intensely careful about how he conducted himself. Conversations with Boaz could no longer be open and honest. He would have to use his Lore skills to set up a special ring of protection around the two of them — and although that would prevent any spiritual being eavesdropping, it could alert them to magic and it would sap strength from him. It would all depend on the being itself. He would have to think on it with great care.

Dawn had also shone brightly into Boaz's bedroom, threatening another hot day, and the Zar had risen immediately and taken a bath in his private chamber.

After his first meal he began reading through some of the day's duties. But Pez could tell the Zar was restless, eager for news of Lazar and keen to think about something other than his council's advice regarding the city's homeless, the need to finance a new cistern, celebrations for the holy month ... the list seemed endless. Under the dwarf's distracting influence and his assurance that it was safe to talk openly, Boaz was soon dispensing with Bin's notes and instead discussing his idea of a picnic for all the new odalisques. It was a charming notion as far as Pez was concerned and he nodded excitedly as the young Zar outlined his plans.

'You'll need at least eight barges, High One, to carry that number of people.'

'At least they're all young and slim. If my father had done something like this he'd have needed twice as many for the same number of women.'

Pez muttered a gentle sound of admonishment. 'Shame on you, Boaz,' he said, grinning. 'The women couldn't help their size. There was nothing else to do but indulge themselves.'

'I know,' Boaz admitted. 'I understand that now and it won't happen in my harem. I'll see to it that the women have plenty to occupy themselves of a more physical nature.'

'Ooh,' Pez said, pulling a face of mock embarrassment.

Boaz looked momentarily mortified. 'I didn't mean that,' he replied archly. 'I meant —' Whatever he was about to say was interrupted by a knock.

'Come,' he called as the dwarf began rolling around the room like a ball, yelling 'kick me!' to the Zar.

'What is it, Bin?' Boaz asked, ignoring the tempting invitation.

'Forgive my interruption, Zar Boaz,' the young man said, bowing low. 'But you asked for any information on Spur Lazar to be delivered immediately.'

'What news?' he demanded and even Pez rolled to a stop.

'A runner has been sent from the Spur's house, my Zar. His manservant has returned, we're told, and he's blind drunk.'

'Jumo, you mean?'

The youngster nodded. 'I think that is his name, yes, High One.' He inclined his head, waiting for orders.

'Is the runner still here?'

'No, we have sent him away, my Zar. I presumed you would want to speak with the Spur's manservant himself.'

'And you presumed correct. Send our own men from the palace to escort him back.'

'Should we give him some time to sober up, Zar Boaz?'

'I want to see him as fast as they can bring him here. No excuses — I don't care how drunk he is. And I mean our men, Bin, not the Spur's soldiers.'

'I understand, Zar,' he bowed again and left.

'Jumo drunk? It's hard to imagine,' Pez commented.

'Perhaps he's celebrating Lazar's wellbeing,' Boaz said hopefully.

'Then why didn't the runner mention the Spur's presence? No, this doesn't sound good.' Pez felt a fresh sense of dread grip him.

Boaz gave a moue of disdain. 'Don't put the jahash on it before we know the situation.'

'I'm not cursing it. I'm telling you what I think.'

'Then keep your baleful thoughts to yourself, Pez. I'm taking this as positive news. If anyone knows where Lazar is, Jumo will.'

Pez kept his own counsel but the feeling of trepidation simply got stronger.

Jumo was brought to one of the Zar's receiving chambers. It overlooked a vast courtyard with an ornamental pool and no windows, only open archways, in order that on hot days cooling breezes could blow through the less formal meeting room. Pez loved this chamber for its beautiful tiled ceiling of blue and white. On the first occasion he had walked into this room he had instantly recognised the work of the Yaznuks, painters who had been captured and brought from the far east along with their exquisitely delicate work, most notably floral designs, that looked almost abstract from this distance. These days those designs, the paints they used and all of their techniques were a closely guarded secret held within three families who, over history, had evolved as the keepers of the art. They alone had royal sanction to produce the Yaznuk style as it was known and could mark their work with the distinctive dragon emblem.

Its beauty so mesmerised Pez that he registered Jumo's arrival by his smell rather than by sight. A stench of liquor hit his nostrils and his attention was instantly dragged from the ceiling to the doorway where the spry man, normally so contained and correct, hung somewhat limply between the grip of two of Boaz's private guards.

Pez was taken aback; as stunned, in fact, as Boaz looked, for this was more than the merry stupor of a man intoxicated. Pez managed to keep up his pretence of disinterest by circling the room and humming to himself, but his focus was riveted on Lazar's manservant who appeared ashen, unfocused and, if Pez was right, filled with grief.

'Let him go,' Boaz commanded, slightly embarrassed for Jumo, and they all watched Lazar's closest companion in life slump and then fall hard on his knees. The guards grabbed for him to keep him upright.

'Is this how you found him?' the Zar asked, dismayed. He had always known Lazar's quiet, exotic friend to be entirely in control of himself.

'No, Great One. He was smelling as highly as he does now but curiously he seemed sober.' The man hesitated as if waiting for someone.

'So what is this? An act for my benefit?' Boaz demanded, irritated more by the look of uncertainty in the man's eyes than any notion of guile on Jumo's part.

The head guard arrived and bowed low. 'Briz, explain what has occurred,' he ordered.

Pez felt a fluttering about his heart, or was it his throat? Either way he felt suddenly breathless with tension. There was something dangerous about this situation, something not right. He watched the head guard take his time to consider his words before delivering them.

'O Mighty One, moments after my men arrived at the Spur's house, so did another messenger.'

'Yes, and?'

Pez's humming got softer and the dwarf became rigidly still.

Briz was noticeably reluctant. 'That messenger brought the gravest of tidings, High One. This is Zafira, Majesty, of the Sea Temple,' he said, nodding to a tiny figure no-one had noticed until this moment when she stepped around and out from behind the guards. She tiptoed closer and bent herself in half to bow with great care to the young ruler. 'Zar Boaz,' she all but whispered.

Pez felt there was no longer any air to breathe. If Zafira was here, then everything had surely gone wrong.

Briz noted the Zar's rising frustration and hurried on. 'The priestess Zafira informed Jumo of his master's death, which occurred last night.'

Jumo let out a heartbreaking groan that gave voice to Boaz's silent, tightly held reaction and Pez's feeling of utter despair.

Jumo spoke. 'She said she would do everything to save his life,' the distraught man wailed softly.

'The Spur is dead?' Boaz queried, uncomprehending, his throat tight with emotion. It was as if the language being used was alien to him and he needed to clarify his initial understanding.

'It is the truth, Great One,' Zafira confirmed, glancing briefly towards a shocked Pez whose only cover now was to close his eyes and hope no-one noticed how still he was.

'Tell me!' Boaz growled, too stunned to make a pretence at civility toward the old woman.

Zafira, trembling beneath her azure robes, stepped further into the room and bowed once more before clearing her throat. 'I tell this tale — as I told Jumo — with the heaviest of hearts.' They all saw her steady herself and blink away the mist of tears in her eyes. 'Spur Lazar took his last breath as a great cloud obliterated the moon during the small hours of this night gone. It was an omen, Highest One, for the darkness that reigned for several minutes signalled death for the Spur from the hideous injuries he sustained at the hands of those who punished him for protecting an innocent.'

It was a cleverly couched yet nonetheless direct insult to the Zar and he knew it, as did everyone in that chamber. Zafira held her chin high, however, no doubt wondering what price she would pay for her candour.

Boaz stared at the old woman, took in the pallor of her skin and her frailty and wondered at the long night she had spent battling to save a man's life. He let the insult pass, almost felt he deserved it. As he glanced towards the once-proud Jumo a surge of pity welled up in him. He registered the shock on the face of the dwarf. And realised they all needed time to digest this tragedy. 'Leave us!' he said to the men.

'Zar Boaz, I think —' began Briz but he was silenced by his ruler.

'I wish to speak to the priestess in private. You may wait outside if you insist — I shall come to no harm from an old woman and a clearly incapacitated man, both of whom I presume have already been thoroughly searched.'

Boaz continued. 'Send messengers to the Valide and the Vizier. They will wait in the antechamber until I summon them. I will give the news to them — no-one is to discuss anything of what has gone on here. Is that clear, Briz?'

'It is, Mighty One.'

'Good. See to it your men obey my command. Help Jumo into a seat before you depart.'

With the men dismissed, the young Zar returned his attention to the old woman who had seated herself — with a nod from Boaz — next to Jumo, presently looking steadfastly at his feet.

As soon as the door closed on the last man, Pez opened his eyes. 'Zafira! I pray this is a ruse.'

Boaz noticed that she did not look him in the eye but shook her head sadly. It was suddenly all too much for her and the old woman began to weep softly. 'We tried everything. It was the poison that killed him.'

'Poison?' Boaz interrupted. 'What are you talking about?' Then more realisation. 'Pez, do you know this priestess?'

Pez nodded gravely. 'I know Zafira and she knows of my sanity. We took the injured Spur to her at his instructions.' He didn't want to say too much more about his connection to the priestess, and he knew Boaz was too filled with despair to ask why the dying Lazar would wish to go to her. 'The whip was laced with poison, High One. We only discovered this at the temple and knew it was a race against time that we would probably lose.'

'Why didn't you tell me?' Boaz yelled, himself losing some control now. 'So that's where you'd been yesterday!'

Everyone was silent for a long time.

Finally Pez spoke the truth. 'It never occurred to me until an hour or so ago that Lazar might not live. In hindsight, not telling you was wrong, Highness. Forgive me but I presumed the Spur would make his own decision about where to lay blame once he recovered. I didn't feel it was my place.'

'Not your place to tell me when you know of an intrigue that not only affects my realm but kills my head of security?' Boaz roared back. And then the anger went out of him. 'But who would do such a thing? The flogging was accepted by everyone as normal punishment for Odalisque Ana's indiscretion.'

'I'm sure the Snake would not have been used on one of your concubines, Zar Boaz,' Jumo said, raising his head defiantly and surprising them all with the vehemence in his voice. 'This was far more deliberate that you are giving credit for.'

'You're forgiven your insolent tone, Jumo, because of your

grief,' Boaz replied mildly, surprising Pez with his maturity. 'Explain the poison,' he demanded of anyone.

Pez signalled to Zafira that she should reply. 'We discovered it was drezden, Zar Boaz.'

'What is drezden?'

'Snake poison,' Pez answered dully. 'The chosen brew of assassins.'

'How do you know how to deal with it?' Boaz said, looking between the woman and the dwarf.

'I have some experience of healing snakebite,' Zafira lied. 'Lazar needed the special tea known as drezia, which is formed from the venom itself. He also needed sewing, for the wounds were savage.'

Boaz shook his head in wonder. 'And you did all this?'

She nodded. 'And anything else I could think of, but we lost him all the same. The wounds were too deep, the poison had had too long to work.'

'He was rallying,' Jumo countered angrily. 'She said if I left he would likely pull through.'

Boaz frowned at Jumo's rudeness, but Zafira jumped in immediately, squeezing Jumo's hand as she did so. Pez saw her reaction and stored it away. Zafira was hiding Ellyana. What were they so afraid of?

'I did think Jumo could be more help back in Percheron, Highness. It occurred to me that his network of contacts might yield more information and be of more assistance in the long run than him fretting by Lazar's side. The Spur was all but unconscious by that time anyway. He was in a delirium before he slipped into a coma and succumbed to the full paralysis of the poison. It was probably best his close ones did not have to witness his end.'

'Who are you suggesting brought this about?'

At this all three pairs of eyes looked wary. Pez shrugged. In his opinion it would not be politic to say the name. Zafira's expression turned blank.

'There are those who were jealous of the Spur,' Jumo answered.

'Name them!' Boaz ordered, again ignoring the man's lack of protocol when talking to his Zar.

'It is not for me to say. I have no proof.'

'Then I'll say it for you, shall I?' Boaz threatened, his ire up again. 'There are only three suspects — my mother, Vizier Tariq or the Grand Master Eunuch.' No-one said a word, so he continued. 'I do not need to defend her but you should all understand that this is not my mother's way. She loves Percheron, its security, and above all, her own. She knew who gave us this security.' He glanced to Pez who was nodding. 'Vizier Tariq has no spine. He is sly and he has ambitions, but he would not dare risk such a death finding its way back to his hands. Salmeo is the most capable of this cunning and despicable act but I can't imagine why he would do such a thing.' No-one answered him. Even Jumo had realised it was a dangerous mire he was negotiating. The accusation would not come from his lips.

The Zar continued. 'No doubt if it was Salmeo it was because he felt humiliated by the Spur undermining his authority. I imagine he wanted retribution for Odalisque Ana's snubbing of harem rules. Except resorting to murder seems an overreaction, wouldn't you say? There is more to this. And I will get to the bottom of it.'

None agreed with his reasoning but not one of them said so, each knowing that it would not bring Lazar back to them.

'Where is the corpse?' he asked Zafira, ignoring Jumo's wince at the harsh word.

'The Spur rallied momentarily before he slipped into his coma. He begged me through his delirium that he was to be given to the sea, my Zar. It was his last wish. We could not argue it for he lost consciousness.'

'Gone?' Jumo was astonished. 'He asked for this?'

She nodded. 'He was determined. I had to agree to a dying man's request. He said nothing else — he knew he was close to death.'

'Where did he die?' Boaz asked, sounding as though it was an afterthought. 'No-one could find him.'

Zafira sighed. She had not taken her hand from Jumo's. 'He died at the Temple. I had his body removed and taken to Z'alotny.'

Pez was surprised. Perhaps Ellyana did not want it known that Lazar had died in her home. He went along with the lie, unsure of why except that he had no reason to doubt Zafira. 'The burial ground of the priestesses?'

She shrugged. 'It is peaceful there and I am familiar with it. In fact it is precisely the sort of place a troubled man *should* take his last rest on this plane,' she said defensively. 'I washed his body and dressed it in fresh robes before I had him rowed out to Beloch. I dropped him out of the boat beneath the giant.' She sounded unsure. 'I thought it fitting it was done there.'

Jumo's anger held him as rigid as the statue of Beloch. 'I should have been there.'

'I couldn't find you, Jumo. I sent a messenger,' Zafira said softly. 'I'm so sorry about all of this, but I have few resources. And the Spur won my promise about giving him to the sea. He murmured something about it carrying him back to his homeland. And then he slipped away from me.'

Jumo's expression softened immediately. Gone was the anger, replaced by something new, akin to fresh pain. 'He was considering leaving Percheron for a while,' he admitted softly.

This seemed to rattle Boaz. 'Was Lazar unhappy?' he asked, confused.

'Not unhappy, Highness,' he said, choosing his words with care. 'He struck me as wistful in the days after we found Odalisque Ana. He was not pleased about being given that task by the Valide, it's true, but when you're out in the desert, Your Majesty, you can start to reflect about life and its possibilities.'

'So he was planning to leave us?'

'No, Zar Boaz. I believe he was simply wondering about his homeland, his family probably.'

'I never asked him about his childhood or life before Percheron,' Boaz replied, genuine regret in his voice. 'I wish I had now.' He rallied himself to the present. 'I will inform those who need to know about this tragedy and then I will declare three days of public mourning. Sadly we will not have a body to celebrate the passing of the spirit but we will send him off nonetheless.'

'And the perpetrator?' Pez prompted.

'And after that,' Boaz repeated, iron in his voice, 'I will have someone ride the needle for this untimely death, so help me.'

Zafira blanched and even Jumo, who had wanted something akin to revenge to assuage his grief, had not expected this.

'Oh Highness, I'm not sure —'

'I *am* sure, Pez. You have all, in not so many words, accused someone connected to the palace with murder. That in itself is abhorrent to me. The fact that the victim was a close friend of mine, someone I admired and respected for most of my life — loved even — makes me more determined to see his murderer pay. I will leave no stone unturned until I uncover the treacherous wretch. And when I do I will visit the penalty of a traitor onto his cursed body and leave him for the birds and insects to devour. He will have no burning ritual from Percheron for he has desecrated my reign with this act.'

Pez had no reply. He had never seen Boaz like this; never heard his tone so terrible or commanding.

'What about the Spur's family?' Jumo asked.

'Yes, we must send a courier, but where? We don't know anything about Lazar.'

'I will go, Highness,' Jumo said and his tone was resolute. 'I have no reason to remain here and I would welcome the diversion of tracking down his family.'

Boaz nodded. 'I understand. Organise what you need at the

palace's expense. Now, the Valide Zara and Vizier Tariq will be waiting. I imagine both of you would prefer not to meet them.' He nodded to Jumo and Zafira.

They both looked grateful.

'Pez will show you how to leave here without using this entrance. May Zarab guide you across the waters, Jumo, and bring you back to us unharmed.'

'Thank you, Highness,' he replied and meant it, bowing low this time in honour of the young Zar who had treated him with courtesy and respect when he probably had not deserved it.

Boaz turned to Zafira. 'I'm not sure how to offer an appropriate blessing to you, priestess, except may your goddess keep you safe and to say my personal thanks to you for doing all that you could to save the life of the man I called friend. I know he didn't die alone or without care. A donation will be made to the Sea Temple to acknowledge your commitment to Lazar.'

'It is not necessary, Zar Boaz,' she said gently, 'and I fear the Vizier will not take kindly to the city donating a single karel to any temple of Lyana.'

'You misunderstand me. The donation will be made from my personal coffers. I understand he died beneath the altar of your goddess. Consider it a private thank you to Lyana for watching over him in his hour of need.'

She nodded. She had not expected such grace or composure in one so young, or such tolerance. He was wise beyond his years to understand that the Valide and her sidekick, the Vizier, would happily have her stoned if they could. Neither had any time for the remnants of a bygone era.

With Pez's subdued guidance, she and Jumo took their leave through a small archway that led into the beautiful but simple Mirror Courtyard, which won its name from the reflection in the grand pool, and through a series of corridors.

Boaz waited for his visitors to be well and truly out of sight before he sat down on a divan and privately grieved. His tears fell silently but his despair at Lazar's loss was intensely felt. With his father and the Spur gone he had no adult male he could confer with — unless one counted Pez, but the dwarf, Boaz understood now, had his secrets including that Zafira was aware of his sanity. Apart from Pez there was now no-one left in the palace to call friend. And then he remembered Ana and his heart lightened slightly. He had promised to bring her news of Lazar as soon as he received it. How would he ever be able to deliver these grim tidings without her hating him and holding him responsible?

A soft knock interrupted his thoughts and Bin entered at the Zar's command.

'My Zar, the Valide is getting ...' He seemed lost for the right word.

'Testy?'

'Yes, Mighty One. She insisted I remind you that she and the Vizier await your pleasure.'

Boaz smiled sympathetically at his servant. 'Please inform the Valide that my day has been interrupted with some urgent news, which I am dealing with. Ask both herself and the Vizier to find some patience. I shall see them as soon as my time permits.'

Bin blanched. 'Are they to wait in the antechamber, my Zar?'

'Yes, pass on no further demands to me from my mother, Bin.' He smirked slightly despite his upset. 'Take a deep breath and give her my message. Then come back in here.'

'Oh this is ridiculous, I'm not a servant to be kept waiting like this,' Herezah snarled at Bin.

The personal attendant made a soft noise of apology. 'The Zar begs your patience, Valide. He has urgent matters to attend to.'

'More urgent than the one he summoned us here for?' Tariq asked, an uncharacteristic insolence creeping into his tone.

'Apologies, Vizier. Please excuse me, I must attend to the Zar's duties,' Bin replied, beginning to back away from his two indignant superiors.

But Tariq had not finished with him yet. 'And what, pray tell, servant Bin, is keeping His Highness from his mother?'

Even Herezah was surprised at the Vizier's defiance. Bin was only a servant but he was the Zar's eyes and ears too and she knew how Boaz was teaching himself to flex his wings, build his own team around him. He might not take kindly to such a pugnacious attitude from another servant, no matter how lofty.

'I am not at liberty to discuss this,' Bin said, again apologetically, albeit firmly, and retreated more hurriedly to escape further interrogation.

Herezah turned to her companion once Bin had disappeared. 'My, my, Tariq, it's not like you to be so belligerent. Aren't you feeling yourself today?' She smiled and the Vizier saw how her amusement mocked him.

It no longer affected him, of course. 'Now you come to mention it, Valide, no, I haven't been feeling myself today.' And then he laughed, equally mocking but gently done so no offence could be taken.

She lifted an eyebrow in query and noticed, as she paid him a moment's genuine scrutiny, that the Vizier didn't have quite the same curve to his back as she recalled. She'd got so used to Tariq's stoop that it never occurred to her that he might have the capacity to straighten ... and yet he certainly seemed to be sitting more upright. 'What an odd thing. You seem to be your full height again,' she said, unable to miss any opportunity to offer a couched insult.

'Thank you, Valide Zara.' His eyes glittered from beneath the bushy brows. 'I've discovered a marvellous new tonic. It's doing wonders for my health.'

'You must share your new potion with me. There's not a woman alive who doesn't want to hear about how to look younger,' she replied, frowning slightly at the new intensity in his eyes. Surely it was her imagination?

'I certainly shall,' he agreed.

'Does this remedy have a name?'

'Oh yes, but it's my secret for now,' and he chuckled softly to himself.

Herezah didn't understand his amusement but she would look into it — if there was a newly discovered herb for youthfulness, then her physic would surely know it.

'Why do you think we have been called by your son, Valide?' Tariq asked, changing the subject.

'I have no immediate idea. I thought it might be about a private meeting he had with one of the odalisques that so incensed Salmeo. But now that you're here, I have to assume the topic is of a more formal nature. Have you any notion?'

He nodded slyly. 'I think the Grand Master Eunuch will have a lot more to worry about than an unscheduled rendezvous by the Zar with a concubine, Valide Zara.'

Her attention was riveted on him now. The Vizier had the audacity to intimate he knew something about her son that she didn't! 'What is that supposed to mean?'

He shrugged but there was a self-assurance evident that troubled her. 'You asked if I had a notion and I do.'

'Tell me,' she ordered. 'If you're going to enjoy the patronage you've always desired from me, Tariq, you'd better start remembering your place. Don't play with me, Vizier.'

'Valide, I would never do such a thing,' he said, feigning surprise that she might think it. 'I just don't want to spread rumours without evidence. It is not my place to comment on Salmeo's position.'

'But you just did!' she hissed. 'Now, what do you know?'

'I only suspect, I know nothing,' he replied and this was true. Since claiming Tariq, Maliz no longer had his omnipotent view of the world. It took all of his presence and energy now to be Tariq, to work his body, to think within him, to effect the mannerisms he had studied for so long. Being the ancient Sewer Rat required such little effort, particularly as the skeletal old man did nothing much more than be still and rot. Over two centuries he had roamed from frail body to frail body, never giving himself entirely over to any of them, simply killing the soul and then hovering within the host, refusing to fully claim it. Although this lack of commitment meant he could barely move these bodies, the freedom did permit him to project himself outside the body for short periods. It was how he had communicated so effectively with Tariq's mind, but not any longer. He was the Vizier now — wholly. The next time he died, he would die in this body and then his spirit would have to lie dormant in another series of frail bodies until he felt the rising of Iridor again. Iridor always triggered his reincarnation. So from now to the moment of his next death, Maliz had only Tariq's eyes to see with and his ears to hear with. He would definitely need to increase the network of spies the Vizier had already set up if he was to keep abreast of even half of the information he'd had previously. Before becoming the Vizier, Maliz had witnessed the conversation between the Deputy Inflictor and the apprentice. It was a chance occurrence — he had been hurrying back to the old man's body when he'd overheard the exchange. There had been no mention of Salmeo in the conversation, of course, but Maliz knew who 'the highest authority' was. He understood the blackness the man's soul, admired him for it.

Herezah persisted. 'I want you to tell me what you suspect, Vizier.'

'Valide Zara, I have no proof but I believe we have been called to hear about the fate of the Spur.'

'Lazar?' He did not miss the tinge of hope in her voice. 'I can't imagine why it's taken so long.'

'Can you not?' He raised an eyebrow now. 'I think the delay is because he has died.'

Shock hit her eyes — the only part of her face he could see. 'What?' she breathed.

'I'm sure his injuries weren't lost on you, Valide.'

She was silent a moment. Her eyes continued to betray her alarm but she did her best to hide her true feelings. 'What has Salmeo got to do with all of this?' she asked with disdain.

'Everything, Valide. I suspect he not only chose the weapon wielded against the Spur, but also who would wield it.'

'You heard what had happened to the Inflictor, what he said.'

'I heard only the excuses of a young man not ready to take on the role of delivering punishment, Valide.'

'And this you say was deliberately contrived?'

He shrugged and annoyed her once again with his secretiveness. Normally Tariq would be falling over himself to share his thoughts with her. Anything to impress. 'I am making a personal observation, Valide. I make no accusation.'

'But Salmeo's absence suggests you might be very much on target.' She said what he chose not to.

'We must be patient. I'm sure we'll learn soon enough.'

He was right. Bin arrived again, bowing. 'The Zar will see you now, Valide Zara, Vizier Tariq. If you'll follow me.'

'About time, young man,' the Vizier grumbled, winking at Herezah. 'The Valide is being kept from the important business of the harem.'

She couldn't believe the audacity of the man. He had never winked at her before, never even acted playful before. What in Zarab's name was happening to the Vizier?

Once they were clear of the Zar's rooms and well away from prying eyes, Pez, who had been singing and skipping since leaving Boaz, led Jumo and Zafira into his own chamber. He became instantly serious.

'Tell us everything,' he ordered the priestess.

'I told the Zar everything in front of you. I have nothing more to tell.'

He pressed. 'Well, how about why you're hiding Ellyana?'

'Or the fact that you said the master died in the Sea Temple when I know only too well he was taken to the Isle of Stars.' Jumo's grief had hardened into anger but Pez was glad to see that the little man had it under control.

She dropped her gaze. 'It is true Ellyana requested that her presence not be spoken about. It is of no consequence that anyone hear about her or the island.'

'Why?' Jumo demanded. 'I hope she hasn't forgotten my promise.'

'That you'd come looking for her?' Zafira asked and when he nodded she gave a sad smile. 'You won't find her, Jumo. She is ...' and Zafira hesitated.

'She is what?' Pez asked, feeling the hairs on the back of his neck stand on end.

'I would have thought you of all people would know,' she replied, looking at her dwarf friend.

He stared at her for moments, thoughts raging.

'What does she mean?' Jumo asked.

Pez had his secrets but the death of Lazar changed everything. He felt he was suddenly part of a covert group. They alone knew the truth about where Lazar had spent his final hours, and why they hid this fact he didn't know. He had always trusted Zafira and there was no reason not to trust her now, and yet she was confusing him.

Jumo was glaring at him so Pez felt obliged to answer. This time he told only the truth. 'Ellyana came to me once. It was a long while ago. I was in the harem and she came in with the Bundle Women. She looked different then. She was not interested in any of the odalisques or wives, not even the servants. She was interested only in me,' he said.

'But everyone thinks you're a dozen goats short of a herd,' Jumo queried, 'so why you?'

'That's my point,' Pez answered. 'She knew otherwise. And it terrified me.'

'What did she say?'

Pez looked vaguely embarrassed. 'Well, I don't really understand it, Jumo.' He hesitated, scratched his large head. 'She said I had to discover who I truly am.'

'And what's that supposed to mean?'

'I don't know.' He decided not to tell either of them about Ellyana's mention of Iridor. Not yet.

'Anything else?'

Again Pez hesitated, considering all the strange events that had occurred recently — from Zafira's admitting that she felt she was part of something much bigger, to Ellyana's return in his life, the odd sensation when he had touched Ana, the voice in his head guiding him to the Temple, the intrusion from the invisible visitor that he could sense and now Lazar's sudden death. Bright in the middle of the mist of his mind, yet to be revealed, was the owl of prophecy, Iridor.

Jumo tired of the protracted pause. He urged the dwarf. 'Lazar is dead because of Ellyana —'

Zafira leapt in. 'That's not fair, Jumo. Ellyana did everything within her power. There are other things afoot. Things I don't understand yet. Ellyana is involved and we should trust her.'

Jumo rounded on the priestess, relishing the opportunity to release some of his anger. 'You're talking in riddles, Zafira. Let's speak plainly here. Ellyana is hiding something and you're helping her to do it. And now Lazar is dead!' His voice cracked on the final word but did not break. They could see how he was fighting his emotions. 'He was rallying I tell you. I could feel it, even if I'm no doctor. That moaning and groaning was Lazar fighting and don't try and tell me otherwise as Ellyana tried. Lazar and I have a bond that goes back a decade. You don't spend as much time together as we did and not know each other inside out. Lazar would not have given up the fight.'

'He didn't,' Zafira said, her voice suddenly cold. 'His circumstances beat him,' she added flatly.

Jumo was not ready to let it go. 'Pez, when I asked you whether there was anything else about Ellyana you hesitated. Do you want to tell me everything, or is this a secret too?'

'Why do you say that?' Pez asked.

'Because I'm sensing secrets all around me. I feel as though no-one is being entirely honest. Lazar is dead, his body already disposed of and Ellyana has gone. Is this not ringing any alarms in your mind, Pez ... or is it just me who smells something rotten?'

Pez smelt it too but wasn't ready to declare it. 'When Ellyana arrived with the Bundle Women she was young, very beautiful, but she kept herself hidden. When we spoke I thought my eyes were playing tricks with me for she seemed suddenly old. No, not old; ancient. It was as if she was giving me a warning about myself and then she was gone. It was most unsettling.'

Jumo said nothing to this, simply held the dwarf in a stare that seemed to look right into his heart.

'I forgot about her,' Pez lied, hating to do this but needing some time to sort his thoughts privately. 'But then she reappeared at the Sea Temple when we all met her. I didn't recognise her at first.'

'Yes, I remember your surprise,' Jumo admitted, frowning. 'So she has been deliberately following you, do you think?'

'I have no idea,' Pez answered truthfully. 'Have you met her previously, Zafira? Be honest,' he added, despising himself for being such a hypocrite.

'I met her for the first time when Jumo did,' she replied, 'although ever since I have felt strangely comforted by her. Do you remember our conversation upstairs in the Sea Temple, Pez, when I said I felt something was happening and that I was involved but I couldn't say what it was or why?'

'I do. You seemed unsettled, unsure.'

'Well, I think it's Ellyana who has the answers.'

Jumo turned away, making a sound of disgust.

'Forgive us,' Pez said, taking Jumo's hand, wanting to give him comfort. 'You have a sad journey to make and are filled with grief. I will give you this promise. Whilst you are away I will find Ellyana and I will seek the answers you need.'

Jumo held him securely again with his gaze. 'I will rely on you,' he said, his tone thick with emotion. 'I would track her myself if not for my duty to my master.'

'Lazar always trusted me. You can too.'

Jumo turned to Zafira. 'I can never forgive you, priestess, for disposing of my master's body without my consent.'

Zafira was equally firm. 'I didn't need your consent, Jumo. I had his.'

'Nevertheless. Nothing I've heard rings true to the man I knew.'

'I am sorry for you in this. Make your journey and after your return we shall talk again when you are more able to understand my position.'

Again Pez noted the strange wording. She was being so careful about how she spoke.

Jumo nodded, too angry to speak about it any further. 'I go. Have either of you any idea where to begin?'

Pez sighed. 'Yes, I do, although this was a secret Lazar shared only with me.'

Jumo's eyes narrowed. There had never been secrets between him and the master. 'Why would he tell you?'

Pez shook his head as if to say he didn't truly understand it either. 'Perhaps so that in the event of this very situation of his death ... that someone knew.'

'Why not me?' Jumo asked, the hurt evident in his voice.

'Because it would have affected your precious relationship with him, Jumo. Lazar loved you too much to compromise the friendship you shared.'

'Tell me!' Jumo demanded, breathing hard suddenly.

Pez looked to the priestess. 'If you'll forgive me, Zafira ... I gave my word a long time ago that I would share this knowledge with no-one but Jumo should the time arise.'

She looked intrigued but put her hands in the air nonetheless in mock defeat. 'I understand. I shall wait outside and then we can return to the Sea Temple together,' she said to Jumo.

He said nothing, and as she left, Pez fixed him with that strange yellow gaze of his and said: 'You believe that Lazar is from a noble line in Merlinea. He liked to pretend he wasn't from an important family but you have always suspected otherwise ... that he was running from them; perhaps a second or third son who hadn't reached his potential, or someone banished for having an affair with the wrong woman.'

'Something like that,' Jumo agreed, his tone giving away nothing.

Once again Pez sighed. 'Lazar's real name is Lucien. Does that give you any inkling?'

The small man shook his head, said nothing, although this news clearly startled him.

The dwarf gave Jumo his final shock for this day when he said: 'Lucien is ... was, not from Merlinea at all. He is the heir to the throne of Galinsea. He is King Falza's eldest son.'

~ 23 ~

Boaz declared three official days of mourning for the death of the Spur of Percheron. Messengers would be sent out into the various quarters of the city to make announcements of Lazar's passing. No actual details of how he had died would be given, even though the Zar knew rumour would become rife very quickly.

At the shocking news Herezah had retired to her chambers and demanded not to be disturbed by anyone. Boaz re-confirmed simply from her reaction, that his mother had nothing to do with Lazar's punishment and subsequent death. The stillness of her body as she received the tidings, the horror she couldn't hide in her eyes and the slight trembling of her voice when she asked a tentative question gave him more than enough proof that the Valide was as devastated as he was — no doubt for different reasons.

The Vizier had been a surprise. There was something different about him; something about the way he listened so thoughtfully before offering comments that would normally be rushing out of his lips in his attempt to impress and be part of any royal conversation. Boaz even found himself appreciating his steadfastness when the Vizier cautioned against overreaction.

'May I humbly suggest you take your time, my Zar. This situation is grave indeed, and if our Spur has, as you imply, been hurried to his death, then it will not do to leap to conclusions. A proper inquiry should be made, formally appointed and delicately handled. Let it take as long as it must until the guilty party is hunted down. The Spur was too admired by too many for justice not be seen to be done … especially so early in your reign.'

Boaz had not expected such level-headedness. He knew of the acrimony that existed between the Vizier and Grand Master Eunuch. It was based on years of jealousy, highlighted since his father's passing, and their collective desire to win his mother's trust. Of course neither man had reckoned on the young Zar wanting to have any involvement in the running of the state. They thought of him as merely a boy, that the mother would rule as Zara until he reached an age when he was ready for such responsibility. Boaz estimated they had counted on at least three or four years of autonomy, by which time it would be hard for the young Zar to wrest back full control of his realm. Well, they were wrong. Boaz had every intention of taking full control now, before misconceptions about his right or fitness to rule could arise.

He had dismissed both his mother and the Vizier but not before he made a point of thanking Tariq for his wise words. Boaz had waited for the usual preening of feathers and plumping of chest; instead he had been surprised once again when the man had hardly blinked at such a compliment. Instead he had bowed graciously and simply said: 'My Zar, call upon me whenever you need.'

Boaz had watched the Vizier gently guide his mother — slightly astonished by the man's graciousness — from the room, careful not to lay so much as a fingertip on her person. The Zar frowned, prompted not just by the Vizier's behaviour but also his straighter bearing. The man's stoop had improved. He would need to talk to Pez about this sudden metamorphosis, he decided now. But first, he must order money to be given to Jumo, then he would need to speak with Odalisque Ana and break the news that would surely shatter her.

Jumo walked with Zafira in a simmering silence back to the Sea Temple. She had the good sense not to try reasoning with him again but she felt her own heart fracture when she watched him finally kneel by Lyana's altar and kiss the dried smear of blood where only yesterday his master had lain dying. It was too much. She took the risk and knelt by the softly keening manservant and put her arm around him, expecting a sharp rebuttal, but none came. His anger was spent; now it was all grief and in this Jumo knew they shared a common despair.

'I'm so sorry, Jumo,' she whispered. 'So sorry for doing this to you.'

They remained there in silence for several minutes before Zafira painfully pulled herself to her feet. 'I shall leave you to your thoughts and private prayers,' she said. 'When you're ready, let me share quishtar with you before you leave.'

Later, as she busied herself with her brew she heard men's voices but did not go down to investigate. Soon enough she heard slow footsteps on the stairs and turned to see Jumo standing in her small room.

'Ready to go?' She tried for a gentle brightness.

He nodded. 'The Zar has sent money,' and she saw a pouch in his hand. It looked heavy. 'It is too much, far too generous. I came to ask you if I might leave some behind ... here? Perhaps you can make better use of it in Lyana's work. Lazar was always impressed by those who serve the Goddess.'

'That's because his people worshipped her more recently than here. It took longer to get rid of us priestesses in Merlinea.' It was not said with any malice.

'Lazar believed in no gods, Zafira. Not yours and not Percheron's.'

'That's sad to learn. It probably means at some time in his life he has been badly let down. It is interesting to me, though, that he was drawn to Lyana that day before you all left to find the new girls for the harem. We spoke then about the Mother Goddess. He felt a special pull to her statue, said she gave him a sense of peace.' She took a step towards him, her tone beseeching. 'Jumo, this needs to be said. I understand the depth of your sadness but you must recognise it as grief not hate. Lazar would not want you to hate me.'

'Not you, Zafira. Ellyana.'

'Please, I beg you, allow some room in your heart — she made hard choices but for the right reasons.'

He shook his head. 'She made choices beyond her authority. I should have stayed. Perhaps he might have lived if I had. And if not, at least I would have been with him as he died. I cannot forgive her. She has no place in my heart. You are a pawn — perhaps I'll find some room to forgive you, Zafira, but not yet.'

It hurt her deeply to hear these words. She wanted to tell him more about Ellyana but fear stopped her. 'Don't leave the money. The Zar is already donating some and you might need it — you have no idea what you're going into, how long you'll be. I presume you now know how far you might need to travel to find Lazar's people?'

He said nothing in response to her mild prying. He was still incapable of believing Pez's tale and had deliberately stopped thinking about it for now. Crossing the Faranel would give him plenty of time for dwelling on this great secret of Lazar's.

Fortunately Zafira was far too sensitive to his situation to press him. 'Keep the money, for safety's sake. You can always leave it later on your return.'

He tucked the pouch inside his robes. 'Then I shall go. I thank you for the offer of quishtar, but another time perhaps when some wounds have healed. I have a ship to find.'

Zafira nodded her gentle understanding. 'Then go safely, Jumo. I shall look forward to a healing quishtar with you on your return.'

And he was gone, his footsteps retreating down the stairs and padding softly across the stone of the temple floor. She watched from the vantage of her window as he emerged into the quiet of the long peninsula and walked away until he was lost in the crowd and action of the busy harbour. She wondered if she would ever see him again or whether Lyana herself would ever forgive her for hurting a good man so deeply.

Zafira steadied her thoughts. She had to find Pez again. She had forgotten to give him something important, something Lazar had insisted upon him having — another aspect she hadn't been truthful about. It frightened her to have it herself. Zafira knew the old stories — what this statue of gold signified chilled her to the marrow.

Iridor was rising. And she was instructed to give this statue to the strange, mysterious dwarf she called friend but knew so little about.

Boaz summoned the Grand Master Eunuch, who was shown in, puffing from the exertion of meeting the urgent call to the Zar's chamber.

Boaz gave no time for polite preamble. As the hefty man completed his bow, the Zar was already talking. 'Did you request Odalisque Ana be readied for a conversation as instructed?'

'Yes, Majesty. She is being prepared now, although I would caution —'

'Salmeo, I am tired of everyone in this palace cautioning me. I shall make myself perfectly clear for the last time to you and to those who would question my authority. I will make my own decisions, good or bad, and should I ever require your counsel, I shall seek it. Until then, just follow my instructions as I have already outlined to you!'

Salmeo seethed beneath the expressionless countenance he had mastered. 'Of course, my Zar. We have only your best interests at heart.'

'Then perhaps you can explain why I have no Spur of Percheron.'

The eunuch looked around him, as if he thought the Zar was speaking to someone else. 'Majesty?'

Boaz reined in his anger. He'd had years of experience watching Salmeo in action. It would be a pity to waste that knowledge so early in their new relationship by showing the eunuch that his Zar could be foiled, pushed into explosions of anger, manipulated in any way. 'Lazar, our Spur,' he reminded calmly. 'I'm wondering if you have any thoughts on how unwise it is that we no longer have Percheron's highest-ranking member of our security force available to us.'

Salmeo appeared taken aback. 'Well, Highness, I suspect there is much healing to be done before he can sit a horse again or command the men.' He struggled to say more, then added to be helpful: 'A few days perhaps?'

'A few days? You were standing quite close, Grand Master Eunuch, I'm sure the extent of his injuries were not lost on you.'

Salmeo affected an innocent shrug. He closed his eyes, as if sympathetic to the Zar's observations. 'Yes, Shaz made a bad job of it, my Zar. I have confined him to his quarters since, not that he's up to much. He himself admits he botched it.'

'And yet you had felt confident he could carry out the sentence,' Boaz reminded him.

'Zar, I didn't have much to choose from. Someone had to do this task. His superior assured me that Shaz was the best available. He is apparently adept with the whip.'

'Yes, the whip, for flogging servants and other dissidents within the palace. Perhaps even for striping a wayward odalisque who needed reminding of her place. He had never even been allowed to touch the Snake before. I'm sure you were aware of this.'

'I could not be sure of this, Highness. Time was short and his superiors were not available for lengthy discussion.'

'Did you know that Shaz has never flogged anyone before, only dummies in the practice courtyard?'

Salmeo shook his head slowly. 'My Zar, this is the first I've heard such a thing. How do you know this?'

Boaz knew when he was being fed an untruth. He ignored it. 'Have you heard any news about the wellbeing of the Spur?'

'No, Zar. But I gather the Vizier has sent out parties of runners. Has he failed you in this?'

'News has arrived, Grand Master Eunuch, but perhaps you've been too busy with harem matters to hear it.'

Salmeo disguised his wrath. He would personally deal with the Elim spies who had not reported such a thing. 'Oh, Zarab be praised. I'm pleased, High One. I did hear that a party of messengers was sent out a few hours ago and I hoped that was to deliver news of the Spur.'

Boaz fixed the fat eunuch with his best stare, one he'd learned from his father. 'Yes, Grand Master Eunuch. New messengers have been sent at my behest to spread news of the Spur's death from his wounds.'

'His death,' Salmeo repeated softly, his hand across his heart.

'Are you surprised?'

'I'm shocked, Zar Boaz. The injuries were bad, I'll grant you, but the Spur was strong, still a young man. If he had the right care the healing might have taken a while but ...' His voice trailed off. 'Dead,' he echoed, still seemingly unable to accept it.

Boaz was confused now, although he worked hard to not show this in his hard expression. He had hoped to confront Salmeo into some sort of confession, or that Salmeo would at the very least let slip some information that might indicate he was behind the murder. Perhaps the Grand Master Eunuch really was innocent and aspersions had been cast without proof.

'It's all my fault, Zar Boaz. If I hadn't stuck to such tradition then the Spur would have been spared. It's me who has killed him. No-one else's fault.' The man was deeply upset and struggled down to his knees. 'I have inadvertently killed him through my actions. Oh my Zar, I was only trying to do the right thing. You are young and we all want to support you, make the transition as easy as we can. I thought that by making an example of Odalisque Ana, we could prevent any further embarrassment to the royal family. Who would think Spur Lazar would take it upon himself to take her punishment?'

Boaz was taken aback. He suddenly felt out of his depth, wishing for once his mother was nearby to offer advice. Was the eunuch weeping? Yes he was. Boaz wanted to look away but knew he mustn't.

'You might have spared the Spur the Viper's Nest, Salmeo. That in itself was unnecessarily cruel and in my opinion a punishment that did not fit the crime.'

Salmeo opened his arms wide in a plea. 'Oh, Zar Boaz, I would have. It was never my idea to use the Snake. You must believe me. I have never called for it before and never would unless there was a traitorous act.'

'If not you, then who?'

'No, Zar Boaz. I take full responsibility. I cannot blame anyone else for this. I permitted it but I promise you from my heart, Mighty One, I was trying to do the right thing.'

'Salmeo, there is more to this dark deed,' Boaz warned and watched the man grow still. His black face was already slick with tears and perspiration but somehow it seemed to darken as his eyes widened.

'What do mean by that, Great One?'

'Please stand,' Boaz commanded, discomfited by the huge bulk of the Grand Master Eunuch imploring him from his knees. The man took several seconds to heave himself back to his feet with the aid of some furniture.

Once again he towered tall and Boaz was relieved that he had himself chosen to stand on a raised part of the chamber or he would have felt as Pez always must. He cleared his throat. 'Lazar's injuries were horrific but we know this was mainly the result of an amateur's work.'

Salmeo nodded. 'He should not have died from them.'

'Well, we shall never know. However, what sped Lazar to his death was the use of poison.'

'Poison?' Salmeo uttered in disbelief.

'Drezden apparently. Have you heard of it?'

'Yes.' It was used by Zars long ago.

'What!' Boaz said, aghast.

Salmeo looked mortified. 'Great One, this is my fault alone. Your father asked me to dispose of the small amount remaining in the palace. It was safely under lock andkey and I had forgotten about it until now.'

'Really,' Boaz said dryly.

'But when did the Spur drink it Great One? If he consumed it before he was taken to the Courtyard of Sorrows, then the perpetrator could be anyone outside of the Palace.'

'This is true. Except one presumes that if it was administered orally Lazar would never have made it to the flogging. He would have died then and there.'

'Not necessarily, High One. Drezden, as I understand it, is a very slow killer. That's the point of it. It gives the murderer time to retreat.'

'I see. Either way, drezden was not swallowed by the Spur.'

'Oh?'

'From what I can gather, the tips of the Snake were dipped in the lethal potion and it entered his body via the wounds from the flogging.'

Salmeo's shock was complete. 'No,' was all he could say, vehemently shaking his head, flesh wobbling tremulously beneath the sober robes he had chosen this day.

'Who chose the Viper's Nest if not you, Salmeo?' Boaz urged.

'I can't —' Salmeo groaned.

'You must, Grand Master Eunuch, or the full blame of the Spur's death will rest on your shoulders. I will not lie to the people about this. Answers are required. Someone must pay for the murder of this man.'

The eunuch wept harder. It was disconcerting enough to watch this normally arrogant man humbled, but to hear him cry was the most uncomfortable Boaz had felt in his life. 'It was Horz, my Zar,' the Grand Master Eunuch suddenly blurted out. 'Horz, the head of my Elim guard. He said he was going to get even with the Spur but I didn't believe it. I kept hoping that in his drunkenness he was just talking rubbish,' Salmeo explained.

'Horz?' Boaz queried. The Head of the Elim was one of the most trustworthy and sober people he knew.

It was as if Salmeo could hear his thoughts. 'Horz had a grudge against Lazar,' he continued.

'What are you talking about? What grudge?'

'Horz is related to Odalisque Ana, Great One. He is brother to her father. He resented that she had been brought into the harem to be made a concubine. Perhaps her father is furious — she mentioned that he did not sanction the sale.'

'Ana's uncle?' Boaz's mind was reeling. 'She never mentioned it.'

'Why would she? Ana is secretive by nature, but I make a point of knowing all I can about our odalisques, Majesty.'

'And he used the drezden? Are you sure?'

'Who else? He has access to it. Only he and I have keys to the dispensary. And once we had heard about Spur Lazar's intentions it was to Horz I turned to help me set up the flogging. I briefed him and left it to him, my Zar. It was Horz who chose the Viper's Nest. Believe me when I say it was a shock to me too, to see that vicious weapon being brought out. But by then it was too late — what could I do?'

'Intervene?' Boaz offered, angry.

'But that would have looked so bad. I have invested my faith in Horz, Great One, as you invest yours in those who serve you well. He has been a model Elim, and ever since taking over as head, he has been exemplary. I trust him completely and so I would never have compromised his position by undermining his authority at the flogging. I was surprised, but having been told that Shaz was the best new Inflictor, I felt it would be handled with caution. Furthermore, once you commuted the sentence —'

'Which you didn't seem to agree with,' Boaz interrupted.

'That is true, Mighty One. I don't believe in ignoring tradition and forgive me if my expression reflected such reluctance.' Salmeo stopped talking, breathing hard from his urgency to explain.

'So Horz had the motive and the opportunity you say?'

'That's right but I thought it was mere talk — the talk of the liquor — it never entered my mind that he would actually fulfil his wish for revenge.'

Boaz sighed, deeply disturbed by all that he had heard. 'Family honour is a powerful thing.'

Salmeo nodded sadly. 'I take full responsibility, my Zar. Horz was appointed by me. He is my man.'

'Don't be ridiculous, Salmeo. You didn't ask him to do such a thing or guide his hand. This is murder — a calculated killing, and I will not tolerate it in my palace.'

'What will happen?' Salmeo asked, a new and plaintive tone in his voice.

'He must pay for his crime. I will require a full confession from Horz by sundown. Bring him to me just before the feast gong. I would prefer not to handle this on a full belly.'

'Yes, my Zar.'

'Salmeo, for the time being this is between us. If I discover that anyone has learned of Horz's actions or our discussion then your head will roll with his. I want to know the truth from his lips before I make my decision.'

'I understand, Zar Boaz. I will prepare him.'

'Will he be honest?'

'He is an honourable man, Great One.'

Boaz nodded. 'I wish to be alone now to consider all that I've heard. I shall see you in an hour. Please have Odalisque Ana brought to me then,' he said mournfully and the Grand Master Eunuch heard the sadness in his Zar's tone.

Salmeo bowed low and then turned to leave. The Zar could not see the way the scar on the Grand Master Eunuch's face lifted with the man's sly grin.

∾ 24 ∾

The man looked sickened. 'Lie to the Zar? Admit to a terrible sin I did not commit?'

'Unless you want your family slain, Horz,' Salmeo warned conversationally. The Head of the Elim looked stunned. 'Or did you think I didn't know about them?' his chief continued, slyly now. 'I know everything, Horz. I know that you were once married and have three children — two boys and a girl, as I understand it. I know that your wife died — your error in making her travel during an illness — and that your brother's family has raised your children whilst you, as a penance of sorts, offered yourself to the Elim.'

Horz's face had drained of all colour. He stood before the Grand Master Eunuch pale and rigidly still.

Salmeo looked at his nails, made a mental note to have the slave do them again this evening. 'I know more. Your children live with one of your brothers — your eldest. Your other brother is a goatherd in the foothills. His marriage is less than perfect but he has five children — one of them is not his. The middle girl is an orphan, adopted by your brother. Her name is Ana and she was found by Spur Lazar, purchased fairly and brought to the palace. Except the negotiations were with the shrewish wife, not your brother, and he is hurting and you are angry that one of your own has been given to the harem. Odalisque Ana recognised you but did not give you away — she's a clever girl. She'll cost me more grief than I deserve, I'm sure, but she protected you, Horz. It was you who gave yourself away. I knew nothing about your brother in the foothills until I began to make enquiries after your reaction at the presentation of the girls. You were so protective towards her I became suspicious and those suspicions were confirmed. It's simple, Horz. I need a scapegoat and you're the perfect solution. I couldn't possibly take the blame myself.'

The Elim said nothing, presumably understanding all too clearly now that he was staring into two pits — both dark, both horrible. One meant death to the family he loved; the other meant death to him. There was no choice really.

'Now if you go along with my suggestion,' Salmeo said softly, his lisp more noticeable as a result, 'I will give you my assurance — a blood assurance if you insist — that I will take care of your children. Your sons will have money and some land or a shop if they wish and a house each of their own in the city. You may choose. Your daughter I will help find a good man for … someone she likes, I promise, someone who will treat her kindly. A rich man. She will want for nothing. Your brothers and their families will receive an annuity each year in gold and camels. Even in your most vivid dreams you couldn't have hoped for this much.'

Horz shook his head sadly. 'This is true.'

'It's how much I value what you will do for me. I pledge it. All this will occur if you'll lie for me … and die for me. You are Elim after all.'

Again the man stayed silent.

'And if you will not lie, Horz, then your family will die. Not just your children but both of your brothers, their wives and all their children between them. I hear the youngest is just a summer old. Pity. There is nothing you can do, there is nowhere they can hide. You should know,' Salmeo said to the proud man who now gazed fearfully at the ground, trembling, 'that I have already sent men to encircle your people.'

Horz looked up sharply, hate radiating from his dark eyes.

'Oh come now, did you expect anything less? Of course I've already despatched men, killers too, but they will not act until they've heard from me. Does your family live or die, Horz?'

Ana was led in by two senior eunuchs and she immediately sensed that the Zar was not in the playful, chatty mood from the previous day. He also did not dismiss her escort. This was a formal meeting then.

She eyed him through the slit of the charcoal veil she wore tonight over her creamy loose pantaloons and billowing chemise. Ana was glad that the veil hid her fear. The Zar's grave countenance could mean only one thing: he had bad news for her. It was obvious. Lazar was not coming back in a hurry.

Why she had held such hopes that he would be striding through the marble corridors within days was beyond her. You didn't have to be wise to see that Lazar's injuries were so horrific it would take months for him to recover. And this was all her fault. Her selfish attitude had brought about his suffering. Remembering how he had looked at her before the flogging, she knew in her heart that Lazar had already forgiven her, but could she ever forgive herself? She doubted it.

Ana swallowed hard and reminded herself that this soul-searching was yet more self-centredness for she was already wondering how she would cope without a glimpse of Lazar or a chance to hear his voice. She loved him. She wanted to tell him. She had tried but he had not been able to see her mouthing the words behind her veil; she could only hope her eyes conveyed her feelings truly. He would laugh and perhaps rightfully so. She was a child in his eyes but he had sold her into the harem for an adult's role. If she could make love to the Zar, she could make love to the Spur.

Oh shame on you, Ana, she chided silently as she watched Boaz approach. *Your wicked thoughts will dismantle you,* she warned herself.

Ana watched Boaz approach and then fell to her knees and

flattened herself as she had been taught, arms spread wide in supplication.

'Please stand, Ana,' Boaz commanded graciously.

She did so, straightening her robes but not giving him eye contact until she was given permission. She intended doing everything the right way from now on, and then she would earn the palace's affection and hopefully Lazar's respect.

'I wish to talk with you privately but I've asked the Elim to remain. Let us move here so we may not be overheard.'

She nodded, wondering at the secretiveness or why Boaz needed the Elim today when he hadn't needed them yesterday.

'You may look at me, Ana. It would please me,' he said and she heard the struggle in his voice.

She decided to help him. 'My Zar, I believe that you have called me here this afternoon to give me news of the man who so generously offered his own skin to save mine. Thank you for keeping your promise.'

Boaz didn't look any happier for the aid. 'Your intuition serves you well, Odalisque Ana. Yes, this is about Spur Lazar but first I must ask you something.'

'I'll answer whatever you wish to ask, Highness.'

'I want your truth,' he counselled and she could see how determined he appeared. 'The man called Horz, do you know him?'

'He is the Head of the Elim, Highness,' she answered immediately but carefully.

Boaz's serious expression did not waver. 'I know this. I want to know if you know him outside of this role.'

Ana blinked. 'He is my uncle,' she said softly. 'I hardly know him but I have seen him once prior to the palace, when he came to visit my father and our family. It was a long time ago but I don't forget faces, Highness.'

'I see,' Boaz replied and she could see a swell of disappointment overcome him. Was this not the honest answer he cautioned her for?

'My Zar,' she began, leaping to the wrong conclusion, 'he has shown me no special treatment. I have hardly seen him since my arrival other than to be presented with the other odalisques and he was in the Choosing Room. He also was in charge of me at the flogging but we did not exchange so much as a word. He pretends not to know me and I him.'

Boaz sighed, knowing Ana could never understand why he had asked this question. 'I thank you for your honesty.'

'You look so unhappy, my Zar. I am sorry for this. Please unburden yourself and give me the tidings of the Spur — the pain is mine, for the fault is mine. I know he was badly hurt and I suspect you are disappointed that he will be out of service for a long while.'

She saw Boaz's eyes widen slightly. There was deep grief hidden in that startled expression and there was pain in the way his mouth twisted, urged itself to say the words.

'Ana, it is my sad duty to tell you that Spur Lazar will not be returning to the service of Percheron.'

She heard him clearly but what he said didn't make sense to her. 'Has he gone away?' she asked, feeling injured that Lazar had not sent word of farewell.

'Yes he has gone away for good you could say,' Boaz admitted. 'He has gone to his gods, Ana.'

She cocked her head slightly as if listening to an inner voice. She couldn't seem to grasp his meaning.

'Spur Lazar died in the early hours of this morning, Ana. It was confirmed by an old priestess from the Sea Temple.'

'Zafira?' she whispered, hardly knowing she uttered it.

'Yes. He died in her arms. She has disposed of his body as he requested.'

Ana was trembling. Boaz signalled to the Elim, who were at her side in moments, preventing her from falling.

'He died from his wounds?' She began to wail softly. 'How can this be?'

'I have no further information,' Boaz lied, not willing to discuss poison or murder at this stage.

'He can't be dead,' she groaned. 'He can't. Have you checked with Jumo, my Zar?'

'Jumo was here with me this morning, Ana. He is as upset as you and has agreed to find Lazar's family and pass on the news with my deepest regrets.'

'Jumo's gone to Merlinea?' she stammered, no longer thinking straight, just talking, saying anything to keep the horror at bay.

'Yes. Ana, you need to lie down. This is a shock for you. The Elim will take you back to your chambers and something will be given to help you sleep. We shall talk again soon.'

'Boaz, no!' she shrieked, ignoring all protocol. The Elim gripped her hard, angry at her manner with their Zar.

'Stop,' he ordered them. 'Be gentle with her. Carry her back to the harem and if I hear of a strand of her hair so much as pulled from her head you will both pay.

'Ana,' he said, gently, not wishing to touch her in front of the Elim but wishing he could cup her face or hold her hand, 'go now. We will know more soon. He would want you to be as brave as he was.' He looked to one of the men. 'Ask her maid to ensure a soporific is given immediately. She must sleep off her shock and someone must be with her the whole time. Pez will do.' He saw their puzzlement. 'He's mad, yes, but he's also company and he can soon alert the harem when she wakes or if she needs anything. Do as I command. Find him and tell him I said he's to stay with her.'

He looked away as the baffled men, unsure of how to order Pez to do anything, ushered the silent, grief-stricken figure away.

Pez took one look at the tear-stained face and understood immediately that Ana had learned the shocking news.

'... and you're to remain here with her, dwarf, do you understand, you fool? Zar's orders,' an Elim was saying.

He ignored the man, humming to himself, but made sure that as the Elim bent down to make his point that he sneezed into the man's face. And then kept sneezing, much to the man's horror and disgust. Pez could see the man's fingers twitching into a fist, desperate to make the dwarf pay for such insult.

'Don't,' the Elim's mate cautioned. 'It's not worth your own skin. He's mad, you know.'

'Sometimes I feel as though he knows exactly what he's doing,' the first one grumbled, wiping his face. 'Come on, let's go.'

Mercifully, they left and Pez was able to turn and lay his hand on the slightly feverish forehead of the restless young woman who moaned softly in a drug-induced sleep. Pez felt it immediately, tingling through his palm and travelling up his arm until it entered his body proper and warmed him throughout. It was such a strange sensation — as though her fever had been passed into his body — and yet it was a comforting feeling. As long as he kept his hand there, the sense of glowing within remained. The sensation no longer disturbed him; it intrigued him instead.

She stirred. Her eyelids fluttered open but she wasn't seeing anything. The warmth running through Pez intensified. He half expected Ana to sit up and then walk in her sleeping state — he had seen others do this — but she didn't. She began to murmur instead. At first he realised she was speaking a language he did not understand and then the words issuing appeared to dissolve into Percherese. He still could not decipher most of it, for she was mumbling.

Then everything changed. Her grip on his hand became intense and there was a sense of urgency; her body was rigid although her eyes remained unfocused.

'Pez.'

Her voice sounded distant, odd. Now he did feel the crawl of fear. 'I'm here, Ana.'

'Tell Lazar I'm sorry.'

He did not want to lie but did anyway so that she could feel safe. 'I will, although he needs no apology.'

Pez frowned as warmth through his body increased.

'The owl is yours.'

'What?' he muttered, close to her ear

'Get the owl, Pez.'

A sudden chill shivered through him, despite the heat he was experiencing. 'The owl?'

'Zafira has it. Get it now!'

'I will, I promise,' he replied, baffled.

Pez watched Ana's grip relax from his wrist, her body became limp again and she slumped into deep sleep, her lips slightly parted, her expression no longer troubled but serene.

'The owl', he said quietly to himself, not understanding any of it. What should he do? He had orders but if he sneaked away now the Elim would just think he was being his usual contrary self. However, these orders came from Boaz and that made it more awkward. Somehow Ana's need felt more desperate. He could claim she would not calm herself until he left her side, or something similar that could not be disputed.

He made his mind up. That searing heat through his body was too strange and frightening to ignore. And anyway, he had good reason to visit Zafira. She was going to tell him one way or another how he would find Ellyana. He had an oath to keep to Jumo.

Boaz had spent the last hour steeling himself for this confrontation. It hurt him to think that he might have to deal severely with a man he admired whilst ignoring the one he despised. Boaz couldn't fully believe Salmeo — not knowing his history as such a cunning man — and yet he could not disbelieve him outright. The fact of the matter was, however, that if Horz admitted to this shocking deed then Boaz would have no choice but to bring the full weight of his crown behind the punishment.

It was treachery of the highest order — not just the slaying of a man of rank but a man close to the Zar, his absolute protector in fact. The people would demand no less than death and nothing honourable about it either. More serious than all of this, of course, was the betrayal from within. That Boaz could be treated so traitorously by one of his own, especially one so close in the prestigious Elim, demanded the most punitive retaliation. If he did not act with the utmost severity it would set the tone for his reign that he was spineless.

Bin sombrely announced the arrival of the Grand Master Eunuch and the Head of the Elim.

'Bring them in,' he ordered.

Bin disappeared momentarily to the study and returned with the two visitors. Salmeo bowed low but Horz prostrated himself.

'Stand,' Boaz ordered and watched the Head of the Elim return only to his knees, head bowed. 'Horz,' he began, glad his voice was free of all the tremors he had feared. 'The Grand Master Eunuch has shared — most reluctantly, I might add — some information that has devastated my feelings about the Elim. I gather you know what I refer to?'

'I do, my Zar, but I beg you not to blame the Elim for this deed. Its honour is intact, for the act you refer to is all my own doing.'

'So you admit it?'

'I admit that it was my sole doing, High One.'

'Say it aloud so we are clear, Horz,' Boaz stressed.

The man swallowed hard and Boaz could see his hand trembling. 'I killed Spur Lazar with poison that I stole from the apothecary. Without the Inflictors' knowledge, I dipped the tips of the Viper's Nest into the lethal potion known as drezden.'

He fell silent. Salmeo nudged Horz with his toe and the man began speaking again. 'I had already blackmailed the head Inflictor into leaving his post on a pretend excuse; the deputy, Rah, was ill. It left only the apprentice, Shaz, who I was sure would botch the flogging, particularly using the snake whip which

I insisted he use.' The man was speaking with the detachment of someone reading a prepared script.

'Stop!' Boaz commanded. 'Grand Master Eunuch, would you leave us for a short while. I wish to speak with Horz alone.'

Salmeo gave a soft, bouncing bow, although Boaz did not miss the glare he threw towards the Elim.

'Look at me, Horz,' and the man reluctantly lifted his head.

Boaz looked at the angry eyes and the defiant set of the mouth that belied the humble tone and the willing confession. It didn't take much to put the scenario together in his mind and he regretted deeply now not sending a runner to fetch Horz far earlier and confronting him with Salmeo's claims as he stood before the Grand Master Eunuch. He felt suddenly empty. 'I thought as much,' he said sadly. 'What has he got over you, Horz, that you would lie for him? It can't be loyalty, for what you're admitting to surely goes against everything you stand for, have always stood for.'

They both knew what he meant.

Horz took a moment to compose himself and when he spoke it was evenly said, no wrath flavouring his words. 'I am not lying, Highness. I am honourable in this confession.' His eyes silently said something different.

It broke Boaz's heart but he was helpless. It was obvious that Horz had somehow been compromised but the man was openly and determinedly confessing to a murder and it was he alone who must take the full blame. Bin was called and told to readmit Salmeo, who flounced in confidently but was careful to keep his expression sombre as he bowed yet again.

'Is everything all right, my Zar?'

'Yes, everything is perfectly as you described it, Grand Master Eunuch,' Boaz replied archly.

Salmeo inclined his head in thanks and Boaz had no choice but to allow the Head of the Elim to continue to weave his sad lies.

It was done. Boaz imagined Salmeo was inwardly gloating, although his expression betrayed nothing but intense sympathy for the kneeling figure.

'We will require a formal witness from my council for sentencing,' Boaz said. 'Bin?'

The manservant stepped forward from the recesses of the chamber. 'My Zar?'

'Fetch the Vizier, and I suppose you had better fetch the Valide Zara too.'

The servant bowed and left the room, urgently calling runners. Boaz excused himself but without much courtesy. He could no longer bear to look at Horz or the smug Grand Master Eunuch without wanting to hurt both of them for thinking he was so gullible.

But, as his father had constantly counselled, information is power. Boaz knew about Salmeo and the eunuch no doubt understood this. It gave Boaz some satisfaction to know that the fat man was now in his debt and might never feel as comfortable again in the Zar's presence.

Bin was surprisingly swift in rounding up the Vizier and the Valide prior to supper.

He returned again to the study. Horz had not moved from his kneeling position, although Salmeo had deliberately distanced himself from the criminal. Boaz felt the flutters of anger again at the chief eunuch's audacity but he damped them down, knowing them to be a useless waste of energy.

'Mother, Tariq,' he acknowledged and both bowed. Once again he was struck by the new posture of the Vizier. His eyes were definitely deceiving him for the man seemed ever straighter, taller than he had just a few hours previous — even his complexion looked less pasty. His mother, by comparison, looked deeply unhappy in her dark garments with no adornments whatsoever. She looked almost as though she were in mourning.

He wasted no further time on courtesies. 'You are here to witness the sentencing of Horz, Head of the Elim, who has confessed to the premeditated murder of Spur Lazar.'

Herezah gave a soft sound of shock. Not much surprised the Valide but this statement had. Tariq, Boaz noted, said nothing and in fact barely flinched at the news, suggesting either he didn't care or, more likely, the man knew more than he was sharing.

'Grand Master Eunuch has assisted in winning this confession,' Boaz replied, his words couching the silent threat to Salmeo.

'And what reason, my Zar — if you don't mind my inquiry — has Salmeo wrung from Horz for wanting to murder our Spur?' It was said innocently enough but Boaz looked sharply at the Vizier. It seemed Tariq had already discounted Horz's involvement in Lazar's death too.

The eunuch demurred. 'It is not my place. I shall leave that to our Zar to explain.'

Boaz briefly filled the newcomers in on the facts.

'Because of that girl!' Herezah exclaimed, angry now. 'She is more trouble than she's worth — first the escape, then the Spur's flogging and now we learn he's been slain because of a father's anger on her behalf.'

'Mother, please,' Boaz calmed.

But Herezah could not let this go. Her anguish at the realisation she would never again look upon the Spur had crystallised this past couple of hours and her sense of self-pity at losing him had turned to anger. She could not forget Joreb's counsel to her to keep Lazar close to their son. Now she was fearful for her little lion and especially for her position and power that she had worked so long and so hard to attain. It spilled over. 'She's a goatherd's daughter, a peasant! We've lost Lazar because of her.'

There were too many underlying agendas for Boaz's comfort. The myriad feelings emanating from the various people in this room had very little to do with sorrow that a good and senior man had lost his life to deceit.

'Silence!' Boaz said, more harshly than he intended. 'Bin, you will record this and name the Valide Zara, Vizier Tariq and the Grand Master Eunuch, Salmeo, as witnesses.'

Bin nodded in the background, preparing to scribe the details.

'Horz, please stand.'

The tall man finally stood.

'You have confessed to the murder of Spur Lazar and thus you will be taken from here to the Palace Pit where you will await execution. You are viewed as a traitor to Percheron and will be accorded the appropriate punishment.' He glanced towards Bin, who looked up quizzically.

Boaz no longer cared for sensitivity. 'Horz, you will ride the needle at the bell of midday tomorrow. Until then you will be given no food, water or companionship. You will not address the Elim, and you will not be permitted to speak with any family members. You have betrayed your Zar and your country. Thus your corpse will rot on the needle to be a warning to all who choose to betray me.'

Boaz could hardly believe the vehemence in his own voice, although the pain reflected in Horz's face almost undid him as he understood how harshly his words injured a man who had never been untrue to his Zar.

He would privately see that Horz had retribution, but sadly not in this life. Horz would have to enjoy his satisfaction from Zarab's Kingdom.

'Begone from me,' Boaz added. 'May Zarab offer you the sanctuary that your Zar cannot.' And he knew Horz understood his careful words of regret.

~ 25 ~

She turned at the sound, rising from her chair. 'Oh it's you.'

'You knew I would come, Zafira.'

'Can I offer you something?'

'Information only this visit. I can't be away long.'

'Then sit, Pez, you're making me nervous.'

'Have you reason to be?'

He noticed how she rubbed her hands against her robe. 'Why would you ask such a thing?'

'Because you're uncomfortable and I've never known you to be anything but entirely relaxed in my presence.'

'Sit, Pez.' She sighed. 'This has been a difficult few days.'

'I can imagine,' he replied, seating himself on the only comfy chair in the room.

Zafira lowered herself back into one of the harder, upright chairs at her table. 'You want to know where Ellyana is,' she said, reading him accurately.

'I gave my word to Jumo.'

'Please, Pez, I can't answer any more questions.'

'Why, Zafira? What are you scared of?'

'You would be scared too,' she groaned, turning to face him now and, despite her anguish, marvelling again at his likeness to a bird. She knew which one now and it struck her as uncanny that it had taken her so long to see this.

'If I knew what?' he demanded.

'Why I have been told to give you this,' she said quietly, reaching into her robe and bringing out a small gold sculpture. Her hand trembled as she held it out to him.

Pez frowned. How could Zafira know that this was why he was here? 'An owl? It doesn't belong to me.'

'It does. It always has. It just has to find you each time.'

Pez shook his head. 'I wish I knew what you were talking about, Zafira.'

'This statue was given to Ana in the bazaar before she was formally taken into the palace. She asked Lazar to look after it for her because she knew she would not be permitted to keep it in the harem. Ana told Lazar that it was to remind him of her. She did not expect to see him again.'

'She was wrong.' He didn't mean to sound so petulant but he was feeling frustrated and scared.

Zafira nodded. 'Lazar kept the owl. He planned to keep it close as Ana had begged, but at the island,' she faltered slightly here in her telling. Pez stored this moment away to think on later.

'Yes?' he prompted.

'He tried to give it to Ellyana.'

'Because he knew he was dying?'

Zafira shrugged.

Pez tried not to show his dissatisfaction at her evasiveness. 'You're going to tell me she refused.'

'She did. Ellyana said the owl makes its own journey to whom it seeks. She told Lazar that Ana had made her choice who to pass it to and Lazar must now make his choice. She cautioned that it must pass forwards, never backwards.'

'I see. How was Lazar to know who was the next recipient?'

'Ellyana said his heart would tell him — he must follow his instincts.'

'Lazar chose me,' he said flatly.

She nodded slowly, her eyes locking now with his.

'I have no idea why,' Pez said airily. 'I've never seen it before and I'd prefer not to keep something so obviously valuable about me.'

'Pez,' she urged, her voice hard now. 'Let me tell you in whose image this statue has been crafted.'

He knew he didn't want to hear what she was going to say next. He heard the warning bells in his mind, felt the beat of his heart warning him to flee, but he was trapped in the chair as if the weight of the world was pressing him down into its cushions. He also knew who the owl was.

'This is Iridor. And he belongs to you.'

As if mesmerised, or under some sort of hypnotic spell he'd witnessed Yozem practise against gullible folk, Pez reached out his hand. Everything inside screamed at him to refuse it but he watched in dread awe as the red jewels of the eyes sparkled with what seemed to be their own fire.

Accept me, Pez, it urged in his mind, and whether he thought he was imagining that voice or not, he answered its call, taking the owl into his palm and closing his fingers around its searing warmth.

Then he vanished.

He was in the desert and he could hear his own panicked breathing but he could not see anything for it was night and it felt as though the Samazen was whipping up about him. He didn't feel frightened though; strangely enough he felt comforted by the warmth burning within him.

What had just happened? Feeling stupid he called out Zafira's name but his voice was fractured and carried away on shifting sands that seemed to swirl about him.

There was nothing to do but exist there. He wasn't sure whether he was still sitting or whether he stood. He couldn't move for fear of what might occur; perhaps he was on a precipice or at the top of some great dune. He had no idea and, fright aside, he had no inclination to move. It felt oddly safe here amid the sounds of the Samazen with a fire burning inside, but soon enough the noise of the sand and wind died away. The clouds that he thought had been covering the moon were not there, perhaps never were. The great silver orb hung low and beautiful in the night sky whilst millions of stars winked at him. Pez sighed out a long breath of pleasure. Wherever he was he wished he could remain here.

Pez.

He replied instinctively. *Iridor?*

Thank you for knowing me.

Why am I here?

To fight her battle once again.

The Goddess?

He imagined whoever owned that voice nodding. *Lyana must prepare for her war but the Messenger must rise first.*

And I am the Messenger?

Yes.

I don't understand.

You have been chosen, Pez, as others have been chosen before you.

What is my role as Messenger?

You are wise counsel to those who protect and nurture Lyana. You are their friend. You are eyes and ears for them, for her. You tell her what she needs to know.

But that is you, Iridor, not me.

We are one.

How can that be?

Because you are chosen. Release me from the statue. Let our spirits combine.

How?

You have already opened your mind to me. Now open your heart. I am friend, not foe. I will never hurt you or those you love, but we together are warriors for the battle.

Against Maliz?

336

Yes.

Has he begun remaking himself? Pez asked, astounded, remembering the old story.

Yes, it is done, but he does not know who Iridor is for this fight.

How will we know who he is?

You will discover, as he will discover you.

The notion of what was being discussed suddenly felt too large. It overwhelmed Pez. *Are you sure it's me? You can see me, can't you? An ugly dwarf, a supposed imbecile? What can I possibly do, how can I—*

Hush, Pez, the voice soothed. *You were born this way in order to be Iridor. You learned early how to hide your true self. You have known your abilities since very young . . . and you have hidden them well. Accept me fully, Pez.*

Is that my name?

Your earthly name, yes. Your heavenly name has always been Iridor and all of us who worship the Mother see nothing but your beauty.

At this Pez thought he might have wept. He couldn't be sure. The voice talking to him was gentle. It demanded nothing. It simply asked him to join the fight, make use of the powers he had been gifted.

Do I belong to Lyana?

Of course, you always have. She loves you and you are her closest friend.

The calming words, the gentle voice, the warmth throughout his being, told him to accept this special task.

I won't let her down.

You never have. When you awake we shall be one but you cannot come into your full power yet, though it will be soon. Until then you will still have questions. Listen closely to those who can help you.

And the desert night blazed into a silvery fire.

He sucked in a huge breath and realised Zafira was standing over him, her face a mask of worry.

'Pez!'

'What happened?' he said, mostly out of a shocked response to her nearness and concern.

'You tell me. One minute we were talking and the next you became silent, rigid in the chair. I couldn't reach you. I was talking to you and pulling at you but you were like the statue you grasped so hard in your fist.'

He relaxed the white-knuckled grip, his hand opening slowly to reveal a silver owl and the jewel eyes that were no longer red. They glittered yellow now, as if all the gold from its body had been absorbed into its eyes. He realised they were the colour of his own eyes; his strange yellowish eyes that had always fascinated and repulsed people.

Zafira gave a sound of exclamation. 'What's happened to you, to it?'

'I don't know how this has happened,' he claimed truthfully. 'I . . . I felt like I was travelling.'

'When? Just now when you were like stone?'

He nodded. 'I can't remember what occurred,' he added, deciding to lie now. He was not ready to share his secrets with Zafira and his mind was suddenly aware that an ancient knowledge lay within. He couldn't touch it yet for it sat dormant as the spirit had promised. He wondered when would be his time.

Zafira was still talking anxiously. 'You called my name but then I felt as though I'd lost you.'

Pez was silent. He knew he was shaking. 'I can't remember anything,' he reiterated, wondering why Zafira herself looked as shocked as he was feeling. 'I do remember what you told me though. I have some questions.'

'Ask them,' she said, no sign of her concern dissipating.

'The old woman in the bazaar who gave the owl to Ana —'

She knew what he was going to ask. 'Yes, it was Ellyana.'

'She was also my Bundle Woman.'

'I know.'

'So she deliberately sought me out and then with the same intent went after Ana and Lazar. Why not just give me the owl when we first met?'

'Pez, I don't know as much as you think I do but I gather that Ellyana was drawn to all of you as she was to me. She was compelled you could say. The owl finds its own, as I have explained. And when Ana approached her, Ellyana realised this was the young woman she was seeking. Lazar, I'm not sure. He could have simply been a bystander.'

'Then why would she try and save his life?' he prompted. 'It doesn't make sense.'

'Compassion?'

He snorted. 'Don't play me for a fool, Zafira. I'm not suggesting that Ellyana's cruel but she is obviously very focused. Her mind is set on one thing — whatever it is — and it involves me and Ana and I'd suggest Lazar as well as yourself. There was nothing coincidental about her arrival at the temple and there was nothing casual about her decision to aid Lazar. She wanted to save his life, needed to save his life. He is as involved as the rest of us. But now she's lost him — that's where it all falls apart. How did she react to his death? It must have been a shock'

Zafira shrugged, looked awkward. 'I was too upset to take much notice and it's not as though we had much control over poison.'

'Yes, but you recall she was so calm at the temple and even mentioned that she should have guessed something like this would happen. She was perturbed but not terrified for his life as the rest of us were. It was as though she knew something we didn't. And still he died.' He shook his head. 'It just doesn't make sense. Didn't you talk to her? Hasn't it struck you as odd that she's turned up now?'

'Yes. But, Pez, I lack your inquisitiveness. Since she arrived at the temple my feeling of being unsettled has disappeared. She is a fellow priestess and her quiet presence has calmed me. I am enjoying not questioning my existence any more.'

'So what has she said to ease your anxiety?'

'That we are sisters and that I have already contributed to the Mother.'

'There must be more,' Pez pushed.

She hesitated.

'Tell me,' he urged.

'She said that Lyana was coming again. She knew because Iridor was rising. Ellyana assured me that my work was just beginning and I would be instrumental in aiding Lyana for the battle ahead.'

Pez had no response to this. It was as disturbing to him to hear this as it was for Zafira to repeat it. They were both involved, then, in the resurrection of the Mother. They stared at each other, helpless.

'And I'm Iridor,' he said finally. He still didn't want to believe it. Still couldn't, in truth.

'Yes, that's what I think Ellyana must have wanted you to understand, why she gave this to Ana presumably, hoping it would find its way to you in the harem. But Ana gave it to Lazar ...' Her voice trailed off.

'And still it found its way to me,' he finished her thought for them both. Pez sat forward and took her hand, a plea in his voice. 'But how do we know this is truth? What do we know about Iridor? How can we possibly accept that I am this ... this —' He couldn't bring himself to say it.

'Demi-god?'

He nodded.

'So tell me what you do know of Iridor.'

He sat back, despondent. 'Very little. An owl apparently.'

She looked suddenly excited. 'He hides himself from others, listens, gathers information and he takes the form of a silvery-white owl at will.'

He feigned a smile. 'Well, I fit the bill on the first three but that last item surely counts me out. I ask you, Zafira, do I look like a bird?' His voice was filled with amusement at such a notion.

'As a matter of fact you do,' she surprised him.

He snorted his derision. 'A silvery-white bird?'

'Come with me, Pez,' she said softly.

'Where?'

'Over here,' she said, standing and walking towards a small bureau that had her comb and brush, her chain with the Cross of Life pendant and a few other possessions, including a pretty ornamental hand mirror worked in silver. She picked it up. 'Look at yourself.'

And Pez did, taking the mirror from her hand and staring into it aghast. He had never cared much for his reflection at the best of times but now he was stunned.

'My hair's gone white!'

∽ 26 ∽

When Ana woke the following morning, Pez was back at her side. He was wearing a madly coloured knitted cap, which hugged his squarish head to make him look all the more ridiculous in the multihued clothes he was wearing.

'Do you like my new garb?' he asked.

She gave a wan smile. 'No-one will miss you in them.'

They both looked sadly at each other for a few moments and Pez reached to take her hand.

She looked earnestly into his strangely yellow eyes. 'Is it true? Not just a bad dream?'

'Lazar is dead,' he said as gently as he could, although the words still caught in his throat. It felt as though he was speaking a lie, no doubt because he wasn't ready to believe in such a loss either. 'Jumo sailed yesterday to find his family. And Horz will pay with his life today for murder of the Spur.'

'Horz?' she exclaimed, fully awake now. She sat up. 'He did not do such a thing.'

Pez gave a small shrug. 'No-one knows the truth, child. He has admitted it to the Zar in front of witnesses.'

'Then he has been forced into speaking a lie.'

'I'm sure that notion hasn't gone undetected, but there is nothing to be done about this. And it should not be something that affects you anyway.'

'The death of an uncle?' she said, her voice hard and flat. 'No wonder Boaz asked me to confirm it.'

'Call him the Zar, Ana. It's important you keep your head very low now. Are you telling me Horz was kin to you?'

She nodded, glad for the admonishment. 'I promise you I will be careful.' Her eyes filled with tears. 'Yes, Horz is my father's brother, but we kept it secret.' She shrugged. 'Neither of us said anything about it when we first saw each other in the Choosing Room and we kept it that way. Pez, I'm not sure I want to live. My life is stretching out before me. It looks long and pointless in the harem. And now with Lazar dead because of me ...' She couldn't finish.

He pulled out a spotted silk square. 'Dry those eyes, Ana, and bury that hurt, I beg you. There is no-one in this harem who cares about you now but me. I will protect you as I promised Lazar. Lazar is gone, though, Ana, and he would have been gone for you anyway. You would not have been permitted to see anyone other than the harem members or the Zar. You must accept it. Put it from your mind.'

She looked at him as though he spoke in a different language. 'Put him out of my mind? How can you ask this of me? I loved him,' she said fiercely.

He was not shocked by her admission. Pez glanced around and made a hushing sound. 'So did I, child. And whether or not it was the same sort of love, it matters not. I will miss him, so will Boaz, so will Jumo, but we must all get on somehow. You must rise above your pain and forge a new life, for you would never have been permitted to love him except as a distant memory. I gather you've already caught the Zar's eye — that in itself should give you hope.'

'To be his concubine, you mean? At his beck and call, to service his sexual needs?'

Pez gave a tutting sound. 'You do view it dimly. Give the young Zar a chance. You may be surprised. He is not obsessed with carnal pleasure. He is actually something of a scholar, and charming company. I was thinking of something way beyond concubine for you, Odalisque Ana. I see no reason why you will not be a wife, if not Absolute Favourite.'

'It doesn't change anything, Pez,' she said morosely. 'I'm still a prisoner.'

'Only of your own mind. The Zar is talking about change. He's planning a picnic for the girls — and that's just the beginning.'

She looked at him. 'You mean I can effect change through him?'

He grinned. 'Good girl. Look ahead, Ana. Pretend Lazar is not dead. Just tell yourself you can't see him any more. It's what they would have done to you anyway. Time will heal that pain in your heart, I promise. Make your own destiny, child.'

His words roused a new sense of hope. 'Has anyone ever told you that you look like a bird?' she said suddenly and regained a small sense of her amusement at the look of surprise that claimed his face.

After the previous day's unpleasantries Boaz was taking his first meal late, slumped in a small alcove off his main study. It was an eating chamber that his father had built a few years prior so that he could take a private meal during a working day.

It was fully tiled — every last inch of wall was covered in beautifully glazed squares, each bearing a fruit. It had been quite a daring design for its time, and in fact still was, and yet it was one of Boaz's favourite chambers in the whole palace. He loved that it was his, even though he was not paying it his usual sense of wonder.

The Zar munched absently on the meal that Bin had personally laid out for him, the intuitive servant deciding that the last thing the Zar wanted was a team of fussing attendants, putting out food and waiting on his every whim.

Bin had assumed correctly and once again Boaz was grateful to his servant's ability to anticipate his needs. He was replaying

Horz's confession over in his mind as he chewed on some roasted lamb smeared with a pungent garlic and yoghurt sauce. It was delicious, cooked specifically for the Zar much earlier this morning in the private kitchens of the royals, but he tasted none of it, not even the fat ripe figs also picked that morning. Bin would do the right thing and let the Zar's dining staff know that the food had been enjoyed. They worked hard, striving to satisfy the palate of the youngster who was still not adventurous with his food but needed to develop a sophisticated taste so he could entertain and be entertained in style.

The kitchens never stopped, their fires fanned every hour of every day to prepare hundreds of dishes for the countless people in the palace who needed to be fed. They took up one whole wing; a dozen huge chimneys billowing smoke all day and all night in separate units that were linked by short corridors. The harem was normally serviced by three of these units, one devoted exclusively to the Valide Zara and the wives. These had not cranked up to full output yet, of course, for the new harem, but it would not take long. Another eight were given over to dignitaries, soldiers, the Elim and all the other people attached to the palace. The final one stood alone in a closed unit. This was for the Zar's food. He had his own vegetable and herb gardens. He even had his own orchard. No food ever crossed from any of the other units into this one. The kitchen staff was hand-picked and trained rigorously, not just in cooking, but in discretion as well as security. Bin was aware that a good relationship with the kitchen team meant they would always go to extraordinary lengths to please their Zar. It also meant they would be vigilant and never permit strangers to have any access to his food. This last point was of paramount importance.

Bin mentioned it now to the young Zar as he entered to re-fill Boaz's glass. 'My Zar, the Vizier has made a suggestion that I think has merit. Perhaps you'll permit me to mention it?'

'Oh yes? What does he suggest for me?'

'Well, my Zar, Vizier Tariq is mindful that without the Spur our security is compromised. Until we find a worthy replacement —'

'There is no worthy replacement,' Boaz cut in. 'There is no replacement at all in fact. I am not ready to accept his death and so I have no intention of putting another man into that position.'

'Of course, Great One. Well, in the absence of that position Vizier Tariq wants to throw a permanent guard around your kitchen. He thinks it's a fundamental aspect of palace security, that everything connected with the Zar is checked, double-checked and triple-checked and nowhere is more vulnerable than where your food is prepared.'

Boaz was surprised. Tariq showing concern? If anything Tariq had treated him with not very well hidden disdain when he was nothing but a prince and even around his father's death the man was condescending. 'And when did he suggest this?'

'Last night, my Zar.'

'Who does he think should do this?'

'He believes there is no-one more trustworthy than the Elim. He thinks the Valide should select the team. She knows all of the more senior members of the Elim.'

'He says this even though one of the Elim has proven to be a traitor?'

Bin said nothing to this but when Boaz glanced at the man's face he could see that Bin and presumably the Vizier believed the story of Horz's treachery almost as much as when Pez told them all once that he could fly.

'I should like to see the Vizier.'

'I shall summon him immediately.'

Vizier Tariq was announced and there was none of the usual flouncing bows that Boaz expected.

'My Zar,' he said softly, and he touched his hand to his lips and heart as he bowed graciously.

Boaz immediately noticed how sombrely the Vizier was dressed — this in itself was unusual. But the surprise was noticing that gone were the tinkling bells and sparkling jewels from the beard. In fact the beard was no longer forked. It ended in a neat plait. The normally ostentatious affectations were vanishing before his eyes, Boaz decided.

He couldn't help mentioning it. 'Vizier Tariq, are you well?'

'I am, thank you, High One,' he said, straightening.

'No, I mean, you don't seem quite . . . er, yourself.'

'How odd, my Zar. Your mother suggested the same thing only yesterday.'

'Nothing's wrong?' Boaz enquired.

'Not at all. I don't believe I've felt better in fact.'

'Good,' the Zar replied, unsure of what else he could say. 'Please, join me,' he added, gesturing towards a long cushion on the floor opposite him.

'This is a wonderful chamber,' Tariq said. 'Your father had such fine taste in art forms.'

'Yes. I wish he hadn't worked so hard to hide it.'

'I'm not sure he did. Just look at this room,' he said, sweeping a hand gently around him, 'it is so advanced for the age. And consider all the additions he made to the palace — each has superbly enhanced its beauty but paving a way for its future rather than looking to its past glory. His wives, especially your mother, were chosen with an eye not just for their exquisite looks, but for their intelligence. Whatever his own desires were in terms of whom he spent his time with, he was again looking to the future. He wanted heirs with nimble, shrewd minds.'

Boaz had never heard an observation from the Vizier in all the years he had known him. Tariq was usually one for agreeing with the powers-that-be.

Tariq was not finished. 'And his faith in his own judgement has been borne out in you, my Zar, if I may say so. From what I know of you, there is a very good blend of the finer qualities of both of your parents.'

'Oh yes?' Boaz replied, amused now. 'What have I won from my mother?' He knew the Vizier would normally lavish him with praise now but he was intrigued to know how the man would handle this question.

'Her looks obviously,' he said matter-of-factly. 'But from what I can see, since you've assumed your new role you also have her intuitiveness. And that is a quality to be admired.'

Sparse, direct, brief. Boaz was amazed. 'And my father?'

'Well, your father was shrewd indeed. I'll admit his interest in life around him lapsed towards the end of his reign but he will be remembered for his incisive decisions. Joreb — may Zarab keep him — was never one to shirk making his stand. Right or wrong he made decisions swiftly. You showed that same courage yesterday, my Zar, if you don't mind me mentioning it. That was a very difficult situation — and not one any of us would like to have faced. No-one present could be anything but impressed with your composure and ability to make that toughest of all judgements. Sending a man to his death is easy if you have little conscience.'

There, it was said. Boaz had to swallow his desire to leap onto the Vizier's comment, carefully couched to suggest that it was clear Horz was lying and taking the blame for a dark deed he played no part in.

'It weighs heavily on my mind nonetheless,' Boaz followed up, equally careful not to commit himself one way or the other.

He saw the recognition of this flash briefly in the Vizier's eyes before it was shrouded. The man was applauding him. 'It was the right decision to make, my Zar, if that helps.'

'I've been struggling with it ever since,' Boaz admitted in spite of his suspicions over the Vizier.

'As you should. If you didn't that would be more curious. Of course the whole business of the Spur's death is a curiosity, wouldn't you say, my Zar?'

Tariq cut a path deep into Boaz's pain. He felt powerless to hide his own feelings with the Vizier using such honesty. 'I will not rest easy until I have the truth,' Boaz confirmed, glad that he didn't overreact to such a brutal question.

'So you doubt Horz?'

'How can I? The man has confessed.'

The Vizier said nothing but the searching look said droves.

'I suspect there is far more to the truth than we have learned,' Boaz answered more fully. 'That is what I will search for in my own way and over time. For now the people will be satisfied that justice has been seen to be done.'

'Bravo, my Zar. You are thinking like a pragmatist.'

For the first time ever Boaz felt proud to be complimented by the Vizier. 'May I offer you some zerra, Tariq?'

Tariq smiled inwardly. 'I would be delighted, High One, thank you.'

Bin, who had been quietly attending from the shadows of the room, now lit only by two hanging oil lanterns, emerged from his dark corner to pour out a glass for the Vizier.

'Thank you, my Zar.' He sipped and his expression of pleasure said enough about the quality of the zerra. 'There are some changes I'd like to effect. If you would permit I would like your kitchen to be permanently observed by the Elim.'

'Bin mentioned this. Is it really necessary?'

'I wouldn't say it if I didn't think it was important, my Zar,' Tariq said, belatedly realising what a contradiction that was for anyone who knew the old Vizier. This was confirmed by the grin that the Zar could not force back. 'Do I amuse?' Tariq asked, knowing full well he did in this instance.

'Forgive me, Tariq, whatever this change is that has come over you, I just want you to know that I appreciate our conversation. Are you aware of how different you sound?'

'My Zar, may I be candid?'

'Please.'

Tariq sipped again. 'I respected your father enormously but it served my purposes to behave the way I did in the past. I can't put it any plainer than that. Your father came to his throne a grown man, quite set in his ways and with a lot of experience under his belt. I was newly appointed and I had to quietly assume my role, ingratiate myself with the right people to win their trust. That has taken years.'

Boaz couldn't help himself. 'Tariq, my father didn't respect you very much. I know he didn't like you,' he said, more bluntly than he had intended.

'Did you think I didn't know this?'

'I must say I have to wonder when I consider some of your ... shall we say, affectations,' Boaz admitted. He was confused by Tariq, mainly because he'd spent a lifetime ignoring the man, disliking him in truth, but now found himself impressed by his calm counsel and insightful comments.

'That's all they were, High One. Affectations. It helped me to disappear ... don't you see?'

'No, frankly I don't.'

'Sometimes, Zar Boaz, people will portray themselves a specific way with the deliberate intent to shield others from their true selves.'

'Why?'

'Defence. Invisibility. The peacock you saw was all that you saw. You never knew behind that facade worked a shrewd mind.'

'A modest one too,' Boaz countered.

Tariq shrugged, sipped again, a smile at his lips. 'I'm merely explaining it for you.'

'So it's all been an act?'

'That's perhaps exaggerating it. I have always done my work diligently — I'm sure your father never complained about that.'

'No, not at all. In fact, I heard him say on countless occasions that as much as he disliked your presence he couldn't fault your efforts.'

'And the reason I climbed to the position I have,' Tariq replied, as if this justified his behaviour.

'Wouldn't it have been easier to be yourself and earn respect along the way?'

'Perhaps, but then I wouldn't have learned as much as I have.'

'What do you mean?'

'Zar Boaz, my presence at the palace is only part of what I do. My real job is to listen in on the streets, to hear what your people are grumbling about, their needs. I have a network of contacts to run and it has suited me to appear flamboyant and shallow because people never took me seriously. They talked around me, over me. They thought my appointment as Vizier a jest but figured I was someone who could be easily compromised.'

'And can you be?'

At this Tariq smiled. Boaz could honestly admit that he felt he was conversing with an entirely different person.

'Zar Boaz, I am revealing the true Tariq to you so that we start out truthfully in your reign. You are young — I don't mean that as insult — and you need sound counsel. Your father never needed someone like me in quite the same way as you do. I am offering myself up honestly to you. I hope that we can work closely and that you'll trust my judgement, hear my advice, include me in your decision-making.'

Boaz took several moments to consider the Vizier's request. He wanted to be sure he chose his words carefully. 'Vizier Tariq, until yesterday I intended to begin distancing myself entirely from you. I disliked you even more than my father did, for I didn't even respect the role you played.'

He watched the man nod in humble acceptance of these harsh words.

'But you have surprised me. I would be lying if I didn't admit that I feel as though I am sitting here tonight with an entirely different man.'

'Does that mean we have a future together, Zar Boaz?'

'That's precisely what it means. It will not happen overnight, of course, Vizier. You must earn my trust and respect. But what I want most is for you to understand that it is me who sits the throne of Percheron and not my mother. I think too many people are getting this around the wrong way, yourself included.'

'You have made yourself perfectly clear, Zar Boaz. Perhaps I might begin our new relationship by organising for the guard around your kitchen?'

Boaz nodded.

'Is there anything else I can do?'

'Keep me informed.'

'My Zar?'

'I want to know everything you do. All that you learn from the streets I want shared with me. You are the one promoting this partnership, so prove it. Show me that I can trust you.'

'And what's in this for me, Zar Boaz?'

Boaz's eyes flashed darkly. 'That's the old Vizier talking!'

'No, Highness. The old Vizier would not have had the nerve. You've proven yourself to be pragmatic, so continue in that vein. Nothing in life is free, my Zar. You might think it is because of the wealth you own and the power you command, but everything comes at a cost ... everything.'

'What do you want? Riches?'

Tariq laughed. 'No. I want the title of Grand Vizier.'

Boaz was no longer surprised. He could now see where this was leading. 'Equal status to Salmeo.'

'Yes, my Zar. Too long I have been treated as his inferior. I want the same privileges and freedoms he enjoys.'

Boaz nodded. If Tariq continued to impress he would not find it difficult to agree to such a request. 'We have a bargain, then, Vizier. Earn my trust and my respect and you will earn yourself a promotion.'

'Thank you, Zar Boaz.' He raised his zerra. 'To your reign, High One. I will work diligently and unrelentingly towards your goals.'

'You do not know them yet,' Boaz replied a little mischievously.

'Oh, but I intend to learn them, my Zar. I shall begin by learning more about the last hours of the Spur. Is that a good beginning?'

Boaz raised his cup to the newly reinvented Vizier and the curious alliance they had made tonight. 'To new beginnings,' he replied and drained his wine.

And deep in the shadows someone, that neither man knew was there, grimaced.

↝ 27 ↜

Salmeo brooded in his chamber. Horz had been immoveable but he could sense the anger and suspicion emanating from the young Zar nonetheless. It was not directed at Horz either. It was levelled quite obviously at himself. This meant he was not free from the Spur's blood smears just yet.

'I am an impetuous fool,' he murmured to himself, regretting for the umpteenth time his rage that had led to the poor decision to bring drezden into the equation of the Spur's punishment. As it was, Shaz had done a far uglier job than even Salmeo could have imagined and it was highly likely that the Spur would have died from his injuries alone. The risk taken with the drezden, having to use others, incriminating himself, had been for naught.

It was not at all like him to act so recklessly. Now, in the calm after the storm of proceedings, he could see how careless he had been and how close he had come to ruining his life. He had thought drezden undetectable — damn the interfering priestess! How she could have identified it was beyond him.

He needed to cover his tracks. The Head Inflictor was still away in the far north, which was convenient. His deputy had been compromised with similar threats to his family and a small parcel of land. He had been easier than Horz, who had no need for land or wealth, but of course everyone can be bought if you threaten those they love. That's why no-one could ever

354

compromise the Grand Master Eunuch — he loved none but himself. With Horz taking the blame, the Deputy could be kept quiet. That left only the youngster, Shaz, who might possibly know something. Presumably the lad had quailed at the job, which meant he must have asked questions of his superior. Salmeo's agile mind thought it through. The Deputy had to tell him something and most likely would have ordered him to do as he was told and that they had no say in this. Shaz was young but not mindless — he could work it out for himself that the only person capable of giving an order that could not be questioned was the Grand Master Eunuch himself.

Salmeo pulled a grape from the glistening bunch of black fruit one of his attendants had delivered with a plate of shelled carrack nuts. He bit down on the grape, enjoying the explosion of juice, letting it trickle down his throat as he considered his position. He spat the seeds out. Yes, he knew what he had to do now.

Boaz was feeling uplifted by the Vizier's visit. It was such an odd sensation to actually like the man and yet Boaz couldn't help it.

Just then Bin emerged looking slightly uncomfortable. 'It's the Grand Master Eunuch, my Zar. He seems very agitated.'

'Important, you think?' Boaz asked.

The man nodded. 'I believe it is.'

'Show him into my study. I don't want to see him here.' Bin turned to leave. 'And he is not to know that I've been with the Vizier,' Boaz added as an afterthought and regretted it by the crestfallen look on his servant's face.

Boaz knew Bin was far too discreet to do such a thing but Salmeo had a way of finding out anything and everything.

Bin reappeared. 'He awaits you, my Zar.'

Boaz nodded, made the eunuch wait another three minutes before he stepped into the study. 'You asked to see me, Chief Eunuch,' he said, knowing how Salmeo preferred to be addressed by his grander title.

'Forgive me for the interruption, my Zar,' the huge man replied, bowing.

'I imagine it must be important.'

'It's about the Spur.'

'I thought we'd settled that. I want to put it from my mind. It is not easy passing sentence on a man's life, especially one as seemingly loyal as Horz.'

Salmeo fixed a chastened expression on his face. 'I can only imagine. But my conscience weighs heavily, my Zar.'

'Explain why.'

'Thank you, High One. I've been wondering how Horz could achieve such an act as dipping the thongs of the Viper's Nest into the drezden without an accomplice. You see, my Zar, although the Head of the Elim would have access to the dispensary — and thus the poison — he would not have such ready access to the whips. These particular instruments are looked after by the Inflictors alone.'

'Well, we've established that the Head of the Inflictors was away, am I right?'

'Yes, my Zar, he still is.'

'So that negates his involvement. And his Deputy was unwell?'

'That's correct, Zar Boaz. Rah was running a high fever. I sent my own physic to care for him,' he lied. 'The physic can corroborate how sick the Deputy Inflictor was.'

Yes I'm sure he can, Boaz thought viciously. 'Is he any better?'

'The fever has run its course, Zar Boaz, but he is still unable to work. At the time of the Spur's flogging he was unable to hold himself upright.'

'So that leaves us with who?' Boaz asked, knowing with a deep sense of pity whose name was about to be announced as an accomplice to murder.

'There is only one other person, my Zar, who could open the weapons bureau. That's Shaz.'

'Now why do you think a young man like Shaz would agree to being involved with murdering the Spur?'

'There is only one thing that propels most men into dark deeds, my Zar.' Salmeo's lisp was pronounced now as he spoke softly and with cunning.

Boaz smelled a vague breath of violets wafting over him. 'And what is that?'

'Money, Zar Boaz. Money alone galvanises most men — young or old — into action.'

'What about love? Respect? Loyalty?'

'Powerful indeed but riches are compelling, especially for a man who barely sees more than a few karels a month, Zar Boaz. What if he was promised what sounded like a small fortune?'

Boaz had heard enough. 'Take me to the Inflictors' quarters.'

'Now, my Zar?'

'Immediately.'

'They will probably be resting after practice sessions,' Salmeo risked.

Boaz fixed him now with a look that was hard enough to crush rocks. 'You disturbed my rest, Chief Eunuch, because you felt it was too important to leave until later. Let's sort this now. If we're going to have another execution on our hands, I want them done together and I want this whole matter put behind us.'

Salmeo bowed, hiding the look of relief he was feeling at having taken careful precautions beforehand. 'Of course, my Zar,' he said, straightening, 'let us go now.'

Boaz had very little to say to the eunuch as they made their way to the Inflictors' accommodation. Instead he spoke quietly to Bin, whom he'd asked to accompany them, using the time to brief his secretary on what had transpired.

The few people they met were daunted by the trio and either bowed low as they swept through corridors or flattened themselves against the walls to bow in their wake, muttering words of joy to the Mightiest of the Mighties. Boaz ignored them.

He was in no mood to be generous of spirit and he noted, not for the first time, that it didn't matter anyway. The truth was he could do what he liked, act how he felt. He could slap passers-by if he so wished and he knew, with a terrible sense of destiny, that they would probably thank him for acknowledging them. It was easier to pretend they meant nothing and thus ignore their cringing good wishes.

After crossing several courtyards Salmeo finally pushed open a timber door that led into a small wing of the palace that housed the Inflictors' quarters.

People at their work dropped to their knees as though it was a sickness. It was most unusual for any royal, least of all the Zar himself, to visit these humble accommodations. Boaz fixed a tight smile at his mouth, moving swiftly behind the bulk of Salmeo to step inside the main chamber and startle the Deputy Inflictor.

He visibly paled. 'Grand Master Eunuch, this is —' and then he saw who accompanied Salmeo. It took moments to register that this was in fact the Zar before he fell to his knees. 'Oh Great One!'

Boaz winced. 'Please stand. You are?'

The man trembled. Boaz could appreciate that his arrival might make the Deputy nervous but the man seemed unnecessarily terrified. Was there something to hide? 'I am Rah, Great One, the Deputy Inflictor.'

'Ah, good. Are you alone?'

'My wife and son are inside, my Zar. Is anything wrong?' he stammered, glancing towards Salmeo, who pursed his lips. The sign was enough to alert Rah that this was official business and it didn't taken him more than a moment's consideration to realise what this was about.

'Can we talk somewhere privately?' Boaz suggested, as someone stepped inside the chamber and then hurriedly left when confronted by the trio of men.

'Er, you're welcome to come into my humble quarters, my Zar,' he offered uncertainly.

Boaz nodded. 'Send your wife and son outside — this is not for their ears.'

It was done. The family was hurried away and Rah returned, embarrassed, awkward and betraying his nervousness through twitching hands and a voice far from steady. 'May I offer some refreshment, my Zar, I —'

'No, that won't be necessary. I'm here to clarify something with you, Rah, and I insist that you converse with me in honesty, without fear of reprisal.'

The man nodded dumbly, again glancing at Salmeo.

Boaz was tired of Salmeo's imposing presence. 'Grand Master Eunuch,' he said, 'you may wait outside.'

Salmeo bristled but bowed nonetheless and departed. Boaz watched him carefully for any sign of threat to Rah but the eunuch's face was blank of any.

As he had with Horz, Boaz turned now to the Deputy. 'Do you know why I'm here?'

'No, High One,' the man spluttered, terrified.

'Be calm, man. I am here only to ask you a question.' Rah nodded, wide-eyed. 'I want to know if anyone, bar the Inflictors, has access to your instruments?'

He shook his head rapidly. Boaz, already suspicious, felt his reaction was too swift. Most people would show some consternation at being asked such an odd question without preamble. 'No, my Zar,' and it was laced with a tinge of horror. 'Absolutely no-one has access to the canes, whips or any of our implements of punishment. Why do you ask?'

'Because a man has died. You've heard about the Spur?'

Rah looked thunderstruck. 'He died? Forgive me, my Zar, I have only just recovered from my illness.'

It was either a superbly rehearsed act or the man was telling the truth. 'How did you learn about the Spur being the person who would be punished?'

359

'The Grand Master Eunuch came to see me. He was shocked that I was sick, my Zar, and incapable of doing the job. He already knew that our Inflictor Felz was not even in Percheron city. He was at a loss to know what to do.'

Boaz knew better. Salmeo was rarely at a loss regarding intrigue. 'So he asked your advice?'

The man nodded fearfully again. 'I didn't have much to give. If I could have stood unaided I would have done it myself, my Zar. Forgive me. It was I who suggested Shaz — he was our only option when the Grand Master Eunuch explained that the job had to be done immediately. Shaz has been well trained and is our best apprentice. He knew what he had to do — I assume the mood and the celebrity of the Spur must have unravelled him. I had high hopes he would do all right.'

'Well, he didn't. He was perspiring, nervous, trembling. He was incapable of handling this task. I could see as much and I was the furthest person from him.'

'I can't imagine he killed him though, Mighty One.'

'No, I don't believe he did. I think the poison might have had something to do with it.'

The man's head snapped back in shock. 'Poison,' he whispered. 'You jest,' he urged, forgetting his manners and all protocol.

'I would never jest about something as grave as this. The Spur of Percheron is dead because someone dipped the whip into poison.'

The man's complexion blanched. There was no way, in Boaz's estimation, that this reaction could be contrived.

'Who chose the Viper?'

Rah could barely talk through his shock to answer. Finally he stammered, 'I can't imagine why he would do such a foolish thing, my Zar, but Shaz would have made that choice. The Elim and Grand Master Salmeo have never involved themselves in such a decision. They have always left judgement to the Inflictors.'

'What could have possibly made him choose the hardest weapon to wield on his first living victim?'

Rah shrugged and then caught himself. 'Maybe the lad got excited. Shaz knows he's the best apprentice by far, so it's possible that arrogance could have got in the way of good sense — you know how youngsters like to show off.' And then he caught himself, suddenly realising that he was talking to someone not far off Shaz's own age. 'Perhaps the boy is in debt to someone and he was bribed?' he offered softly. 'I didn't know any of this, my Zar, until now.'

Boaz felt light-headed. Surely not an execution of Shaz as well as Horz? In his heart he knew Horz was not guilty and he couldn't imagine Horz paying a boy to do his dirty work. The Elim were too proud for that. And yet Boaz had no proof of innocence for either, only evidence of guilt. He felt a blood rage threatening. 'I have found what I came for,' he said tightly and turned, angry and distraught.

He stomped out of the small dwelling and strode past Salmeo who stood a little distance from the main door looking grave.

After the Zar had disappeared, Salmeo turned to Rah who had appeared at the doorway still trembling from the episode.

'Did he believe your story? Did you tell it precisely as I instructed?'

All Rah could do was nod and mutter, 'Zarab help me.' He was feeling sickened to his soul at lying to his Zar and now incriminating innocent Shaz, whose only flaw might be that he strove too hard to please those he worked for.

'You have done well. Your family will live ... and they will thank you for your steadfastness.'

Rah began to weep. 'What will happen to Shaz?'

'Who cares?' Salmeo replied and smiled cruelly at the pitiful man. 'Don't worry about him — collect a purse from me tomorrow after it's done. That will ease your troubled conscience, Deputy.'

Shaz was only just beginning to recover from the previous day's trauma. He had not yet heard the news that the Spur had died and he lived in hope that the man he had admired and cut so badly would forgive him. He planned to be one of the first to visit the Spur — if he would give his permission — so that he could make that plea of forgiveness in person. He'd even changed his mind about his profession. He no longer wanted to be an Inflictor. Flogging a man was nothing like flogging the practice dummies. Felz had said all he had to do was remove his emotion and pretend the man tied to the post was just a dummy. But Shaz had been unable to distance himself from the emotion or the reality. He hated what occurred yesterday and had it not been in front of the Zar, whom he also admired, he would have refused to continue after his first few botched lashes, no matter the harsh consequences. It would have been hard enough to complete the punishment with a single whip. Putting the Snake into his hands was a ludicrous order.

He was taking a rest after a practice session when the soldiers came for him. They were angry too. News had flared around the barracks as fast as a raging fire that their leader was dead — killed by the ineptness of an apprentice Inflictor who was also deep in a conspiracy led by debt and greed, or so the story was shaping with each new telling. Salmeo would be pleased at how his fabricated tale was being embellished by gossip.

Shaz was dragged from his bed, slapped and punched, kicked and shoved as the four men moved him, without explanation, from his tiny room to the Pit, where he joined Horz, saddened to hear the young man's cries. It didn't take much for the former Elim to understand what had transpired and to give a nod of appreciation in the darkness of his stone cell at Salmeo's cunning.

He and Shaz would die tomorrow for a deed they were innocent of, but Horz would die proudly, calmly, he knew this. He was ready, had accepted his fate from the moment Salmeo began his threats. The Elim were trained to accept their destiny. This was his. He was only regretful that his death was not enough for Salmeo and that the boy had to die too. Poor Shaz. He sent a prayer to Zarab that the ending of their lives would be swift, if not for him, then certainly for the young man.

❦ 28 ❧

Pez sat in the marble coolness of the palace infirmary and watched Kett hobble back unaided. They were alone.

'Is it working properly?' he asked carefully.

'With the help of the tube,' the boy answered and turned away so the dwarf would not have to share his troubles.

'It's all right, Kett. I won't say I understand — how can I? But I do understand your grief. I think it is important to weep and mourn your loss.'

'The Grand Master Eunuch came to see me,' the boy replied after clearing his throat.

'And?'

'He wants me to present myself for duty tomorrow.'

'Has he given you a role yet?'

'No. I'll just be one of his slaves and my dream of working for Spur Lazar must be buried,' Kett answered, the pain of his shattered hopes clear.

Pez realised yet another person whose life had been touched by Lazar would grieve. 'Kett, be patient. There are wheels turning that I can't explain just yet. I'm optimistic you may have a role to your liking.'

'Oh?'

The hope in the boy's voice was gut-wrenching. 'I will tell you more when I know.'

'Pez, may I be plain with you?'

'Of course, I am with you.'

'Yes, that's what troubles me. You are sane.'

Pez smiled. 'Our secret.'

'The Zar knows, doesn't he?'

'He lied to you only to protect me. He has known since he was old enough to talk,' Pez said. 'And now you know.'

The boy's grim countenance faltered briefly as a grin surfaced but was gone almost as fast as it arrived. He hadn't known Pez long enough to be shocked by the news. 'I am privileged.'

Pez was reminded of the youngster's claim to be the black bird, the raven. He didn't know what this augured but the voice inside counselled that Kett might also be one of the players in the battle ahead. He couldn't know yet whether Kett was a disciple of Maliz or whether he supported the Goddess. His instincts told him it was the latter and Pez trusted instinct. He had to keep this boy close and especially to Ana, if possible. Even in this he had no guidance, only a vague feeling that this was the right path.

'So you will keep my secret.' It was a statement, not a question.

But Kett nodded solemnly, his hand touching his forehead before settling over his heart. 'I shall take it to my grave.' And Pez trusted him.

'I have some news,' he said solemnly. 'You have been recuperating so I presume no-one has told you yet of what has happened to Spur Lazar.'

The boy shook his head. 'What do you mean happened? Is he hurt?'

'Worse,' Pez answered grimly, and with only a vague feeling that he was somehow connected to this child, he proceeded to tell Kett the entire sordid tale.

There was nothing Kett could say when it was told. He stared at the ground, deeply upset and silent. Finally he spoke. 'He tried to have me spared,' he said, voice trembling.

'Yes, Lazar was not one to tolerate anyone suffering. He would have thought your punishment grossly out of kilter with the sin.'

'As was his own. At least I'm alive.'

Pez swallowed his own sadness. 'Good, Kett. That's the spirit, child. You are alive. The gods have spared you and perhaps there is good reason for this.'

'I have a purpose?' the boy asked with hefty disdain in his voice. 'I'll grow fat and act like a woman.'

'I don't notice any fat Elim, and none of them could be accused of acting in any way but fearsomely and loyally.'

'Not their leader, it seems,' the boy countered, his anger still evident.

Pez's own flared. 'Don't be so sure, Kett. There are things in motion here that you cannot understand. If you believe that Horz is guilty of murder then I feel more sorry for you than I already do. You did know Horz, I gather?'

The boy, duly reprimanded, nodded. 'He is as worthy of death as I was to be gelded.'

'That's right. He is taking the blame for someone else's dark deeds.'

'Why don't you say something?'

'Do you suppose that people haven't already guessed as much? The fact is Horz is admitting guilt — that's impossible to counter. And anyway, who would listen to the ravings of a lunatic?'

'But you're not!'

'Very few know that, Kett. It is our secret, one I need you to keep for me.'

'Why is it that you trust me?'

Pez shook his head. 'I feel compelled. I think we were meant to meet. I just wish it wasn't under such circumstances.'

'Will you be honest with me, now that we share this secret?'

Pez nodded slowly. 'I promise.'

'How is it that the guards saw me but neither you nor our Zar?'

The dwarf had been expecting this question. 'Another secret.'

'You can trust me, Pez.'

'I have the Lore.'

The boy's eyes widened. 'The Lore,' he repeated, as if the very word itself was precious. 'Why didn't you hide me then?'

Pez looked pained. 'I couldn't. Sustaining the invisibility for two was hard enough and I knew it would only last for a few moments. They knew someone was behind that screen and I couldn't risk them searching. I couldn't risk the Zar being found. I'm sure you understand.'

'So I was sacrificed,' Kett said sadly.

'You shouldn't have been there,' Pez answered mildly.

'Neither should you.'

'But I had the Zar to consider. It was my fault he was present.'

'So what are you here for?'

'I honestly don't know,' he said, which was partly true.

'Who else knows?'

'Oh you're part of a very elite few. I can list them on one hand,' Pez said, counting off using his fingers. 'Lazar knew, of course. And his servant Jumo, Zar Boaz, Odalisque Ana and a priestess called Zafira all know.'

'And now me.'

'Yes.'

'What is your purpose in keeping your sanity secret?'

'Each has asked this same question. I answer the same way: I don't know. I have acted this way since the moment I entered Percheron as a prisoner. It caught the attention of the men who buy slaves for the palace. I was fortunate that the old Zar happened to be travelling through the slave market one afternoon. He saw me, laughed at my antics and had someone buy me for him. I've been at the palace ever since. That was two decades ago.'

Kett's eyes widened with surprise, 'How old are you?'

'Ancient,' Pez replied, knowing now this was truth.

'I will not betray you,' said Kett.

'And that faith will be rewarded.'

'How?'

'You will see.'

'You are not required to be present, Boaz,' Pez advised.

'But I must be, don't you see. Horz is lying — and he knows I know.'

'I still don't understand.'

'Yes you do. This is about honour. I will honour Horz for his noble sacrifice. What the Elim don't realise is how loyal he is. He is giving his life protecting his symbolic leader.'

'So you accept this is Salmeo's doing?'

'I never doubted it, Pez. I just can't prove it.'

'And now Shaz is to die as well. Must it be so?'

'If I don't Salmeo will spread the word — as cunningly as we know he can — throughout Percheron that I did not punish the co-conspirator. He has hatched this plan to cover his tracks. Now he has rid himself of the two people who might have revealed him, and the other, Rah, has been coerced to the point where he would rather lie to me than risk whatever Salmeo has threatened him with.'

'Justice must be seen to be done — is this it?'

'Precisely.'

'Someone else somewhere will know something.'

'I can't imagine who, but if you can find that someone bring them to me.' Boaz sighed. 'What if I let myself down?'

'You won't, child.'

'How can you be sure?' And Boaz understood. 'The Lore?' The dwarf nodded. 'I thought you said you never wanted to use it.'

'Well, I had to as you know.'

'But again?' Boaz asked with wonder, still fascinated by Pez's skill.

'If you'll do something for me.'

The Zar gave his friend a look of gentle warning. 'Now what?'

'We talked about it before. A servant for Ana when the time is right.'

'Kett, you mean?'

Pez nodded. 'Salmeo's told him to report tomorrow. I'm not sure how much he's capable of just yet but the Chief Eunuch insists he be given his tasks.'

'And you want him trained in the harem? What's your interest in Kett?'

'I feel responsible,' Pez answered, not altogether untruthfully.

'As you should,' Boaz grumbled. 'He obviously knows about you now?'

'Yes, I've shown myself to him.'

'Zarab save us, soon you'll be sharing it over quishtar with my mother and I'll no longer have the worst-kept secret in Percheron! All right. I shall see what can be done — I too feel responsible for his unhappy situation.'

Pez gave a brief bow. 'Thank you, my Zar.'

'It cannot happen immediately. Give it some time. Let him fully heal. Let all of us fully heal from this turbulence that the palace is coping with. Give me up to twelve moons.'

Pez nodded. It was longer than he had hoped but he was not in a position to argue. 'Until next summer, then.'

'You have my word.'

'Thank you, my Zar.'

'Just stay close today, will you? I'm filled with dread and you're the only one I can admit it to.'

'I will protect you.'

The Zar was transported in the curtained, slave-carried karak. They weren't travelling far but their journey was via countless manicured gardens and various gateways — six in all — that had to be passed in order to reach the main courtyard that accessed the city itself. They would not leave the palace grounds proper but stop in the Moon Courtyard where, for centuries, zars had climbed a special royal stairway that led them to the parapet from which they could view public exhibitions, processions, entertainments and executions.

Boaz did not like travelling in the karak, having never quite grown out of his childish nausea at the swaying sensation. It niggled at him now like an unwelcome but familiar visitor as he sat unhappily on silk cushions. Next to him sat Pez, dressed in identical clothes.

'Bit scratchy, aren't they?' the dwarf commented in an effort to divert his Zar from the ordeal ahead.

'Wardrobe thought it fitting that you be seen fully as the fool.'

Pez spoke softly so he could not be overheard. 'Is that so? You should be cautious that they don't inadvertently make you look the fool, my Zar.'

Boaz found a small grin — it felt like his first in an age. Then his expression darkened again. 'How bad is it going to be, Pez? Tell me honestly.'

Pez realised the diversion hadn't worked. He pursed his thick lips, for honesty was probably the last thing Boaz needed right now but it was also necessary. 'Worse than you can possibly imagine. You know of Riding the Needle but, Boaz, you have no conception of how truly shocking a death it is. As for Shaz, he is to be ganched, is this right?' Boaz nodded mournfully. 'Have you seen it occur?'

'No. My father maintained there was more than enough time for me to see sights of this magnitude.'

'Joreb was right to protect you from it and no doubt hoped you wouldn't have to deal with such things until later in life. Spiking is cruel beyond belief, Boaz. They haul the victim up on pulleys on a special scaffolding from which are hung terrible, sharpened hooks. The victim is dropped from a height and the fun of the spectacle for the crowd is to see where on his body the vicious hooks snag. If he's lucky it's across an artery so death is relatively swift.'

'And if not?' Boaz asked, his feeling of nausea suddenly much worse.

'If it's through his belly or chest he takes a long time to die.'

'I'm not going to be able to watch this,' Boaz warned.

'You have no choice.'

'What if I can't help but close my eyes or look away?'

'I won't let you. My magic can compel as skilfully as it repels, my Zar.' The swaying karak halted. 'We are here,' Pez added unnecessarily, sneaking a look outside.

The sound of the people's excited murmuring from the other side of the thick walls was loud enough to tell them that a large crowd had gathered for the executions.

'Why do they want to watch this?' Boaz murmured.

'Morbid curiosity, dark fascination, macabre entertainment.'

'Then I make myself a promise to provide new entertainment for my people. We are a nation that prides itself on culture, Pez, why . . .' He couldn't say any more.

'Boaz,' Pez began firmly as the Zar began to gulp air. 'I applaud your sentiment. But public execution has its place. It is a valuable reminder, if nothing else, that life — no matter who you are or what your situation might be — is precious. Any potential law breakers watching will know after today that you do not tolerate anyone who thinks they are above your laws.'

Boaz nodded but Pez wasn't finished. 'Your subjects will know after today, High One, that whilst you could so easily have covered up the crime within your own palace, you have been ruthless with one of your own. No-one will miss this point.'

Boaz hardly heard his friend's words. He was sure he was going to vomit. Pez fixed him with a fierce stare, which somehow gave Boaz strength, then the dwarf rolled out of the karak squealing.

Boaz fought back his fear and emerged sedately, squinting slightly at the harsh light of the hot morning, a drier one, aided by a soft breeze. The sky was a bright canvas for the sun to splash her golden rays across, interrupted briefly by a few scudding clouds — leftovers from the previous days of overcast skies. But there would be no rain today to wash away the blood or the stench of death.

Boaz was already sweating into his formal robes, and the wrapped silk about his head made him feel even hotter but this had little to do with the weather. Pez rolled back to him and took his hand, acting like one of the monkeys Boaz used to be so amused by in his father's zoo.

'Beware, my Zar. Salmeo has plotted another surprise.'

Ana and a few of the girls had been assembled in a large airy chamber that enjoyed a sweet breeze that blew in off the Faranel through the huge square courtyard adjacent. Most of the young women were enjoying sitting around the grand stone fountain with its gentle spumes of water coming from sculpted fishes' mouths. But Ana remained in the chamber itself, admiring the exquisitely pretty tiles depicting the tree of life. She was feeling sorry for three of the youngest odalisques, who were barely out of childhood and found some small comfort in each other. They stood apart from the rest of the girls who were all of similar age. One of the three was only nine summers and looked permanently terrified, and with good reason, Ana thought, knowing full well the hated Salmeo would not have spared young Eishar his special private exploration of her body.

'Did you sleep well, Eishar?' Ana asked, trying to ease the child's fear.

'No, I'm frightened they'll come for me at any time,' the girl half sobbed.

'They?'

'The Zar's people,' she answered, her voice small and frightened.

'You must stop worrying,' Ana reassured her. 'I've met the Zar and he's really a very gentle man. He's quite young ... about my age, and he will not be looking to call any of you three — not yet, not for a while anyway.'

She hoped she was telling the truth; she had no real idea about the Zar's tastes or desires, but if her judgement was sound then Boaz was not interested in children; he wasn't even interested yet in sexual congress for he could have commanded her to do his bidding when they were first alone.

Eishar reminded Ana of her small sister and she wondered how her family was getting on. The Samazen could come at any time and her father would have to bring his two small herds closer to their dwelling. He wouldn't have her help this year and that saddened her deeply. She loved time alone with her father, especially when he would relate the tale of how he found the prettiest of babies in the scrub of the further reaches of the foothills, just before they yielded to the desert proper. A pain knifed through her when she understood that she would never see her beloved father. And that sense of emptiness reminded her of the only other man she'd loved and that he too would never look upon her again. At least her father was alive, she comforted herself — providing he hadn't died of heartbreak — but Lazar had died for her, because of her selfishness.

All the girls turned at the sound of the Elim arriving. Most of the older girls were excited at the prospect of being taken to the main bathing pavilion, whilst the trio of children would have liked nothing better than to be allowed to play beneath the cypress trees.

But the two Elim who arrived had not come to explain anything and the entrance of the Grand Master Eunuch set off a palpable tremor of fear amongst the girls.

'Sisters,' he lisped.

Everyone watching the huge man became deathly still.

Ana glanced at Eishar and the youngster looked ready to wail.

'Welcome to your first proper day in the harem of Zar Boaz. I'm afraid to inform you that today's activities will have to be postponed. It was my intention that you begin your formal training. However, something rather important has arisen that involves one of your number.' He let that statement sink in before he continued. 'We've come to collect Odalisque Ana,' he finally said softly, almost sounding apologetic. 'Where are you, Ana?'

Ana could have guessed as much that it would be her name to be called and yet she had no idea why.

'I'm here,' she said, making no particular effort to reveal herself.

Salmeo turned, his scar lifting slightly in a fleeting grimace. 'Ah, there you are. Hiding were you?'

'No, Grand Master Eunuch. I was merely keeping the younger girls company. It is all still rather frightening for them.'

'But not for you, eh, Ana?'

'I think you've already done your worst,' she replied evenly and noticed Eishar's glance of awe at her audacious behaviour.

'Oh my dear,' he tittered, 'I've hardly begun. Come now, you have something to witness.'

'Another of your spectacularly unpleasant shows?'

'Careful, Ana,' he warned. 'I am tolerant because these are still early days. But once your formal training begins, the discipline will become stringent.' He spoke to the wider audience now. 'You should all be warned. Odalisque Ana is being shown some leniency today because she must face something ... well,' he searched theatrically for the right word, 'shall we say unsavoury,' and he enjoyed watching the alarm betray Ana's composure.

A murmur passed through the girls. 'Fret not, my lovelies, Ana will be returned to you shortly, unharmed.' He smiled, his tongue flicking briefly through the gap in his teeth. 'Come, Ana,' he added, firmly this time, and she knew not to disobey.

After being dressed and appropriately hidden behind a long dark veil, Ana was led by the same two Elim beyond the main entrance. They assisted her into a tiny curtained karak and carried her swiftly through the beautiful series of manicured gardens. She chanced pulling back the curtains a mere crack and realised they were taking her towards the Moon Courtyard. It felt as if a lifetime had passed since she was last here and yet it was only mere days ago. In a moment of crystal clarity it came to her that taking her life might be easier than facing the dullness that stretched out before her. No Lazar, no meaningful conversation with the girls who would soon see her as enemy rather than friend as the jostling for the Zar's attention began. Thinking about Boaz gave her some hope — his intelligence, his youth, his desire not to imprison the girls of the harem but to find new ways to entertain and educate them. And dear Pez . . . perhaps her lifeline.

The karak was settled on the ground and Ana became aware of a constant murmur of voices. One of the Elim opened the curtain. 'You must accompany us now.'

'Why are we here?' she asked, keeping her voice light and with a hint of playfulness in it. She was learning fast, although Ana suspected the Elim had seen every approach over the years. This one, however, was young and perhaps not as experienced because he did respond.

'There's to be a public execution today, Miss Ana. You are required to bear witness.'

Ana gasped, shrinking back into the karak. Why hadn't she guessed this? Salmeo was going to ensure she paid many times over for her challenge of him. She hadn't learned anything from Pez's careful warning — she had even baited the fat eunuch again today, impressing the younger ones and enjoying the shocked glances from the older girls. It was stupid of her and all it had served was to intensify Salmeo's power over her. He enjoyed it too. Enjoyed it especially because he knew she could never win — no amount of defiance would ever usurp his authority over her and the power he held on her life. She was his to command.

'I can't,' she implored the waiting Elim.

Now his companion, an older man, looked in, irritated by the delay. 'Hurry,' he snapped, 'the Grand Master Eunuch awaits.'

'You must come now, Miss Ana,' the young one repeated with sympathy.

She shook her head but the older Elim reached in and all but pulled her from the karak. 'You will behave, Odalisque Ana. I am answerable to the Grand Master Eunuch and if you give us any trouble today I will personally make your life as unpleasant as I can.'

And so the chain of misery passed down the line of command from Salmeo to his Elim. 'It can't get any worse,' she said.

'Be very sure that it can, Odalisque Ana. Now hold yourself erect and do not let the harem down.'

Boaz felt his throat close tighter still at Pez's warning. He looked up at the great wall that surrounded the Stone Palace and its grounds. He instantly recognised the enormous bulk of Salmeo and next to him a petite figure in dark sombre robes. It was too small to be his mother, and no servant of hers would be permitted to leave the harem for the purposes of a public execution. There was only one other person who would be forced to witness this event — it had to be Odalisque Ana. Salmeo obviously intended to crush Ana's spirit well before it took flight and gave her any delusions that she might survive the harem with her integrity and personality intact. Even his mother had learned to play to Salmeo's rules and it would be no different for Ana — unless he himself made it different.

There were special steps cut into the wall which every Zar had mounted at one time or another, usually to make some proclamation or simply to observe his people going about their daily lives. Today these steps would afford him the best possible view of suffering. He wished with all of his heart he didn't have to be here, but there would be no escaping this today. He could see Pez waiting at the top for him, going about his silly antics and raising guffaws from the crowd.

The Zar of Percheron took a deep breath and began the long climb, his steps matching the rhythm of a single haunting drum that announced his impending arrival.

In the throng awaiting the two barbaric executions stood a person in a dark grey jamoosh, holding the hand of a lad, no more than ten. The youngster looked fearful, glancing up every few moments toward the intense gaze of his companion who had eyes only for the top of the palace walls and the various figures that stood upon them.

'That's her, that's Odalisque Ana, standing next to the Grand Master Eunuch,' whispered the boy.

'I gathered,' came the reply.

'And the Valide Zara is here today as well. She stands near the Vizier. Can you see him?'

'I can, although I would not have recognised him out of his garish silks and showy beard.'

'The drum is sounding for the arrival of the Zar.'

'Thank you, Teril,' the person said and in the tone was a gentle admonishment to suggest that this was not news.

The youngster was not deterred. 'Should we get closer?'

'No. I think you'll regret being here soon.'

'I've attended many floggings,' the boy boasted but not convincingly.

'I know,' the person said a little sadly. 'But this is far, far worse and you know the prisoner. Have you ever seen someone die slowly in excruciating pain?'

The boy shook his head.

'Well that's what's ahead for young Shaz. Perhaps we shouldn't stay.'

'But you asked me to bring you,' the boy said, confused.

'I did. But I have entirely different reasons for being here, which have nothing to do with an execution.'

'Because of her?' the boy asked, nodding at Ana.

'Yes.'

'You cannot speak to an odalisque. You should know this already.'

'I don't intend speaking to her. I simply needed to see her for myself, that is all. Do you see the dwarf prancing around?'

'Yes, his name is Pez.'

'I want you to get a note to him from me. It's very important, very urgent. Can you do that? I will pay you.'

'I will not accept money. You should know this too after what we've shared.' The person nodded and the boy read thanks in the intense look from beneath the jamoosh. 'Where is the note?'

'Here.' The figure pressed a small folded parchment into the boy's hand.

'Now?'

'As soon as you can, Teril.'

'I may have to wait until the dwarf comes back down those stairs.'

'I can never thank you enough for helping me in this way.'

'Then our debt is settled?'

'Fully.' The figure put a hand on the youngster's head. 'Be careful. No-one else must read this but the Zar's jester.'

'I understand. But how will you walk? You needed my help before.'

'I shall manage,' came the brusque reply and the lad gave a brief farewell before melting away into the crowd.

The figure in the jamoosh glanced up at Ana, turned unsteadily, the pain of exertion hidden beneath the veiling garments, and then hobbled away on two gnarled walking sticks.

∽ 29 ∽

Boaz was given a tumultuous welcome from the city of Percheron. It was not often they saw their ruler in person and the fact that this was their new Zar prompted great cheering and excitement. He stood, suddenly tall and lean, but with broad shoulders, not at all like his stout father of later years. Although few had ever seen his mother they knew her by reputation to be an incredible beauty and this young man's dark curly hair and altogether handsome appearance suggested he resembled the new Valide's famed looks. Many in the crowd had been surprised but also delighted to hear of the young Zar's proclamation of not one but two public executions so early into his reign. There had been rumours that the young man was studious, bordering on scholarly, and those rumours had gathered momentum to suggest that he was also squeamish in nature. Several of the more outspoken city leaders had tactfully queried amongst themselves whether this prince was cut out for the role of Zar and whether he could rule with a firm hand. Others had replied, quite rightly, that his father — once so feared in his prime — would have chosen carefully from the many heirs on offer. Joreb would not select a boy unable to summon the kind of strength needed to hold Percheron in his grip.

And now Boaz was seemingly proving his father correct. To onlookers the young man seemed far from timid as he acknowledged the crowd's welcome.

'All right?' Pez whispered to his Zar, even though no-one stood close enough on the parapet to overhear him.

'Yes, surprisingly. Are you using it on me?'

'Not yet,' Pez lied. 'You are handling yourself perfectly. I'm proud of you.' Pez was channelling his magic so gently that Boaz could not feel it. Soon the Zar might be more conscious of the Lore but for now Pez wanted to instil confidence in this young man.

'Do I keep smiling at everyone?'

'You're giving them precisely what they want. Soon you will call for silence so that your executioners can proceed.'

Boaz raised a hand and on that signal a hush washed across the crowd. He nodded gravely towards the fearsome-looking palace executioner. 'He did this for my father for so many years,' he uttered softly to his friend.

As the man began to announce the sentences Boaz looked surreptitiously away towards Ana.

'It's not right that she's here,' he whispered angrily.

'I don't know why you're surprised.'

Boaz grimaced. 'I thought that with Lazar's flogging and subsequent death it was over between Salmeo and Ana.'

Pez frowned. 'Don't be naive, Boaz. It's only just begun.'

They stopped talking as a small gate was opened in the palace wall and the two victims were led out. One walked proudly, the other was jabbering and crying, needing to be all but carried between the two Elim who escorted him.

'Oh Zarab! Poor Shaz,' Boaz whispered, his tone fraught, and Pez knew the gentle channelling was done with.

Herezah leaned towards Tariq. 'Is it really necessary for me to be here?'

'Forgive me for imposing upon your goodwill, Valide. I felt our young Zar needed your support today.'

She stared at the Vizier for a long time, long enough to make him frown. 'Tariq,' she finally said, 'I don't know what to make of you at the moment.'

'What do you mean, Valide?' he asked softly, ignoring the executioner's drone below, the apprentice's hysterics and the excited whisperings of the crowd.

'I mean that I cannot make you out. There is something about you that doesn't fit with my image of our Vizier.' He chuckled deep in his throat. It was a nice sound to her ears, unlike anything she'd heard from Tariq in all the years she'd known him. 'And there's that laugh. I've never heard you make such a genuine sound of amusement, Tariq.'

'And how has it been before, Valide?'

'Like a sycophant,' she answered directly. 'I've watched you calculate your fake chortles for years. In fact everything about the Tariq I recall is calculated and controlled.' She shook her head. 'Your amusement just now sounded utterly genuine.'

'It was,' he replied, glancing down to where Shaz was wailing as he heard his sentence.

The Valide bit her lip beneath her veil in thought. 'I've also never thought you cared much for Boaz.'

'I didn't.' He smiled at the obvious shock registered in her eyes. 'What I mean is, until a short while ago your son was simply another heir ... another prince in waiting. Suddenly he is our Zar, the Chosen One. I do care about our Zar, Valide, and I especially care that this one is still young enough to need guidance from those who have some wisdom to share.'

'You see, Tariq, this doesn't sound a bit like you,' she whispered.

He smiled once again and it was flirtatious, his eyes, seemingly younger, sparkling as they never had before. 'I can't imagine who I sound like then.'

'It's as if there's an intruder. Someone has stolen Tariq's body.'

The Vizier had to temper his desire to throw back his head and laugh loudly. 'Perhaps someone has. Would you like me to go by a different name?'

It was Herezah's turn to stare quizzically. 'No, that will not be necessary. I can't say I'm not impressed though. I like the curious metamorphosis you seem to be going through, I like it very much and I can only put it down to the brew you are taking. I see your stoop is all but gone — it is clearly working.'

'Thank you. I do feel stronger than I have in a long time.'

'And I'm especially pleased that your concern is, for once, not selfishly shown,' she added, ignoring his wry glance which suggested her feelings were somewhat hypocritical. 'I do think Boaz has been especially brave in his decisions regarding these two about to die — they were necessary and he made the right choice — but I know this will be taking every ounce of his courage to stand here and bear witness.'

The Vizier looked thoughtful. 'Boaz will make a great Zar with the right people around him. He has his mother's extraordinary looks and poise to charm people, combined with the warrior bearing of his father to intimidate them. It's a prized mix.'

'I would never have thought it but I think you're right — these last few days he has reminded me strongly of a young Joreb.'

'We must remember, though, that he is still young enough to be influenced and we have no idea who is influencing him.'

Herezah was taken by surprise. 'What do you mean by that?'

'Nothing sinister. I may have taken little more than a cursory interest in him previously, but now he is Zar I will be taking a far more proprietorial interest on behalf of the Percherese. Who does he defer to? Where does he go for advice? I need to know more about him.'

'I can't believe we're having this conversation, Tariq. You've known the boy since he was born — you'd know as well as I that his two great friends are the hated dwarf and the Spur. Now Lazar is gone and my son is left with a halfwit as his closest companion.'

Tariq turned and stared at Pez who was standing on one leg, threatening to overbalance into the crowd beneath, clearly in his own world.

'I had Yozem, my crone, do a blood reading on him, you know,' Herezah added casually.

'And?'

'Nothing. Pez is blank to her. She is unable to read him at all.'

'Is that common?'

Herezah snorted. 'She has never failed me previously.'

'I see,' Tariq muttered, distracted, a vague sense of gentle magic swirling about him. He tried to follow it, lock onto it, but he couldn't. It was as though it knew it was being hunted. He had no idea where it was coming from. He returned to his thoughts and focused on the dwarf. *I must take more interest in you too, Pez,* he thought to himself. *Perhaps there's more to you than meets the eye.*

On the wall, still dancing, Pez prayed to the Goddess that she would protect him from discovery as he carefully channelled his magic.

Everything formal that had to be said was now spoken. Above the pitiful moans of Shaz, the executioner turned to Boaz for the next item of theatre before they got down to the serious business of killing two men.

Boaz took a deep breath. He had one last hope of saving a life today whilst not allowing anyone present to doubt his sincerity of intent. 'Good people of Percheron,' he began and the crowd below became silent. 'The law of the Zar has been proclaimed. Shaz the Inflictor and Horz of the Elim have betrayed me and they are now under the shadow of death for their treachery. That said, I am mindful of the old traditions of our nation, too many of them lost in recent times. I am hopeful that together we might rekindle some of our passion for the rituals observed by our ancestors that have made us the wealthy, educated and cultured people that we are today.' Whistles and cheers rippled through the people.

Boaz raised a hand for silence. 'To this end, and as Zar Baelzeemen did three centuries ago, I hand over the power of the

Crown to the people.' This won more applause, even though no-one in the mob understood what he was referring to.

But the Vizier did. Maliz had lived long enough to have known the reign of Zar Baelzeemen. 'He's far cleverer than any of us have credited,' he said.

'What do you know?' Herezah demanded.

'My history — as does your son. The Zar he refers to had a habit of allowing the crowd to show mercy when there were two or more executions planned on the same day.'

Herezah had no time to reply because Boaz was speaking again.

'People of Percheron, if there is ever an occasion during my reign when more than one person is to be executed on the same day, I will allow you to overrule, if you so choose, and show mercy to the condemned. Zar Baelzeemen was a compassionate man and I intend to rule with the same sense of humanity. I cannot forgive these two prisoners for what they have done — I must not, in fact — but you can reprieve one of the sentences if you so choose.

'Raise your hands, people, if you wish to see Horz of the Elim suffer the consequences of his dark actions,' he shouted, emotion lacing his voice as he hoped against hope that they might spare the older man. The crowd roared its response back, their arms raised in unison.

Horz would die today.

Boaz swallowed his disappointment. It had been too much to ask for. He called upon them again and now even Shaz had stopped his groaning to find out if the Percherese had any sympathy for his plight and pleas of innocence.

'Having heard his deeds, raise your hands if you wish to see Shaz the Apprentice Inflictor pay the price I am exacting for his part in the Spur's demise.'

There was an embarrassed murmur followed by an awkward silence as only sixty or so hands from the two hundred or more present shot into the air.

Pez began clapping from relief but he turned it into a joke, mugging for the audience, making whooping sounds as though he didn't really understand what his excitement was for. Boaz laid a hand on his companion's shoulder and the dwarf became still immediately.

'See how he can control him,' Herezah whispered to the Vizier. 'No-one else can.'

Tariq nodded, intrigued now by Pez. He stole a glance at Salmeo who scowled in his direction. Tariq smiled back. He knew how much the Grand Master Eunuch would resent the Zar's overturning of Shaz's punishment. It would leave a loose thread for the eunuch to tie off later.

'My people have chosen to spare Shaz the Apprentice,' Boaz called, working hard at not showing his delight.

The crowd below were not so circumspect and the roar of approval was deafening. Shaz himself looked confused, unable to believe that he had cheated death as it knocked so loudly against his door. He looked at Horz who nodded, a soft and sad smile about his lips as he silently congratulated the lad on his reprieve. Then the rough hands of the executioner's aides were pushing Shaz back through a gate and into the Moon Courtyard. There he began hugging every soldier, every servant, even one of the executioner's team. Then he saw a familiar face in the distance — it was Teril, one of the youngest apprentices of the Inflictors — and waved, too ecstatic to speak. The lad returned the gesture; he would see Shaz soon enough but he had a task to fulfil first.

He looked away from Shaz and up to the top of the wall where Pez was doing one of his famous jigs.

'Hey, boy, you're not allowed here! Our Zar is up there,' a soldier said, approaching hurriedly. 'You'll get yourself knifed for less.'

'I have a special note for the dwarf,' the lad mumbled. 'It's important.'

The man laughed. 'What? And you think the fool can read it?'

The youngster looked suddenly uncertain. 'No. I just promised one of the priests that I'd get it to him. I don't care if he understands it or not.' The lie about the priest came easily.

'Let me see it,' the man said, slightly chagrined now at the mention of one of Zarab's holy men.

'No, sir. I cannot,' the boy said. 'I cannot do that. This is a private note between the priest and the dwarf.' Then he hurriedly moved on from his lie. 'I am wearing my palace uniform, you can see I am allowed to be in its grounds.'

'Show me your mark,' the man said, not fully suspicious but, with the Zar thirty feet above them, he knew not to take any chances.

The lad rolled back the loose sleeve of his shirt to reveal the special branding that all palace servants were forced to endure when first accepted onto the staff. The man nodded. 'Who is your direct superior?'

'Rah,' the boy answered. 'I am returning to him now once I pass on the note. You can watch me.'

'I cannot let you go up there and you may not remain here.'

'Will you let me win his attention at least and if he is prepared to accept the note he can signal that to both of us?'

'The dwarf wouldn't have a clue —'

'I know, sir. But I gave my oath.'

'All right,' the man said, feeling a bit sorry for the lad. He had a son of similar age and understood how important it was to instil a sense of duty into boys of this age. The lad was only trying to see a task to its proper end. Furthermore, all the soldiers were happy to hear of Shaz cheating death; none believed he'd had any part in the downfall of their Spur. It couldn't hurt to show a bit of the same generosity of spirit that their own Zar was promoting. 'Go on then, see if you can win his attention, although I'll have to search you.'

The boy beamed and permitted the search. Once given permission he whistled and as fate would have it the noise had dwindled almost to silence outside the walls as preparations were underway to have Horz ride the infamous needle.

His sound pierced the air. Both figures above heard it and turned. 'You've been magnificent. Don't ruin it now. Keep looking ahead,' Pez cautioned his Zar and then looked down again with irritation to see the young lad beckoning him. 'What's this?'

'Who is it?' Boaz hissed.

'I've no idea. I don't recognise him from here but he obviously belongs to the palace.'

'What does he want?'

'Me, I think. I can't tell. Shall I find out?'

'No. Let him wait. I don't want you to leave.'

'I won't. He's waving something at me. Let me just get it.' Pez disappeared down the steps, pausing regularly to maintain his semblance of madness.

'Well, you're in luck, lad. The fool has fallen for it,' the soldier said as they watched the dwarf descending, grabbing at the flying fruit he was muttering about loudly enough for them to hear.

'I like Pez, he's funny.'

'Funny, yes. He's also mad. I can't see what this Zar or the old one could see in having that thing ranting by their sides all day.'

Pez grinned when he finally arrived. 'Is it dinner already? Are we eating the elephants from the zoo?'

'Go on,' the soldier said, nudging the lad.

'Er, Pez, sir,' the boy began, unsure how to address the court jester, never having spoken to him before.

Pez stared at them both, as he scratched his crotch. 'Did you see all those flying pomegranates just now? I had no idea they could sprout wings or talk.'

'The, er, lad has a note for you, Pez,' the soldier said, deciding to speed things up a bit.

Pez stared at the proffered scroll. 'Is this my dinner?'

The man looked at the boy with sympathy. 'Just put it in his hand and you can tell your priest that you fulfilled what was asked of you. If the idiot eats it, that's his problem.'

The youngster did as he was told, pushing the scroll into the strangely oversized hands of the dwarf, trying not to gape at the huge knuckles and long fingers. 'I was asked to give this to you.'

Pez smelled the note and then began to dribble from the side of his mouth, his eyes fixed vacantly on something beyond.

'Go now,' the man urged the lad and he watched him hurry away.

'And the elephants?' Pez asked, seemingly returning to himself.

'Soon,' the soldier said and also took his leave.

Pez clutched the scroll. He felt a chill crawl up his spine. No-one had ever written to him. The only person who might would have to know the truth about him. That meant someone on the outside of the palace had asked the lad to get this note to him. Was it Jumo? He couldn't write but he could have had it scribed. Zafira perhaps? Or even Ellyana? He couldn't read it now — it would be too obvious. He sniffed it again instead, knowing others were watching him. Then, after nibbling the edge and spitting the fragments straight back out again, he tucked the note into his shirt and climbed the steps to watch Horz. He had not allowed the Lore magic to wane whilst he was occupied but he could feel Boaz's anxiety level increasing. It seemed the executioner's team was ready to begin what was the most hideous method of execution known in Percheron.

∽ 30 ∽

Boaz's complexion had blanched so pale Pez wondered if the boy would pass out. The Zar seemed to be staring at one spot, his eyes glazed. Pez increased the wave of magic and his friend seemed to recover some equilibrium.

'Pez,' Boaz muttered, swaying slightly. 'How can I let an innocent man die?'

The dwarf ignored the question and increased his channelling. Boaz was going to have to learn about situations of intolerable cruelty.

Pez looked down and felt his own gut twist at the sight below. Horz — naked except for a small piece of linen tied around his hips — was being laid out on the ground.

'I've read about this in the books in the library. Do you know it was invented by one of the zars?' Boaz seemed mesmerised and repulsed at the same time.

Pez could feel the boy leaning into the magic, trying to take more because of his fear. 'Boaz, you must teach yourself how to let go,' he cautioned. 'I have you. You are safe. I can make you blind to it if you wish, but I think that would be cowardly. Think of Odalisque Ana standing over there alone, watching her uncle die hideously and with nothing to help her, save whatever courage she can muster from within.'

It was the right thing to say. Boaz stood straighter, taller, at the mention of the girl's name.

'Now let go as I say, and I will keep you safe. You will not disgrace yourself.'

'What about Ana?' he whispered, taking slow breaths.

Pez felt the greedy grip on his magic lessening. 'Ana is strong. Hate for Salmeo will get her through this.' A further lessening on the hold. He had to move quickly. There was no more time. 'Now, Boaz, I must go.'

'Go?' Boaz exclaimed.

'Hush, child, I want to say goodbye to Horz.'

Boaz blushed. 'He's a good man. I had hoped they would pardon him. Can your magic not help him too?'

'No, I won't use magic,' was all Pez would say, keen to be gone. 'Just stand there and focus on me. I'll be near him so it will look as if you're watching the condemned man. The Lore will not fail you, Boaz. Trust it.'

The Zar nodded miserably. 'Tell him I'm sorry.'

'I think he already knows,' and Pez was climbing down the steps once again.

The bindings around Horz's wrists and ankles were being tightened. Four men took hold of these straps on each limb and pulled so that the Elim was now spread-eagled on the ground.

The executioner looked up to his Zar who sadly lowered his head as the signal to proceed.

The hush in the crowd was so thick it was oppressive as Pez emerged from one of the gates, snarling and running at the onlookers. They backed away, unsure. Was this part of the entertainment? Or was it just the oddity of the infamous dwarf? It was not often they got this close to the Zar's famed jester but his reputation preceded him; he was known to be contrary, one moment happier than the birds at dawn and the next dark and angry like a gathering storm. And it looked to them as though dawn had come and gone — the storm was surely brewing. Pez was hissing at everyone, including the executioner. 'I want to kiss him goodbye,' he suddenly moaned, breaking into sobs. He kept repeating it like a child determined to have his way.

The executioner had been handed a thick, vicious pole, sturdy and fearsome. It was sharpened to a savage point and now he positioned the sharp end between Horz's spread legs. It was just moments from being used to impale the trembling yet silent man of the Elim.

Pez increased his volume until he was shrieking.

The executioner looked suddenly rattled and turned once again to his Zar for approval. The young man, standing alone, trembling in tandem with the man about to die, nodded and the executioner stepped back, allowing Pez his request to kiss Horz goodbye. Everyone near the front of the mob and those on high watched the dwarf change instantly from hysterically angry to smiling and serene. He bowed to his Zar, then to the executioner before waddling over to kneel by Horz and whisper close to his ear.

'You are the bravest man the Zar knows,' Pez said. 'Go to your god with a clean conscience, friend,' and Pez silenced any reply by placing his mouth on the lips of the innocent man.

When he lifted away Horz stared back at him in shock, for two reasons. The dwarf had tricked them for all of these years! He was as sane as Horz was — he heard it in the words, could see it in the intense yellow gaze of the man. There was another surprise too that he was deeply grateful for.

'Shh,' was all Pez would say, a finger to his lips, and then he was cavorting away, grinning and clapping. 'I kissed him,' he yelled and his bemused audience could only shake their heads as they watched his short figure cartwheeling and skipping back to the small palace gate and disappearing through it.

Their attention diverted by the dwarf's madness, no-one saw Horz die as he bit down on the pellet Pez had passed into his mouth. The poison was swift, his heart was stopped in a matter of seconds, and he sighed softly to his death with his eyes open and not so much as a twitch of his bound limbs. It was a peaceful, painless end to cheat the executioner of Salmeo's victory.

Everyone marvelled at the brave Elim who didn't even struggle when his supposed torment began. Their awe at his courage when he didn't scream as the pole was rammed into him was so palpable it was like a living, breathing entity of its own. A few people were violently sick as the executioner used a huge mallet to ease the pole's passage through Horz's body, and even two of the men stretching his limbs looked away when the tip of the pole burst through flesh and bone to emerge at Horz's shoulder.

The shrieks of disgust in the crowd quietened to reverence for this heroic man who, although condemned as a murderer, would live on in the history books as the Elim's most famed warrior, almost godlike in his stoicism.

'Raise him,' the executioner called, he too taken aback by the lack of noise or struggle.

Horz was raised, impaled on the pole which was now set into the ground. He would remain there for three days until the smell of his corpse offended the palace and then he would be removed to a special mound on the fringe of the city where he would rot fully, reminding the Percherese for a long time of their Zar's intolerance of any treachery.

Ana had closed her eyes to the terrifying scene below and refused to open them even when the fragrance of violets told her that Salmeo was leaning close.

'Your uncle is a stunningly brave man,' he lisped. 'Not even a sound. I must say that impresses even me and I've seen the bravery of the Elim over the years.'

'I hope his spirit never lets you rest easily again,' Ana replied.

Salmeo laughed, despite being infuriated by the proceedings. Not only had Horz died courageously but Shaz had been released and posed a very real threat to the eunuch's secret. 'Come, Ana, you will learn that I am not threatened by spirits. Now let us really begin your training as a slave.' He licked his lips. 'I have so much in store for you.'

In the karak back to his wing of the palace, Boaz felt what was a mild headache gaining in strength.

'It's the after-effects of the Lore,' Pez said matter-of-factly. 'You should tell your aides that you wish to be left in peace.'

Boaz shook his aching head. 'I am humbled by Horz's bravery.' He stared absently into the silk screen that hid him from the view of palace passers-by.

'We all should be. I told him what you said,' Pez lied.

'And?' Boaz asked eagerly, desperate for some relief from his guilt.

Pez gave him the release. 'He offered thanks.'

There was a difficult silence between them for a few moments.

'I am going to see more of this in my life, aren't I?' Boaz said eventually.

'You will see suffering, yes.'

'Next time I will be as brave as the Elim. I will emulate Horz and not call upon the Lore.'

Pez nodded. Boaz was growing in stature with each day. 'I am proud of you for that.'

Boaz sighed. 'It's over then.'

'What is?'

'The business with Lazar.'

'Not for me,' Pez muttered bitterly to himself. He called for the Elim to stop, tumbling out of the karak before the men could halt fully. He laughed maniacally before sticking his head back through the curtains.

'What was that for?' Boaz whispered.

'You need time alone. Rest. I shall take supper with you later if you wish.'

The Zar nodded absently. 'Can you get a message to Odalisque Ana for me?'

Pez nodded, the mention of a message reminding him of the folded note pressed against his chest. 'Of course.'

'Tell her I'm sorry she had to witness that. Tell her I will keep my promise about the picnic.'

'I'll go and find her for you now.'

Boaz touched the little man's gnarled, claw-like hand. 'Thank you, Pez.'

～ 31 ～

Pez returned to his own chamber, the parchment scratching against his skin as he closed his door on the day's events. For no reason he could explain he felt all of his skin itch in anticipation. It was not the note, it was something else, as though every inch of his being was prickling with expectation.

Checking first through the windows that no-one was around outside, he took the extra precaution of sitting on the floor next to a huge painted chest of drawers that held his silks. It completely covered him from view if someone decided to suddenly look through those windows.

He remembered now as he unfolded the note why the youngster who brought it was familiar to him. He had been present in the Courtyard of Sorrows. He was Shaz's assistant, who had carried the Viper's Nest behind the apprentice. He did not know his name.

A fresh wave of foreboding washed over him. Pez opened the note, recognised with a chill the handwriting despite the scrawl, and finally, hardly daring to breathe, read its terrifying contents.

He couldn't know how long he had stared at the note. Many minutes had passed, he was sure, as he had read and re-read in disbelief.

'The note tells no lie,' said a familiar voice and Pez looked up to see that a dazzling young woman stood before him.

He could not tell whether she'd just appeared or silently slipped through his door. 'Why am I not surprised to see you?' he said, anger simmering not only for what he'd read but for her audaciousness in coming here again.

'I sense your distress,' she answered levelly.

'Oh, I wouldn't call it anything so mild as distress. Betrayal is the word that leaps to mind, treachery perhaps. A good man died today.'

'So I saw,' she replied softly.

'And it had no effect on you, I see,' he said darkly.

'What I noted most is that he didn't suffer. It was one of your best performances.'

'Losing life before one's time is not suffering?'

'I won't debate this with you now, Pez,' she said as if suddenly losing interest. 'There are more important things to discuss.'

'More important ...' His voice trailed off into silent rage. He pointed a gnarled finger. 'I'm not part of your intrigue, Ellyana. I will not be coerced as you have done to others. I'd suggest you keep an eye out for Jumo.'

She sighed. 'Yes, I imagine he would be vengeful.'

'Ready to kill in fact. And with every right after what happened and how you manipulated him and everything connected with Lazar's death.'

'I understand your anger —'

He interrupted her with a sound of disgust. 'Where?' was all he said.

'You will know.'

He nodded. 'Leave me. I want nothing more to do with you.'

'Not before I finish what I came here to tell you. Hate me all you wish, Pez, but I am not your enemy.'

'Who needs enemies?' he bit back.

'You have one. He is already hunting you — he senses you.'

'I don't know what you're talking about,' he said, less sure now.

'Yes, you do. You have the owl. It has marked you. I know

you've lied that the white streak is only achieved with dye. It is there — it is her permanent mark. You remember the dreamscape too — I can see in your eyes how it haunts you. You know who you are.'

'I am Pez,' he growled.

'You are hers! You are Iridor!' she hissed back at him and her beauty faded with her angry demeanour. Her creamy complexion turned to translucent, parchment-like skin; her eyes, originally a startling blue, were milky now and she shrank before him. She blazed power but he was not cowed.

'Who are you, Ellyana?' he demanded.

'You know enough now about yourself to understand that the rising of Iridor is prompted by a visit from the crone.'

'The Mother?' he exclaimed, shocked.

'An embodiment of her, a messenger for her, a servant. Call me what you will,' she said, suddenly gentle. 'I repeat, I am not your enemy, Pez. We are allies in the same struggle.'

'For the Goddess, you mean.' He finally said what had been troubling him since the frightening dream at the Sea Temple. It turned his blood to ice to say it aloud. 'Go on, admit it,' he urged, hating the way Ellyana spoke such provocative words without ever explaining herself.

'Yes, it's true. For the Mother Goddess. Iridor is almost fully risen, Pez, and he heralds her next coming.'

'I don't understand any of it,' he said, waving her away in a desperate bid to rid himself of this frightening new responsibility.

'You won't understand . . . not until you change.'

'Change?'

'It's what I came to finish telling you. You must transform fully.'

'Into what?' he asked, astounded.

'Iridor's true form.'

And that's when it all fell into place. There was no sound but he sensed a click in his mind, as if a final jigsaw piece had slotted into position. It was as if he knew. Had in fact known it all his life. Her words felt as though they suddenly completed him. It was as if his previous life was simply a vessel and now that vessel, no longer required, lay shattered in hard, jagged bits about him. He knew in his heart she said the truth but still he had not been ready to hear it even though his whole life had been lived to get to this particular point.

'The owl?' he whispered, still not wanting to believe.

'Look in the mirror. You're almost there.'

Pez tried once again, adopting his more regular sarcastic tone. 'I am a shrunken, deformed, mad dwarf, Ellyana, or hadn't you noticed?'

'You are Iridor for this battle,' she said softly and with such affection it almost reduced him to tears. 'You are also Pez, dear one. You don't have to give up who you have been but you must accept who you are. Don't be afraid — it is your destiny. You have been chosen, as all of us have.'

Another dark thought struck. 'And Maliz?'

She nodded grimly. 'Has risen. He is amongst us.'

'Already?' Fear drove him now. 'How will I know him?'

'You won't. Not yet. It's always the same. But by the same token he doesn't know you either — not yet. But he is looking for you and when he knows you, you will lead him to her.'

'Her?'

'Lyana.'

He dared not say it as he frowned, repeating the beloved, revered name in his head. 'Who is she?'

'I do not know. None of us does. The Mother works in mysterious ways. But Lyana will reveal herself in time and you must protect her. Be her eyes, her ears.'

'How do I become Iridor?' he asked, running his short fingers through his whitened hair.

She nodded gently at his acceptance. 'Go to the Sea Temple. There you will find answers.'

'Why don't you know?'

'I am a merely a messenger, like you. I know only what I'm told. We serve, you and I, that is all. Go now and don't be seen — may Lyana bless and keep you safe in the perils ahead.' Ellyana touched his face with fingers that felt feathery against his skin, or was it the other way around? 'I must go,' she said.

'I'll show you a way out,' he said, reaching for the door, keen to have her gone and some silence to think.

Ellyana smiled. 'No-one saw me come and no-one will see me leave. You keep yourself safe. You are the critical link now. Trust no-one in the palace, not even your friend the Zar. For all we know Maliz could have taken him.'

Pez grunted. 'I would know, I think.'

'Not necessarily,' she warned. 'Be suspicious of all. Now go, Lyana awaits.'

Pez made his way to the Sea Temple as if in a stupor. He had changed out of his normal comical clothes into a soft sand-coloured jamoosh, beneath which he was naked save for his white linen wrap. Pez rarely wore the traditional clothes of Percheron but now it afforded him the anonymity he needed. He required none of his art of guile as he ran, every fibre of his being tingling with his new knowledge from the note and in anticipation of the change Ellyana spoke of.

He arrived breathlessly at the Sea Temple and stood a while dragging in deep lungfuls of air. As Pez looked up, sucking down the salty air, he noticed for the first time the tiny balcony that ran around the bright blue dome of the building.

How odd, he thought, that I haven't seen that before. Doves and the occasional seabird called from the balustrade where they were afforded a magnificent view of the harbour and the city. Pez's attention was diverted to the dark doorway; he knew that when he stepped through it his life would change. He had no real notion of how or what his new role was to be but he understood that he had no choice in this. It was his destiny. He cast a single glance out to sea, his gaze falling across Beloch and Ezram, and reminded himself to visit the giants of the harbour. He had been meaning to since he had first talked to Boaz about them. He made a promise that whatever happened today he would make that visit in the next few days.

And then Pez was climbing up the stairs into the cool darkness where Lyana was waiting for him. The soft smile at her lips seemed broader today. Was that a faint blush at the cheeks? He knew he was being fanciful but he suddenly felt very aware of being in the presence of the Mother Goddess.

He knelt, bent his head and reached a short arm to touch the folds of her robe, and that's when Lyana spoke to Pez, her new Iridor, her Messenger.

∾ 32 ∾

There was no sign of Zafira. He couldn't understand why, for she had never been away for his visits before, but as quickly as the surprise of her absence came, it left him.

Lyana had spoken to him in his mind. At first he had thought he was imagining it but the sincerity of the beautiful voice and her obvious love and gratitude were all too real. He began sobbing within moments of her musical tone welcoming him and thanking him for the gift of his life.

Pez had hazy memories of childhood. Perhaps he had blocked most of them out, but the echoes of torment and humiliation sometimes called to him across time. He had learned very young to be thick-skinned, to turn people's taunts back on themselves and to use humour to make people enjoy him rather than detest him. He recalled joining a travelling circus. Most of the people performed acts of great daring or trickery. His job was simply to make people laugh, and it wasn't hard, considering his stature and looks. When he was captured by the slave traders, he had been with a small breakaway group of the circus troupe who had made a roving journey through the less travelled but fabled lands of the Faranel to seek new acts. Pez was not his true name. It was the name he had adopted for the circus and it had stuck. It suited him. He wanted no memories of what had come before the happiness and companionship of the troupe.

Life had been good ever since. He could hardly complain, but Pez had never been loved by anyone — not Joreb, and not even Boaz if he was truthful. And yet, while on his knees, crying like a baby, a goddess was telling him how much she loved him — all of him.

And now he walked as if in a trance to the top of the temple, past Zafira's tiny living area, through another small trapdoor and out onto the roof.

Trust me, my old friend, Lyana had beseeched.

And when he had tentatively explained that what she asked of him was very frightening, she had filled his body with the warmth of her soft tinkling laugh. *We always have this conversation, Iridor. You are always fearful and yet we never let each other down. Trust me now as I trust you.*

It was a leap of faith he was going to take as he undressed on the rooftop to the sound of cooing doves. He unwrapped the linen from around his hips and laid it on the discarded jamoosh. His skin trembled slightly but he wasn't sure whether it was from the caress of the warm wind or the terror of what he was about to do.

Naked, Pez climbed onto the balustrade as a small flock of doves flapped away in irritation at the disturbance. He balanced there, willing himself to find the courage.

For me, Pez, she whispered into his mind, and he knew he could not ever let her down.

Pez, court jester to the Zar of Percheron, opened his short arms as if in supplication to the Goddess who urged him to this feat, took the deepest breath of his life and then, like the doves before him, launched himself off the Sea Temple towards what felt like certain death but what he hoped would be eternal life.

He waited for the ground to meet him and imagined in a few seconds people would gather about his dying, mangled body, muttering to each other about the waste of life. But the ground never came; instead he became aware of a comforting sensation of buffeting warm air.

Pez opened his eyes and could feel nothing but elation.

He was an owl. Silver-white, majestic, beautiful. And he was flying.

Iridor had risen.